MW01519076

PROXY

LAUREN E. RICHARDS

ISBN: 978-1-4834-5086-5 (sc)
ISBN: 978-1-4834-5085-8 (e)

Lulu Publishing Services rev. date: 5/11/2016

To M

ACKNOWLEDGEMENTS

There are so many people that I would like to thank, as their support and encouragement really motivated me in the process of writing this book. I would like to thank my parents, who have been wonderful in their dedication and kindness while they supported me in all the writing I have done. I would like to thank Kristen, my little sister. She has always been there for me and supported me, and I would like to acknowledge that. I would like to thank my teacher, Bob DeLibero, for his continued support and guidance with my writing. I would like to thank my teacher, Mr. Wood, for offering support and encouragement in my writing. I would like to thank my friend Katie, who sat with me every single day during lunch while I wrote my book. I would also like to thank my friend Adam for supporting my writing. I would like to thank my friend Kendra, who is an amazing writer and encourages me to continue writing. Lastly, I would like to thank my cat Sparks, who has provided emotional support and comfort while I was writing about a very difficult topic. Thank you to everyone!

CHAPTER

1

I t's been three months, twenty-one days, four hours, and twelve minutes since Daddy left. I'm keeping count in my pink notebook with hearts and "Girl Power" stamped all over it. I don't even know what "girl power" is. And I hate pink. And hearts, except the ones that really mean something, like the ones that Daddy drew on the side of my bookshelf, or the ones we made with our hands, half his, half mine, when I sat on his lap. Those kinds of hearts I like. I wish my notebook was green with plants on it like my name, Fern. But the pink hearts and "girl power" notebook was the one on sale at Wal-Mart, so that was the one I got for my seventh birthday present.

Daddy left three days after I turned seven. He told me months before that he was going to live somewhere else, but he said he wanted to stay for my birthday. By then, he and Mommy weren't speaking. Mommy used to bake my cakes before she got mad at Daddy, chocolate cakes with green icing. She always said green looked "revolting" and made my teeth look moldy, but Daddy told her "It's the kid's birthday, Beth. Give her whatever kind of icing she wants." So Mommy did, and by the end of it all, Daddy and I usually got her to smile a little bit by spreading green icing on my nose. If he stuck it in my ear, she would even laugh sometimes.

This year, no one asked what kind of cake I wanted. Mommy picked one up from 7-11 on her way home from work. It was smashed a little on the edge and it didn't have even one speck of green on it, not even flowers with green leaves and vines. It was vanilla, plain vanilla that tasted too sweet in my mouth. I didn't spread frosting on my nose or in my ear. Somehow, I knew Mommy wouldn't have laughed anyway. Daddy tried to keep the mood happy by telling me how big I was getting, but we both knew that was a lie. I have always been little, and this year I don't think I grew at all, not even an inch. Finally, Mommy and Daddy got tired of glaring at each other from across the table and said it was time for presents. I was glad. The cake stuck my lips together like cement. It also tasted like glue. I know what glue tastes like because when I was in daycare, Benjamin Neely shoved me against a wall and made me eat some. Daddy gave me a little plant with pointy leaves.

"David, are you insane?" Mommy asked. "Fern can't take care of a plant! She'll spill the dirt everywhere! She'll kill it!"

I opened my mouth to tell Mommy she was wrong, but Daddy said, "Come on, Beth, she's seven! Fern has a green thumb too, don't you, Fern?" I looked down at my thumb. It wasn't green.

"That means you're good at taking care of plants" Daddy whispered to me.

"Yes!" I said loudly making sure Mommy knew how serious I was. "I have a green thumb! Actually, I have two green thumbs! Actually, all my fingers are green! My toes, too!"

Mommy got all quiet then, like she does when she's sad or annoyed, and left the room. I climbed into Daddy's big lap. "How come Mommy's mad at me?"

"She's not", Daddy answered. "She just gets that way sometimes. It's her fault, not yours."

"Why did you give me a plant if you knew it would make Mommy sad?"

He looked past me at the direction that Mommy had gone. I looked too, but I didn't see anything.

"Because it reminded me of you. I wanted to find a Fern plant, but they don't really sell those at stores. This is an ivy plant."

"Is Ivy a name too?"

"Yes."

"Do you like the name Ivy better than Fern?"

"Nope, Fern is still my favorite." I gave him a hug. My arms couldn't even reach all the way around him; that's how big and strong he is.

I climbed out of Daddy's lap and went to the freezer. "I've got something for you."

"What is it, a Popsicle?" he asked.

"Nope. I couldn't think of anywhere else to put it." I lifted my present out of the freezer and wiped of the layer of frost that had collected on it. "It's a picture of me and Mommy, so you won't forget us when you leave."

He took the picture from me and looked into the frame at my smiling face, but not at Mommy's. "So you can remember both of us", I said.

"Thank you, Fern", he said. But now he seemed sad too.

I went to my room and flopped on my bed, clutching Pox in my hand. A moment later, there was a knock on the door. It was Mommy. She handed me a pink notebook with hearts and "Girl Power" stamped all over it. "Happy birthday", she said.

I said "thank you", even though I didn't like the present. She always told me it was very important to do that.

"It was on sale", she told me, and closed the door. From the kitchen, I heard yelling, Mommy's voice hysterical and whiny, and Daddy's voice, angry and low. I tiptoed to the door and pressed my ear against it to hear what they were saying. Mommy was tired of me and Daddy ganging up on her. That's what she said. We weren't, though. Were we? I felt sick. And I still had the taste of glue in my mouth.

Daddy packed his clothes first. Some went into his suitcase, but most went into the box labeled "Salvation Army". I thought that was funny, because we always buy our clothes there, and now The Salvation Army was *getting* our clothes! What if Mommy took me there and we saw some of Daddy's clothes for sale? That was sad, because he was my Daddy. He didn't belong in pieces all over the Salvation Army so strangers could take bits of him home. He belonged with *me*. I reached into the "Salvation Army" box and pulled out the first thing I touched. A white t-shirt with black oil smears. Probably from when he fixed the engine of his car. He got all dirty then, and Mommy wouldn't hug him until he took a shower and washed his hair. I smelled the shirt. Oil, but still Daddy.

"Can I have this?"

He held it to his nose, like he was also remembering the time he had to fix the engine and Mommy said, "You smell horrible, David! I don't even want to see you until you don't resemble a grease monkey!" I don't know what a grease monkey is, but it's probably bad because of the way Mommy said it. But she makes everything sound bad. Even mint chocolate chip ice cream.

"You can have the shirt if you want it", Daddy told me. "But it's just a rag."

It might have been just a rag, but it was special now that he was leaving. I planned to wear it all the time, or at least until Mommy told me to change into something "decent", like she does when I wear my green camouflage shirt. Mommy doesn't like it because she thinks it makes me look like a boy. After I helped Daddy pack the last of his college yearbooks, it was time for him to leave. Mommy stayed in her room. I don't even think she had said goodbye. Daddy hugged me with his big arms. I still miss his hugs. Mommy never hugs me, and even if she did, it wouldn't feel the same, because Mommy's skinny like me.

"Take care of your plant", Daddy whispered to me. He wiggled his thumb, and I wiggled mine back. It wasn't green on the outside, but I could feel the color spreading through my bones like a plant stem. I hugged him again, smelling his jacket.

"I wish I could keep the way you smell", I told him.

"You can." He opened his suitcase and pulled out a silver bottle. "Here. My aftershave."

"What's that?"

"Aftershave is like cream you put on your face. Smell it." I did, and the aftershave smelled *exactly* like Daddy! I still wear it, but I only use a little bit at a time, so it will last, because I know Mommy would never buy me another bottle.

The day after Daddy left was a Saturday, so I didn't have school. Mommy was taking a bath, even though she is always clean. She said she needed to "relax because work is so stressful and get away from any kids", even though I am the only kid she sees normally. She doesn't even work with kids, so it's not like she's taking care of them a lot. She works at a place called "The Happy Hour Casino", and I know she doesn't see any kids there because the sign on the outside door says "Must Be At Least 18 To Enter." I'm not even allowed in, even though Mommy works there. She made me stand outside once when she couldn't get a babysitter. Five strangers stopped and asked if I was lost.

When Mommy takes baths, she brings smelling salts, books, and candles into the bathroom. Sometimes wine too, or sherry. That Saturday, she had just gone into the bathroom with all the stuff she uses to take a bath, so I knew she wouldn't be out for a long time. I walked around the house because I didn't have anything else to do. The doorway to the guest room was open. Daddy moved into the guest room after he and Mommy decided they didn't love each other anymore.

When Daddy left, he moved everything, but in the middle of the guest room floor was something that he must have forgotten. It was the picture I had given him. Out of all of his things, that was the only thing he had forgotten. Except he hadn't forgotten all of it. I was ripped out of the picture. He must have taken that part with him. The part with Mommy in it was lying on the floor like a leaf that had just drifted off a tree. I picked up the picture of Mommy. We were at the beach and Mommy looked beautiful. She was wearing a green swimsuit and her hair looked like a mermaid's, all swishy and floating away in the wind. When Daddy left, he put all of the things from Mommy in the "Salvation Army" box. I don't think he took anything that made him think of her. I also don't think that leaving the picture behind was just a mistake.

Now it's been three months, twenty-one days, four hours, and thirteen minutes now since Daddy left. All that time I was remembering stuff about him, and it only took a minute. I think it's funny sometimes how if you think for a long time about something, time can pass really fast or really slow. I guess it depends on of the memory is happy or sad. Are my memories of Daddy happy or sad? I don't think I know. He's coming soon, though. The bad people in the courtroom who took him away from me are giving him back for three hour every two weeks. Mommy says that time means nothing to a little kid, but I have the days Daddy is coming back written down to the last minute. Maybe that means I'm not a little kid. He's coming in eighteen, no, seventeen minutes now. We're going to see a movie, just me and him. Mommy comes into the room with a bottle of window spray. Whenever she gets in a bad mood, she cleans and complains how dirty I am. I press my nose up against the window and say "Daddy daddy daddy daddy" under my breath so I can try to block Mommy out of my head, because she's never nice to me when she knows Daddy is coming. I think she might be jealous.

"I love you too", I say, so she won't feel bad that I'm leaving her for a while to go to the movies with Daddy.

"Hmmm", she says, scrubbing the coffee table in the same spot for ten seconds. I wait for her to say she loves me too, but she just keeps rubbing.

"I think that spot is clean now", I say helpfully.

She throws down the rag. "Just stop it, Fern."

"Stop what?" What was I doing?

"Stop trying to make me happy. You can do everything in the world, but as long as that awful man you call your father is still around, I'm not smiling."

My stomach is scared now, like it gets sometimes when Mommy's mad and I don't know exactly why. It's twelve-seventeen. Daddy gets here at twelve-thirty to take me away from Mommy's sharp voice.

"Daddy's coming at twelve-thirty", I say to Mommy. I'm not sure if she's glad to see me going or if she wishes I could stay with her. "You can come with us if you want", I tell her, so she won't feel left out. At first, I really hope she says no, but then I think it might be nice for all three of us to go to a movie like we used to.

"Don't be stupid, Fern", she says. Her voice makes my stomach jump a little. If I was an apple and Mommy's voice was a knife, I'd be sliced right in half. "You know your father and I don't get along."

I know that, but why? Who could possibly not love Daddy? "Why, Mommy?" I ask.

"I told you before, Fern, I don't like being called 'Mommy'. You're seven years old, for God's sake. Grow up. I'm *mother,* you got that? *Mother."*

I always forget. Or maybe I just don't want to hear her, because calling her 'Mommy' makes me feel a little bit safe. Calling her 'mother' makes me feel like she's not even my real mother. Most times I just call her nothing, but sometimes I slip. It is now twelve-thirty four, and Daddy still isn't here. I wonder if he forgot me on purpose, like he forgot my picture on purpose. Mommy tells me to get away from the window because my hand are greasy and they leave smudges on the glass. That must mean my hands are dirty, so I go into the bathroom to wash them and make faces in the mirror while I wait for Daddy. I can make really good faces now that my two front teeth are gone. I lost one a week ago, and the other one a few days before that.

When I lost my first tooth, Daddy told me a story about a fairy who would come into my room at night and take my tooth and leave me fifty cents. Mommy told him not to put stupid ideas in my head and that if I ever believed in the Tooth Fairy, I was even dumber than she thought. She said she would take my tooth and give it back to when I stopped believing stuff that Daddy told me. She said my tooth was safe with her. But the next day, I found it in the trash can next to an empty packet of Kraft macaroni and cheese. I took my tooth out of the trash and cleaned it off really good, with water and lots of soap so it would smell nice. I still have it. I keep it locked in my little green box, where I keep all of my special things.

It's twelve-thirty seven now, and it still don't hear Daddy's car coming to pick me up. I come out of the bathroom, and Mommy is still cleaning. I pick up a rag and start scrubbing too. Maybe that would make her happy, if I helped her. She tells me to put the rag down, because I'm not helping, just pushing dirt everywhere.

Twelve-forty one. I hear Daddy's car. He doesn't park in the garage like he used to. Daddy rings the doorbell, and I feel sad, because it makes me think he is just someone visiting and not my Daddy, who never used to ring the doorbell. The ding-dong noise makes the house feel empty, even though Mommy is in the living room cleaning and I am standing right by the door. I open it, and my Daddy is standing on the front porch. He looks different, and it scares me a little bit, but I hug him anyway, because I know he is still my Daddy. His face has more hair on it, like little spikes on a cactus and his eyes have dark circles around them, like Mommy's sometimes do when she doesn't sleep. He's skinnier, too. Maybe there isn't any food where he lives now. I have to remember to give him a box of Poptarts before he leaves, so at least he can have those.

As I hug him, he presses the movie tickets into my hand and whispers "Don't let your mother see."

There are words printed on the tickets: CHILDREN OF THE CORN: GENESIS. One child, one adult. They also both say RATED R. I whisper into Daddy's coat "Is this the sixth one?"

"Yep", he tells me. We've seen all the Children Of The Corn movies. And all the movies that came from Stephen King books. Daddy has read all the books out loud to me, from *Pet Sematary* to *The Shining*, but we don't ever get scared. Mommy doesn't know, because it's a secret between Daddy and me. She would be mad if she found out. Or maybe she just wouldn't care. I think that maybe not caring would be worse.

Mommy marches into the room and says to Daddy "You're late." Her voice sounds like knives. I wonder if Daddy is scared too. "I'm only fifteen minutes late, Beth", he says.

"Eleven", I say, because I've been keeping track.

"Shut up", Mommy tells me, and my stomach shakes a little.

"Don't talk to her like that!" Daddy's voice us angry, but not at me. I can tell. If Mommy's voice is a sword trying to slice me open, Daddy's voice is the shield protecting me.

"The traffic was just awful, Beth," Daddy says. "Bumper to bumper. The snow's held everything up."

"You're still late."

"Just a little. We'll still make it to the movie on time." Daddy sounds a little bit scared now, so I grab his hand and squeeze it. He leads me to the closet and says "Your coat, m'lady", while he holds it out so I can put my arms into the sleeves. He used to do that kind of stuff a lot more.

Mommy grabs the coat from him and pushes it back into the closet. "Fern isn't going anywhere."

At first, I don't think I'm hearing her right, so I shake my head really hard to clear my ears and say "What?"

"I said, you're not going anywhere with him." Mommy's head jerks toward Daddy, and she glares at him.

"Why not, Beth?"

I've noticed that when Daddy is mad at Mommy, he uses her first name a lot, but when Mommy is mad at Daddy, she *won't* use his name. That's how I know they're both angry now.

"Why not, Beth?" Daddy asks again, and I can almost see the anger in his voice. Red. If his words were a color, they'd be red.

"Because you were *late*", Mommy answers. If her words were a color, they'd be blue. So it's blue versus red now, and I'm wondering who'll win. Maybe we can all mush together to make purple and be a family again. But Daddy is fire and Mommy is ice, and I know for a fact that fire and ice can't live with each other.

"I was only a few minutes late", Daddy says. "Just let me take her."

"No. I'm the parent here. You, you're just...irresponsible. You're not in charge of the kid. I am."

I can see my time with Daddy ticking away on the hall clock.

"Please, Mommy, let us go see the movie. I'll be home with you afterward, I promise."

She shoves me aside. "I could care less if you're with me or not. And I'm not 'Mommy'."

"Mother, I mean. Mother! Please let me go with Daddy!"

She smiles now. I think she's glad to have both me and Daddy begging. One simple word can change our entire day. If she says that one word, then ice wins and fire burns out.

"No."

My head feels like it's on a merry-go-round, and I hear echoes of angry words from Daddy, but I can't tell what they are. Through all the dizziness I hear Daddy yelling to me.

"Fern, go upstairs! I don't want you hearing this! *Go upstairs!*"

I trip up the staircase as Mommy shouts "See? Why don't *you* just take the little brat? She listens to you better anyway!"

It is hard to breathe now. I am pressing my ear against the vent upstairs so I can hear what they're saying. I eavesdrop a lot. I want to stop listening, but I can't because I need to *know* things. My cheek is resting against the carpet, which feels scratchy and burns a little.

"Two hours!" Daddy is yelling at Mommy. "I get to see my own kid for two hours every two weeks! That's four hours a month! And you get her every single day, but you don't even care!"

"I can't afford a kid!" Mommy yells. "Take her, if you want! Just take her! I don't care!"

She doesn't care. I have known this for a long time now, but hearing Mommy say it makes it more real. *She doesn't care.*

"Someday," Daddy says. His voice is fire now. "Someday I will! I may be the only thing that can save her from you!"

"Save her?" Mommy screeches. "Save her? What, do you think I don't take care of her? I feed her! I give her a place to sleep! I give her clothes! I send her to school!"

Daddy's voice gets quiet, but I can still hear him loud and clear when he says, "You may do all that, Beth. But do you really *love* her?"

Mommy doesn't answer. My head is spinning again, and the smell of the carpet is making me feel sick. All that floor cleaner. The movie tickets are still in my hand, but CHILDREN OF THE CORN: GENESIS has left my mind a long time ago. I rip up the tickets because I know my time with Daddy is over. Mommy ruined it. I am crying now, but I don't realize I am crying until suddenly my face feels wet and my eyes sting. I heard the front door slam after I smelled the floor cleaner on the carpet. Daddy is gone, and I'm alone again with Mommy.

CHAPTER 2

U sually, the memories of being with Daddy are enough to block out the mean stuff Mommy says. They're like a shield. But now, I have no shield, and Mommy is still ready to fight. I crawl under the covers of my bed where it is hot and stuffy. Pox is there, and I remember when I got him, when Daddy gave me the ultimate shield against Mommy's words.

I was four, and sick with the chicken pox. Mommy told everyone who called her on the phone that day, "Oh, Fern is *so* sick, poor thing. Yes, I'm taking care of her. You know how hard it is to have a sick kid...mmm-hmmm. The girl's father does next to nothing, so it's almost like being a single mother with a sick kid, and the Lord knows that's near impossible!" After the seventh time she repeated those things, she shouted up the stairs at me that she was going to work and I "had better not get out of bed and infect the house, or else!"

I slept for a while after that, and when I woke up, Daddy was knocking on my door saying "Fern? You awake, Sweetie?"

He was holding a box of Popsicles and a stuffed rabbit.

"I came home to take care of you", he whispered.

And he did take care of me. He took my temperature (102 degrees), and gave me the box of Popsicles. Grape, my favorite flavor. I was a little bit scared to have one, because grape Popsicles turn your mouth purple. That's why Mommy doesn't let me have them. She says it makes her seem like she has a slob for a kid, and even if she does, she doesn't want other people knowing that. So I never get grape Popsicles, except with Daddy. I took a little lick, and the cool felt good because my whole face was so hot. Then I looked over at Daddy, and he had the Popsicle stuck right in his mouth. There was purple juice running down his chin. The skin around his mustache was already purple. So we had a Popsicle party that day in my bedroom. Daddy and I ate the entire box and both got tummy aches, but somehow, I felt better, even if my stomach hurt a little. Then Daddy gave me the stuffed rabbit and said, "If I have to be at work when you need someone, now at least you have Rabbit." I told him Rabbit was a very boring name, and he said "Well, what do you want to name him then?"

"Pox", I said. I was tired then, so I lay down with Pox next to me. When I rubbed Pox's ear, I didn't feel so sick anymore. And that was how I got Pox.

I must have fallen asleep, because now it is dark out. I am rubbing Pox's ear, and I suddenly really want something grape flavored. I tiptoe to Mommy's room, but I stop outside the door because I hear crying.

Sometimes, on nights when she is remembering Daddy, Mommy cries in her room, so I have to make dinner by myself. I always toast Poptarts. If we don't have any, I don't have dinner that night, because I don't know how to cook anything else.

Then I bring Mommy her cup of tea. I put extra honey in the tea to make it sweeter so maybe she'll feel better. On the nights when she just glares at me and says, "Where's my tea?" I don't give her anything extra, not even a saucer for her cup.

Tonight, though, I think she is sadder than normal, but I don't know why. I feel weird inside, because I don't want her to be sad, but I'm also mad at her because she ruined the day for me and Daddy. I decide when I bring her the tea, I won't give her extra honey, but at least I will give her a saucer.

Tonight, I think she would like chamomile, because that kind relaxes you. I know all the names of all kinds of tea, even the names that are really long. I also know how each tea makes you feel better. I think I am a tea doctor. I give Mommy her favorite cup, the one with light pink flowers, and a saucer to match. I change my mind about giving her honey and squeeze a bunch in, because maybe she deserves it and is just having a hard day today. Then I squeeze some honey onto a spoon and lick it, because I love the taste even more than chocolate milk.

I bring Mommy's tea to her door and hold it in one hand while I knock and say, "I've got your tea!" Then I remember to call her *'mother'*, so I say, "Mother! I've got your tea! Mother?" But she doesn't open the door. I wonder if she's so mad at me that she's ignoring me. I don't really see why she would be mad at me, but she always says I'm just a little kid, so what do I know? I hear footsteps toward the door, so I hold out the tea and put a smile on my face. The smile isn't real, but right now, it's the best that I can give to Mommy. She opens the door just a crack and glares at me. Her eyes are red, so I am positive that she has been crying for a long time.

"Go away, Fern."

"But I brought your tea..."

"I said go away. I'm having coffee tonight." She takes a long sip from Daddy's old coffee mug, the one that says "MOUNT SUNAPEE" on it. That doesn't make sense, because Mommy hates coffee. She says it's bitter. I think she just doesn't want to take the tea that I made, maybe to make me feel bad. And it works, because I feel like there is a hole in my chest and she has stuffed it with hurting words. Mommy has a blue photo album of her lap that she closes when I come in. The photos in there must be making her cry, because she is holding the album like it is something sad. Sometimes her face looks almost guilty, but I'm not sure why. I am pretty sure the pictures are from her and Daddy's wedding. Mommy was beautiful then. I know because Daddy showed me a picture of them on their wedding day. I don't mean that Mommy isn't beautiful now, but back then, she even more pretty. She had light blonde hair and she was laughing in every picture that I saw. She doesn't laugh now; maybe that's why she isn't quite as beautiful as she was when she married Daddy. I don't know what to say to her now, so I ask, "Can I have some dinner?"

"Dinner?" She looks at me and her face seems confused.

"I'm hungry", I tell her. She looks back to the photo album.

"Yes, you can have some dinner." I stand by her door and wait for her to get up. But she doesn't.

"What?" she asks me. "What are you waiting for? If you want dinner, go make dinner."

Poptarts again. I pull a box of Cookies 'n Creme out of the cabinet. I wonder why they spell 'Creme' that way, because I know it's not right. I can tell with word like that, because I read books a lot and then the words glue themselves into my head so I have no choice but to remember them. If I didn't have so much to think about already in my brain, maybe I would write a letter to the Poptart company and ask them to explain that spelling to me. I toast the Poptarts and sit down at the empty table. Maybe someday Mommy will teach me to make French toast.

When Mommy goes downstairs to get more coffee, I sneak into her room, even though she has always said never to go in there. The blue album is sitting on her bed, and I want so badly to look in it and see proof of when Mommy was beautiful and happy. There is a tiny corner of a picture sticking out of the side of the album, so I make sure Mommy isn't coming. Then I take the photo out. It isn't of Mommy and Daddy's wedding. It is a school picture of a girl with dark braids. She's tiny like me, but her face looks older, maybe ten or eleven. She is wearing a school uniform and frowning at something in the distance. I wonder who this girl is. It can't be Mommy, can it? The smell of coffee is traveling up the stairs, so I slide the picture back into the album and run to my room, still wondering about the mysterious little girl.

Daddy doesn't call the next morning. This makes me worried, because he always calls the day after he visits me. But yesterday was a very bad visit, like a dark cloud in the room, so I would think that would make him want to call me even more. I take the phone from the kitchen and bring it to my room, so if Daddy calls, Mommy can't answer and hang up when she realizes it's Daddy. She always does that if I don't get to the phone first. By one o' clock, I am worried. Maybe Daddy got into a car accident. Maybe he got attacked by one of the scary-looking men that stand outside The Happy Hour Casino and smoke. Maybe the last thing he remembers is Mommy yelling at him and me running upstairs like a baby. Maybe he doesn't even *want* to call. If he doesn't call in the next ten minutes, I will try to be brave enough to ask Mommy for his number so I can make sure he's okay. The phone rings in my hand then. It is so sudden, it makes me jump and drop it. I answer it, because it must be Daddy.

"Hello?"

"Who is this?" The voice on the other end is deep and growling and definitely not Daddy.

"This is Fern."

"Oh", the voice laughs. "The kid. Right, Beth told me about you."

"Beth?" Why would this man call my Mommy by her first name?

"You don't even know your mother's first name?"

"I know it", I say. "Her name is Beth. Who are you?"

"Just get Beth, kid." I go to Mommy's room, where she is on the computer but I don't get to see what's on the screen because she blocks it with her hand when she sees me coming, like she doesn't want me to look. "Someone's on the phone for you. It's a man." I wait, but she tells me to go away, so I lay outside her door with my ear up to the crack, and I can hear every word.

"Brian? Hey, baby. You coming tomorrow?"

Who's coming tomorrow? And why on earth is Mommy calling him 'baby'? I want to open the door and ask this, but when you're eavesdropping, you can't do that, so I keep listening.

"Did you pick it up?" She listens for seven seconds. I time it.

"Yeah, get orange. Or blue." Orange or blue what? My mind is spinning with questions. I hear footsteps coming near the door, and I back away so Mommy won't know I was listening. Later, Mommy goes to the store like she does every week, and I get to pick out three bottles of Gatorade. I'm not sure why Mommy lets me get it, but she says, "You can get some Gatorade, Fern. How about Blue Cherry? And orange? And, oh, Tropical Cooler? That one's green. You'll like that." I wonder if this has something to do with "getting orange or blue", like Mommy was saying on the phone. Maybe she was telling the man to bring Gatorade. But that wouldn't make sense, because we just bought some. I decide not to think about it and just be happy that I have a special treat that turns my mouth different colors. On the car ride home, Mommy tells me that if she has a friend coming tomorrow and that if I am very good, I can have some Gatorade then.

"Man or woman?" I ask, because I want to know if Mommy has a boyfriend. I hope she doesn't.

"What?"

"Your friend. Are they a man or a woman?" Mommy smiles, but not at me. It's a secret kind of smile, like she's happy about something but she doesn't want me to know what.

"A man", she says. I know better than to ask anything else.

When I wake up the next morning, I hear two voices in the kitchen, and I pretend for a moment that the voices are Mommy and Daddy, and they are together and happy and making me breakfast. Then I remember that Mommy's man friend is coming today. I don't like the word boyfriend because it makes me think of getting married, and I absolutely do not want Mommy and her man friend to get married. They sound happier together than Mommy and Daddy ever did. This makes me hate the man friend already. I hear the sound of something being poured. Tea for Mommy probably, and maybe coffee for her man friend. They are laughing. I can't remember the last time Mommy laughed.

My door opens without anyone even knocking, and Mommy comes into my room. And then I see the man friend. He is very big and tall, and as strong as Daddy is, but my Daddy is the good kind of strong. Mommy's man friend looks like the bad kind. He has brown hair on his arms and legs and face. And he has a lot of hair on his head, except this hair is yellow. It looks gross. His eyes are dark brown and squinty. I decide he has dyed his hair because I have never seen anyone with brown hair on their body and yellow hair on their head. Also, when I look closely, some parts of his hair at the very top of his head are still brown. He reminds me of a poster of a surfer in California. I saw a poster like that at The Happy Hour Casino. I wonder if that's where Mommy met him.

It is a little weird that Mommy brought him into my room while I was still in my pajamas. I have been wearing Daddy's old white oil-shirt as pajamas. Usually when company comes, Mommy makes me put on a dress and tights and a bow and sit on the couch and smile like I'm about to get my picture taken. That's when I decide that Mommy's man friend must not be company. He must be my enemy.

"Fern", Mommy says. "This is Brian." Brian looks at me, and his mouth twitches at the corners. Then he smiles, but it's not a friendly smile. I try as hard as possible to keep my face very still.

"I talked to you on the phone yesterday, kid", Brian says.

I know he did; he doesn't have to tell me that. I want to tell Mommy how rude he was to me, but then I see how happy she looks. Her face is all lit up like a flashlight. Or maybe fireworks. If Brian makes her this happy, maybe she won't be mad at me all the time. I don't want to ruin it.

"Brian and I have a surprise for you", Mommy says, kneeling down so she looks me in the eye. I move back because she has never done that before, and it scares me a little.

"Wait here, kid ", Brian tells me. He and Mommy leave the room, and I hug Pox tight, wishing Daddy was here. He would know what to do about Brian. But Daddy still hasn't called.

A tray is at my door now, and Mommy is carrying it, with Brian behind her. On the tray is a plate of scrambled eggs, which I hate. There is also a tall glass of blue Gatorade, so I guess I have been good enough to get my special treat.

"Breakfast in bed!" sings Mommy, putting the tray down. I stare at her, because Mommy has never done anything like this before. Then again, she has also never had a man friend in the house whose hair on his head doesn't match the hair on his body. This is a very weird morning.

"You like scrambled eggs, right?" Brian asks, but I think he knows I don't, because he is smirking.

"She *loves* them!" Mommy tells Brian, her eyes sparkling like scrambled eggs are possibly the best thing in the world. They're not. I'm more of a dry cereal and Poptarts kind of kid.

"I don't usually eat eggs…" I start to say, but Mommy interrupts me.

"If you eat them, you can have that Gatorade".

I do want that Gatorade. I practically love anything that is fruit flavored and will turn my mouth different colors, so I take a bite of the scrambled eggs, trying not to taste them. Mommy and Brian sit in my room while I choke down the disgusting eggs.

When I've eaten about half of them, Brian takes the plate away and Mommy says, "Now you can have your Gatorade, Fern."

I am all too happy to have my Gatorade. It tastes different than I remember, probably because I haven't had it in so long. The blue stains my mouth, and I think of Daddy and the grape Popsicles.

"Drink it all, Fern", Mommy says.

"Eggs make you dehydrated", adds Brian.

"What's that mean?" I ask. He smiles in a mean way that makes me want to stick my Gatorade straw right up his nose.

"Oh, I forgot. You're just a dumb little kid. It means that eggs make you thirsty. So drink up!"

I have had enough Gatorade now. The glass they gave me was huge, so I lay back down.

"Finish it!" Mommy says. Her scary voice is back.

"I'm full", I tell her.

"Look, you little brat", Brian snarls. "Your mother bought you that Gatorade, and you won't even finish it. Do you even know how wasteful that is?"

"Can I finish it later?" I plead. I don't know why they want me to finish the Gatorade so badly. It's true that Mommy is strict about wasting things, but she doesn't care *that* much. Both Mommy and Brian are staring at me now and my heart starts beating very fast in my chest. The room is spinning, but somehow I know I am still. I feel the straw against my lips and Brian's rough hands as he holds it there and yells, "Swallow! Swallow!"

I see blue, bright blue, behind my eyes and I hear Brian and Mommy and I feel my throat closing and my heart pounding. Then then I don't see or hear or feel anything at all.

CHAPTER
3

I wake up in the back of a car. It isn't Mommy's. She keeps her car clean as the day she first bought it. I'm not allowed to eat or drink in there and I have to sit on towels so I don't get dirt on the seats. This car smells like beer and grease from McDonalds. There are empty hamburger bags on the floor, and I can see sticky marks all over the windshield. It must be Brian's car. I look around me and I see that I have thrown up the blue Gatorade. It is sticky against my chest and my face, but no one has wiped it off. Mommy and Brian are sitting in the front of the car, and I am wrapped in a blanket in the back with no seatbelt. I think I might have fainted. Everything is still spinning, but at least I can focus my eyes. I can breathe again too. My head feels heavy. Not as heavy as before, but I am still tired. I don't know what happened. I look at the blue Gatorade vomit stains on Daddy's oil-shirt. What if...

I must be moving in the backseat, because Mommy turns around. She is smiling. Maybe she likes seeing me hurting. Thinking that makes me hurt even more.

"What happened?" I ask Mommy. She doesn't answer me.

"Brian, Fern's awake", she says. He turns around.

"She puked. Nice." I don't know if he is one of those people who says something that really means the opposite, or if he really does think it's nice that I threw up. I'm surprised Mommy doesn't scold him. She hates the word 'puke'. We are in a parking lot now, and everything around me is blurry, so I can't see where we are.

"Where are we, Mommy?"

"I'm 'mother', Fern."

"Sorry."

"We're at the emergency room", she says. "I don't know exactly what happened to you, but the doctors might. Be sure to tell them everything that's wrong, okay? They can't fix you otherwise."

"Okay", I answer. Brian opens the backseat door and Mommy scoops me up. I am still stuck in the blanket like a burrito. I hate burritos.

"I can walk", I tell Mommy. She doesn't answer me, so I wiggle around a little bit, but she just holds me even tighter. I don't like her touching me at all because it feels like she is about to drop me.

The emergency room at the hospital has automatic doors, so when Brian rushes in front of us to open the door for Mommy, and the door opens by itself, he looks like a very silly man. I giggle a little bit.

"Shut up", Brian growls at me.

"Stop laughing", Mommy snaps. "You're sick, so stop laughing."

She walks very fast to the front desk, so everything in the hospital is moving around me like I'm in a car on the highway. "My child is sick", Mommy gasps to the lady at the front desk, who is wearing a flower-printed hospital shirt and has a name tag that says "Janice".

"What seems to be the problem?" Janice asks. I like her voice. It's soft, like Pox. Pox. I remember that Pox was in my bed with me. I want to hope that Mommy remembered Pox, but I don't think she would have.

"Did you bring Pox?"

"What's Pox?" asks Brian, even though I wasn't talking to him.

Mommy rolls her eyes. "It's Fern's stuffed rabbit", she explains.

"What kind of name is 'Pox'?" Brian wonders.

I am not about to explain the story of how Pox got his name.

"No", Mommy snaps. "I didn't bring that stupid stuffed rabbit. You're too old for it, anyway."

"What's the problem?" Janice asks again.

"Well", Mommy takes a deep breath. "My daughter, Fern, just passed out. I don't know if it was a seizure or what, but she threw up..."

"I see that." Janice looks at Daddy's oil-shirt, which is am still wearing. The throw-up is almost dry now. "Did she hit her head?"

"No, but her heart's racing, and she can't breathe, and-".

"I can breathe now", I say. "I feel a little better."

"Janice, she doesn't know what she's saying!" Mommy nearly shouts. "Can you just get a doctor to look at this kid?"

Janice hands Mommy a slip of paper with the number 133 on it. "Sit down, please. When your number is called, a doctor will see you." Mommy gets right into Janice's face, and I feel sorry for Janice, because you never want to be the one Mommy is mad at.

"We need a doctor!" Mommy yells. I think she must be only two inches from Janice at this point. "We come to the emergency room, and we can't even see a doctor for my sick kid?"

"There are a lot of people waiting", Janice says. "Some of them have been here for hours. We can't just drop everything to take care of someone who walks in the door. It wouldn't be fair."

Janice is very brave. Or maybe just very stupid. Mommy stomps across the waiting room floor. I feel the shake in my body every time she puts her foot down. She hold me tight to her chest as she sits in the plastic chair, with Brian next to her. She is holding me too tight and I don't like it. Her sharp fingernail is pressing into my chest. I try to get up, but Brian puts his large hand on my leg and hold me down.

"You're sick", Mommy says. "You're not going anywhere."

I guess I'm not, with both Mommy and Brian holding me, so I look around the room. There are a bunch of plastic chairs like the ones we are sitting in against the walls. A person is sitting in each one, except for the kid in the corner who is lying down and taking up two chairs. They all look sad. Some kids are crying, but not very loud, because their mothers are rocking them and whispering to them. I wondering if they are whispering "shut up, or you'll be sorry", like Mommy does when I cry. The walls of the room are light blue in some spots and light green in others, like someone didn't finish painting.

In the middle of the room, there is a round table with picture books on it. I wish I could have one of them to read, even though I usually read chapter books. The mother next to us is reading to her son. I try to listen too. I close my eyes and imagine that mother is mine and she is reading to me.

"Too tight", I gasp to Mommy, because her bony hands are digging into my chest, but she ignores me.

I watch as Brian looks around the room at other people's cards with numbers. The numbers are being called by a doctor behind a glass window at the front of the room. Each time someone hears their number, a nurse comes to the door and takes them away. I wonder where they go. I wonder if it hurts. I kind of hope they call our number soon, because I don't know if anything the doctor can do would hurt worse than Mommy's beige-finger-polished nails digging into my skin like little knives. Brian stops at the edge of the room and I know what he is looking at, even though I can't see all the way over there. I think he has spied a card with a lower number on it. The man who owns the card is talking to the woman next to him, so he doesn't see Brian take his card, 27, and replace it with ours, 133.

"Mommy", I say. "Look!" I know she won't be happy with Brian when she sees him doing that, but it's the right thing to do. Mommy is strict and kind of mean, but I don't ever remember her cheating on anything.

"Shut up and stop staring at him!" Mommy hisses.

I think maybe she didn't see the same thing I did, so I say "Brian stole that man's card, Mommy!" She digs her nails into me so hard I know it's on purpose.

"Shut *up*, Fern."

Brian is coming back now, smiling and holding card 27. I hate him. I want to punch him right in his smiling face, but Mommy is holding me too tight. I feel sad for the man who now has card 133, because his elbow is twisted in a way that I have never seen an elbow twist before, so I think he needs to see the doctor more than I do.

"Sir!" I call out, and all the people in the room turn and look at me. I open my mouth to tell the man with the funny elbow about the hard, but the doctor behind the glass calls "27!", and Mommy tosses me over her shoulder and practically runs out of the room. As we leave the waiting room, I see the man with the funny elbow look at his card like he is confused. Then he shrugs sadly, and it makes me want to cry for him and hit Brian and scream, all at the same time.

The nurse who is standing next to the waiting room door is pretty and young, kind of what I think Mommy used to look like from the pictures I've seen of her from when she was in high school. She told me that she was so pretty, everyone thought she should be prom queen. The nurse smiles at me, and I see that she is chewing gum. I want a piece of gum now, because my mouth still tastes sour, like throw-up and Gatorade.

The hall she leads us down is long and covered with windows. It is raining outside and it is sort of dark, even though it is the middle of the day. There are doors on the sides of the hall. They lead into rooms with beeping machines and people that look dead. The dead-looking people have tubes up their nose and wires stuck in their arms. I hope the doctors don't do that to me. I am scared now, and I want Daddy.

Before he left, he used to take me to the doctor every year. Daddy never missed a single one of my check-ups. Mommy never went. Daddy took me to a doctor for kids. There were no numbers or plastic chairs or dead-looking people. When they wrapped a Velcro band around my arm and pumped the ball at the end to test my heart, they let me put on a pair of headphones and I got to listen to a band called Simple Plan. I miss that music. I tried playing it at home, but Mommy told me to "turn that noise off before it kills my eardrums, Fern!" I told her it was music, not noise.

"Listen to the words", I said.

"I can't hear the words", Mommy shouted, "Over that awful drumming!" But I don't think that was true, because I could hear the words fine, and Mommy wasn't trying very hard to listen anyway.

The nurse stops in front of an open door and says, "The doctor will be in to see you in a few minutes."

Then she leaves me alone with Mommy and Brian, and I want to grab her white clothing and say "stay here with me!" because Brian makes me nervous. Mommy does too, but I'm used to that.

The room we are in has a bed that's raised way up on some kind of metal legs that can make it go higher or lower. There are a few machines, but not as many as the other rooms have. I guess kids don't get tubes and wires. There is a sink, a stack of little cups, and a box of plastic gloves. It smells like hand sanitizer, the kind I used to get when they gave it out as free samples at the mall. I collected the little bottles in my room, but Mommy found them and threw them away, because she said she couldn't have one more thing cluttering up her house. Mommy puts me on the bed, and my stomach shakes.

"I'm going to throw up", I say.

"Get to the bathroom!" Mommy screeches, but I don't know where the bathroom is, or even if there is one, so I just throw up on the crinkly paper I'm laying on. The throw up is still blue.

"Gross kid", Brian mutters, but I don't care, because I feel even better now. Not quite normal, but like I just got something bad out of me.

"I guess your stomach is empty now", Mommy says. She hands me a paper towel from the dispenser on the wall. "Clean it up yourself."

So I start scrubbing the throw-up around on the bed. A man in a doctor's coat is at the door now, and Mommy grabs the paper towel from me and starts acting like she was cleaning up after me this whole time, even though she wasn't. She was kissing Brian on the neck. I saw. It looked gross, because Brian has brown hair on his neck, and who wants to kiss that?

"The poor kid just threw up again", Mommy tells the doctor. "I was just cleaning her up, but..."

The doctor smiles at us, and I like him, because his eyes remind me of Daddy, even though Daddy has green eyes, and not brown like the doctor.

"Don't worry about it", he says. "I've seen much worse, but for goodness sake, kid, what on earth did you have that was so blue?"

"She had Gatorade", Mommy says, and I like the doctor a little less now, because he called me 'kid', just like Brian does. It wasn't mean, though, so I decide not to hate him right away. He sits in the chair across from the bed.

"I'm Dr. Warner", he tells us. "Do you mind if I ask a few questions?"

"Not at all", Mommy says, smiling huge. I don't remember the last time I've seen her this happy. "Call me Beth", she says. Dr. Warner looks a little bit embarrassed.

"Okay. Why are you here?" he asks.

"She fainted", Mommy says, putting her hand on my shoulder.

I try to shake it off, but she stays firm. "Then there was vomiting, heart racing, blurry vision, throat closure, and chest pain", she says.

"Wow." Dr. Warner finishes writing on his yellow notepad. "When did this happen?"

"Today, Doctor. It happened today, after breakfast."

"What did she eat?"

"Well, I gave her eggs, and some Gatorade as a special treat."

"And when did she faint?"

"Later on."

"Yes, but when? I'm just trying to determine if it might have been a case of food poisoning."

Mommy shakes her head so hard I think it might fly right off her shoulders.

"No, it's much more severe than that. I mean, with her symptoms? It could be a chronic illness."

"What's a chronic illness?" I ask.

"It's when you don't get better", Brian says. "You just get sicker and sicker until you die."

"I don't have that!" I say, but my heart is racing again.

"We don't know", Brian says.

"Don't worry, kid", Dr. Warner says. "You'll be just fine."

"My name is Fern", I tell him, because in kind of like him and I don't want him to ruin it by calling me 'kid'.

"Sorry. You'll be just fine, Fern", Dr. Warner tries again. He turns to Mommy. "Does she have any history in hospitals?"

Mommy turns to Brian, and her face looks like a question mark. Maybe this is all too much for her and I need to help her, so I say, "No history of being in the hospital. Except when I was born."

That makes Dr. Warner laugh, but I don't know what is funny. Dr. Warner talks some more then, but I don't listen because I am suddenly very tired.

"You can lie down, Fern", Dr. Warner tells me gently. So I do.

"See?" Mommy is saying loudly. She is mad and she is using her knife-voice again. "Don't you see how sick this kid is? She can't even stay awake to answer some simple questions!"

"I'm awake", I say. "I can answer questions!"

"I want her tested", Mommy continues, ignoring me. "And I want her kept here overnight!"

"Well, we'll certainly run some tests", Dr. Warner says. "But they should be done by tonight, so you can take her home then. I doubt Fern wants to spend the night in a hospital."

"She doesn't know what she wants!" Mommy yells. "She's delirious! I want her kept here overnight, and if this hospital refuses to provide the care needed, I have a mind to sue!"

I think Dr. Warner is getting nervous now, like I do around Mommy. His words come out choppy, like ticks on a clock.

"We will certainly provide the medical attention needed to care for Fern", he says nervously. "But all I'm saying is that it may not be necessary to keep her overnight."

Brian calls Dr. Warner something then, something I am not allowed to say. Dr. Warner's face turns red. "Perhaps it would be best if you two would sit out in the waiting room", he says. "I'll run some tests on Fern and let you know the results. Then we can determine if overnight placement is appropriate."

"It is!" Mommy yells as she and Brian leave. "This is the worst hospital I've ever seen! My kid could die on your watch, and you wouldn't even care!"

I am alone in the room with Dr. Warner, so I am allowed to cry now. He doesn't tell me to shut up or that I'm a baby. He just hands me tissue after tissue and waits for me to feel better. Then he says not to be scared, that they are just going to do a few tests.

"A few parts might hurt a little", he says, and I like him for that.

At the doctor's office that Daddy used to take me to, they always said "This won't hurt a bit", right before sticking a big needle in my arm.

"It's okay", I tell him. "I'm okay with a little hurting."

Mommy does a lot of hurting at home, only she does it with her words.

Dr. Warner tells me I am very brave, but I know I'm not, because Mommy calls me a wimp all the time.

CHAPTER 4

The first thing Dr. Warner brings out is the Velcro band with the rubber tube and the pump attached to it. This one is plain black, not red and blue with airplanes on it like the Velcro band at the doctor's office where I went with Daddy. Dr. Warner says the pump will test my heartbeat. He wraps the band around my arm and squeezes the pump until the band is filled with air and I can hear the little Velcro teeth ripping. He does that while I am lying down, then sitting up, and then standing.

"Is your heart beating fast, Fern?" he asks me. I put a hand over my chest.

"Yes, I think it is."

Dr. Warner writes something down and moves out of the room.

While he is gone, Mommy and Brian come into the room. They are being quiet, like they will get in trouble if someone sees them. Brian is carrying a bottle of orange Gatorade. When I see it, my stomach feels tight. I never eat or drink anything that made me throw up. That's why I don't ever have tomatoes, mayonnaise, cheese, or spaghetti.

"Thought you might be thirsty, kid", Brian says, uncapping the Gatorade. He takes a plastic cup from the counter and fills it with sweet, colorful liquid. "Drink up."

"I don't want it", I say, looking at Mommy.

"Do what Brian tells you, Fern", she says. "Drink that Gatorade."

"But I think it might have made me throw up," I protest. "You know I can't eat anything that makes me throw up! Like tomatoes, and mayonnaise, and-"

"That's stupid", Brian interrupts. "I've eaten things that made me throw up. Hell, I've eaten a double cheeseburger, puked, and eaten another double cheeseburger a few hours later."

"Drink it, Fern", Mommy insists.

"No."

I press my lips together. I'm not going to drink it. The only way they'll get that Gatorade past me is if they force my mouth open and pour it in themselves.

But then they do. Mommy nods to Brian, and Brian nods to Mommy. He grabs my nose and holds it so tight that I can't breathe with my mouth closed. But I won't open my mouth, so I try to scream with my lips closed. It comes out sounding like "Hmmmfffff!" I am running out of breath. Is this what drowning feels like? My head pounds. It feels like there's a thousand-pound weight on my skull. I have to open my mouth. Maybe it I take a quick gulp of air, I can close my mouth again and keep it closed until Dr. Warner comes back. I try to gulp, but Mommy is even quicker than my mouth. She holds my lips open, and Brian dumps the Gatorade in. I feel the sticky-sweet liquid in my mouth, and it tastes like horror because it makes my mind flash like lightning to the time when I first saw Brian come into my room with the Gatorade. Brian holds my nose closed again, and Mommy hold my mouth. I have no choice but to swallow. So I do.

"Think that's enough?" Brian says to Mommy. She nods.

"For now."

They both let go of me at the same time, and I fall backward on the bed, my mouth opening and closing without noise. My chest hurts, and as I am crying out in pain, I see them slip out the door like shadows. Dr. Warner comes in with a set of needles and some baby wipes. Dr. Warner. Can he save me from Mommy and Brian? Can he be my superhero? He sees me curling up my body to try to squeeze out the pain, and he rushes over.

"Fern! What happened?" I hear voices out in the hallway and I know that Mommy and Brian are coming back.

"Don't...let...them..." I say, but Mommy lets out a very loud yell that makes Dr. Warner drop the needles.

"Oh, my god!" Mommy yells, clutching Brian. "Oh my god, she's having a seizure!"

"No, she's not!" Dr. Warner leans over me and whispers into my ear. "Fern? Fern, can you hear me?"

I nod, because I can hear him, but he sounds so far away, like he's yelling to me through a tunnel. "Is she dying?" Mommy whispers.

"Is she, doctor?" Dr. Warner shakes his head. "No, she's not dying, but did either of you see what happened?"

"Well", Brian starts. "She just-"

"We didn't see anything", Mommy interrupts. "How could we? *You* were the one who left her here alone. We were just sitting in the waiting room and we heard her yelling. Then we came in here to find this." She points at me.

"I'm going to throw up", I say, and this time, Dr. Warner gets me a bowl in time. He looks at it when I'm done, which is gross, but maybe that's his job as a doctor.

"Orange! That's odd, very odd. She hasn't had anything to eat or drink since she last got sick."

Mommy leans against Brian and covers her face. She makes crying noises, but I can tell she's not really crying, because real crying isn't that loud. I know her real crying. It's when it's nighttime and she's looking at pictures that she won't show to me, and I have to bring her tea and make myself dinner. That's real crying.

But Dr. Warner doesn't know any of this, so he says, "Don't worry, Beth, we'll find out what's wrong." Then he pats her on the arm, and Brian slaps him. Hard, across the hand. I see Dr. Warner shaking his wrist like he's trying to shake the pain out. Why did Brian do that? Maybe he's just a very bad person, the kind of person who hits doctors.

"Hands off her", Brian snarls, pulling Mommy into a hug.

"I'm sorry", stammers Dr. Warner. "I didn't mean-"

"Brian." Mommy looks at him with a cold stare that sends a shiver through my body. "Go outside now."

Brian nods, and leaves the room.

"I'm so sorry", Mommy says to Dr. Warner in a sugary voice, as sweet as the Gatorade. "I don't know what's gotten into him."

"Let's...let's focus on Fern." Dr. Warner seems like he wants to run, but no one runs with Mommy in the room. Dr. Warner cleans my arm with a baby wipe.

"I'm going to test her blood", he tells us as he's cleaning. "We'll check for anything unusual. It might explain the vomiting, or perhaps the results of the last test. Her heart rate is unusually high, and while it's not uncommon for children to have high heart rates in a hospital setting due to nerves, it still may be something we want to check out."

"Of course it's something you want to check out!" Mommy snaps. "Now take her blood! We need to find out what's wrong!"

"Don't worry. We will." Dr. Warner slides a needle into my arm, and I watch as the clear plastic tube fills up with red blood.

"It's less scary if you don't look", Dr. Warner says. But I keep my eyes focused right on the tube. If I looked away, I would feel the pain and maybe not know what was happening, and I always like to know what's happening. After a while, I get used to the feeling of the needle in my arm, so when Dr. Warner takes it out, I jump a little, because it hurts.

"Fern, stay still!" Mommy barks. "How does the blood look?" she asks. Dr. Warner squints at the glass tube, and he looks like a scientist, the crazy kind who make potions that blow things up.

"Too soon to tell", he says. "I'll send this to the lab to have it tested." I knew it. He must be a crazy mad scientist.

"What's the lab?" I ask. If Dr. Warner is crazy, I should probably know before he does any other tests on me.

"It's where they check blood and other test results", Dr. Warner tells me. "No big deal."

"Of course it's a big deal!" Mommy says. "Don't tell her everything is fine! She could be seriously ill!"

"Beth." Dr. Warner leads Mommy out into the hallway whispers to her about not scaring me and making me feel safe and comfortable. He says he doesn't know what's wrong, but he doesn't want to assume the worst. I can hear what he's saying as I listen at the door. He and Mommy come back into the room, and Mommy looks like I do when I'm in trouble. She sits down in a chair and puts her head in her hands. Then she starts to fake-cry again.

Dr. Warner looks like he doesn't know what to do. "I have to go check with the nurse about what we should do next", he says, moving toward the door. "I'll be back in a little bit, okay?" He puts the blood sample on the counter and leaves. Mommy lifts up her head as soon as he's gone. Her eyes look normal and not puffy, and there are no tears on her cheeks. I knew she was faking.

"He forgot the blood sample", she says. "I'll go give it to him. You stay here, Fern, got it? Don't move an inch. Remember, you're sick."

"But I feel a little better", I say.

"Don't move", she repeats. I watch her close the door. I hear her footsteps moving quickly, almost like she's running. Then I hear her coming back, but there are two sets of feet walking now, and neither comes into the room. I stand up and walk to the closed door. I hold onto the doorknob and kneel down. I hear voices outside, so I press my ear against the door and listen. "I told you we couldn't talk in there! Not with all those people!" Mommy's voice.

"Beth, no", says someone else. "Not now. It's too risky." Brian.

"If we're going to stay together, you have to help me with this. You do want to stay together, right?" Mommy asks. Brian must nod, because Mommy says, "I thought so. It's in the cafeteria. Just grab some packets. At least ten."

I hear Brian walk off, and I wonder what he is getting packets of that could be in the cafeteria. And why would it be risky? There are running footsteps now, heavy ones, and panting.

"Okay", Brian says. "I got them."

"Good."

I hear paper being ripped, and a top being unscrewed. Then shaking. "Keep the cap on!" Mommy whispers. "Harder! Shake harder! There can't be any on the bottom." Any what? What are they trying to mix? "Now go!" Mommy says, and she opens the door just as I crawl back into bed. She is still carrying the blood sample. I stare at her. What did I hear out in the hallway?

"I couldn't find him", Mommy says, setting the blood sample down exactly where Dr. Warner left it. I keep looking at her. Maybe if I look hard enough there will be a clue on her face that will tell me what I heard. "Why are you staring at me?" Mommy asks. I want to ask her about the packets and the shaking. Dr. Warner comes in and looks at the blood sample carefully, and hands it out the door to a nurse.

"Well?" Mommy demands.

"We're going to see how the blood sample turns out", Dr. Warner tells her. "In the meantime, can I ask you and Fern a few more questions?"

"What more do you need?" Mommy says. "You've already asked about our insurance, Fern's past health, the symptoms...what else do you need to determine that she's sick? It's pretty clear to me that's something's not right."

"I want to ask about your family", Dr. Warner says. Mommy looks furious, and I feel sorry for Dr. Warner. He's a nice man. He shouldn't have to have Mommy be mad at him.

Just then, the nurse comes back to the door and says, "Doctor, we need you in the lab right away to look at Fern's blood samples. Something is off." As Dr. Warner rushes out of the room, I swear I see Mommy smile.

"The results of the blood test are quite alarming", Dr. Warner is saying. "The sodium content in her blood is dangerously high. I'm not sure what's causing it, but she needs to stay here for the night so we can monitor her. I would like to do some other tests to determine if there might be anything toxic in her blood, but unfortunately, the lab doesn't have the equipment to perform those tests."

He tells me I will be moved to the cancer unit as soon as they can send over a stretcher. "Cancer?" gasps Mommy. "Relax, she doesn't have cancer", Dr. Warner assures us. "The pediatric ward is full. The only bed we have is in the cancer unit." By this point, Mommy is hugging me and squeezing my chest so that I gasp in pain.

"Oh, you poor thing!" she cries. "See how she's gasping, doctor? There is something seriously wrong here!"

"Too...tight..." I say.

"See, she's trying to tell you that her chest feels tight", Mommy explains. She shoves my head in her lap, and I don't like it, but my head feels so heavy that I can't move it away. I keep one eye open so I can see what's going on, but after a few minutes I find out that it's very hard to sleep with one eye open, so I give in and close both.

I start feeling things after that. I feel myself being lifted onto a stretcher, but not by Mommy or Brian. The hands that lift me aren't skinny and clawing like Mommy's, or smelly and greasy like Brian's. It must be Dr. Warner. Then I know we are going down a hallway, because I can feel things moving around me, even though I am completely still. I hear a beep and a moving sound, like an elevator, and I guess it was an elevator, because the next thing I know, I am moving up. The elevator stops, and the doors open. Noisy voices hit me like a wave, and I wake up from my half-sleep, when I closed my eyes and felt things, but I didn't see. Mommy is hurrying right along next to the stretcher, murmuring "How could this be happening? Fern, are you still with us? Fern!" I sit up. "Lie down", whispers Mommy. "You're sick. Lie down *now.*"

I do, and the world continues to spin around me as I get more and more dizzy. Why do I feel like this? I never got dizzy before. I never threw up unless I had the stomach bug. I never felt my chest burning so tight. I never felt so tired. Never...until I drank that Gatorade.

My room in the cancer unit in smaller than the one in the emergency room, but it has a lot more machines. I might as well be one of those dead-looking people. I *feel* like one. A nurse lifts me from the stretcher and puts me in the bed. This one has sheets and a pale blue blanket. Dr. Warner tells Mommy she'll have to leave now, because it have to stay overnight and visiting hours are over, but she can see me first thing tomorrow. Mommy points her finger right in Dr. Warner's face.

"I'm going", she says, "to sort this mess out with someone useful!" She storms off with Brian. I am alone with Dr. Warner.

"Fern," he asks me. "Is there anything I can get you?" I think of what I need right now: Pox and Daddy.

"My Daddy", I say. Dr. Warner nods. "Okay, I'll get your Daddy."
My heart smiles. Daddy is here? How?

"He's in the waiting room with your mom, isn't he?" Dr. Warner asks. "My heart is frowning now. In fact, it may even be crying.

"No", I say. "That's not my Daddy. That's Mommy's man friend."

"Her...man friend?" Dr. Warner wonders. "You mean her boyfriend?"

"I don't like that word", I say. "It makes me think of getting married."

"Okay, sorry. Her man friend." Dr. Warner leans back on the stool and looks at me. "Fern, do you mind if I ask *you* about your family? Your mother seemed angry when I asked her."

"Okay", I agree. "What do you want me to tell you?"

"When did you meet your Mommy's 'man friend'?"

I am thinking now, thinking about whether I trust Dr. Warner. If I decide I do, I will tell him everything he wants to know. If I decide I don't, no one can make me talk. I make two lists in my head: things I like about Dr. Warner, and things I don't like about Dr. Warner. The "like" list fills up quickly, and the "don't like" list is empty except for the fact that he called me 'kid.'

"Mommy brought her man friend into my bedroom this morning", I say. "That's how I met him. It's weird, because she usually makes me dress up for company, but when I met Brian, I was wearing what I am now. Minus the throw-up. It's my Daddy's oil-shirt."

"That must be very special to you", Dr. Warner says softly.

I nod. "It is. And now it has throw-up stains on it. I know how to do the laundry, but not how to get stains out."

"We can take care of that", Dr. Warner says. "I can give you some hospital pajamas, and we can use some stain-remover on your Daddy's oil-shirt."

"Thank you", I say, because no one has ever tried to help me with taking care of the things that Daddy left me. I wonder if Dr. Warner has any aftershave. I'm almost out. "Can you tell me about your Daddy?" Dr. Warner asks. I swallow hard, because when I talk about Daddy, it's like he's sitting right here with me, but I can't quite reach him, and that makes me sad.

"He gave me Pox", I say. Then I explain how Pox got his name. "Daddy left me and Mommy", I tell Dr. Warner. "I've been keeping track of how many days and hour and minutes he's been gone in the notebook Mommy gave me for my birthday. Daddy gave me his aftershave. I put I little bit one every day so I can remember him."

Dr. Warner smiles. "I wondered why you smelled like Sandalwood Summer."

I try to stop talking, but I can't. It's like Dr. Warner has popped a balloon in my head that holds everything I know about Daddy, and now it's all spilling out my mouth. "He took me to horror movies and he read me all the Stephen King books. Mommy didn't know. It was a secret. Don't tell her, okay?"

"I wouldn't dream of it", Dr. Warner says.

"Before he left, I gave him a picture of me and Mommy so he would never forget us", I say. "And guess what?"

"He forgot it?" Dr. Warner guesses.

"Yes, he ripped the picture in half and took the half with me in it" I say. "But I think he may have forgotten the other part on purpose. Which isn't really forgetting, is it?"

"No, I suppose not." We are both quiet for a moment, and wonder what Dr. Warner is thinking.

"What about your Mommy's 'man friend'? Can you tell me about him?"

"I don't like him", I answer. "He calls me 'kid', even though he knows my real name is Fern. And he smells bad. He kisses Mommy, and I don't like that. It's like Mommy's kissing a trash can. One filled with McDonald's wrappers and greasy stuff."

"I see." Dr. Warner is writing on his yellow notepad again. I try to read what he is writing, but his handwriting is so bad I can't even figure out a single letter. Maybe doctors make their handwriting really bad on purpose so people who try to spy on them can't see their notes. It makes sense when you think about it.

"Does Brian ever say or do things that upset you?" Dr. Warner asks.

"I only met him this morning", my voice says, but my head is saying yes, yes he does say things that make me scared and mad but I can't do anything about it because I'm just a kid and he's a grown-up. Plus, Mommy's on his side. Brian makes Mommy happy, I can see that. But he stole number 27 from the man with the funny-looking elbow. He forced my mouth open so I would have to drink the Gatorade he poured. Telling anyone these things would get Brian in trouble, and even though I want him to get in trouble, telling on him would make Mommy mad. So I keep my mouth shut, just like Mommy's always told me to do.

There are voices out in the hallway. Two angry ones, and one calm one. Brian, Mommy, and a nurse. Dr. Warner is still. I think he is listening like I am.

"I have a right to see my own daughter!" Mommy's voice, angry.

"Yes, but visiting hours are over. She may already be asleep." A nurse's voice, calm.

"We don't have to deal with this crap. Let us stay!" Brian's voice, angry. I close my eyes and hope that the nurse wins and Mommy and Brian will go away.

"We have to hook her up to an IV", the nurse says. "Most parents get nervous watching that."

"I won't", Mommy insists. "She *needs* an IV. Why would I get nervous if you're doing your job?"

"I'm sorry, we can't let anyone in at this time." I hear Mommy's fake crying. "I just want to see my little girl!" she sobs. "She could be *dead* in the morning, and I won't even have gotten to say goodbye!"

"I promise you, Fern is in good hands", the nurse says, but I can tell that she is backing down. "Can you make an exception just this one time? For a desperate mother?" Mommy pleads. The nurse sighs. Mommy can usually talk anyone into anything.

"I'll ask the front desk, but if they say no, that's final. Okay?"

The nurse walks off, and I hear Mommy whisper to Brian, "We've got them, baby. Just you wait and see."

They must be kissing now, because I hear lips smashing together and gross smacking sounds.

"I knew you'd help me", Mommy whispers.

"We've got this idiot right where we need him."

I look at Dr. Warner. "I didn't hear any of that", I say. He sighs deeply, looking very worried.

"I'm concerned, Fern. I may have to check into this." Now I must be the one to look worried, because he says, "But it's not yours to worry about, okay?"

CHAPTER 5

I can't help thinking about all the grown-ups in my life. Dr. Warner. Mommy. Brian. Daddy. I can't puzzle them out. I've heard so much that I shouldn't have heard, and it's all sitting in my head in a tangled mess. Mommy and Brian come in, so I guess they were able to talk the nurse into letting them stay. They are followed by two doctors, a man and a woman who is wheeling stand with a bag on it and holding a set of needles. A nurse follows them. She is wearing plastic gloves and carrying a clear, thin tube that looks like a curly straw. The doctors introduce themselves. They are Dr. Trellis and Dr. Norms. I like Dr. Trellis right away because she smiles at me, but Dr. Norms seems kind of scary because he has a pointed noise and really big eyebrows. He looks like a cartoon character, the villain kind, not the hero.

"We looked at the blood again", says Dr. Trellis. "And an IV will be necessary to keep her hydrated with that amount of sodium in her blood."

"Oh my god!" Mommy rushes to my side and clutches my hand. Her nails bite into my skin, leaving half-moon shaped marks. Mommy makes whimpering and hurting noises like it's her and not me that's getting a needle in the arm. It hurts a little when it slides in, but then I forget it's there.

"You can bend your arm now", Dr. Norms says, and I guess I didn't even realize that I was holding it out straight. That must be why my shoulder aches. I bend my arm, and it burns like fire inside my blood. I don't want to think that Dr. Norms lied to me, because maybe he just didn't know. On my arm, there is a bandage that covers a tube that goes into my body. The tube is thin and clear and I thought I would feel it whenever I moved, but I haven't yet. The tube is long and it is connected to a plastic bag that is hanging from a metal pole. In the bag is something clear that looks like water.

When Dr. Warner has checked my IV, he says to Mommy and Brian, "You have to leave now. We made an exception so that you could be with Fern while she was getting her IV. It's in, and she's doing fine. You can see her tomorrow." Dr. Warner means what he says this time, and Mommy knows it. Still, she tries one more time.

"Please, doctor, is it so awful to want to stay with my sick child? It's just so *difficult* to leave without her. I never imagined she could get this sick."

"We're keeping an eye on her", Dr. Trellis says. "It's time to go now."

"Please, Beth", Brian says from the corner where he is standing with his hands in his pockets. "Let's just go."

Mommy grabs his arm and marches him away, like she does to me when I'm in trouble. I listen to their footsteps go down the hallway. Mommy's heel shoes make a click, click, click sound, and Brian, wearing old sneakers, walks thump, thump, thump. Mommy is talking as they walk, so I listen. "I was almost there!" she yells. "And you went and blew it! You know I do the talking! Don't tell me when we should leave! They were about to let us stay, I know they were!"

"I'm tired of this, babe. I'm sorry."

"You'd better be. One more incident like that and you won't be calling me 'babe' for much longer."

As I hear the door slam, I look at the doctors and the nurse. They glance and one another with red cheeks, and continue working like they heard nothing.

"Geez, nervous much?" Dr. Trellis comments. "Just another hysterical parent. Well, don't worry about it, Fern. She's coming back tomorrow. You'll see your mommy soon."

"You're a lucky girl to have a mother who's so worried about you", Dr. Norms says to me. I nod to him, but inside I am shaking my head. Mommy hates spending time with me when I'm sick. Why does she want to be with me all of a sudden? Can't the doctors see that it's not always like this? I want to tell them, I really do, but what if they mention it to Mommy?

At exactly 9:31 p.m, a nurse comes into my room and asks if I need anything. I need Pox, but I think she means something in the hospital, so I ask for some grape juice. I can turn my mouth purple now, since Mommy isn't here, and that makes my heart a little bit happy. I just wish that Daddy was with me, dribbling purple down his chin and onto his shirt. Then we could both have stained shirts together. The nurse tells me they don't have any grape juice, and asks if cranberry would be okay. I nod, but when it comes, with a green straw and lots of ice, I can't even take one sip, because it looks just like the blood that Dr. Warner took from me, and even though blood doesn't scare me, I don't want to be drinking it.

At 9:47 p.m, Dr. Warner brings me a set of hospital pajamas. They are white and blue-striped with a string in the back that ties around my neck. I think the sleeves are only supposed to reach the end of my shoulders, but they go almost to my wrists and the top hangs on me like Daddy's oil shirt, way too big. The IV must be working, because I am feeling almost normal.

At 10:00 p.m, a nurse comes into my room and says it's time to turn my light out.

"Do you want a night light?" she asks.

"No thanks."

"Are you sure? We have a bunch of them for when kids get scared of sleeping in the hospital. It's nothing to be ashamed of. It's frightening to be away from your parents in a strange place like this."

"I'm not scared", I say, which is true. The only times when I am scared are the times when Mommy is around. The nurse tells me that I am a very brave girl, but I don't quite believe her. Not being scared isn't the same as being brave.

The hospital is very quiet at night. I thought it would be just as noisy as it is in the day time, but I guess the doctors and nurses do a good job of keeping those people quiet, because the only thing I hear is the beeping of what they told me is my heart monitor, and the soft crying of someone in the next room. It sounds like a kid. Maybe she's scared and the nurse forgot to give her a night light.

I am very tired, but my mind is buzzing so much that I don't think I'll ever sleep. I close my eyes, but I keep seeing Mommy and Brian and the blue Gatorade and Dr. Warner and the IV and the blood and the needles in my head until they all start spinning around like a top and I feel dizzy.

There is a knock on my door and a nurse comes in. She turns the light on and I see her face. She has brown hair on her arms and legs and yellow hair on her head like Brian, but her face is Mommy's. She smiles at me and says "Drink up, Fern! Drink up!" Then I see that my IV bag is not full of the clear liquid anymore. It is full of bright blue Gatorade. I can feel is going into my body and turning my blood sweet and fruit-flavored. My arms and legs start to glow blue where the Gatorade is flowing, and the nurse cackles. Then she says "I've got her right where I want her, Honey! Right where I want her!" and runs out of the room. I feel the Gatorade taking hold of my body and making me shake and throw up and twitch, and then I lie still. There is someone else in the room with me. Not someone dangerous. I can sense it. I can't see very well, because everything looks like I'm seeing it through fog, but the other person in the room looks like a skinny girl with dark braids. She is wearing a white dress with blood stains on it.

"Get out", she says. "Don't let Mommy hurt you. She hurt me and I was stupid. I never did anything about it. You have to *do something!* She rushes toward me and grabs my shoulder, shaking me. *"Stop her before it's too late!"*

I open my eyes, and it's just Mommy, shaking me awake.

"Fern?" she says. I blink and look around. Dr. Warner is standing with Mommy and Brian.

"See how late she slept?" Mommy demands. "You need to take another look at that blood sample, doctor. Sleeping so late isn't normal."

Dr. Warner looks at his watch. "It's ten-thirty. That's perfectly normal."

"Not for a kid who wakes up at six o'clock every morning! Even on days she doesn't have school, she's always awake before anyone."

"Wait", I say. "What day is it?"

Dr. Warner checks his watch again. That watch must do everything. "Monday."

"I have to go to school", I say. Even I know how dumb it sounds. I am lying in a hospital bed and class started two and a half hours ago.

"You're not going anywhere", says Mommy. "You're *sick,* Fern, and if I have to chain you to this bed to keep you here, so be it!"

"Let's take another look at her blood", Dr. Norms says. "Why don't you two get some breakfast?" he suggests to Mommy and Brian. "There's a cafeteria downstairs."

Mommy opens her mouth to say something, but Brian pulls her out of the room, saying "I'm hungry, Beth. Come on."

I hear Mommy yelling at him all the way to the elevator. Dr. Warner cleans off my arm with a baby wipe. "Do you mind if we take a little more blood?"

"Go ahead," I say. I'll say okay to anything, just as long as Mommy and Brian are gone. I watch the tube fill with red again, and Dr. Warner looks at me like I'm weird, but he doesn't say anything.

I am thinking about my dream. Daddy once told me that you dream about everything you remember most about the day. The Gatorade,

Mommy, Brian, the nurse, and the IV make sense, but what about the girl? Where did she come from? She looked familiar to me, like I've seen her before, but not really *her*. Have a seen a picture of her? Why did she appear in my dream? Maybe it was from the crying I heard from the next room right before I feel asleep. How could just hearing someone cry make me think of a whole person who tells me to get out before Mommy hurts me? Mommy wouldn't hurt me, would she?

"I heard something last night", I tell Dr. Warner. "Someone was crying. It sounded like a kid."

"Next door?"

I nod.

"That's Leah. She's been here for a few months."

"Why? Does she have cancer?" I ask. I hope that doesn't sound rude, because maybe Leah doesn't want me knowing what's wrong with her, but Dr. Warner doesn't seem to mind.

"Leah has leukemia", he says. "She gets sad sometimes at night because her parents aren't there."

"Oh", I say. I want to tell Dr. Warner that I understand, but I don't get sad that Mommy and Brian aren't here. I get sad that Daddy's gone, but it's not quite the same.

"Okay, we'll get this blood tested right away", Dr. Warner says. "Take it to the lab please, Dr. Norms." As Dr. Norms leaves with my blood, I see Dr. Trellis come in.

"How do you feel this morning?" she asks me.

"Better", I tell her. "Just a little dizzy. And tired. And-" I put my hand on my chest. "-my heart is still going fast, I think."

"There's someone who wants to see you", Dr. Trellis tells me. "It's Leah."

"Leah?" Dr. Warner looks surprised. "I was just telling Fern about Leah."

"She's been the only kid in the cancer unit for nearly a month", says Dr. Trellis. "I told her you came in yesterday, and she's been waiting to see you since then. The poor kid hasn't seen anyone her own age for a long time."

I haven't either, so I sit up straight and grab the bed while I stand up to make sure I don't fall.

"Whoa, Fern", laughs Dr. Warner. "You can go see Leah for a few minutes, but only if she's awake. I'll have to check."

"Okay." I start to follow Dr. Warner out the door, but Dr. Trellis holds me back.

"We need to bring your IV pole", she says. "And a wheelchair."

"I can walk", I say. I jump a little bit to show her, and fall down. I guess I was dizzier than I thought.

"Exactly."

Dr. Trellis tells me to wait on the bed, and soon she comes back with a wheelchair. "Sorry, we don't have any kid-sized ones left."

I don't like the wheelchair. It's way too big. My feet can't even reach one of the many foot rests, so I keep my legs tucked under me. The wheelchair makes me think there's something *really* wrong with me. It makes me feel guilty. Like a faker. It turns out that it's hard to wheel an IV pole along the floor at the same pace as a wheelchair. I drop the pole four times by the time we get to Leah's room.

Leah is sitting up in bed with about a million pillows behind her. Her eyes are big and brown. Good brown, chocolate brown. Not like Brian's mud brown eyes. She is bald and wearing a red and black hat that looks like someone knitted it for her. Maybe her mother, or her grandmother. When she sees me in the doorway, she smiles, and I see that she is missing her two front teeth, like me. I wonder if her mommy told her the tooth fairy wasn't real.

"Hi", Leah says. I can't really hear her, so I move the wheelchair a little closer to her. The IV pole comes crashing down on the table that is next to her bed, spilling ginger ale everywhere. Leah giggles.

"Sorry!" I say, trying to get out of the wheelchair to pick up the IV pole, but Dr. Trellis beats me to it. "Sorry, I'm not really used to wheelchairs. They're kinda crazy."

"You're funny", Leah says. "What's your name?"

"Fern."

"I'm Leah. I'm nine."

"I'm seven." I don't really know what to say after that, so I tell her, "I like your hat."

"Thanks", she replies. "My grandma made it for me. She's made me thirty-nine hats so far, one for each month I get through chemotherapy. But this hat's my favorite. Do you have grandparents?"

"Nope." I shake my head. "My Daddy's parents died before I was born, and my Mommy's parents died when I was three."

"I'm sorry", Leah says, and suddenly I think of how wrong it all seems. She's the one who's had leukemia for so long, and she's feeling sorry for *me*, because I don't have grandparents?

"I'm sorry you have leukemia", I tell her.

She smiles. "Don't be. My Mom says I was put on this earth to be here for as long as God needed me to be. And when He doesn't need me to be here anymore, Mom promises that Heaven will be very beautiful."

I just stare at her, even though staring is "*disgustingly rude, Fern*", according to Mommy. I've never heard anyone talk about death like that. All of a sudden, I really want to meet Leah's mommy. I want to hug her and have her whisper nice things to me and let me sit on her lap. I can easily imagine her doing those things with Leah. But Leah needs a nice mommy, because she is so sick. I should be able to be okay on my own.

"What's your diagnosis?" Leah asks. I don't know that word.

"What's a diagnosis?"

"It's your sickness", Leah explains. "You can't have cancer, because you've still got hair. What do you have?"

"I don't know", I answer. I really don't. "I started throwing up and then I guess I fainted and then they brought me here."

"Do you feel better?"

"Yeah."

"Are you going home?"

"I don't know. My mom wants me to stay."

Leah crinkles her nose. "That's weird. My mom always wants me *out* of the hospital. In fact, she gets so excited, we stop at Dairy Queen for ice cream every time I'm discharged."

"What does discharged mean?"

"Sorry. You're new to this. I know all the medical terms because I've been here so long, but I guess most people don't know what I'm talking about", Leah says. "Discharged means they let you leave the hospital when you're better."

"Oh." I can't imagine Mommy taking me to Dairy Queen.

"What's your favorite ice cream?" Leah asks. "I always get a soft-serve chocolate with butterscotch dip."

"I don't know my favorite", I tell her. "I guess I like flavor that make your mouth colored. Fruity stuff."

Leah smiles. "I like those too."

A nurse pokes her head into Leah's room. "Fern, Dr. Warner wants you back in your room now, please."

"I'll see you again", I promise Leah.

"Bye", she whispers sadly.

Back in my room, Mommy and Brian are sitting with Dr. Warner, who has my second blood sample. Dr. Trellis has my first. Mommy glares at me.

"Where *were* you?" she hisses.

"Visiting Leah", I explain. "She's in the next room. She has leukemia."

"Just what she needs", mutters Brian. "An annoying kid like you bugging her when she's trying to recover."

"She *liked* seeing me!" I protest. "We're friends!"

"Fern." Mommy is using her knife-voice. "You're here because you're *sick*. You're not here to make friends. You could have caught something from that kid. And I'm not pleased that Dr. Warner let you go, either. From now on, I don't want you leaving this room. You're just making yourself sicker, do you hear me? You're already going to be in the hospital for a long time."

"Actually", Dr. Warner clears his throat. "That's what I wanted to talk about. The results of Fern's second blood test came back. She's perfectly fine! The symptoms you were describing are a bit troubling, but we can chalk them up to the sodium increase in her blood. Her second blood test contained normal sodium levels. The sudden increase could have been caused by a number of things, and I want to make sure it doesn't happen again, so I'm going to prescribe some medication. She should be fine to go home in a few hours!"

"*What?*" Mommy looks furious. "This child is still sick! Don't you see, she *needs* to be in the hospital!"

"We've provided the necessary care", Dr. Warner says calmly. "You should be happy, Beth. She's going to be okay. Now I'll stop the IV flow, and we'll take out the tube."

"You useless doctor!" Mommy yells. "We need help here, and you're just turning us away!"

Before I can stop her, she grabs my IV and rips it from my arm. The pain sears like the time Mommy burnt me with a hair dryer. I still don't know if that was an accident of not. The needle from the IV drops to the floor, leaking the liquid from the bag. I clutch my arm, but Mommy grabs me in one hand and Brian in the other. She pulls us out of the room and out of the hospital.

CHAPTER

6

Dumping me into the backseat of Brian's car, she yells at him, "If you had helped me in there, we'd be all set! You're a moron, a clueless man who won't even help out his girlfriend!"

"Babe, please-"

"Don't call me that, you disgusting creature! Look at you! You're a mess! And as soon as you take us home, you're leaving. I'm not staying in this damn filthy car a second more than I have to!"

Mommy grabs a great handful of French fry wrappers and beer cans and flings them out the window. The word litterbug flashes through my mind, but I don't say it. Instead, I wonder where the word came from, because bugs don't litter. Only humans do.

Brian is driving very fast. I see the needle on the speedometer going up, up, up. Past seventy now, past eighty. It settles on 83. The speed limit is 65. I wonder if Brian will get stopped by the police, because if a person is driving too fast, the police will stop them. I don't think that sort of thing would send Brian to jail, though. Too bad.

We are almost home. We pass all the places I know- the bank, where they once gave me a grape lollipop but Mommy took it away because she didn't want my mouth turning purple. The grocery store, where I always slip a box or two of poptarts into Mommy's shopping cart. The hairdresser, where I never go because Mommy says it's cheaper to cut my hair at home. The pharmacy.

"Stop!" Mommy yells. "The pharmacy! I need to pick up Fern's prescription."

She whispers something to Brian. He nods. "Still pissed at me?"

Mommy's eyes flash like lasers.

"Yes", she snaps. "But since we're here, you might as well make yourself useful."

"Stay here", Brian orders me like a dog.

I "stay there" as Mommy and Brian walk into the pharmacy. They aren't holding hands like they used to. This makes me happy and guilty and the same time. Happy, because we are getting rid of Brian now. Guilty, because I feel happy about it.

Mommy and Brian are in the pharmacy for a long time, and I wonder how long it takes to pick up medicine. When they come back, Brian is holding four full bags. I ask what's inside the bags, but Mommy won't tell me. I don't think she knows I'll probably find out anyway, because I find out pretty much *everything* just by listening.

We are all quiet as we drive back to the house. Brian puts the bags on the counter and I try to peek at what's inside, but he shoos me away. Then he leaves, slamming the door behind him. Just like Daddy did.

Daddy. Daddy... I look down at the hospital pajamas I am still wearing, and I realize the Daddy's oil-shirt, my little piece of him, is still at the hospital, throw-up stains and all. Mommy starts crying as soon as Brian slams the door, so I run to the kitchen to make her tea. She takes it without saying thank you. Mommy tells me I need to get into bed, because I'm sick.

"Why don't we go to Dairy Queen, Mommy?" I suggest. "Since I got discharged from the hospital? We could celebrate."

Mommy looks at me with her eyebrows all crooked and her lips tight, the same way she did when I suggested that she have another kid, because I've always really wanted a sister. Or a brother; that would be okay too, I guess. She looked furious then, like I was absolutely crazy. That's how she looks now.

"Are you stupid or something?" she says. "There's nothing to celebrate! If we had gone to a proper hospital, you'd still be hooked up to that IV. Now I've got you home, and I don't even know how to make sure you don't pass out again! Get in that bed now! I don't want to tell you again!"

I get into bed. I guess I won't be getting to try a soft-serve chocolate ice cream with butterscotch dip today. Mommy opens the bottle of pills and holds one out to me.

"How about these, Fern? That's your medicine from now on."

The pill is about half the size of my pinky finger. It is two colors, blue and red. Those have to be the worst two colors to put on a pill, because the red makes me think of blood, and the blue makes me think of blue Gatorade.

"It looks so big I could almost play tennis with it", I say. "I can't take a pill that big."

"Too bad", replies Mommy. "I wasn't really giving you a choice, you know."

She shakes five pills into my hand and gives me a glass of water.

"Take them."

"Five?" I ask. "Isn't that a lot?"

"You're sick", says Mommy. "You need at least five pills, believe me. Now take them and stop whining about it."

Just looking at the pills makes me feel like I'm choking. "What if we crush them up and put them in something?" I suggest. "Like pudding or yogurt?"

Mommy shakes her head. "You need to get used to taking pills, because I have a feeling that you're going to be taking them for a long time. You're not going to get better quickly, Fern."

I take the pills, one by one. The fourth one gets stuck in my throat, and I start to taste it. It has the flavor of chalk dumped in chili powder. I take the last one, and my throat is still burning.

"What exactly is my diagnosis?" I ask, swallowing again and again to get rid of the pill taste. Mommy frowns at me.

"What's up with you?" she asks. "How come you know all these fancy hospital terms? First discharged, and now diagnosis. Where'd you learn those?"

"Leah", I say. "She's been in the hospital for a long time, so she knows."

Mommy sighs. "Just what I need. Another sick kid teaching my sick kid the ways of the hospital."

"What's my diagnosis?" I ask again.

"Beats me". Mommy says. "You could have cancer like Leah, for all I know."

I wake up a few hours later from another awful dream, but this time, Leah was in it. The pills were it in too, but this time they were the size of soup cans, and Mommy was forcing them down Leah's throat. Brian stood over her, laughing and eating a soft-serve chocolate ice cream cone with butterscotch dip. Leah was calling me to help her, but when I tried to move, my feet wouldn't work, and when I tried to yell, my mouth wouldn't work either. I heard the saw the little girl again, the one with dark braids and a white dress. She was standing next to me, and I couldn't quite see her face, but she was yelling at me and Leah to run. Then Dr. Warner pulled an IV out of my arm, and it hurt so much that everything went black.

The house is quiet, so I get out of bed, because I am *so* thirsty. It feels like I haven't had anything to drink in days or maybe even weeks. I'm really tired too. My legs and arms feel like they weigh a thousand pounds, and when I try to lift them, my head spins. I don't think I've ever been this tired, not even after Daddy took me on a hiking trip and we got lost. We walked for seven hours before we found the car. I try to think about why I feel like this, but my mouth is so dry that my tongue feels like a crinkly piece of paper in my mouth. After getting back into bed, I stare at the ceiling. I can still taste the pills in my mouth and in my throat, and they still taste awful. The pills. It must be the pills. But why would Dr. Warner say I should have pills that make me tired and even sicker? I hope Mommy gave me the medicine he told her to give me.

"Mommy!" I call, but then I remember that she doesn't like being called that. "Mother!" The house is still quiet. I can't hear Mommy anywhere. I can usually tell when Mommy is in the house, even if I don't hear her, because the house is scary when she's in it. It feels like everything is made of glass, and if I even move, everything will break and Mommy will yell at me. When Mommy isn't home, it just feels like an empty house. Like now. So Mommy must not be home. But I have to ask her about the pills. On the refrigerator, there is a note. *Fern, if you wake up and don't feel well, drink this.* I open the refrigerator and there is a pink milkshake with a green straw. It smells like strawberries. I wonder when Mommy made it, because I must have slept right through the noise of the blender, even though that sort of thing would usually wake me up. Mommy's note doesn't say anything else. Not where she is or when she left or when she'll be home. Maybe the milkshake will give me some energy, and I'm still so thirsty. I take out a spoon and dig through the milkshake, looking for bits of pill powder. The only thing I find is chunks of strawberry. The milkshake looks really good. I carry it upstairs, which is not easy, because I am so tired I have to crawl. Mommy doesn't normally let me have food upstairs, but she isn't home, so it's probably okay.

The milkshake tastes just as good as it looked. After I finish it, I put the glass on my nightstand and wait for whatever was on the milkshake to make me feel better. But I just feel more tired and even thirstier. I wonder if there's a sponge in my stomach. I can barely keep my eyes open, so I hold them with my hands and try to stay awake, because maybe Mommy will come home and give me the right medicine.

Just then, a thought hits my brain and wakes me up. I don't feel better because there was nothing in that milkshake to make me feel better. There might have even been more of the pills that made me so tired in the first place. I peer in the bottle. I remember Mommy pouring the pills out. There were thirty-three, and if I took five... I normally love math, but not when it involves pills and being sick and tired and thirsty. I rest my forehead on the bathroom floor. It feels cool and it helps me think. Thirty-three minus five is twenty-eight. There should be twenty-eight pills in the bottle now. I count and there are twenty-six. I'm sure I didn't count wrong. Two pills are missing. I fall asleep then, right on the bathroom floor, not wanting to believe that Mommy might have tried to hurt me on purpose.

The front door opens, waking me up. I'm still tired, but I keep myself awake and listen very carefully. There are two voices. Mommy and a man. At first I think it is Brian, but this voice is quieter than Brian's booming way of talking that sounds like he's throwing rocks at my head whenever he says 'kid'. This voice sounds like a waterfall, all the words connected together. The voices are coming up the stairs now, and I know they will see me, because I'm in the bathroom. I try to see what the man looks like as I watch his face come into my sight when he stumbles up the stairs, but my eyes are blurry with sleep and who knows what else, so all I see is brown skin and black hair. And then Mommy, coming closer and closer to the bathroom door, which is open. She looks at me lying on there and before she takes the man into her bedroom, she kicks the door shut so he can't see me. I wait in the bathroom for a while, too tired to get up.

When I wake up, it is morning and I have marks on my cheek that look like the bathroom floor tiles. Maybe Mommy and The Man Who Wasn't Brian last night was just a dream. But then I hear voices, and I know it wasn't.

"Beth, I'm so sorry. I don't normally drink like that, I promise you. It was wrong of me to stay with you in that state. I really am sorry."

This man is *nothing* like Brian.

Mommy answers, "Raymond, you made the right choice. Come on, stay here just a little longer."

"Beth, this really isn't right. You have a boyfriend. You told me about him last night, remember? I-I can't do this. It's wrong."

"No, it's not. He doesn't have to know. Besides, we had a fight."

"I still don't feel very good about this."

"Oh, come on. Get up. I'll make you breakfast."

"You really don't have to-"

"Fern!" Mommy yells. "Go make some coffee!"

I really just want to lie down, but Mommy will get mad at me if I don't make the coffee, and I kind of want to see The Man Who Isn't Brian. He has a nice voice, like Daddy. I hold on to the staircase railing as I try to make my feet move, but they are so tired that they shake and then I feel myself go down.

Whenever I fall, it's like I know what's about to happen, and I think to myself that I could have stopped it, and then everything is in slow motion. I hear a crash as I land at the bottom of the stairs and I wonder what it was. Then I realize it was me landing on the wooden floor.

For a second, I feel nothing, and then my body feels like it's being stabbed with a thousand needles, especially my head. I know there is blood, because when I try to move my hand, it lands in something sticky and wet.

I hear footsteps and Mommy yells "Fern! The coffee! Come on!"

Then she must see the blood, because she says, "What the hell happened?"

"Oh my gosh", The Man Who Isn't Brian says, rushing down the stairs. "What happened?"

Mommy answers for me. "She has seizures. It's draining, Raymond, but I'm the only one who can raise her, so I have to live with it."

"Seizures?" I don't have seizures.

Raymond touches my forehead, and even though it hurts a lot, I like his fingers because they are rough and smooth at the same time. I don't really know what a seizure is, but I don't think it's falling down the stairs.

"She's awake", Raymond says. "I don't think it's a seizure, Beth."

"It's got to be."

"Beth, I'm a doctor. I told you that when we first met. I know it's hard to trust someone else with your child, but I've been trained to know what a seizure looks like, and what we see here certainly isn't it."

"We should take her to the ER, right?"

"Well", Raymond leans over me to look at my head. "She hasn't vomited, that's a good sign that it's not a concussion, but yes, we should probably get her checked out, just in case."

For some reason, Mommy seems excited about this. Her face lights up like a firework in the sky, and her eyes get that happy sparkle in them. Raymond notices. She grabs his arm and cries, "Will she be all right, Ray? Will she?"

"I think she'll be fine," Raymond says.

I may be fine, but I'm really tired. Raymond's strong hands lift me into Mommy's car. I hope I don't throw up, because Mommy's car is just as clean as the day she bought it, and one time I got in trouble for eating a bag of dry Cheerios in the backseat. Mommy complained that the Cheerios smelled 'dusty' and that they left crumbs, so I don't even want to imagine what she might say about throw-up.

As we drive, I hear Mommy fake-crying and Raymond trying to calm her down, but soon their voices blur together and then they are nothing at all.

I wake up when I feel the car stop moving. I am still wearing the hospital pajamas from yesterday. I hope Dr. Warner is keeping Daddy's oil-shirt safe for me. Maybe Leah has a new hat.

Janice The Nurse is at the front desk again, and she looks surprised to see us. At first, I think she didn't expect to see me again so soon, but then I realize she is looking at Raymond.

"Dr. Ray?" she asks. "What are you doing here?" I am confused too. Does Raymond work at the hospital?

"It's all a bit complicated, Janice", Raymond says. "We've got a bit of a problem here, though. This little girl..."

"Fern", Mommy tells him. "Oh God, Raymond, I'm so bad! I didn't even tell you the name of my kid!"

"Fern", Raymond continues. "Janice, Fern fell down the stairs and hit her head. There was no vomiting, which leads me to believe there is no concussion, but as you can see, there's a bit of blood. My recommendation would be to have a doctor check her our right away, since she seems very lethargic also."

Janice smiles. "Haven't lost your touch, Dr. Ray."

"Excuse me." Mommy pulls Raymond away from Janice. "How do you know this woman?"

"I'm sorry, Beth", Raymond says. "I should have introduced you to her. You see, I used to work at this hospital until I got offered a better position at another hospital. Janice and I are friends. We met through work."

"Oh." Mommy looks like she just swallowed a lemon. "I see. You're just friends?"

"Yes, Beth, we are just friends. I promise."

"She bumped her head, you say?" Janice asks. Mommy nods and glares at her, which I think is mean, because Janice didn't do anything wrong. "And you two are...together?" She points at Mommy and Raymond.

Raymond opens his mouth but Mommy says loudly, "Yes. Yes, we're together. Then she squeezes Raymond's arm so hard he almost drops me.

"Sorry", he whispers.

"It's okay", I whisper back. "Just don't marry Mommy."

"What?" he laughs.

"What's with the whispering?" Mommy snaps. "Janice, we need some help here."

"Of course. Friends of Dr. Ray get special privileges in my world."

Mommy's eyes light up and I also think I there must be glitter in them, because they sparkle. I know she likes the words 'special privileges'. Janice leads us to a small room with a table covered by a crinkly piece of paper.

"I'll have a doctor look in on her in a minute", she says. "I'll also get you some pajamas." "She's already wearing some", Mommy says. "The poor kid is always sick. There's just no use even getting her dressed."

I can tell that Janice is embarrassed, because she nods quickly and leaves. Mommy helps me onto the table.

"Fern", says Raymond. "When we were leaving, your Mommy told me to get some blankets from your room, and I found this." He holds out Pox. "I thought it might be special to you."

I grab Pox and say "Thank you. Thank you!"

"Oh, for goodness sake", Mommy says. "Stop acting like a baby, Fern. You don't need that old thing. I bet Ray wouldn't have even brought it if he knew who gave it to you." She takes Pox from me and starts to toss him aside, but Raymond stops her.

"I don't care who gave it to her", he says. "Sometimes kids just need something to cuddle, Beth. Especially in hospitals. I work in one, so I would know. You wouldn't believe how much difference a stuffed animal can make."

I can tell Mommy wants to fight with Raymond and tell him that I'm too old for Pox, but she doesn't.

"Fine", she says. "But when Fern is ten and still sucking her thumb, it's all on you, Ray." I don't suck my thumb, and Mommy knows it. She just said it to make me mad. Raymond smiles at me, and I think he winks too.

CHAPTER 7

A few hours later, a nurse comes in. She's tall and thin and very pointy. She says her name is Dr. Teresa, but it doesn't matter because in my mind she is Pointy Woman. Pointy Woman measures the beating of my heart with a squeeze pump and cleans off my forehead with something that stings.

"How did this happen?" she asks as she puts a bandage on my cut. "I fell down the stairs", I say.

She laughs, and even her laugh is pointy. If she was a plant, she would be sharp- like a cactus.

"Weren't looking where you were going?" she asks. Mommy makes a growling sound in the back of her throat like she's unhappy.

"This is nothing to joke about, Dr. Teresa. Fern had a seizure. She was convulsing at the bottom of the stairs when we found her, the poor thing."

Pointy Woman turns to Raymond. "What's your say, Dr. Ray? Or have you gotten too good for us, now that you're working for a bigger hospital?"

She laughs, and Raymond smiles. "Of course I'm still happy to help in any way that I can, but I really don't think it was a seizure", he says. "She was still when we found her."

"That's not what she said." Pointy Woman jabs her finger at Mommy, and her finger is pointy like a needle.

"Ray", Mommy says, and I can see that her teeth are pressed together so her voice comes out tight, like a stretched rubber band. "Why don't you go wait outside?"

"I'll be right out there if you need me", Raymond says, closing the door behind him. Mommy tells Pointy Woman how sorry she is, but the men in her life just don't understand how hard it is to have a sick child. Pointy Woman nods, but I don't think she's really paying attention. Mommy must think that too, because she says, "Are you even *listening*, doctor? This is important!"

Pointy Woman takes a seat next to Mommy and puts her hand on Mommy's shoulder.

"I know it's hard", she says. "But we're doing the best we can. We have to do a blood test. Is that okay?"

"Of course!" Mommy says. "Anything you can do to get Fern better is absolutely okay. Better than okay, in fact. It's wonderful. Last time we were here, it was just a disaster. This useless doctor sent us home early! I just *know* that won't happen this time, right?"

Pointy Woman nods and leaves to get the needles to take my blood. Mommy turns to me.

"Look, Fern", she says in her tight rubber band voice. "There's something wrong with you. Show them that. Tell them how you feel."

"Tired", I say. "And dizzy. And my head hurts."

"Did you drink the milkshake I left you?" Mommy asks.

I nod. "Yes, but it didn't help."

I turn my head back to the pillow then, but before I close my eyes, I think I see Mommy smile like a snake that just spotted an extra fat mouse to eat. I feel something in my arm a few minutes later and it turns out to be a needle when I open my eyes. My blood is going into a tube, and since this has happened to me before and I'm not scared of it, I just close my eyes again.

Mommy is asking Pointy Lady all kinds of questions, like how my vital signs are, and what my pulse is, and if any of it is abnormal. I don't know the words 'vital' and 'pulse' and 'abnormal'. The blood sample is back now, and labeled with a piece of tape and a Sharpie pen. Eyes must have a mind of their own, I decide, because mine open wide and look around when the blood comes back from the lab. Pointy Woman is standing over me, and I see that she has a very long and very pointy nose with a few hairs in it.

"Can we bring Dr. Ray back in?" she asks Mommy. "There's something we all need to discuss." The look on Mommy's face says no, but her mouth must not be paying attention to her face, because her mouth says yes. Raymond comes back in and sits down.

"This is very troubling", Pointy Woman growls. "It seems that there are traces of sleeping pills in Fern's blood. How could that have happened?"

We all stare at her, and she says "I'm serious. How did this happen?"

"I really don't know", Mommy says quickly. "I need a word with Fern, please. Alone." Once Pointy woman and Raymond are gone, Mommy kneels down next to my bed.

"Fern, you need to tell them that you swallowed those pills by accident."

"But I didn't!" I cry. "I don't even know how I got those pills in me!" Then it hits me. I *do* know. Mommy gave me those huge red and blue pills. Why?

"But it wasn't an accident," I tell Mommy. "You gave me those pills, remember?"

Mommy breathes right in my face, and for a lady who spends so much time using mouthwash and mints, her breath stinks.

"You can't tell them that", she says. "You say that you found them and thought they were candy."

"But they're *not* candy. They're pills.""

But you can't tell them that."

"Why not? Why do you want me to lie?"

Mommy sighs. "Just do it, Fern."

"I can't. It's not the truth."

"You'll do what I say, or..." Mommy's face goes dark, and I can tell that she is thinking. "Or you can't see Daddy anymore."

"Yes, I can!" I say. "I can call him or find him or..."

"Get real", Mommy snaps. "You're just a kid. You can't do anything."

I want to cry. I can feel tears behind my eyes, but I squeeze them back and set my mouth into a straight line so Mommy doesn't know I'm upset. "I can still see Daddy anyway", I say.

"No, you can't", Mommy growls. "Not unless you cooperate."

I can't risk losing Daddy.

"Your choice." Mommy gets up to call Pointy Woman and Raymond back in. She's knows what I'll do. I know too.

"Fern will explain to you about the sleeping pills", Mommy says. Pointy Woman looks at me with a pointy stare.

"I found the pills", I say. "I thought they were candy. I didn't know they would make me sick." I sound like a robot. I cross my fingers behind my back so I feel better about not telling the truth. But it doesn't work.

"You know, Fern, you're too old to be eating things that you don't know are safe", Pointy Woman says. "Sleeping pills can be very dangerous. A few more of those and you could have been in seriously hurt."

"Isn't it serious already?" Mommy asks, sounding a little bit too hopeful.

"Not too serious", Pointy Woman replies. "We're going to give her something to make her vomit. To clean out her stomach, so the sleeping pills don't stay in there. Then we're going to put her on an IV to keep her hydrated, because she's going to vomit quite a bit and lose a lot of fluid."

"Okay", Mommy says. "Let's get to it, then."

Pointy Woman pushes a button on the wall, and a voice crackles on and says "How can I help you?" It reminds me of the thing they call the 'intercom' at school. I call it 'The Lazy People Machine', because everyone just talks to each other through it instead of actually getting up and telling the other person what they want.

"One dose, please", Pointy Woman says. She asks me what flavor I want.

"Grape", I start to say, but Mommy interrupts me and says it doesn't matter. They send strawberry. It's pink and really sweet smelling. It looks like the strawberry milkshake that Mommy put the sleeping pills in, and suddenly I never want to have strawberry milkshakes, or even strawberry anything, ever again.

"Drink it, Fern", Pointy Woman says, putting a tray next to me. I don't want to drink it and I don't want to throw up again.

"No", I say. "I don't want to get sick."

"For God's sake, Fern, do what Dr. Teresa tells you!" Mommy exclaims.

I fold my arms over my chest and stare at it. Gross pink bubbles swim to the top of it, and just the smell makes me feel sick already. Raymond pokes his head into the room.

"Everything okay in here?"

"Ray, can't you get her to drink it?" Mommy asks. "You're a doctor."

Kneeling down next to me, Raymond looks me right in the eye. My face burns because I feel like I am about to cry. Raymond is the only person in the room who I like, and I'm letting him down.

"Fern", he says gently, "you don't want those pills in your stomach, do you?"

"Will they hurt me?" I ask. If they will, then I'll drink it, but if they won't, then the pills can stay right where they are for all I care.

"Tell her they'll hurt her!" Mommy snaps. "She might die if she doesn't drink it! Tell her that, Ray!"

"She won't die", Raymond says quietly. "I'm not telling her that, because it's not true. But Fern, those pills need to be out of you as soon as possible, which is why you need to drink it." He hands me Pox.

"Would it help you to hold your friend?"

"His name is Pox", I say.

"Interesting", Raymond replies. "Right after you drink it, I'd like to know how Pox got his name."

Squeezing Pox really tight usually helps when I'm scared, but not today. I need something more. "I want Daddy", I say. "I want him to hold my hand."

Mommy blows air out of her mouth. "Your father isn't here, Fern. And he's not coming. I don't even know where he is, and furthermore, if he knew you were in the hospital, he wouldn't even come to see you. You know how he is."

"Daddy's not like that!" I cry. "And I need him!" Then I feel someone's hand in mine. It is rough and smooth at the same time, and I know who it is without even turning around.

"Can I hold your hand?" asks Raymond. "I know I'm not your Daddy, but it might help."

Raymond is trying to help, which I like, so I close my eyes as tight as I can and squeeze his hand. I pretend he is Daddy. Then I drink it. It only takes a few seconds for it to start working. Pointy Woman said it would make me throw up, and it does. At least Raymond is still holding my hand. He doesn't let go until I lift my head from the tray and flop back on the pillow. I feel like all my insides have been squeezed out, and now I'm just a shell with nothing inside me at all.

"I'm thirsty", I say.

"You should be", Pointy Woman replies. "Vomiting forces a lot of liquid to leave your body. I'd give you something to drink, but that wouldn't be sufficient. We're going to put an IV in to give you fluids, so after a while, you hopefully won't feel as thirsty, okay?"

I'm too weak to talk, so I nod.

"Have you ever had an IV before?" Raymond asks.

Before I can answer, two doctors walk through the door.

"Dr. Warner?"

He smiles. "What in the world are you doing back here, Fern?"

"She had a seizure", Mommy replies.

She keeps saying that, even though everyone knows it isn't true. Dr. Warner looks at Raymond, asking a question without words. Raymond shakes his head, and I am pretty sure he is answering no, I haven't really had a seizure.

"This is Nurse Horn", Dr. Warner says, pointing to the woman next to him.

It's weird that her name is Nurse Horn, because horns are pointy like Pointy Woman, but Nurse Horn isn't pointy at all. In fact, she is round and smiling. Like jelly, I think. Jelly Lady. Jelly Lady takes a wipe and cleans the area right on the inside of my elbow. The wipe is wet and it makes my arm twitch.

"Scared?" Jelly Lady asks, but not in a mean way.

"Not really", I answer.

As she slides the needle into my arm, Jelly Lady asks, "So what brings you here, Raymond? Thought you'd left us, yeah?"

"No way, Diane", Raymond says. "It's good to see you again."

"This lady here?" Jelly Lady looks over at Mommy, and I wonder how she can look away from my IV and not put it in the wrong place, but the needle goes in right. "She's your girlfriend, yeah? Your special someone?"

Jelly Lady winks at Mommy, but Mommy doesn't wink back. She glares like there are pointy swords in her eyes that can jam right into Jelly Lady's round, happy stomach.

"It's a bit complicated", Raymond says.

"Yes, we're together", Mommy says, putting her arm around Raymond. "Absolutely together. It takes a toll you know, having a sick kid."

"Mmm-hmm." Jelly Lady puts a pink bandage with purple hearts around my IV. I would rather have green, but I don't tell her that, because Mommy has always told me to keep my thoughts to myself. "What was flying through you head, Sweetie?" Jelly Lady asks. "Sleeping pills? Those could harm a little thing like you, yeah?"

"I thought they were candy", I say.

I don't think I sound like I'm telling the truth, because Mommy slices me with her eyes and mouths "If you want to see Daddy..."

"And you!" Jelly Lady turns to Mommy. "What were you thinking, keeping the pills where a child could reach them? Be more careful next time, yeah?"

"I'm so sorry, doctor", Mommy says. "I suppose Fern thought that since she's sick all the time, pills might make her better."

She laughs, a dry kind of laugh. The kind of laugh you make when you're not really laughing. My face gets hot, and it must be red too, because Mommy has just made me feel completely stupid. Of course I wouldn't take pills that she didn't give me!

"Visiting hours are only till seven, yeah?" Jelly Lady says to Mommy and Raymond.

"Oh no, please!" Mommy cries. "You have no idea the hell I've been through! It's *so* hard raising Fern, and I just *need* to be with her! I can't leave her! Please let us stay! Please!"

Jelly Lady's face crinkles up like bread dough. "All right", she says. "All right. I'll see if we can make an exception this one time. I have three boys of my own, and I know it's hard to leave them when they're sick."

"Can I sleep here?" Mommy asks. "Right next to Fern?"

I don't know why Mommy wants to stay with me, because she told me one time that I was a mistake. She and Daddy had just started to not love each other. If two people can feel love toward each other, can they feel the *opposite* of love toward each other also? Daddy stormed off after he and Mommy had a fight. I had asked to take ballet lessons, and Mommy said it was too expensive, but Daddy said we would find the money. I didn't know who to believe, so I asked. That was when they started yelling and Mommy's face turned white because she was so mad, and Daddy's face turned red. Mommy said "she'll become a spoiled brat" and "she doesn't *need* it", and "if you're so set on that kid taking dance class, *you* find a job and *you* pay for it!" Daddy yelled back that just because a kid doesn't *need* something doesn't mean they shouldn't have it, and that Mommy should be glad that he was a stay-at-home father so he could spend time with me. Then Mommy screamed, "Well, I *wish* you'd get a job, you lazy ass! It's bad enough that I have to bring in *all* the money, but you just sit around and spoil that kid all day!" Then Daddy yelled some words I'm not supposed to say. He got into his car and drove away. Mommy must have still needed someone to yell at, so she came into my room where I was listening against the door and told me that I was a mistake. That her life would be easier without me. I started crying since I knew that was true, because isn't every parent's life easier without kids to take care of? Mommy told me I was a crybaby as well as a mistake, and then she closed my door and turned out the light. We didn't see Daddy again till morning.

Mommy follows Jelly Lady and Pointy Woman and Dr. Warner to find a cot to sleep on, but Raymond stays sitting down. He leans forward and rests his chin in his hand.

"I know you didn't think those pills were candy", he says. "You're too smart for that."

A warning buzzes through my body, but it tells me to trust Raymond. I want to tell him everything, but I don't know how much time I have, so I just nod yes, I knew the pills weren't candy.

"What's the deal then?" Raymond asks. "Why did you take those pills?"

I study Raymond. My head hurts, and I'm still tired.

"I don't know", I say.

"Yes, you do", Raymond replies. "I know you do. You don't have to tell me, but I won't believe for a second that you have no idea how those pills got in you."

Raymond is smart, I think. Much smarter than Brian, and much nicer. There is a crash in the hallway, and I hear Mommy yell "Damn it! That was my foot!"

"Language!" whispers Dr. Warner. "There are children on this floor".

"It's okay!" I call. "I hear bad words all the time."

Mommy glares at me as she and Dr. Warner come into the room holding the front end of a cot. Jelly Lady and Pointy Woman hold the back end. They put the cot right next to my bed. Mommy pats my head, which is weird, because she has never done that before. She says that she doesn't like touching little kids, because they have germs.

"It'll be okay now, Honey", she says. "I'm here."

"Why are you staying, Mommy?" I ask. If she calls me "honey", which I hate, I'm going to call her Mommy.

"Mother", she reminds me. "I'm 'Mother.' And I'm staying because I *care* about you, Fern. I want to see you get better." She sighs and lays back on the cot.

"Will she ever get better? All of you are doctors, so there's got to be an answer somewhere. Will she?"

"Yes", Dr. Warner says. "Fern will be okay. We just need to keep her hydrated. It's very important at this point."

Mommy sniffles and nods, but I know the sniffling is fake, and I don't know why she's doing it. "May I get us some dinner?" she asks. "I'm sure poor Fern is starving."

I suddenly realize that yes, I am very hungry.

"There's a cafeteria downstairs", says Pointy Woman. "You can get something and bring it back here for her."

Mommy rushes out of the room without even asking me what I want.

"Your Mommy knows what you like, yeah?" says Jelly Lady.

"I hope so", I say.

"What do you *want* to eat?" asks Dr. Warner. "If you could have anything, Fern, what would it be?"

"A Popsicle", I answer. "Grape."

Dr. Warner smiles. "I think that can be arranged, if you eat what you mother brings you."

I promise that I will, even though the thought of Mommy anywhere near my food makes me feel funny in my stomach.

Suddenly, Raymond jumps up. "I'm a bit hungry too", he says. "I think I'll get something with Beth."

He looks at me as he leaves the room, and I can't quite read his face, but I think that look says "I'll protect you." When Raymond and Mommy come back, Mommy is scowling and muttering under her breath.

"Liquids, Beth", Raymond is saying. "Fern needs liquids to keep her hydrated. Trust me on this, okay? I just want to help."

"She's not going to get better by drinking milkshakes!" Mommy says, and I think my heart actually stops beating for a second. *Milkshakes?* No, not again.

"She needed those French fries!" Mommy snaps. "And that burger! She needs some meat on her bones! For God's sake, Ray, the kid weighs less than forty pounds! She's sick, and she needs food to get better!"

"Greasy, salty food will do the opposite of what we want for her", Raymond says.

What we want for her? Suddenly, I don't feel quite so good about Raymond. Brian and Mommy were planning something, and now it sounds like Raymond is part of it. And I don't think that the plans are good for me. There is a button on the side of my bed. I press the button on the side of my bed, and a tray pops up. Raymond puts a tall glass in front of me. It looks like a chocolate milkshake.

"It's a chocolate milkshake", he says.

"I don't like milkshakes", I tell him. This isn't quite true, because I like milkshakes, but the last one I drank had sleeping pills in it, so I'm not sure if I ever want a milkshake again.

Mommy glares at me so hard that I think lasers will shoot out of her eyes and zap me into a million pieces.

"Fern", she growls. "Raymond bought you that milkshake. And you will drink that milkshake."

I look at Raymond for help.

"It's okay", he mouths. "Drink it."

I think I have gotten to be quite an expert at reading people's lips. Along with having really good hearing, this could help me be an awesome spy someday. The milkshake sits in front of me. It's so thick and cold, it's almost like ice cream. I want it. I really do. Raymond nods at me, and I pick up the spoon. When I finish, I am cool and tired, and I also have a frozen headache. It's late, and Raymond says that he needs to be going now. That's when it hits me that there's only one cot in the room. No place for Raymond to sleep. I guess I didn't expect him to stay at the hospital with me, but now that he's really leaving, I'm terrified.

CHAPTER

8

"Don't go!" I blurt out. Then I cover my mouth, because I don't know why I said that. Everyone turns to look at me, and I feel like a zoo animal.

The first time he came to see me after he left, Daddy took me to the zoo. He told me that the judge suggested the zoo. I don't know who the judge is, but I decided right then that I hated him, because anyone who suggests the zoo can't be good news. It was really cold that day, so I had to wear my winter coat. By the time we got to the gate, my ears were freezing and my teeth were chattering, and even Daddy looked cold too. We went in anyway. It was sad, seeing the animals in their cages. The signs said "NATURAL HABITAT", and I asked Daddy what that meant. He said it meant that the cage where the animal was kept was made to look like where the animal would live in the wild.

"It really doesn't look like that at all", I said. "It just looks sad."

Daddy agreed. We tried everything we could to cheer ourselves up, but I was still remembering how Daddy had just left, and I guess he was remembering it too, because neither of us smiled even once. The animals staring at us from their cages just made it worse. Daddy bought me a green balloon, and I tried to imagine like we were one of those families you see advertised on billboards for the zoo. Two parents, two kids, four smiles. Everyone holding balloons and eating cotton candy. Our family couldn't be like that anymore. I didn't even think it ever was. I asked Daddy if we could please go, and he seemed relieved, because he said yes, and when we reached the gate, I said a prayer that all the animals would be let go and spend their lives in their *real* natural habitats, not the lies on the signs. Then I let my balloon go, and watched it disappear into the gray sky.

They are still looking at me. Nothing's changed, except I have my mouth slightly open, like I always do when I'm remembering something. I also always tilt my head to the left. I don't know why.

"Fern!" someone is saying, so I close my mouth and straighten my head. It's Raymond.

"I'll stay", he says, taking both my hands in his. "I'll stay."

"Oh, Ray", Mommy gushes. "You're too good to the kid." Then Raymond says that he and Mommy need to have a *grown-up talk.* He looks right at me when he says that, so I think he knows that I eavesdrop. How could he know that, though? It's seems like he knows everything. Kind of like Santa. Except Santa isn't real. Mommy told me that when I was three.

Dr. Warner and Pointy Woman and Jelly Lady say that I need my rest and they'll let me sleep now. Just before she leaves, Jelly Lady asks if I still want the Popsicle.

"If you have one", I say.

"We'll work on it, yeah?" She winks at me, and the door clicks shut.

As soon as they leave, I drag myself out of bed and to the door. Hospital doors are really thick, so it's hard to hear through them. I think they do that so if someone's screaming in pain, everyone else doesn't hear it. I heard Leah crying, though. But like I said, I have very good ears.

"Look, Beth", says Raymond. "I'll stay this one night, because Fern wants me to. If I can help her, I will. But you need to understand, there can't be anything going on between you and me. It just wouldn't be right."

Mommy's cell phone rings. "Single Ladies" is her ringtone, which I think is kind of weird, because she dates so many people, so she's never single like they sing in the song. I don't like that song anyway. It makes me feel bad to be a girl.

Mommy must look at the screen to see who called, because she barks "What, you jerk?" into the phone, so she can only be talking to one person. Daddy. She listens for a minute, and I wish I could hear what Daddy is saying on the other line, because I haven't heard is voice in what seems like a million years.

"You *what?*" says Mommy. "You got *fired?*"

I know what that means. Daddy lost his job. Mommy told me that when a person loses their job, they don't get any money so they can't buy food and then they die. What if Daddy doesn't have any money anymore and he can't buy food or even gas for his car and then he can't come visit me anymore and Mommy won't take me to visit him and so I never get to see him, and all the while, he's starving to death?

"You better still send the child-support checks", Mommy says.

I know what those are. Daddy told me they are checks that you can trade in at the bank for money to help raise your kid. Mommy told me that they're a tiny bit of cash that a deadbeat father sends to try to make up for the fact that he abandoned his family. I like Daddy's version better.

"You *can't?*" Mommy snaps. "What do you mean, you *can't?* Use the money you've got in the bank!"

Daddy must say no, because Mommy yells, "You have to, you jackass! It's the *law!*"

She is quiet while Daddy talks, but she is breathing heavy, and when she talks again, she uses her knife-voice that probably slices right through the phone and cuts and cuts everything it finds.

"Send the next one, or prepare to meet my lawyers." She slams the phone shut.

I don't think Mommy actually *has* any lawyers, but knowing her, I'm sure she could get some. Mommy can tell anyone to do anything, and they usually do it, because they're all scared of her.

"Beth?" Raymond asks. "Is there anything I can do?"

"Yes", Mommy breathes. "Stay with me, Ray. Stay with me. I can't take care of Fern on my own. Please."

Raymond sighs, and he says something to Mommy, but I can't hear what, because at that moment, I hear footsteps and a voice saying "Excuse me!" right outside the door, so I crawl back into bed. Jelly Lady comes in, holding a purple Popsicle in her hand.

"Found one for you, yeah?" she says.

"Thank you", I say. The Popsicle feels good in my mouth, and I still want to hear what Mommy and Raymond are saying. But I can't listen at the door with Jelly Lady standing right there. It doesn't matter, though, because the Mommy and Raymond come back in then.

"She should go to sleep when she finishes her Popsicle, yeah?" Jelly Lady says.

"We'll make sure she does", says Raymond.

"You're staying, Dr. Ray?" Jelly Lady asks.

"Yes", Raymond sighs. "I'm staying. I'm off work for a few days, anyway."

"And I'm very grateful." Mommy squeezes Raymond's arm. "I could never manage Fern by myself."

"She's not a particularly difficult kid", Jelly Lady says. "Very polite, yeah?"

She says "Goodnight, Fern", and suddenly I wish she was my grandmother. She is the grandmother type.

"We'll check on her in the morning", Jelly Lady says, and turns out the light.

It's quiet then. Mommy lays down on the cot, and Raymond sleeps in a chair. I think it would have been nice of Mommy to offer him the cot because he offered to stay when he didn't even have to. But she doesn't offer it to him, and soon, I hear Raymond's breathing become slow and steady and I know he's asleep. I feel a little bit scared in my stomach, because when he was awake, Raymond made me feel safe, and I haven't heard Mommy's breathing sound like sleep, so I know she's awake, and we're lying awake together in a dark room, staring at the ceiling. I wake up and see Mommy slip out the door. Quietly, like a shadow. I wonder where she is going. Raymond doesn't move. Maybe Mommy just went to the bathroom, but I still have a very bad feeling about this. I lie on my back and listen for footsteps outside the door, because Mommy has to come back sometime. I rub Pox's left ear, like I always do when I'm nervous.

Being alone in the dark makes all kinds of things swim through my head. What if Daddy can't pay the child-support check? What if Mommy's right and I'm really, really sick? What if Brian comes back? The worries fill my head. Soon, I think it with explode with all the thoughts I have in it. Eventually, I hear Mommy come back, but she is stomping like she is angry.

Raymond must wake up easily, like me, because he says, "Beth? Is that you?"

The footsteps stop, and I hear a single word outside the door, whispered by Mommy. "Damn."

"What's going on?" Raymond asks. "What are you doing?" He checks his watch. "It's two in the morning!" A little piece of moon shines through the window and hits the silver of the watch, making it sparkle. I like it. I've always wanted a watch, but I've never asked for one, because the only watches that I ever see are the expensive ones, the kind that. Mommy can't afford. But there must be kid watches out there somewhere. Ones that are cheaper and made of plastic and hopefully green. Maybe Raymond would buy me one, but I would never ask him, because like Mommy says, it would be "the epitome of rudeness."

"What are you doing, Beth?" Raymond asks again.

The light from the doorway lets me see. Mommy's face, and it is red. She looks like me when I've been caught eavesdropping.

"I sleepwalk", she says like scissors. Snip. Clip. And Raymond is cut silent.

Mommy doesn't sleepwalk. In fact, when I was six, right when Mommy and Daddy started fighting, I had trouble sleeping at night. My mind would start to spin around like a blender with Mommy and Daddy's angry voices. I closed my eyes tight, but my head spun even more, so much that I almost felt dizzy.

After a few days of that, I told Mommy that I wasn't sleeping, and she said "You better not have insomnia, Fern. And you better not sleepwalk. Or sleep-talk. Or do anything besides sleep. Nighttime is for sleeping. People who have those problems are just freaks. Got it?"

I said yes, I got it, but that night, I stayed awake until I saw the sun coming up. I heard Daddy get up to go to the bathroom, so I called out to him, and he came and held my hand until I fell asleep, just as it became morning.

"You sleepwalk, Beth?" Raymond asks.

"Yes, I do. Drop it, Ray. I don't want to talk about it."

Raymond apologizes and closes his eyes again, but I can't help seeing what Mommy has clutched in the hand she is holding behind her back: a fistful of salt packets from the cafeteria. My eyes are wide and my mouth is open, and even though my body should be trying to get rid of the sleeping pills by sleeping, I am wide awake and thinking with every cell of my brain. I didn't know the cafeteria was open all night. This hospital practically has its own time zone, but one you can't even define, since everyone in it seems to be on their own schedule. My mind keeps going back to one thing, like a magnet being pulled very hard and giving me a headache. Why did Mommy have that salt? I get more and more tired as my brain tries to figure out the mystery of the salt, but I have no answers. Something is off a bit, like a crayon scribble outside the lines that I just can't see.

I wish I could never fall asleep, because when I do, another awful dream is waiting for me. I am standing near a field full of salt. Across the field, there is that same girl with the dark braids, waving me over and yelling, "I need to tell you something! Hurry, it's important!" I look around but there is no way to get to the girl if I don't go through the salt.

It burns my legs like hot lava, and I scream and fall down. The girl starts shouting "No, Fern! No!", but the salt is sinking me deeper and deeper and soon I am under a giant pile of white salt that looks like snow. My whole body is burning and I start to twitch. Then I feel hands on my body, shaking me awake. I open my eyes and Raymond is standing over me.

"What happened?" he asks. "Bad dream?"

"Yes." Then I notice that something is missing. Mommy isn't in the room.

"Where's Mommy?" I ask Raymond.

"She went to check in with the doctors", Raymond says. "I didn't want to leave you alone while you were asleep, but I really have to go now."

"Go where?"

"I have to go home, Fern."

"Will I see you again?" I ask. There are tears burning behind my eyes. Water and salt. Burning salt tears.

"I don't know", Raymond says. "I'm not your Mommy's boyfriend, Fern."

"You mean her man friend. And I *know* you're not."

"Good." Raymond smiles. "I think you know that better than she does."

"Do you really have to go?" I ask. "I don't want Brian to come back."

"Look, Fern", Raymond sighs. "I get the feeling you don't feel very good around Brian. Or your mother. Is that right?"

"Sort of", I say in a small voice.

"Okay." Raymond sighs again. "Here's what we'll do. I'm going to give you my phone number, Fern. Can you make calls at your house?"

"Mommy usually doesn't let me."

"Is your mommy okay with you calling friends?" I look at the floor. It's really shiny and clean, even though a lot of people walk on it. They must use a ton of cleaning supplies here.

"I don't really have any friends", I say.

"Oh." Raymond is quiet for a moment, and then he says, "So what we'll do is this, okay? If you feel scared or you need anything-anything at all- you can call me, all right? And I'll answer you. I promise."

"What will I tell Mommy if she catches me on the phone?"

"Tell her you're talking to a friend. Because you are. We're friends, right?"

"Yes", I say. I take the number he has written on the notepad that Dr. Warner uses. "Can I hug you, Raymond?"

He laughs. "Yes. And I'll hug you back." Raymond is strong like Daddy, but not quite as big. I try to smell his clothes, but I can't really because everything smells like hospital by now.

"What kind of aftershave do you use?" I ask.

The corners of Raymond's mouth move upward. "Winter Pine. Why, Fern? Thinking of growing a beard?"

"No, just wondering." I pretend there is a notepad in my head and write down "Daddy- Sandalwood Summer. Raymond- Winter Pine." Summer and winter. Opposites.

"Okay." Raymond stands up and stretches his arms above his head so he looks kind of like a tree when I squint. "I'm going to check in with the doctors as well, before I leave. Your Mommy should be right up." He kneels down next to me. "You should probably tuck that phone number away. No use in your mommy seeing it, right?"

I nod. Raymond is right. I need to hide the number somewhere where Mommy won't see it.

"Goodbye, Fern", Raymond says. "I'll talk to you again, okay?"

"Bye."

As Raymond walks out the door, I feel the burning salt tears behind my eyes again. I've got to find a way to hide Raymond's phone number. There is a jar of pens on the counter, so I take the blackest one I can find and press it into my skin. I write the numbers on my right shoulder. My hospital pajamas cover them, so Mommy won't see them, but I can see them any time I want to. I just have to remember not to wash my right shoulder when I take a bath. I count the minutes that go by as I wait for

Mommy to come back. Twenty. Twenty-one. She comes in twenty-two minutes and thirty-three seconds.

"Where's Ray?"

"He had to leave."

"Where?"

"He said he had to go home."

"He just ran off like that? My God, Fern, why didn't you come get me?"

I shrug. Suddenly, Mommy slaps me hard across the face. Her hand comes in like a fly swatter, and I am the useless, annoying fly. There is burning in my cheek. My throat is closing in very tight, but I keep the tears away, because in will never let Mommy know she can hurt me. In the mirror, I see a red handprint across my face. I try to brush it off before realizing that I can't do that, because it's the mark of Mommy's hand. I see Mommy behind me in the mirror, and she looks shocked, like she can't believe she just slapped me.

"Mommy?" I ask. Suddenly, she springs into action like a jack-in-the-box toy that I never got to play with when I was little because Mommy said they were for babies and they were creepy besides.

Mommy jerks open the drawers under the counter, saying, "We've got to cover that up! I need powder!" She pulls a box of baking soda out of the bottom drawer and stuffs her hand into the orange box. Baking soda spills all over my bed, but for once, Mommy doesn't seem to care about making a mess. She shoves a handful of white powder on my face and rubs it around. I twist away from her, because she is rubbing the red handprint and it feels like it's on fire now.

"Stop it!" Mommy grabs both my arms and pins them to my sides. I feel the IV poke my insides, and I remember how it hurts to bend my arm.

"Listen to me!" Mommy hisses. "I'm going to put this on your face to cover up the handprint. Don't look at me like that, because you know you deserved it. If anyone asks...don't tell them, no matter what."

"Why?"

"Because I said so!" Mommy's fingers grip my arm as she shakes me. "And if you tell anyone...a lot more than your face will be hurting."

Mommy softens her voice the tiniest bit. "Look, I lost my temper. But you pushed me! You deserved it!"

"I'm telling Daddy", I say. She grabs my arm and twists. I scream out as my skin feels like it's being torn off.

"Hurts, doesn't it?" she asks. "It will be a lot worse if you say a single word to anyone about this. You love me, don't you?" She doesn't wait for an answer. "Then you won't tell."

She smears more baking soda on my face and stuffs the box back into the drawer just as Dr. Warner comes in. He is holding a clipboard and smiling. Mommy shoves me down on the bed so that the hurting and burning side of my face is against the pillow.

"Good news!" Dr. Warner says. "You get to go home this morning, Fern!"

I stay lying down, so Dr. Warner can't see my face. If he does, he'll know that Mommy hit me, and then she'll hurt me more.

"Fern?" Dr. Warner asks. He turns to Mommy. "Is she awake?"

"I don't think so", Mommy says, even though I am awake and she knows it. "And I really don't think she's ready to leave. I know she isn't."

"The sleeping pills are out of her system. She's hydrated. That's all we need to do."

"She needs to stay, don't just turn us away like you did last time! I want to find out what's wrong with her!"

I hear Dr. Warner sit down on the creaky chair. "Perhaps while she's asleep, Beth, you could tell me a few things."

I hear Mommy's breathing change. Usually, when she's feeling okay, she just breathes so I can't really hear it. When she's mad, breathes loud and heavy, like pebbles being dumped on my head. When she's scared or nervous, she breathes short and fast. Right now she is breathing short and fast.

"Tell you what things?" she asks.

"I'll be frank with you", Dr. Warner says. "I talked to Raymond before he left. He seemed very concerned with how you treat Fern."

CHAPTER 9

I gasp, and Dr. Warner must hear me, because he comes over to the bed and says, "Fern, I know you're awake. Sit up, please."

I don't move. There are two forces in this room, Mommy and Dr. Warner. Each of them wants me to do something different, and either way, it won't end well for me. My heart pounds like a drumbeat in my chest. Who should I listen to?

"Fern?" I sit up. "What in the world...?" Dr. Warner exclaims. He looks at my cheek, and then at Mommy. "Beth, why is there a handprint covered with baking soda on Fern's face?"

I guess the baking soda didn't make my face look normal. And how did Dr. Warner know it was baking soda, anyway? Doctors must know everything they keep in their drawers, even though that's a lot of stuff to remember. I can see myself in the mirror, and the side of my face really does look awful. It's red and covered with white powder. Part of the skin is turning purplish, like a giant bruise handprint.

"She must have slept on it funny", Mommy says quickly.

"Don't try to lie to me, Mrs. Kyros. I know what happened here."

"She could have been resting her hand under her cheek. She has very odd sleeping positions, doctor."

"What about the white powder?"

"There must have been something on the pillow", Mommy says.

"And why was she trying to hide it from me?"

Mommy doesn't have an answer for that question. "Look", she finally says. "It's probably part of her illness. A facial rash. Maybe she's allergic to something. We should really check for allergies before she leaves."

"Beth, you can stop making excuses", Dr. Warner says. "I know what happened. I know you hit her."

I am frozen between the forces. Then I remember Mommy's fingers twisting the skin on my arm and the burning and the tears and all the pain mixed in with everything, like chocolate chips in cookie dough, so I say, "No, she didn't hit me." It's true. She *slapped* me. There must be a difference, or else I'd be lying.

"You realize, Beth, that I have to call Child Protection Services."

"No, you're not! I didn't do anything to her! And Raymond doesn't know what he's talking about! He's a drunk, do you hear me? A drunk!"

"I can assure you that Raymond was at no time under the influence of any alcohol."

"Oh, please! Did I mention where I met the man? At a casino bar!"

"He said he doesn't normally drink," I say, remembering my face pressed against the bathroom floor when I first heard Raymond's voice.

"And how would you know that?" Mommy asks me. I suddenly remember that I know because I was eavesdropping. My face turns red, and I don't answer.

Dr. Warner reaches for the phone that is hanging on the wall, and Mommy yells, "Let's go, Fern! Move it!" She yanks the IV out of my arm. It is bleeding a little bit, and I don't have a band-aid. I spit on the cut to stop the bleeding. Mommy picks me up, and the IV pole falls to the ground and clatters behind us as she walks out the hospital doors with me in her arms.

"Where are we going?" I ask Mommy.

"You're going home", she replies. "And I'm going to the pharmacy. I need to pick up a few things."

"Can I come?"

"No. You're not leaving the house, do you hear me?"

Mommy stops the car stops in front of the house, and says "Get out. I'll be back in a while."

I walk through the rain to the front door, but I don't really want to go inside. The rain feels nice and cold on the spot where Mommy hit me. I see a little white river running down the front of my hospital pajamas, so the baking soda must be coming off. The drops sting my face for a little bit, but after a while, the sting feels good. I start thinking about how I wish things could be the way they were before Daddy left. I wish I had been there on the day that Mommy and Daddy got married, so I could see how happy they were. Mommy told me once how she and Daddy first met. She stumbled into my room, holding a wine bottle. I didn't like the smell, but Mommy must have liked the taste, because the bottle was almost empty. She looked funny that night. Her eyes were puffy and red, but not like she'd been crying, and her face looked sad and very real. She was walking like she might fall down, and she held on to the edge of my bed and sat on the floor with a thunk. But I don't even know if she was really Mommy that night. She could have been anyone.

"Fern", she said, and her voice sounded funny too, all her words blended together. "Do you know how I met your Daddy?"

"No", I said.

"Well." She patted the pillow, like she was going to tell me a bedtime story for the first time I could remember. "I met him at a movie, Fern. I was waiting in line to see "Bridesmaid Wars", and he was waiting in line to see "Children of the Corn". He knocked into me and spilled my popcorn everywhere. Then he offered to buy me a new bag. We got talking, and he convinced me to see "Children of the Corn" with him. It was an awful movie, Fern. Just awful."

"Then why did you see it?"

Mommy laughed. "You'll understand someday, Fern. It wasn't the movie I wanted to see, it was him. He held me during all the scary parts, and since pretty much the entire thing was scary, I was in his arms the whole time."

"He held you in his arms on the day that you met him?"

"Yes, it was like magic. Like we were made for each other." Mommy was quiet for a minute, and I thought she had fallen asleep, but the she said, "He loved me, Fern. And I loved him."

"Don't you still love him?" I asked.

She yawned. "I thought so, Fern. I thought so. But I think things are changing now."

"How?"

"I don't know." She laughed, and her laugh sounded scary because she threw her head back and took a sip from the wine bottle. It spilled down the front of her dress and looked like blood. She laughed harder. "I guess we'll see, Fern. And by the way, don't ever see "Children of the Corn". It's too scary."

"Okay", I told her. I had already seen it three times with Daddy, but Mommy didn't know that.

"Good girl", Mommy said, and laid her head down on my lap. I patted her earrings because they were sparkly green stones that I wished I could have.

"Do you think anyone will ever love me like magic, Mommy? Like when you met Daddy?" I asked.

But Mommy was already asleep and snoring. That was the only time that I think Mommy had called me a good girl.

The next morning, she was in a grumpy mood. She yelled that I was useless and ugly, but she had called me a good girl the night before. So I hung on to that good girl for a long time, like it was last piece of chewing gum. But then one day, she yelled at me again, and that time, her words threw out the "good girl". I guess I'm not good anymore to Mommy.

I hear a car in the driveway, and I realize I've been standing in the rain for a long time. Pox is still in my hand, and he is all wet. Mommy doesn't see me, and the car comes closer and closer, until she glances in the window and I am standing right in front of her with my face tilted up to the sky, all the baking soda washed off. The car jerks to a stop, and Mommy slams the door shut.

She is carrying a bag, but I don't get to see what's in it, because she grabs my arm and says "What were you doing out in the rain? You could get sicker than you already are?" She keeps saying I'm sick, but I don't know how.

"What do I have?" I ask.

She ignores me and goes inside. The door shuts, so I guess Mommy doesn't mind if I stand in the rain after all.

"Listen here, Fern", Mommy says. I am at the bathroom counter. She is spreading some type of powder all over the handprint on my face. It's called "foundation", and it's skin-colored. No one will be able to see the handprint if there's foundation on my face, which is burning up again. The mark is disappearing though, with each powdery layer that's rubbed on my face. I look in the mirror. Everything seems different, like my reflection isn't even me. I have short blond hair and blue eyes and freckles. I still have all that, but I look more tired and there are dark circles under my eyes. My skin is a mess. My hair hasn't been washed in at least a week. Normally, I hate taking baths, but right now I really want one, because maybe I could scrub away everything bad that's happened, and when I pull the plug, it would all go down the drain like soap bubbles. Mommy catches me watching myself in the mirror and barks "Listen!" again.

"I need you to do something for me", she says. Her voice is soft and too sweet, like cotton candy. I hate cotton candy. And I hate her talking to me like I'm a baby. "The foundation is going to clear your face up", Mommy continues. "And then we'll give you a bath and brush your hair. I'll find a dress for you to put on."

"Why do I have to wear a dress?" I ask. "There might be some people coming to see us", Mommy says.

"Child Protective Services?" I say. Mommy might think I don't pay attention, but that's not true. I hear everything. I'm not sure what Child Protective Services is, but it doesn't *sound* like a bad thing. It sounds like a service that protects children.

"Are they coming because you slapped me?" I ask Mommy. Her voice turns hard. The cotton candy has become too sweet, hardened into a shell, and cracked.

"That's none of your business. It's none of their business, either, but they're going to ask you about it anyway."

"Okay."

"No, Fern, it's not okay. I need you to tell them that I never hit you. Tell them what a good mother I am. I buy you ice cream every Friday and take you to ballet class, got it?"

"But you *don't.*"

"But you'll tell them I do. Or else you'll get taken away. And put into an orphanage where they'll hit you all the time with a whip. You don't want that, do you?"

"No", I say. I don't know if such a scary orphanage is out there, but I don't really want to find out. I let Mommy give me a bath, and scrub my head so hard it hurts. I let her brush my hair. It looks the same to me as it always does, but Mommy tells me I look almost pretty. I take her words and stick them in my brain. Mommy goes to my closet and pulls out a pale blue dress with a white ribbon around the middle. It's the only dress I have. There was a Christmas party at The Happy Hour Casino one year, and everyone was invited to bring their kids. They even took down the NO ONE UNDER 18 ALLOWED TO ENTER sign and let all the kids run around while the grown-ups drank funny-looking drinks with olives out of wide glasses. I was the youngest kid there. The second youngest was a nine year old boy wearing a purple tie. He ate seven brownies and threw up. I didn't want to talk to him. So instead, I stood outside of a circle of teenage girls and listened to every word they said. By the end of the night, I knew all about boyfriends and dating and sex, so the one good thing that came out of that party was that Mommy and Daddy don't have to have any serious talks with me about that stuff, which is better for all of us anyway.

The Child Protective Services don't come that day, or the day after. Daddy doesn't call, even though he is supposed to be visiting me on Friday. I want to call Raymond, but Mommy watches me every second. She makes me sit in a chair by the door with my hand folded in my lap, with my hair fixed and brushed. Wearing the blue dress with the white ribbon. I feel like I'm waiting for a party that will never happen. "I need to go to school", I tell Mommy on the third day of waiting. I'm all dressed and ready, so I might as well be doing something. "Not until all this is over", Mommy says.

I am about to ask her "Until all *what* is over?", but at that second, the doorbell rings. Mommy tells me to stay put, and then she answers the door. I know right away that it's the Child Protective Services, because the man and woman at the door are wearing badges that say "CHILD PROTECTIVE SERVICES-SPRINGFIELD".

"We should have come earlier", the man says.

"No worries!" Mommy laughs, and I feel like me and Mommy are characters in a play, pretending everything is fine. I also feel like we're not very good actors.

"May we come in?" the woman asks.

"Of course, of course!" Mommy opens the door wider, and the man and woman step into the house. The man is kind of short and stumpy-looking. That's a nicer way of saying fat. He has a bunch of extra skin around his neck that makes him look like a frog. The woman is tall with moles all over her face. Mole. That would be a good name. Why isn't that a real name? One mole has hair sticking out of it, and I have to look away, because it's kind of gross.

"You're Beth Kyros, correct?" Frog asks. He checks a clipboard and nods. His extra skin moves up and down too.

"Yes, I am", Mommy says, smiling. "What can I do for you?"

"We're from the Child Protective Services", Mole says. "We'd like to talk to Fern."

Mommy pulls up a chair and sits next to me. "Talk away."

Frog clears his throat. Croak, I think. "We need to talk to her alone", he says. Mommy's eyes turn dark for a second, then flash back, like a shadow that comes out when the sun hits it, then disappears. I guess Mommy does have superpowers, because it's almost like her eyes can talk to me.

"Remember", she whispers. "Tell them what a good mother I am. Don't forget about the whip at the orphanage."

I swallow hard and follow Frog and Mole up the stairs.

"Can we talk in your room?" Frog asks.

"Okay", I say. I sit on my bed, grateful to be near Pox. Mommy didn't want me holding him when I waited by the door because she said he was "dirty". I don't have any other places to sit in my room, so I ask Mole and Frog if they would like to sit on the bed with me, since that's the polite thing to do. Mommy would be proud of me already.

"That's okay", Mole says. "We'll sit on the floor."

She and Frog sit down. It takes Frog a while, and I wonder of he'll be able to get back up again. It doesn't look like it.

"Are you comfortable, Fern?" Mole asks.

"I guess so", I say. Right now, I'm thinking about how Frog does *not* look comfortable. I'll probably have to help him up.

"Okay, I'm just going to ask you a few questions", Mole says. "I'm Meg, by the way, and this is Fredrick."

I nod, but they'll always be Mole and Frog in my head. "Do you live with your Mommy?" Mole asks.

"Yes."

"What about your Daddy?" Frog says.

"Not anymore", I tell him.

"Hmm." He rubs his chin.

"Daddy left a while ago", I say. "I can even tell you exactly how long, because I'm keeping track in the notebook I got for my birthday. Do you want to see?"

"That's fine", Mole says. She writes something on her notepad. I lean over to see what it is, but she blocks it.

"You don't need to see that, Fern."

"Sorry."

"Do you love your Daddy?" Frog asks.

"Yes!" I exclaim. "He comes and visits me, and we go places."

"Where?" Mole asks.

I know if I tell them about how Daddy and I like to watch Stephen King movies, I might go to the orphanage with the whip. "The zoo", I say. "We go to the zoo."

"How often does your Daddy come visit you?" Mole says. She is writing the entire time she is talking, and I wonder how she can do that. Maybe she had to learn it at Child Protective Service School.

"Once every two weeks", I tell her, remembering what Daddy yelled at Mommy the night we were going to see CHILDREN OF THE CORN: GENESIS.

"For two hours. Four hours a month."

"Has your Daddy ever hurt you?" Frog asks.

"No", I say. "Never."

"Okay." Mole writes something on her notepad about. "Are you sure, Fern? You can tell us. We just want to help." I am mad now, because everyone always thinks that Daddy has done bad things when he's way nicer to me than Mommy.

"*No!*" I say again. "Daddy wouldn't hurt me. Ever!"

"What about your Mommy?" Mole asks.

I suck in my breath, because this is the part where I have to lie, or they take me away to the orphanage where they use a whip. "What about her?" I ask.

"Is she ever mean to you?"

"No", I say. Orphanage. Whip. Taken away. "She's never mean to me."

"She's never hurt you?"

I touch the side of my face that burns, the side that Mommy covered with foundation. I don't think anyone can see the bruise. "She's never hurt me", I tell Mole.

"Or touched your privates?"

"No."

"Or said mean things to you?"

I want to tell them yes, Mommy had said mean things. She's said that I'm a baby and I'm stupid and that she didn't even care if I went to live with Daddy. And I'm a mistake.

"No", I say, looking Mole right in the eye.

"Does your Mommy ever do nice things for you?" Frog asks.

"She takes me to ballet class. And out for ice cream on Fridays."

"That's nice of her."

I keep my fingers crossed behind my back.

"That's a nice dress you have on", says Mole. "Does your Mommy buy you dresses like that?"

"I don't like dresses", I say.

"Are you ever hungry, Fern?"

I am stuck. Mommy didn't tell me anything about how to answer that. What would sound normal? "I like Poptarts", I say. "And Popsicles."

"Is that all your Mommy gives you to eat?" Mole's forehead wrinkles up, and I know I've said the wrong thing.

"No!" I say quickly. "I just have those things sometimes. For dessert."

"Okay, good." Mole writes that on her notepad. I don't see why she should care what I eat.

"Does your Mommy give you enough food?" says Frog, and I suddenly understand. They want to make sure Mommy isn't starving me to death, like Daddy is starving because he got fired.

"I have enough food", I say.

"What grade are you in, Fern?" Frog asks.

"Second."

"And you go to school every day?"

"Every day that I'm not sick." Which is almost like the truth.

"Do you like your teacher?"

I don't like Miss Bimmons at all, but I nod anyway.

"Is there anything you want to tell us, Fern?" asks Mole. "Anything at all?"

"No." because that's what Mommy would want me to say. Mole sighs. I can tell she wants something that I am not giving to her, but I don't know what it is.

"We've heard", Frog says, "that your Mommy hits you and calls you names."

"That's not true", I say, crossing my fingers extra-tight, because this is a very big lie.

"Are you sure?"

"Yes."

"Okay, Fern, I think we're done here. Thank you."

Did I do well enough to stay with Mommy and not get sent to the orphanage?

"I'm going to talk to your Mommy for a little bit", says Frog. "Meg will stay here with you, okay?"

Frog moves around on the ground, but like I thought, he can't get up. I reach out and take his hand, but he's really heavy, so I end up on the floor too.

"Thank...you...Fern..." he says. "I really need to get into better shape."

"Obviously", Mole says, smiling.

I was hoping Mole wouldn't stay, because I had planned to listen at the door. But I can't do that with Mole right here. That would get me in trouble for sure. Instead, I sit on the bed and fold my hands in my lap and listen very closely, because maybe if I'm quiet enough, I can hear what they're saying anyway. There are two sets of feet in the hallway, and I hear the sound Mommy talking to Frog, but I can't hear the words. Since I can hear the voices and not the words seems almost like they're teasing me. And I hate being teased. I notice that Mommy is using her hostess voice.

That's the voice she uses when we have people visiting and she wants to look good for them.

There is a knock on my door and I know it's Mole, because Mommy never knocks. She just comes right in, because she says that she doesn't need permission to come into my room.

"May we come in?" Frog asks.

"Yes", I call. "Thank you for knocking!" I hope that Mommy hears that and takes the hint.

"Fern's so polite", Frog says as he and Mommy come in.

"Yes", Mommy says in her hostess voice. "Manners are very important to me."

"That's good", Frog says. "I'm glad to hear it. Things look okay, Beth. Better than okay, in fact. They look very good. Fern seems well taken care of. She's very polite, as I said, and seems comfortable with adults. Now, about her father…"

Mommy jumps in. "He left us a while back. It's hard to take care of Fern on my own, but I do my best. In fact", she smiles as she says this, "he's missed the last two child-support checks. And I really need the raise money. Surely there's something you can do about that."

I want to defend Daddy, because it's not fair for them to gang up on him when he's not even here, but Mommy glares at me, and her eyes tell me to keep my mouth shut.

"We'll look into it, Beth", Frog says. "It's important for a father to keep paying child-support checks. However, we're going to need to come back a few times to make sure that everything is still running smoothly between you and Fern. We can't ignore the allegations we got, but we don't have any proof to act on the claims. We'll be back in about a month."

Mommy's mouth twists into a straight line, and she looks like I do when I've been caught eavesdropping. Which is almost never, because I'm a very good spy, even though Daddy caught me twice. He didn't tell.

Mole checks her watch. "Let's go", she says to Frog.

They walk down the stairs. Mommy follows them, and for the first time, I notice that when she uses her hostess voice, she moves like a butterfly, around and around everyone, but never close enough to touch. She opens the door for Mole and Frog, which is very good manners, according to the book she gave me for Christmas called "Manners for Kids: The Complete Guide". I didn't want to read it, but one day I was really bored. I asked Mommy to take me to the library, but she said no, because she was cleaning the house. I was afraid that sticking around might make her think I wanted to help, so I went upstairs. Then I felt guilty for not helping Mommy, so I figured the least I could do was read the book she got me. It was so boring that I feel asleep right after reading the part about opening doors for other people.

Mole and Frog leave, and the door clicks shut. Silence. Mommy turns to look at me, and she's as scary as the monsters in the movies that Daddy and I watch. I back away, afraid. There's no one here to help me now.

CHAPTER
10

"Fern", Mommy comes closer. "You did a good job".

She hugs me, and for the first time, I feel her hands holding me without pinching and clawing to make me behave. I am stunned, like she just zapped me with a laser.

"I...what?"

"You were a good girl for me."

I was a good girl. I made Mommy happy. I want her to call me a good girl again. I hug her back.

The next day, Mommy says I'm going to school. She spreads more foundation on my face and I get into my uniform. It's warm out for February, and I don't even need my jacket. As I am getting a package of Poptarts out of the cupboard for my lunch, Mommy hands me a brown paper bag.

"I made your lunch." Mommy has never made my lunch before, so I'm surprised. I normally take a pack of Poptarts or Keebler peanut butter crackers. Mommy's probably still proud of me for being so good for Mole and Frog yesterday.

"Don't forget", I tell her as I am leaving. "Daddy's coming to see me after school." I'm really excited to see Daddy. I need to tell him absolutely everything. He'll have answers for me, I know that.

I've been out of school for a week, but no one notices when I walk up to the bus stop. That's okay with me, because I'm used to being ignored by other kids. The bus driver notices, though. I've always liked her. Her name is Naomi, and she lets us call her by her first name, even though no other grown-ups at our school let us do that. Naomi has skin the color of chocolate and hair the color of black licorice. She smells like chocolate too. That's because she keeps a Twix bar in her purse every day. I know this because I heard her tell Mrs. Scott one day when I was pretending to drink from the water fountain, but I was actually listening to them talking. Also, the time that Nick Sylvester told me that Daddy doesn't love me because he left, Naomi gave me half a Twix bar as I sat crying in the back of the bus. Naomi told me that Nick was just being mean, and of course Daddy loved me. She said her parents split up too, so she knew how hard it could be. Then she told me that she wasn't supposed to say mean things about kids, but she thought Nick Sylvester was a jerk who would probably end up working at McDonalds. We thought about that while we chewed on Twix bars, and Naomi drove the bus to a big field where all the other busses were. Then she brought me home in her silver jeep, which she said was named Sylva, since it sounded like silver. She said she was probably getting a new car soon, a brown one that she would name Ginger, but I liked her silver jeep. Sylva smelled like peppermint.

"Feeling better, Fern?" Naomi asks as I climb on the bus.

"Yes", I say. "Thank you." I sit in the back of the bus, even though it's the bumpiest. I always get a whole seat to myself, since everyone wants to sit with their friends, and I don't have any of those.

Mrs. Bimmons hands me a stack of work to do by tomorrow. I don't think it's fair that I have to do a whole week's worth of work in one night. Mrs. Bimmons only likes girls with a lot of friends, and girls who wear pink and sparkles and have millions of friendship bracelets on their arms. Those girls she gives stickers and little erasers shaped like strawberries to. She sometimes even lets them skip their work if they are out. But I don't care, because the work is easy. Besides, stickers are stupid and those strawberry erasers don't even work, they just leave gray streaks on the paper.

At lunch, I sit by myself at a table in the corner. I like being in the corner because I can read without people telling me to switch tables because they want to sit with their friends and I am in the way of that. I unpack the brown bag that Mommy packed for me, a peanut butter sandwich and pretzels. I look for signs of jelly but there is none. Next time, I'll tell Mommy to bring home grape jelly, and then we can go in the kitchen and make sandwiches and get all messy with peanut butter and grape jelly. Mommy will laugh and put a spot of jelly on my nose, and I will reach my tongue up to lick it off, but my tongue isn't quite long enough. And Mommy will take out her phone and snap a picture to show all her friends how much fun we have. Except I did that once with Daddy, not Mommy. And Daddy didn't take pictures, so all I have are memories, which is why they get mixed up sometimes. I eat the peanut butter sandwich and the pretzels, and then I am thirsty, but Mommy hasn't packed any water or juice. The school water fountain has a funny taste.

I am still thirsty in class after lunch, and even more on the bus ride home. Naomi says I look tired, and she gives me a sip from her orange plastic water bottle. Mommy never lets me share any food or drinks with her, because she says she doesn't want my "sloppy, little-kid mouth" on everything. She also says I backwash, which is when a person spits back into the water bottle after drinking from it. I don't do that though, and Naomi knows it. I thank her, and get off the bus. My house is the last stop, so I get to be alone with Naomi for a while every day. I've missed her since I've been in the hospital. Mommy is waiting for me at the front door. She never does that. Naomi waves to her, but Mommy doesn't wave back.

"I have something to tell you", she says.

"What?" I can tell it is big news.

"We're moving."

"We're what?"

"We're moving, Fern." Even though she's said it twice, I don't believe her. Why would we move? Suddenly, a thought jumps into my head like popcorn.

"Are we moving in with Daddy?" My mind starts spinning. We could be a family again, the kind of family that other kids have. Raymond could come visit us, and Leah too. I could have a bedroom with green walls. The house could be really old and big, with all sorts of secret passages that I could hide in to listen to people. We could-

"No. We are most certainly *not* moving in with your father, Fern. But there will be someone else living with us."

"Raymond?"

"Brian." It takes a moment for this to click in my brain, but when it does, I am tearing away from Mommy and running up the stairs, not even bothering to take my shoes off, because it doesn't even matter anymore. Nothing does. I hold Pox tight in my arms and cry. Mommy doesn't come to find me for three hours and forty-seven minutes. I keep track in my pink notebook. Like always, she doesn't knock on the door.

"Sit up, Fern." I sit up.

"We're going to live in Rockford", Mommy says. "At Brian's house. He said there's plenty of room."

"But you and Brian had a fight", I say.

"He called me today. Said he was sorry for...well, he said he was sorry."

"For what?"

"My God, Fern. You don't need to know everything. It's grown-up stuff!"

I look at Mommy. Maybe I can make her change her mind.

"Why are we moving in with Brian?"

Mommy rubs her forehead and sighs. "Because it's better there, Fern. This town isn't any good. And in Rockford, we'll be able to get you the help you need."

"What help? I don't need any help!"

"You're sick, Fern. I'm not sure what's wrong, but hopefully Rockford will have some doctors that will know. We can't keep seeing Dr. Warner. The man's a complete idiot."

"I like him."

I know why Mommy wants to move. Mole and Frog said they'd be back in about a month, and Mommy doesn't want to be here then. If them coming back means I have to go to an orphanage, I don't want to be here either. But I also don't want to live with Brian. I mash my face against the pillow.

"I don't like Brian", I say in a muffled voice.

"I'm sorry", Mommy says, even though she doesn't look sorry at all. "But Brian's going to be around for a long time, Fern, so you might as well get used to him. He's better than your father."

"No one is better than Daddy!" I shout. "No one!"

Mommy grabs my arm and twists, just like she did when she told me not to tell about the handprint on my face.

"You'll cooperate", she says. "Just like you did with Child Protective Services. If you don't cooperate...you'll be very sorry, I can tell you that."

Suddenly, I sit up. "What about Daddy? He was supposed to pick me up three hours ago!"

"He must have forgotten", Mommy says. "See, this is what I mean. Do you really want a father who forgets about you?"

"He *didn't* forget me", I insist.

I know he didn't forget me. He wouldn't forget me. Something must have happened, but there is no way for me to find out what. I use a little extra aftershave that night. Since Daddy didn't come get me, I need to be reminded of him a little bit more. Sandalwood Summer fills my nose. The tube is almost empty.

A week later, I am in my room again, except this time, there is nothing in it but boxes. Three boxes, to be exact. One says "CLOTHES", one says "BOOKS", and one says "OTHER". There is no box that says "TOYS". The only toy I have is Pox, and I have been holding him so he will keep me company. Mommy is downstairs yelling at the men who came into our house. They were dressed in blue jeans and orange shirts that said "Prime Movers". Mommy's yelling at them because she thinks they're not being careful enough with her stuff. It's all packed into boxes and labeled too, except Mommy has a lot more stuff than me. I hear her downstairs without even eavesdropping.

"Be *careful* with those, you! Do you even know how much they cost? No, because you couldn't afford them, but that's no excuse to treat them like they're the stuff from the dump you live in!"

If I were on of the Prime Movers, I decide I would drop Mommy's crystal wineglasses on the pavement by the driveway. On purpose. She's even yelling at them about being careful with her clothes, and clothes can't break. Daddy hasn't called me to say why he didn't come on Friday. He didn't write me a letter, either. At least, I don't think so. Mommy has stopped letting me get the mail. She says I've gotten too nosy to be trusted with mail, so she drives to the mailbox every day and puts all the mail in her purse so I don't see it.

"Fern!" Mommy calls. "Let's go!"

I look around at the room I've lived in since I was born. I had a family here. Mommy and Daddy and me. I guess this is just one more sign that things will never be the way they used to be. I take my ivy plant from my window sill. Mommy won't let me take it, because she says the dirt will spill everywhere and the plant will get squished. I said it wouldn't if we took in in her car and I held it in my lap, but she said there was no way a dirty plant was going within ten feet of her car. So I have to leave it here. I set the plant in the corner of the room and write on the wall "PLEASE TAKE CARE OF THIS IVY PLANT. MY DADDY GAVE IT TO ME." I don't know who I'm writing to, but someone will find it eventually.

I look around the kitchen for something to eat, because I haven't had any breakfast, and it's almost noon. It seems like Mommy packed all our food too. Then I remember my secret box of Poptarts. Daddy and I were at the store one day, and we saw limited edition grape Poptarts. Daddy said that limited edition meant that they wouldn't be around for long, so we had to buy them. But instead of eating them, I stuffed the box behind the washing machine so if we ever ran out of food, I would not starve.

I reach behind the washing machine and sure enough, the box of Poptarts is still there. It's old. It must have been two years at least since we bought it. But Mommy says that Poptarts could survive a nuclear attack. I'm not sure what a nuclear attack is, but I think it means that the Poptarts are safe to eat. I open a package and bite into one. One of the Prime Mover men, the one named "Stan", I know for his nametag, goes upstairs to get my boxes. I try to follow him so I can help, but he says, "it's okay, little buddy, I got it." I shake the box of Poptarts at the other Prime Mover man, James.

"Want one?"

"Thanks, kid."

"My name is Fern", I say.

"Okay. Man, I haven't had one of these since I was your age. How old are you, four?"

"I'm seven." Mommy comes into the kitchen and glares at James.

"What are you doing? You're supposed to be moving boxes! I'm not paying you to stand around and eat Poptarts with my stupid kid!"

"Sorry", James says. He sprays Poptart everywhere when he says this. A little piece lands in my hair, but I pretend not to notice.

Mommy looks disgusted. "You're revolting", she tells James. "Prime Movers Company will be hearing for me about this for sure!"

James hangs his head and shuffles up the stairs.

"Pick up your feet!" Mommy yells. She looks at the Poptart I am eating. "You better finish that, Fern. You know I don't allow food in my car."

The drive to Brian's house is three hours and fourteen minutes, so I have a lot of time to think. Our car is driving in front of the Prime Movers truck. I think they're going to follow us all the way to Rockford.

I'm supposed to go to second grade in a new school, one that's ten minutes from Brian's house. The work from Mrs. Bimmons is easy, and

I finish the entire stack in one hour and twelve minutes. Maybe they'll have harder work at the school near Brian's house.

I stare out the window at the clouds. They look different in winter than they do in summer. In summer, they're big and puffy and I can see all kinds of shapes in them. In winter, they're thin and grayish, and I have to work my head really hard to see anything in them. Winter and summer clouds are like string and cotton balls. The weather is supposed to be warmer in Rockford. Mommy says that's one of the reasons why we're going, even though I know that's not true. I hate when people talk about the weather making them feel a certain way, because it's just weather. We still exist no matter if it's hot or cold. When I grow up, I want to live in a place far, far away with no weather at all. Is that even possible?

Mommy pulls into a gas station and gets out of the car. I can tell she's annoyed, because at this gas station, a person actually has to get out of their car and pump their own gas. Mommy likes to have someone else do it for her. While I watch the numbers on the little gray screen near the pump change, I wonder if Daddy is okay. Then I see Mommy's cell phone sitting in the cup holder in the front seat. I know I shouldn't, but my hand must not be connected to my brain today, because while Mommy's back is turned, I reach for the phone and open it. I have used Mommy's phone before, when she wants me to call for a salad from the pizza parlor. That's how I know there's a contacts list. If I push an arrow key and then hit enter, a bunch of names come up. The first one is "Nicky's Pizza Parlor". The second one is "David". That's Daddy's name. I push the arrow key, and then the enter button. I hear a ringing as I hold the phone up to my ear. Any second, Daddy will answer and I can ask him if he's okay. I hear the ringing one, two, three times. No one picks up.

"What the hell are you doing?" I look up, and Mommy is looking over the drivers seat right at me. I know she can see the screen, which still says "Calling David". I guess the phone answered her question for me.

"You're calling your father?" Mommy whispers. Then her volume must get turned up really loud, because she yells. "YOU'RE CALLING YOUR FATHER?" She grabs the phone from me and looks at the screen.

She shakes the phone in my face. "See, Fern? Still ringing. He's not going to pick up. He left you, Fern! He's forgotten us! So you might as well give up!" Tears leak out of my eyes and I shake my head.

"He hasn't forgotten."

"You're pretty dumb, you know that?" Mommy says. "If he loved you, he wouldn't have left." The other people at the gas station are staring at us.

Mommy slams the car door and drives off faster than I've ever seen her drive. On the way out, she sticks up her middle finger at the mother and daughter who are whispering and looking at us. I don't know why she does that. Maybe she is trying to point them out to me, but people normally use their first finger when they point to something. Mommy is quiet for the rest of the drive. I am quiet too. I really have to pee, but I am afraid to say anything, so I just hold it. I realize that I am folding my hands in my lap like I do when I am behaving for Mommy. Am I really that afraid of her? The car slows down, and I see we have stopped in front of a big house. It's not old like I hoped, because the roof is only tilted one way, and old houses never have roofs like that. The front lawn is really dirty. I guess Brian doesn't believe in recycling, because there are beer cans and wrappers scattered all over the brownish grass. The house is an ugly color, bluish gray. The windows don't have curtains.

Mommy once told me that men have no sense of what's pretty or ugly, but when she steps out of the car, she says "Oh, it's beautiful! We're so lucky, Fern." I'm not sure what we are, but don't think lucky is it. Mommy walks up the front steps. The doorbell is missing, and I see it in the yard, like it was thrown there. Did Brian throw it? Why? All that's left on the side of the house is a square hole with a bunch of wires. It turns out we don't even have to use the doorbell, because Brian comes to the door and opens it. I think he was watching us through the window, which is kind of creepy, even though I would do the same thing. Brian kisses Mommy on the cheek, and I don't know how she can stand it and not pull away, because his mustache is disgusting. It looks like there's little pieces of bacon in it.

"Come on in, Beth", says Brian. He doesn't say anything to me, so I follow Mommy. The house smells like beer and grease and sweaty man. I'm sure that after I spend an hour in here, I will smell just like Brian.

"I've cleared out a dresser in my room", Brian says. And bought a new mattress. King size."

"Do you have a closet?" Mommy asks. Mommy loves closets. Her closet at our old house was like a giant mirror that opened and it was so big, you could even walk inside. All her shoes were lined up by color. So were her dresses. It smelled like the perfume counter at Macy's, the place that smells so strong that I have to hold my breath whenever we walk by that part of the mall. But I would rather deal with the perfume counter smell every day than live on Brian's house.

"I'm going to need a closet, Brian", Mommy says. "I need a place to put my clothes."

"But I've only got one, and all my hunting trophies are in there." Mommy puts her hand on the doorknob.

"We can leave if you don't want us." I know she won't leave.

"No, of course I want you, Beth!"

He doesn't say anything about me, but I had already guessed that he didn't really want me in his house. Mommy crosses her arms and lifts one eyebrow, an expression she does very well. I tried to do it once, but Mommy told me to stop it because I looked like a freak and Daddy asked me if there was something in my eye.

"The closet?" Mommy asks, still in her crossed arms and eyebrow lifted pose.

Brian sighs. "I can move my hunting trophies and clothes to the dresser. You can have the closet. Just promise me one thing, Beth. Don't ever leave."

"I won't", Mommy says. "For now."

There is a knock on the door, and Stan and James are standing on the front step, holding boxes. It looks like Stan's is heavy, because he is groaning and shifting from foot to foot. I want to help him, but I know that if he's having trouble carrying it, the box would absolutely crush me.

"What happened to your doorbell, man?" James asks Brian.

"Ex-wife was giving me some trouble", Brian says. James looks embarrassed, and he doesn't ask anything else. I think he's scared. James and Stan bring the boxes in quickly after that, like they want to leave right away. I don't blame them. No one mentions where I will sleep. So I ask.

"Where am I sleeping?"

"Oh." Brian looks at me like he's forgotten I am there.

"I brought her mattress", Mommy says.

"I don't have another bed, kid", Brian says. "There's an extra room upstairs. I guess you can put your mattress there."

"What do you say, Fern?" Mommy reminds me.

"Thank you", I say, but I'm not exactly sure what I'm thanking him for. An empty room with no bed?

Mommy tells me to take my boxes upstairs and unpack before dinner. Then she grabs Brian by his shirt collar and drags him toward the bed. I don't even bother eavesdropping, because I know I won't hear anything anyway. When Mommy is in bed with a man, there is never any talking. Just moaning.

The upstairs is really more of an attic than a floor. There is a long hallway with one room on the end. I guess that's where I'll be sleeping. The room is so tiny, it may even be a storage closet. The floor is shiny wooden, and the walls are made of bricks. There is a chimney, but I'm guessing Brian will never make me a fire. Daddy used to. I feel like I'm in a giant oven, even though the room is very cold. I look around the room for heating vents. I don't see any, and that's bad for two reasons. First, that means there is no heat. Second, I can't eavesdrop. Vents are very good for eavesdropping. I take the books and clothes and other stuff out of the boxes, but I have nowhere to put them, because there are no shelves in the room. I stack the books against a wall and pile my clothes in the corner. I don't bother folding them, even though I know how. I decide that this room could really use a cat. *I* could really use a cat. But there is no way a cat would survive in this house. The smell would kill him on the first day. At least I still have Pox. I held him all the way here.

CHAPTER 11

"Fern!" Mommy yells. "Dinner!"

The staircase is very narrow, and I almost fall going down. The smell is a lot worse downstairs. Mommy and Brian are sitting at a table. Mommy is drinking wine, and Brian is drinking beer. There are only two chairs at the table.

"I'm here", I say. They both look at me. "For dinner."

Mommy gets up from the table and whispers something to Brian. He nods, and Mommy goes to the counter and gets a paper plate with pretzels on it.

"Here." Mommy and Brian have plates of pizza. I see a box on the counter with three slices left.

"Can I have some pizza, please?"

Brian sneers at me and makes an ugly sound, like a growling dog. "That's pizza for the adults, kid."

"Does it have alcohol in it?" I ask. When grown-ups say that something for is adults, that usually means these is alcohol involved. Brian and Mommy laugh, but I don't see what is funny. Then Mommy's face gets serious.

"You hate pizza anyway, Fern. It has tomatoes."

I didn't think Mommy cared that I hate tomatoes. I don't think she wants me to have any pizza.

Brian and Mommy won't let me sit at the table with them, because it is their "grown-up time". Brian digs a hard plastic chair out of the closet and lets me sit there while I eat my pretzels. It is sticky on my legs. I finish the pretzels right away, because they didn't give me very many. I don't like pretzels that much, because they make me thirsty.

"Can I have a drink, please?" I ask.

"No", Brian says without looking away from Mommy.

"Why not?"

"The water here is bad. It will make you sick."

"What about some juice?"

Brian laughs, a mean laugh. "This isn't a nursery school, kid. Go upstairs and leave your mother and me alone."

I drag Pox upstairs. My stomach is still growling, because all I've had to eat today are some Poptarts and a few pretzels. And nothing to drink. I wonder how the water here can be bad. Is it poison? Will I have to go back to the hospital? I could get water from the sink in the bathroom, but I don't want to risk it. Then I remember something.

"What now?" Brian mutters when I walk back down the stairs.

I ignore him. I'll have to learn to do that if I'm ever going to survive living here.

"How will Daddy know where I am?"

"He won't care", Mommy answers, taking a sip of wine. "He doesn't give a damn where you are, Fern."

"He DOES!" I shout, and run back upstairs. I forget how narrow the stairs are, so I trip on the way up and my knee starts to bleed.

Before Daddy left, he covered my knee with a Band-Aid whenever I scraped it. A batman Band-Aid. He said I was strong like Batman because I never cried when I got hurt. I didn't even care that when we bought the Band-Aids, the lady at the checkout said, "We have Wonder Woman Band-Aids too, sweetie. Didn't you see those?" I did see them, but I don't like Wonder Woman because I don't think she ever wears enough clothes. So Daddy put a Batman Band-Aid on me every time I got hurt. Then he tied a towel around my shoulders as a cape and said I was a superhero. I still want to be a superhero, but there's no one to tie my cape anymore.

I dig through my pile of clothes for Daddy's oil-shirt, because maybe it will make me feel better. But Daddy's oil-shirt is still at the hospital. I wonder if Dr. Warner ever washed it like he said he would. Maybe he could send it to me, but how would he know where I live now? I put on my nightgown instead. It's green and blue. I got it when I was four, but it still fits me because I haven't really grown.

When I was four, me and Mommy and Daddy used to go shopping all together. I get my clothes from the Salvation Army, and one day we all went there to find pajamas, because Mommy sold my old ones at The Happy Hour Casino garage sale. Those Green Lantern Superhero pajamas just happened to get stuffed into a bag along with my old baby clothes, and I know it wasn't an accident, because Mommy hated those pajamas. She said they were for boys. According to her, I'll never be a superhero.

At the Salvation Army, Daddy and I flipped through racks of cool superhero pajamas while Mommy looked in the girls section for white and pink nightgowns. "There's no way I'll have a child wearing any of those", she said when Daddy and I came over to her, carrying the pajamas we picked out. Mommy and Daddy had a fight then, right in the middle of the store. I hid in a rack of shirts and listened. The rack smelled like mothballs.

Mommy was yelling that she wanted me to look *nice,* that I was an embarrassment to her. "Beth, no one is going to see her pajamas anyway!" David said.

"She's ugly enough as it is!" Mommy snapped. I remember pulling my shirt up and looking at my stomach, trying to see if I was ugly. There was a mirror near the rack, so I crawled on my hands and knees and peered out. I didn't think I looked any different than normal. I hadn't washed my hair in a few days, but I didn't think I was *ugly*. I listened to Mommy and Daddy argue. Eventually, they agreed on a long nightshirt that was blue and green. Mommy made mad growling noises all the way home.

I pull the nightshirt over my head. I might as well go to bed, since I'm tired anyway. Mommy brought my mattress up here and put it in the middle of the room, but I don't like it in the middle of the room because it's not like it was in my old room. The mattress is heavy when I push it against the wall. There is no pillow, but that doesn't matter so much. Too many pillows hurt my neck anyway. I lie down and stare out the window. I see the stars out, but they don't twinkle like it says in the "Twinkle Twinkle Little Star" song. They just shine, no matter what. The house where we used to live didn't have this many stars, but Brian's house is in the middle of nowhere, so the stars can just be themselves. They're the only pretty things around here. I don't even mind anymore that I don't have a curtain, because I would never want to block out the stars.

It's cold lying on the mattress with no blanket. I pull my knees inside my nightshirt and curl up into a little ball. Then I dream. I am in a house that I don't recognize. There is a long hallway with pictures. At the end of the hallway, there is a closed door, and for some reason, it is glowing. I hear screams and moans. It sounds like a kid. There is no one else around, so I run to the end of the hallway and bang on the door with my fists. The screaming goes on, and the voice inside yells, "The doorknob, Fern! Come and help me!" Then the screaming stops. I put my hand on the doorknob, which is so loose it rattles in my hand. What's on the other side of the door? Where am I? Who is screaming? I open the door. The room is empty, except for a single bed. I see someone lying there on her back. The girl with the dark braids. I think she is dying. Her face is so pale it's almost gray, and there is blood running out of her mouth and down her chin. She is wearing white, like she always is when I see her. I want to run, but she reaches out her hand and says "Stay with me, Fern." I don't ask how she knows my name. I grab her hand, which is cold, like she hasn't been outside in weeks. She squeezes, and I squeeze back. We keep squeezing each other's hands until she stop squeezing and her hand goes limp. I put my ear to her chest, and I can feel all of her bones. She isn't breathing anymore. My mind tells me I need to get help, but the door somehow locked itself and I am pounding with my fists so hard my hands bleed. I am crying and screaming and no one comes. No one will ever come.

I wake up because something sharp is sticking me in the side. I don't ever remember watching someone die in a dream before. My hands are still shaking, and I slap my knees and arms to make sure I'm not dead too. The thing is still digging into my hip, but it feels like it's something in the mattress. Maybe it's nothing. Maybe I woke up because my stomach is still growling and my mouth is so dry it feels like it's full of sand. I don't care if it makes me sick, I need a drink. But first, I need to find out what's in the mattress. There is a zipper on the side where you can unzip mattresses and refill them with whatever mattresses are filled with. I unzip it. At first, all I see is fluff that looks like snow. But then, I see the corner of something. It looks like a red book. I push my hand into the fuzz, like I'm digging someone out of a snow pile. How come I never felt this before? I've had the mattress for as long as I can remember. Or maybe the red book was at the bottom of the mattress, where my feet don't touch, so I never could have felt it. Then it moved when the James and Stan put it into their truck. My hand comes out of the fuzz, holding a red book. It's plain, no title, no picture. Maybe it's blank. I open the front page, and a school picture falls out. A little girl with dark braids. The same school picture Mommy had in the blue album. The same little girl I see in my dreams. Who is she? Why do I keep seeing her? Why is she always telling me to escape? The first page of the book says "Holly". Holly. That must be her name. This must be her diary. But why is her diary in my mattress? I turn the page, and there are words, words that Holly wrote in writing that looks kind of like mine. "My name is Holly. I am eight. I am not sick." Why would she write that she isn't sick? Did someone think she was sick? I keep reading. "I don't have any brothers or sisters. But I want a sister. Mom says that she'll never have another kid because I'm enough to deal with already. Mom tells everyone I am dying. She says that I have a sickness called epilepsy and eventually I will die from seizures." Seizures. That's what Mommy said I had! Holly and I seem to have mothers that are a lot alike. Are there really that many mothers out there who say things that aren't true? "I have never had a seizure. I know what one is, too. I looked it up on Mom's computer when she was at work today. She works at a place I'm not allowed to go in." Something about this sounds very familiar, like it's happened to me. I know there's a fancy name for that, but I can't think of it. A few words on the page bring my eyes right back, like a really strong magnet. "Mom works at The Happy Hour Casino." I gasp out loud and cover my mouth, because what if Brian and Mommy heard? Then I remember that I'm on a whole different floor. I could tell and stomp my feet and they wouldn't hear me then, not even the tiniest bit. "There is a sign on the door that says you have to be eighteen to go in. I don't like Mom's uniform. The skirt is way too short and the shirt shows her belly button. She has to wear a lot of fake plastic jewelry too, and a name tag that says Beth." No. I squeeze my eyes shut, but when I open them, the words are still there. "A name tag that says Beth." I can almost hear the wheels inside my grain turning and spinning. Pretty soon, smoke will be coming out of my ears, I'm thinking so hard. Holly's mommy works at the same place my Mommy does. She says the same kinds of things. And she has the same name. When Holly wrote that she wanted a sister, I don't think she realized what I am thinking now. She *is* my sister. Or half-sister, if she doesn't have the same Daddy, which she probably doesn't, because there's no *way* Daddy wouldn't tell me if I had a sister. But Mommy might not. This leaves me with a million questions burning in my mind, but one keeps popping out into the front of the whole mess. *Where is Holly?* I look at the date on the top right corner of the page. Holly first wrote in the diary fifteen years ago. So she would be in college now, or maybe even have a job of her own.

"Mom makes me take pills all the time. The pills make me drool, and drooling is something you do when you have a seizure, according to the internet. I am not allowed to go to school. When a police officer came to our house, Mom explained that I was too sick and she was homeschooling me. But she doesn't homeschool me. She doesn't teach me anything at all. We have a service that delivers books for me to read from the library. Mom told them I can't actually go to the library because I'm too sick, so they bring the books to me. I guess I teach myself, because I ask them to bring math and history and science textbooks. Stories, too. Stories are my favorite. They help me forget that I have to stay in bed all day. I want to be a writer when I grow up."

I should ask Mommy about Holly, but something inside me is pulling at my brain and telling me not to. Maybe I shouldn't have read the diary. It's sort of like eavesdropping, and I never tell Mommy when I am eavesdropping, so why would I tell her about the diary? I zip it back into the mattress and promise myself that I will read more tomorrow, right after I get home from my first day at a brand-new school.

Mommy does not wake me up the next morning for school. I don't really worry about it, because she sometimes forgets when she has had a lot of wine the night before. And I think she had a lot of wine last night. I feel the diary under me. I will always keep it where I can feel it, just so I know it's there. My head aches and I want water. My stomach sounds like it's crying. Maybe Brian has some cereal. Most grown-ups only have the kind of cereal that looks like little twigs or tree bark, but Brian seems like the kind of person who would have something with a lot of sugar. I can almost see a bowl of Captain Crunch in front of my eyes as I try to get up. And water, I need water so badly. Or juice.

I dig through my pile of clothes until I find my school uniform from my old school. It's wrinkled, but that doesn't matter. I don't know how to use an iron, and I would be very surprised if Brian has one anyway. After I put on my uniform, I think of something. Maybe I'm too sick to go to school. After all, I feel absolutely awful. My throat is dry, and my head feels like it has its own heartbeat. But I'm just hungry and thirsty, and

I can't spend the day here in Brian's house. I might as well go to school. Then I see the note on my door that says "You are not going to school." The door is locked. I listen for Mommy or Brian, but I don't think anyone else is in the house. They probably went to work. Mommy and Brian work at the same place, The Happy Hour Casino. That's where they met. Mommy is a waitress at the bar and Brian's job has a funny name. He's a bouncer. I didn't know what that meant, so I asked Mommy, but Brian must have overheard me, because he said that a bouncer is "a tough guy who keeps the scum out of the bar, kid. Scum like you."

I looked at Mommy. "Brian just called me scum."

"My God, Fern, can't you take a joke?" Mommy said, but I don't think Brian was joking.

My knees are shaking, so I lie back down and wonder when they will be back. There's really nothing else to do, so I unzip the mattress and tug Holly's diary out of the fuzz. My eyes are blurry and I can barely keep them open, but I read.

"Today I tried to stand up, but my legs just wobbled and I fell down. I think that's because I haven't gotten out of my stupid bed for so long. Mom said that if I wanted to leave the bed, I needed a wheelchair. So tomorrow I'm getting one." My eyes close, and just before I fall asleep, I shove the diary under my pillow so if Mommy and Brian unlock my door, they won't see it.

It goes on like this for days. Three, to be exact, but it feels like eternity. I try to stay awake, but I'm so hungry and thirsty that I always fall asleep and dream of Holly trying to talk to me, but I can't hear what she's saying. I must always be asleep when Mommy and Brian open my door, because when I wake up, it's always night, and my door is locked again, but there is a plate with some crackers and a plastic cup of juice. I finish the juice and crackers each day and bang on the door, but either no one hears me, or they're ignoring me. Why are they locking me in here? What did I do wrong? I get hungrier and thirstier each day, so hungry and thirsty that I can actually see my hands shaking when I read Holly's diary. I feel like I know her now. She's keeping me company in this little room. Well, her and Pox, who I hold in my weak fingers every day and squeeze him as hard as I can. The words of Holly's diary flow through my head like the water I want so badly, but I can't understand them, because my mind feels like it's been stepped on and squished and dried out. On the fourth day, I realize something. I've been sleeping at the wrong times. Mommy and Brian lock me in this room every day, but they have to open it to put out the juice and crackers. They must put it out in the evening, and I'm always asleep in the evening, because I try to stay awake all day while I wait for them. So I have to become like a bat. Bats are nocturnal, which means they sleep during the day and stay awake at night. So the next day when I wake up, I see that it is morning. After eating the crackers and drinking the cranberry juice that was set out, I squeeze my eyes shut again and try to fall back asleep. It isn't hard. What *is* hard is seeing Holly all through my dreams, because these dreams tell me something I don't want to know: Holly is dead. I see her die nearly every time I dream about her. I see her spinning around in a cloudy place with no floor or ceiling or even anything in between. Is it Heaven? There are some things I know about Heaven. It's supposed to be the best place ever.

There was a church in the town where we used to live. We never went to church, but when I was five, they had Children's Day, which meant that kids got to come and listen to some men in funny robes talk about Heaven while parents drank coffee and ate gross looking cookies called biscotti. Daddy took me. At ten that morning, a bald man wearing a white robe and a necklace with a cross came to the church playground where we were waiting and said, "Come, my children", which was weird, because we weren't his children. He took us into a building with a tall ceiling and lots of wooden benches that he said were called 'pews'. We didn't get to sit on the pews, though. We sat on the floor in front of a table the Bald Man called an 'altar'. I sat next to a boy wearing a purple skirt and a white shirt with a sparkly green heart. He was the only other kid close to my age. He smiled at me when I sat down. I smiled back

"I like your shirt", I said to the boy. "Green's my favorite color too."

"My favorite color's not green", he said. "It's purple. But I like this shirt 'cause it has sparkles."

"Oh. I like sparkles too."

"Why are you here?" he asked. "I'm Chris, by the way."

"My Daddy brought me", I said. "And I'm Fern."

"My Daddy brought me too", Chris said, and he looked sad about that. "He thinks that if I come here, they'll teach me to be more like a boy and not like dresses and purple and sparkles anymore."

"But the bald guy up there is kind of wearing a dress", I pointed out.

Chris smiled. "His head looks like an egg."

"Why doesn't your Daddy want you to wear dresses?" I ask. "I wear dresses. I don't like them, but I wear them sometimes. And my Daddy is okay with it."

"But you're a *girl*", Chris replied. "So it's okay. My sister's a girl, and Daddy lets her wear dresses. But not me."

Bald Man started talking to us then, so we had to be quiet. He told us about Heaven. He said there are sparkling white gates there they you have to go through and it's all made of clouds.

A girl raised her hand. "If it's all made of clouds, don't you just fall through?" she asked. "Clouds can't hold a person."

"True." Bald Man smiled. "But in Heaven, you can fly."

I decided right then that I wanted to go to Heaven. I listened to Bald Man talk more about angels and harps and Jesus meeting you there, but my mind was already forming my own version of Heaven. Lots of green hills. And green houses with fern plants growing along the street. Cats, too. All the grape Popsicles you could eat. And it would be warm, and Daddy would be there.

I looked at Chris, and he was staring at the ceiling with his mouth open, like he was thinking about what he thought Heaven should look like too. I wondered if he thought Heaven should be purple, with lots of sparkles. After Bald Man was done taking, he said we could go to the Children's Hall and get juice and cookies. An older boy raised his hand.

"What about Hell?" he asked. "Aren't you going to tell us about that?"

"Not now", Bald Man said.

"What's Hell?" Chris asked.

Bald Man smiled down at him. "Who wants cookies?"

It didn't actually matter if Bald Man told us about Hell or not, because when Daddy and I got home, Mommy asked me what I learned. I told her all about Heaven and how wonderful it sounded and how I couldn't wait to go there. Then Mommy said that not everyone went to Heaven. And she told me all about Hell, and she said that if I wasn't a good girl, I would go there. She said it was hot there, like being thrown in an oven, and you were forced to work and suffer forever. And burn, too. She said they had hot metal spikes that they stabbed you with over and over, and it hurt worse than dying, because you were already dead, so you couldn't die again anyway. I hope that if Holly is really dead, she went to Heaven.

CHAPTER 12

In my dream that night, Holly is begging with me. She is wearing a white nightgown with bloodstains on the front. She is telling me to leave.

"Leave where?" I ask, but she keeps saying "Leave, leave, Fern, please leave."

Now she is saying it with her eyes too. Her eyes are also begging. We are standing in a locked room. She is tied to a bed with ropes that I can't break through. I've already tried, but she pushed me away, saying, "I'm fine, I'm fine, just leave, Fern." Then the doorknob rattles, and a shadow comes in, but no person. Just a shadow. Holly screams, and I see her face turn paler and her chest stop going up and down. There is more screaming, but it can't be from Holly, because she just died. I realize it is me, and I am still screaming when I wake up. The sun outside my window is just starting to set. I did it. Mommy and Brian should be opening the door soon with my juice and crackers. All I have to do is wait until then.

But there is a hole in my plan. What will happen when they open the door? What will I say? I hadn't thought about that, I had just wanted to leave the room, but what if they won't let me out? And then there's Holly. What did she mean by "Leave"? Where?

I pull out the diary and read.

"It is my birthday today. I'm turning nine at 6:03 in the morning. Right now it's five-thirty. I like to wake up early, and I can never sleep in on my birthday, because I like to see the clock numbers change so I can officially be nine years old at an exact second. Mom is still asleep. She said not to bother her until she wakes up, and not to get out of bed. She still tells everyone I have epilepsy and I can't walk. She says I am getting a big surprise for my birthday. Here is my birthday list: markers, colored pencils (crayons are for babies), a sketchbook, a cat. And one more thing. I want to know who my Dad is. Mom told me that as soon as she got pregnant with me, he left the state. I think that was wrong of him, because now Mom doesn't have anyone else to be with at home, and I don't have a dad. Mom is lonely, I can tell. She tells everyone that I have epilepsy and that I am "bed-ridden", and then she makes me lie in bed while people bring her flowers and get-well cards for me. She smiles when people visit, and cries, but I know it's fake crying. She lets visitors touch my cheeks and say they wish there was a cure. I wish they would stop touching me and giving me cards. I have a wall full of cards with pictures of smiling animals and the words "Get Well Soon!" I hate smiling animals, and the cards just make me think of how Mom is lying, and that hurts my stomach. I hear something. I think I hear Mom getting up now. More later. Holly."

I hear something too. It's the click that a key makes when it's put into a lock. And it's coming from my door. I zip Holly's diary back into the mattress and sit up very straight, so Mommy will know I'm awake. Also, she will be very proud of my "good posture." Good posture is very important to her. The door opens a crack, and I hear whispers.

"She asleep?"

"Shut up, Brian. Let me check." The door opens wider, and I see Mommy's face. Even though she's the one who locked me in here and didn't give me enough to eat and drink, it's been four days since I've seen her, and I want to jump up and run to her and cry, but I am too tired to get out of bed.

"Mommy?"

"Fern", Mommy says softly, like there's someone else hiding in the room who might yell at her for talking too loud. "How do you feel?" She bends down and kisses me on the forehead. "You were so sick, Honey. We were worried."

Who is this Mommy? The kissing, the "Honey", the worrying. It doesn't fit my Mommy. But it *is* my Mommy, standing right in front of me, pretending to smile and care about me. I think she's pretending, because if she wasn't, she wouldn't have locked me in this room.

"Why did you lock me in this room?" I ask. Brian comes in, holding a glass of cranberry juice. "Is she gonna tell, Beth? You said she wouldn't."

"Shut *up*, Brian". Mommy turns to me. I like how she's being nice to me and telling Brian to shut up. It's a good change. "We locked the door so you would stay safe while Brian and I went to work. We brought you food every day, but you were always asleep."

"But you locked the door even when you got home from work", I say. "Why?"

Brian and Mommy look at each other, and I can tell they are searching for an answer that neither of them has. "The door wasn't locked", Brian says finally.

"Yes, it was. I checked it every day."

"You got up?" Mommy snaps. "Fern, do you even realize-".

"Hang on, Beth", Brian says, smiling. "There's a perfectly logical explanation for this. The kid's got weak fingers because she's sick, right, Beth?" Mommy nods, and I think they both understand something now, something that will prove that I am wrong.

"Right", Mommy says. "Her hands are weak. There's no way she could turn a doorknob. So she must have thought it was locked when it really wasn't."

She kisses me again. "Fern, Honey, why would I lock you in a room for four days? Why didn't you just yell for me?"

"I did", I insist. "No one answered."

"It's these walls", Brian says, pounding the brick with his fist. "Can't hear anything through them."

"Then why'd you put me here?" I ask.

"So you wouldn't disturb us", Mommy answers. "We didn't lock the door, Fern. Don't go making up stories. We checked on you. It's not our fault you were asleep."

But I know they locked the door. If they hadn't, why did I hear the click of a lock being opened with a key? It's true, my fingers are shaky. So shaky, in fact, that when I hold them in front of my face, they wobble and I sort of feel like they're not even part of my body at all. I don't even feel like *I'm* part of my body.

"Can I please have something else to eat?" I ask Mommy. She feels my forehead with her hand. Her fingers have shiny red nail polish. They usually do, and it's never chipped.

"You have a fever", she says.

"I do?"

I feel my cheeks. They're cold.

"You can't tell, Fern, but you're burning up. Isn't she Brian?"

Brian is busy looking at Mommy's chest, which is weird, because it's not like she has an interesting shirt on.

"Oh, yeah", he says. "The kid's got a fever. Definitely."

I don't believe him, because he hasn't even felt my forehead.

"What's that saying?" Mommy wonders. "Feed a cold, starve a fever? I know I read that in a medical magazine."

"I don't think you did", I say, because I don't want to starve, and besides, Mommy never reads any magazines except for the ones about celebrities and clothes and how to lose weight fast. Mommy leans in close to me, but not to kiss me this time.

"Are you calling me a liar, Fern?"

"No", I say, but my mind is screaming yes, yes you're lying! All of this is a lie! You lied to me about Holly! You said I'd never have a sister or brother, but I did! And you never told me! And something is wrong here, but I don't know exactly what! My mind screams all those things so loud that I'm afraid Mommy will hear.

"Apologize to your mother", Brian growls.

"Sorry, Mommy."

"Excuse me?"

"Mother, I mean. Mother. Sorry, Mother."

"Brian and I are going to bed now", Mommy says.

"Are you going to sleep already?" I ask. It just got dark out, and grown-ups *always* stay up later than kids.

"Man", Brian laughs. "This kid's stupid, Beth. Of course we're not going to sleep. We're going to *bed*."

I don't see the difference, but I don't want Brian to call me stupid again, so I don't ask.

"We've got champagne", Brian says, putting his hairy arm on Mommy's shoulder. "And some kick-ass romantic music, and-".

"Shut *up*, Brian", Mommy says, but she is smiling, so I don't feel as good as when she said "Shut *up*, Brian" before. They turn toward the door.

"Wait", I call, and I realize my voice is barely louder than a whisper. "Can I have something to drink? Or eat?"

"No", Mommy says. "Gotta starve that fever",

Brian smirks. I hate his smile more than anything right now. His stares at me, squinting. His eyes are too small for his face.

"Although", Brian pauses to rub his stomach, "I could really go for something to eat right about now." He licks his lips, and my stomach howls like a dog at the moon. "Maybe some buttery, fluffy waffles dripping with syrup", Brian says. "Or a jelly donut. You like jelly donuts, don't you, Fern?"

I love jelly donuts. They're always the ones that nobody bothers to eat, because they're "too dry" or "too boring" or "just plain gross." Jelly donuts remind me of the last kids picked for kickball teams. That's why I love them.

"Or ice cream. Rich, creamy chocolate fudge with pieces of brownie and lots of chocolate sprinkles." Brian sneers at me.

He knows what he's doing. And I hate him.

"And to finish it off", he says, showing his yellow teeth, "a nice, cold glass of tangy juice. With a curly straw."

"Stop it!" I yell. I try to make my hands into fists, but I'm shaking so much from the hunger, I can't do it. "Stop it!"

"Oh, lighten up, Fern", Mommy says. "He was just joking, weren't you, Brian?"

"Yep."

I think of the words in my head before I say them, and they seem perfect. When I talk, it's like spitting out knives. Hopefully one will hit Brian in the chest.

"Well, I'll just go downstairs and get some juice or something. You can't stop me!"

"That's where you're wrong, Fern", Mommy says. "That's where you're wrong."

I want to ask what they mean, but they walk off, pausing in the hallway. My door is open, so I lean forward in bed and listen as hard as I can.

"Should we shut the kid in?" Brian is saying.

Mommy laughs, a tinkling laugh, like a fairy. And not the nice kind of fairy, either. "Hell, no. She's been practically without food or water for four days. She won't even be able to get out of bed. And she might die if we keep her there much longer. I'll take her in tomorrow."

Take me where? I'm dying to hear more, but Brian and Mommy's footsteps go down the staircase, to Brian's room, and there is nothing else to listen to. Will I die? Will I go to Heaven, like Holly?

Holly. Something about her is sticking in my brain now. My last dream, in the locked room. She was telling me to leave. My sister was telling me to leave, and for the first time, I understand her. I will leave.

Deciding to leave is a lot easier than actually doing it. It's hard for me to get out of bed. Someone must have spun the room around me when I wasn't looking, because it won't stop turning, not even when I close my eyes. Mommy told Brian I wouldn't be able to get out of bed, but here I am, leaning against the door. Out of bed. This must be my first step away from Mommy, and I feel very free. Thirsty, hungry, and tired, but free. The staircase is in front of me now. It looks like a cliff, and it's about as steep as one, too. I sit on the top step and bump my way down the stairs. It hurts a little, but falling would hurt a lot worse. Every three steps, I stop to listen for Brian and Mommy. But I hear music floating around the house, and when I reach the bottom of the staircase, I see that their door is closed. Safe for now. I crawl on my hands and knees to the kitchen. Before I go anywhere, I need to get something to eat and drink. I remember Mommy, leaning in close and saying "That's where you're wrong, Fern", when I said I would get something from the kitchen. A metal chain is hanging from the cupboards and fridge. Where did Brian and Mommy even *get* chains? The roof of my mouth feels like sandpaper, and I'm too tired to think about the chains. I'm also too tired to try to pull them off, even though I know they're locked. But Brian's wallet isn't locked. It's fat and leather-brown and sitting in the edge of the counter. I take a twenty-dollar bill. The next step of leaving may be hard. I've still got Raymond's number on my arm, but his number won't tell me where he lives, and Mommy seems to get super-ninja hearing whenever I'm trying to use the phone. So Brian's computer is now my friend. I want to go home, but I know no one will be there to help me. But I have to leave, and Raymond will make me better. He's a doctor, and they help people, right?

No password, I think as I crawl to Brian's computer. Please, no password. If I can't get into Brian's computer, then I might as well be back in bed. Except there's no way I could get up the stairs, and I guess I don't know what would happen if I just lay here. Maybe Holly can help me from Heaven, if that's where she is.

I remember Bald Guy at the church saying something about people in Heaven answering prayers for people who are still alive. I don't really know how to pray. Bald Guy didn't teach us that. Maybe it's something like writing a letter, only it's in a person's head. *Dear Holly,* I think. I close my eyes to make the floor stop spinning. *Dear Holly, I am going to leave, like you told me to. I am going to find Raymond because he will help me. I just need something. To find Raymond, I need to use Brian's computer, and I can't do that if there's a password lock on it. So please don't let there be a password lock. Thank you. Love, your sister Fern.*

There is a big chair near the computer, the kind that spins around. Before Daddy left, he had a chair like that. I used to sit on it with my knees tucked under me, and he would spin the chair until I yelled and laughed at the same time, and Mommy snapped that the chair wasn't a toy. One day, though, Daddy spun me a little too hard or a little too fast, and I couldn't stop. Even when I kicked my legs out and swung my arms, the chair kept spinning, and Daddy was laughing, because he didn't know that I wasn't having fun anymore. I remember a second when everything seemed to blur together, and then I was in the air. I landed on the wooden floor. My back hurt so badly, all I could do was scream. There was a splitting and pushing feeling, like my bones were coming right out. I rested my forehead against the floor and moaned. Daddy was kneeling next to me, saying "I'm sorry, Fern, I'm sorry!" but I couldn't answer. He tried to rub my back, but pain shot through me when his finger touched, and I screamed.

Mommy came in and yelled, "Now you've done it, David! Now you've done it! She's gonna be crippled for the rest of her life, so how fun does your stupid chair seem now, huh? My God, if she broke her back, you're taking care of her, do you hear me, David? 'Cause I'm not taking the fall for this!"

I wanted to tell Mommy that it wasn't Daddy's fault. He was just trying to play with me, he didn't know that I would get hurt. But I ached all over, and I could only groan. I didn't break my back, but the doctor told me I had to rest for a few days anyway. Mommy took away Pox for a month, because she said I should have been more responsible, and now she had to pay for a visit to the doctor because of me. After that, no one spun me anymore.

I climb into Brian's spinning chair. It wobbles, and my back twitches a little. I really don't need any more spinning today. My hand are shaking so badly, I have to put both hands on the mouse. No password, no password. I jam the ON button, and the computer screen lights up. No password. Thank you, Holly. I am in. I don't use computers much, but I know what the google screen looks like. I type in "Raymond Beacon, doctor". I hit ENTER, and I see that Raymond is very popular, at least on the internet. Finally, I find the website of the hospital he works at. It says he's one of their best doctors. I smile a little when I see his picture, because it's almost like he's looking right at me. Under the picture, there are words. I can't read them all, because I think a lot of them are hospital words, like "discharge" or "diagnosis." The hospital could have its own language, I think. Toward the bottom, there it is. Raymond's address. 701 Lighthouse Street, Kansas. I open a new google page and type in MAPS. From where I am now, sitting at this computer, Raymond's house is two hours and seventeen minutes away. But what if he's not home? I click back to the hospital's website. "Raymond Beacon works Monday-Friday, 5:00 a.m- 5:00 p.m." I sigh. He'll be at his house. But how can I get there? I think of Brian's wallet on the counter. I'll take another twenty. I can buy a bus ticket in the direction of Raymond's house. It won't take me *right* there, but I'll be close enough. Maybe I can even get a taxi! I've never been in one before. There is a bus station about ten minutes away, and a 7-11 even closer. I take another twenty from Brian's wallet and leave the house, closing the door behind me.

CHAPTER
13

The sunlight makes the world in front of my eyes go black. My knees shake. Why is everything in me shaking? I try to walk. My throat burns and begs for water, and my stomach screams for food. I can't see Brian's house anymore. I will be at the 7-11 soon, where I will get a drink and a snack. Grape soda first. I need energy, but there's no way I'm drinking Gatorade ever again.

The sun blurs everything around me. There is sweat on my face, but I am cold, very cold. It's the middle of winter, and I don't have a coat. I am going to fall. That's when I see her in front of me. Holly. She's wearing her bloody nightgown, but she doesn't look cold. When I blink, she is gone. I don't know how far I get exactly, or even if I moved at all since I saw Holly, but I am now lying with my cheek against the pavement. It is cold. There are a lot of things going on, I can tell, even with my eyes closed. Sirens. Voices. Lots of voices. I open my eyes, and there are a lot of faces looking down at me. A policeman, a doctor, Mommy, and Brian.

But no Raymond. I didn't make it to his house. I didn't even make it to the bus station. I look to the side of all the faces, and I see an ambulance parked on the side of the street. Who got hurt? Why am I lying here? I don't quite remember how I got here, but I should probably find out what's going on. I open my mouth to talk, but all that comes out is "Uhhhhh".

"She's awake", the doctor yells. "She's awake!" I hear someone crying, and I look up. Mommy has her face buried in Brian's coat.

"Oh, Fern!" she wails. "Why did you get out of bed, sweetie?"

I don't want to tell her why, so I just say "I was hungry." I know that Mommy isn't really crying. When someone really cries, their shoulders shake, and Mommy's are still.

"Out of the way, please", a doctor calls. He has something that looks like a bed on wheels.

"Where are you taking her?" Mommy grabs at his coat. "Where?"

"Ma'am, please calm down. We're taking your daughter to the hospital."

"What happened? Why?" Mommy kneels on the ground and looks at the sky, as if the stars will give her an answer, but I know they won't.

Holly is in the stars, and she's on my side. She won't be telling Mommy anything.

"Why my little girl? Is she going to live, doctor? Please tell me she's going to live?" I guess I should have realized it before, but *I'm* the sick one. It's me they're taking to the hospital. Again. And I am sick because of Mommy. Again. "Please", Mommy begs. "Please let me stay with her."

"You and your husband can ride along in the ambulance", the doctor says. "Get in, please."

I want to tell the doctor that Brian is not Mommy's husband, but I'm too tired. I close my eyes, and the voices start talking again. I hear word, more hospital words, like "emergency" and "heart monitor" and "possible seizure." My eyes pop open.

"I didn't have a seizure! I didn't!"

"Okay", the policeman says, his voice soft. "Okay. We're going to lift you up now, okay, Fern?"

128

Being lifted up sounds a lot easier than standing right now, so I nod. I feel strong arms under me. The policeman's metal badge digs into my back, keeping, me awake. He puts me on the bed with wheels, which is pushed up a ramp into the back of the ambulance.

"How are you doing, Fern?" the doctor asks me.

"I want water, please", I say. With every word, my throat hurts in a new way.

"We'll get you some water as soon as we can", the doctor says.

"She's dying", Mommy wails. "I just know she's dying!"

"Ma'am, please", the policeman says. He puts hid hands on Mommy's shoulders. "I know you're very upset, but I'll have to ask you not to say things like that in front of your daughter. It could be very upsetting to hear."

"The kid's asleep", Brian points out, but that isn't true. I just have my eyes closed. This sends everyone panicking. I feel the doctor's hot breath on my cheek as he listens to my heart. He smells like cherry medicine.

"Fern, please don't go to sleep, okay?"

"Why not?" I ask.

"Because we need you to stay awake right now."

"Why? I'm tired."

"Help her sit up", the policeman orders. "Hold her hand and squeeze it to keep her awake."

Even though I don't know why they want me to stay awake so badly, I sit up and let the doctor hold my hand. He squeezes so hard it hurts, but my fingers don't mind being crushed. My whole body is crumbled anyway, so it doesn't really matter. Ambulance rides are weird. When I see the red and blue lights blurring by on the street and hear the sirens, I always imagine there's a lot of blood and screaming inside. In here, it's pretty quiet, but still just as scary. Scarier even, because quiet is always scarier. All I can do now is listen. Listen while the ambulance parks and I am wheeled out and into a bright-lit hospital. Listen while the doctor and policeman describe how they found me and Mommy fake-cries. Listen while an IV is put in my arm. Listen while a machine scans over my body.

The machine is loud, but it doesn't hurt. Listen while Mommy hovers over me when she knows everyone is watching. I want to tell her to stop. A nurse pokes her head in the room.

"Fern?"

"Yes, yes, Fern's in here."

Mommy waves her in.

"Call me Corinne", the nurse says. Corinne is wearing a blue shirt and blue pants that look like a uniform. I decide to call her Blue, but of course I won't say that to her. That would definitely be Bad Manners. Blue sits down across from Mommy and Brian.

"They've got her stabilized, Mrs. Kyros."

"Call me Beth", Mommy says. Blue ignores her. I like Blue.

"What I was saying is that Fern is okay. However, she's severely dehydrated and close to starvation. The scan revealed hardly anything in her stomach. This is very troubling. Why hasn't she had anything to eat or drink?"

Mommy looks at Brian, who nods. "Tell her, Beth. Just like you told me."

"Of course she can't keep anything down!" Mommy says. "Pica will do that to a kid!"

"Pica?" Blue asks. "Fern has pica?"

"You don't even know what pica is?" Brian smirks. "And they actually hired you to work at a hospital?"

I don't even think Brian knows what pica is. *I* certainly don't.

Brian proves my point by smiling his twisted smile at Mommy and saying, "Pica's that disease where...um...you can't...swallow food, right, Beth?"

"Actually", Blue glares at Brian, "pica is an eating disorder in which a person consumes non-food items. You say she has that, Mrs. Kyros?"

"Yes", Mommy nods. "That would explain everything, wouldn't it, Corinne?"

Blue sighs. "Something isn't right here", she says.

My heart beats a little faster. Maybe Blue knows. Maybe she'll save me.

"Why don't you tell me everything?" Blue says to Mommy. "Everything about how Fern ended up unconscious in the street."

Mommy smiles and winks at Brian, but Blue says "Hold on a minute", and leaves the room.

Mommy whispers to me, fast and hissing. "Don't you dare says word, Fern. Let me do the talking, got it? And if I ask you about anything, just agree with me."

But I can't do that, because I don't have pica. "No", I say weakly.

"Listen, kid", Brian growls. "You'll do as your mother says, you hear? Because I have no problem with hitting you to teach you to obey. If you're living with *me,* you're living with *my* rules. And one of my rules is to obey your mother."

One of his rules must also be to lie, but I nod, because I don't think my body can take any more hurt. Blue comes back, holding a cup of water and a plate of graham crackers.

"Why don't you have this, Fern? You need something in your stomach."

I decide that I love Blue. Mommy presses her lips together and glares at everything in the room. I don't know why, but she really doesn't want me to eat. But she can't control that. She can't punish me just for eating. I look at her eyes squinting at me. I smile right at her mean face and take a big sip of water. It feels better than anything I've ever drank, like a cooling all over my body. Water runs down my chin and drips onto my school uniform, which I'm still wearing. Mommy can't say anything. She can't be mean to me, because Blue is right here. I want Blue to stay. The graham crackers taste almost as good as the water. I eat them in seven bites.

"Can I have some more, please?" I beg.

"No!" Mommy snaps. Blue stares at her. "I mean, no, she can't, right? She'll get sick if she eats more, won't she, Corinne?"

I shake my head. No, no I won't.

"To be honest, she might", Blue says. "Her stomach was nearly. empty. We have to give her food slowly. I'm sorry, Fern. I know you're still hungry, and probably still thirsty too, but more food might upset your stomach right now. And we don't want you throwing anything up. After your mommy tells me what's been going on, we'll see about getting you something else, okay?"

Mommy's mouth twists into a mean little smile.

"Okay", I whisper.

"Just one thing", Blue says. She points to Brian. "How are you related to Fern? Only family is allowed in the ER. Sorry, but it's just protocol. So, are you family?"

"No", I say quickly. Then I cover my mouth to try to stuff the words back in, because Mommy will really get me now. But I don't think she heard me. Blue did, though.

She leans closer to me. "What was that, Fern?"

"Of course he's family!" Mommy says. "Why is this even an issue?"

"It's not", Blue reassures her. "He's fine, I just didn't want...never mind. Just tell me what happened."

"Well, Fern has always been a sick child", Mommy says, smiling like she just swallowed a bottle of honey. "Ever since she was born, I've had a hard time getting her to eat. She just threw everything up. We took her to the doctor, of course, and they gave her an IV. But it didn't help. They said she might die. They still say that."

Blue looks shocked, which I think is kind of weird, because she's a nurse. Doesn't she hear about people dying a lot? I'm *not* dying, though. Am I?

"Anyway", Mommy continues. She settles into the hard plastic chair like she's about to tell a really long story. "When she was four, Fern was diagnosed with pica. By that point, she was eating the dirt out of my garden."

Mommy's never had a garden. She says they're too messy and not worth the work. "Then she started eating paper and clay and crayons when I took her to art class."

I've never been to art class. Mommy says it's too expensive.

"I took her to the doctor again, but nothing helped. I made sure there was nothing in the house that could be poisonous. That's when she started eating cloth. Her clothing. I would look at her and she'd just have ripped apart her shirt. I was buying her new clothes every week. We moved here because we were told there would be people to help her. But the new house wasn't child-proofed, and she got into some bleach. Threw it up everywhere. We kept her in bed and tried to feed her normal food- plain, so as not to upset her stomach- but she wouldn't eat or drink. We tried everything. One of us accidentally left the door unlocked tonight and she must have gotten outside and fallen over because she hadn't had anything to eat or drink. We tried, Corinne, we tried *so* hard, but she just wouldn't eat!"

"I see." Blue says. "I also see that Fern's eaten a plate of graham crackers and drank a glass of water without any problems."

"Are you saying you don't believe me?" Mommy gasps. "Are you calling me a liar?"

"Not at all. But I'm worried about her level of dehydration, as it could be dangerous. How long did you say she went without drinking?"

"Four days".

"Juice", I say. I'm trying to tell them that I didn't go *completely* without something to drink. I had a little juice. But I'm too tired to say nothing more than that one word.

"What's she saying?" Blue asks.

"The kid wants juice", Brian says.

"But of course she wouldn't drink any", Mommy jumps in. "She does that sometimes. She says the name of some food, but when we get it for her, she wants nothing to do with it. We wait on her hand and foot, Corinne, but *nothing* works!"

"She needs an IV", Blue says. "Right now. We need to get some saline in her."

"Saline?" Brian asks. "What's that, some drug?" He has the same twisty smile as Mommy. He likes the idea of giving me drugs.

"No, saline will hydrate her", Blue says. "And that's what's important right now. If she still refuses food, we'll need to put in a feeding tube. Dinner's being served in about ten minutes. We'll see if she eats then."

Dinner!

"Can you eat something, Fern?" Blue asks. "It will make you feel better, I promise."

"I can eat", I say. "Please, let me eat."

Mommy rolls her eyes. "You'll see", she says to Blue. "The kid's hopeless."

Dinner is curly pasta and bread and ginger ale, and for dessert, Jell-O.

"Bland foods", Blue says. "Bland, high-calorie foods are what you need now, Fern."

I nod and smile. Dinner tastes wonderful. Mommy glares at me the whole time. One day, her face says. I kept you without food for so long, and they messed it up in one day. With each bite I take, I grin at Mommy as her face grows darker and darker, like a storm cloud. I finish it all. Blue clears my tray and helps me into hospital pajamas. Soon, I'll have an entire collection of pajamas, one from every hospital I go to. I don't want a collection like that.

"We want to check your blood", Blue says. "I'll go get the needle, okay? This will just be a little pinch, Fern."

I can see Mommy look at Brian. "Wait, where's the cafeteria?" she asks Blue.

Blue tells her, but I tune her out and look at Mommy's lips, which are mouthing something to Brian without letting Blue notice.

"Salt", Mommy is mouthing. "Salt."

Something inside me is tugging and pulling at my mind. Salt. Salt is bad. I can't quite say why, but I feel like Holly is trying to tell me something. Or maybe I'm trying to tell *myself* something. Suddenly, I have an idea. Mommy may know how to fake-cry, but I do too. With real tears. I don't use it often, because it feels like lying without words, but it's kind of like my superpower. To fake-cry, I always think of the saddest thing I can, and focus until I feel tears. Now, I think of Mommy's voice, telling me about Daddy when we were at the gas station on the way to Brian's house. "If he loved you, he wouldn't have left you." Almost. I my throat feels tight. "If he loved you, he wouldn't have left you." That's it.

"Mommy, no!" I cry, grabbing her sleeve. "Don't go! I'm *scared*!" I squeeze my eyes closed and open them again so the tears will fall faster. "Please, Mommy, don't go!" I sniffle.

Mommy looks surprised. She tries to shake me off. "Let *go*, Fern! I'll be back in a minute!" I scream as loud as I can.

"*No*, Mommy!"

"Why don't you wait until we take a blood sample, Mrs. Kyros? Then maybe Fern will be calmer." Mommy is like a human tug-of-war. I can tell one side of her wants to go and get salt to do something bad. I know it's something bad.

"Okay, I'll stay. Brian, why don't you go get it for me?"

I hadn't expected that. To be honest, I kind of forgot Brian is here. He's been pretty quiet.

"Get what?" Brian asks.

Maybe he didn't see Mommy mouthing "salt" to him. Or maybe he's just stupid.

"*You know*", Mommy says. "What we talked about, remember?"

"Oh, yeah." Brian leaves. So does Blue.

Mommy and I are alone now. I pretend I am sleep so I don't have to look at her, but I still hear her whisper "you'll be sorry." I hear footsteps in the hallway, but they're light, small footsteps instead of Brian Footsteps. It must be Blue. Mommy mutters something I'm not allowed to say.

"Where *is* he?" she demands. Blue doesn't answer. She takes blood from my arm, the same way they did at the other hospital. When she goes to find a doctor to test the blood, Brian wanders in, eating a cheeseburger. Sauce drips down his chin.

"What the hell, Brian?" Mommy yells. She grabs him and pulls him aside, but of course, I can still hear them. Super Ears. That's me.

"That idiot nurse already took the blood sample to the lab. It's too late! You were supposed to get back here before her!"

"Can't you just put it in and tell them to test the blood sample again?"

"I could, but it would look suspicious. I don't know if I could risk that."

"Risk what?" I ask. Both heads turn toward me.

"Were you listening, kid?" demands Brian.

"She always does that", Mommy says. "Just ignore her. She can't do anything."

"But Beth, she *knows!*"

"She won't if you shut up, Brian!"

Blue comes into the room, smiling. "Good news!" she calls. Mommy and Brian hurry back to their seats.

"It looks like Fern's blood sample is pretty much normal", Blue says.

"What do you mean, 'pretty much'?" Mommy snaps.

"Well, she's obviously extremely dehydrated, but except for that, she's okay. We've decided to keep her in the hospital until she puts on a little weight and gets rehydrated. But I don't see any signs of pica, although after she's discharged, it might be helpful to seek therapy for her."

"That can't be right", Mommy says. "It can't be."

"It is", Blue says. "If you and your husband could leave now, Mrs. Kyros, visiting hours are over. You can see Fern in the morning."

"What do you mean?" Mommy demands. "You must have to do more tests! You can't just tell me she's fine and send me away!"

It takes Blue an hour to make Mommy and Brian leave. Mommy keeps saying "Fern *needs* me, don't you, Fern?"

When Mommy and Brian finally leave, Blue says, "You're lucky to have parents who care so much about you."

Blue is nice, but she just doesn't get it.

"Yes", I say. My voice is as flat as a pancake. "I'm very, very lucky."

Blue leaves me alone then, after showing me a button on the side of my bed to push if I need anything. I stare at the ceiling and think about Holly. As it gets later and later, I get tired, so tired I can't keep my eyes open. So I don't.

CHAPTER

14

There is the sound of someone screaming, right outside my door. "Hide me, hide me!" I jump out of bed and Holly is standing in the doorway. I can see most of her in the moonlight, but she still looks like a shadow. Her eyes have sunk deep into face, like they were just too heavy to hold up. There is blood around the neck of her white nightgown, and her skin is grayish. And she's wearing her dark hair in two braids. It's always in two braids.

"Help me, Fern!" she cries. "She's coming! Don't let her see me! Please, Fern, hide me!"

I don't know who Holly is talking about, but she's my sister. And nobody hurts my sister. "Lie down flat next to my bed", I say. "Stay really still."

She does, and it takes me a minute to realize that she's not breathing.

"Holly?" I whisper, but she doesn't hear me, because there are loud footsteps in the hallway. High heels, going clip-clop, clip-clop like a horse.

There is the beam from a flashlight bouncing around the hallway, but it's red, for some reason. I hear someone laugh. It sounds familiar.

"I know you're in here", the voice says. Mommy. I'd know that sticky-sweet voice anywhere, but is she talking to me or Holly? The red light shines through the door, and I can see Mommy behind it, smiling an evil smile, with the corners of her mouth twisted up. She is holding a bottle that rattles when she shakes it.

"Come on, Holly, don't do this. You *need* to take this medicine, don't you?"

Holly keeps quiet on the floor.

"Holly?" Mommy tries again. "I see you there. Get up!"

Holly doesn't move. Mommy yells out loud, so loud that I'm surprised no one comes into the room. But everything is silent. Mommy takes off her high heel and throws it at the wall. It makes a thump. Then it lies still on the floor next to Holly.

"Damn you!" Mommy shouts. "Damn you, Holly! I've tried everything! What's the matter with you? Don't you *want* to get better?"

Holly sits up. "I'm not sick", she says. "I don't have epilepsy."

"Yes, you do."

"No." Holly's voice sounds stronger now. "I don't. I know I don't. And I'm going to tell! I'm going to tell everyone you're lying! Then you won't make me sick anymore!"

In the red light, I see something on Mommy's face that I hardly ever see. She is scared.

"Fine", she whispers. "Fine. You've made your choice. I warned you. It's over now, Holly. It's all over."

Mommy grabs the pillow from under me. My head flops back onto the mattress, and I watch as she slams the pillow over Holly's face and holds it there. I hear Holly trying to scream and kick, but Mommy is stronger.

"Stop!" I yell. "Stop it Mommy, please, stop it!"

I try to grab the pillow, but Mommy pushes me off. She doesn't even seem to really notice me. I shove her back, trying to get her off Holly, but a kick of her high-heeled foot sends me flying against the bed. My head hits the hard plastic side. All I can do is watch as Holly's screams get quieter and quieter. Then they stop altogether. Mommy waits for a few minutes. Then she slowly lifts up the pillow, and I see that my sister Holly is dead. I let myself cry, but my sadness turns to anger, and I'm yelling, just yelling at nothing. Because then I wake up. Holly isn't lying dead beside me anymore.

There are heavy footsteps out in the hallway. I can't stop crying. A light flickers on.

"Are you okay?" I'd know that voice anywhere. It's Raymond. He is wearing a doctor's coat and carrying a clipboard.

"Fern", he says.

"Raymond", I say. "I can't say I'm glad to see you *here*", he tells me. "But I sure am glad to see *you*."

"Me too. What are you doing here?"

"This is the hospital where I work, Fern. My job right now is to make sure everyone in this unit is doing okay? So, are you?"

"Am I what?"

"Are you doing okay? I heard screaming and crying."

I look down at my lap. I hoped Raymond wouldn't hear me, because Mommy says it's very hard to like a crybaby, and I want Raymond to like me.

"I'm all right", I say.

"You may fool everyone else by saying that." Raymond sits down on my bed. "But you can't fool me, Fern. Something's going on. Bad dream?"

"I guess", I say.

"Want to tell me what it was about?"

That's what daddy used to say. Before he left, I didn't have bad dreams as much as I do now, and Holly was never in them. Usually, I was falling out of an airplane without a parachute. It was thrilling, but scary too, because I knew when I hit the ground, I would die. So I screamed. Daddy always came running into my room in his boxer shorts with red stripes. He held me in his lap and cupped my face in his big, strong hands and said "Bad dream?" I would nod and sniffle, but I wasn't crying. He put his hand on my chest and said "You're heart's pounding like a hummingbird, Fern. What was the dream about?" I always told him. He brushed the hair off my forehead and said, "The next time you're falling, imagine you have wings. You're falling at first, sure, but then I want you to spread your wings and let the breeze take you up into the clouds."

"Will the sky be very blue up there?" I asked.

"Yes", he said. "With sparkly green wind."

I could always fall asleep after that.

"Did my mommy tell you she had another kid?" I ask Raymond.

"No." He looks surprised. "Did she?"

"I think so. A girl. Older than me. She died and went to Heaven. Her name was Holly."

"How did she die?"

"In a bunch of ways. Last time, Mommy held a pillow over her face until she stopped breathing."

"Is that what you dreamed about, Fern?"

"Yes. But it didn't feel like a dream. Holly is real. At least, she *was*."

"Hmmm." Raymond rubs his mustache.

"Do you believe me?" I ask. "Does it make sense?"

"Hmmm", Raymond says agin. "It must make sense in some way, Fern. Just maybe not now. But it will."

He doesn't answer the question about believing me.

"Why are you in the hospital again, Fern?" he asks instead.

If I tell, Mommy will hurt me. Maybe worse than she hurt Holly in my dream.

"I don't know", I say. Brian looks at my face like an answer is written somewhere on there.

"I have a feeling you do know", he says. "You're too smart, Fern. I know you know."

I want to say yes, yes I know! Mommy is telling everyone I am sick with pica. She wouldn't give me food or water. She locked the door,

Raymond, she locked the door! And I tried to find you, but she had hurt me so much I fell, and now I'm here.

"I really don't know", I say.

Raymond sighs. "It's would really be better if you told me. But I have to respect your decision not to. I'm here any time, though, if you need to talk. You know that, right?"

I nod.

"What about my phone number? Do you still have it?"

I roll up the sleeve of my hospital pajamas and show him the numbers on my arm. He laughs and touches it gently.

"That's really not good for your skin, Fern. Why didn't you call me?"

Another question I can't answer. If I do, Raymond will know that Mommy is mean to me. And then Mommy will know that Raymond knows. And then she'll hurt me.

"I was busy", I say. "We moved."

Raymond's eyebrows raise on his head. They look like two fuzzy caterpillars. "You moved? Where to?"

"Brian's house."

"Does he treat you okay?"

I look don't answer.

"Does he treat you okay?" Raymond asks again.

I nod and flop my head back onto my pillow. I don't want to lie to Raymond anymore.

The rest of the night, I do not dream, but I hear whispers. Holly is trying to tell me something. I think she wants me to get her diary and read it. "I can't!" I shout out loud. "I'm in the hospital!" Then sleep finally comes. So do tears.

In the morning, Mommy and Brian walk into my room before breakfast even comes. Blue is putting new liquid in my IV. She calls it 'saline.' Mommy is carrying a bunch of flowers wrapped in tissue paper, and Brian is carrying a little blue box decorated with ladybugs.

"For you", Mommy says, handing the flowers to Blue. "To thank you for taking such good care of Fern."

"Oh!" Blue looks surprised. "Well, um, thank you, Mrs. Kyros. Thank you very much."

"Call me Beth", Mommy says.

"And this is for you, kid", Brian says, putting the ladybug box on my bed.

"I picked it out", Mommy says. "It's to put your medicine in. Surely she has lots of medicine, doesn't she, Corinne?"

"We've given her some vitamins and supplements", Blue says. "But I'm not sure if-".

"You're pretty sick, Fern", Mommy interrupts. "You'll have lots of medicine to put in that box."

"Thank you, Mother", I say, and I am proud that I remembered to call her 'Mother'.

"Ahem", coughs Brian.

"Thank you, Brian", I say, even though he didn't help pick it out.

"Replacing her saline?" Mommy asks Blue.

"Yes." Blue's face looks surprised, maybe because 'saline' is another one of those hospital words that ordinary people don't know.

"I'll assume you're going to give her breakfast soon, right?" Mommy says. "She needs food to get stronger."

"You're right about that", says Blue. I have a list of things we can order for her from the cafeteria." She gives Mommy a sheet of paper.

"She'll just have a piece of toast", Mommy says. "Got to start slow and bland, like you said."

"Actually", Blue looks uncomfortable, "I think we should give her a little more than toast. She's strong enough to handle it now, and her body needs the extra fuel. How about pancakes and eggs?"

"I don't really like eggs", I say.

"Okay, then. Pancakes and fruit?"

"Yes, please", I say. "And something to drink. Juice or water."

"Okay, Mrs. Kyros?" Blue asks.

Mommy's mouth looks like a ruler, straight and thin. There are two sides of her again, fake-nice and mean.

"Fine", she says.

Blue unclips a little microphone from her waist and talks into it. "Pancakes, fruit salad, and juice up to room 636, please."

"And I'll have a breakfast sandwich!" Brian calls.

The pancakes come on a tray that's wheeled into the room, like I'm at a hotel. Brian does not get his breakfast sandwich, so he grabs a pancake off my plate with his big, greasy hands

"Are you all set, Fern?" Blue asks.

"We're fine", Mommy says. "Thank you so much for all your help, Corinne."

Blue walks out the door, calling "Mike, you had better get out those boxes in the cafeteria right now, or I swear I'm going to lose my mind! I'm not going to ask you again!" I stab a chunk of pineapple with my plastic fork, and Mommy glares at me.

"Why don't you want me to eat?" I ask.

Brian closes the door. I'm trapped now.

"Look," Mommy says. "What goes on in this room *stays* in this room, got it?"

"Huh?" What are they going to do?

Mommy takes my tray of breakfast and dumps it in the trash. Then she covers it with paper towels.

"I would have eaten those pancakes", Brian says.

"Why did you throw my food away?" I ask. "I'm hungry."

"That's too bad. You don't eat pancakes. All you eat is clay and dirt and cloth, because you have pica."

"I DON'T have pica!"

Brian slaps his hand in front of my mouth. It smells like beef.

"Shut up, kid! Someone will hear you!"

Mommy digs around in her big pink purse. She never used to carry such a big purse. She had a thin leather one with gold trim that she used before I was born. She said those were the best years of her life. I don't exactly remember when she bought the big pink purse, but she always told me she hated big purses because she thought they made her look like a mother. I guess looking like a mother is a bad thing. But now she has her big pink bag, and she pulls out a carton of salt.

"Why do you have that?" I ask.

Mommy doesn't answer. She snaps open my IV bag and pours some salt in. She grabs the bag and shakes it around. The salt goes back into her big pink bag. Brian stands by the door, looking out for anyone who might be coming.

"Why did you pour salt in my IV?" I ask.

"To help you get better", Mommy says.

"Why will salt help me get better? Shouldn't a doctor be giving it to me, then?"

"No", Mommy says. "*I'm* doing it. Because I care about you, and I want you to get better faster. Salt will do that. The reason the doctors aren't giving you salt is because it will make you better faster, and they want to keep you in the hospital as long as they can so they can make more money."

That makes sense. Mommy doesn't like to spend a lot of money.

"But you can't tell", Brian says.

"That's right. You can't tell anyone", says Mommy. "Can I trust you?"

Can she trust me? I think the better question would be, can I trust *her*? Something inside me is telling me that I shouldn't. I need to tell Blue that Mommy put salt in my IV. But she's my mommy. Maybe she feels bad about locking me in that room, so she's trying to make up for it by making me better extra-fast. That must be it.

"Can I trust you?" Mommy asks again. I look at her face. She's got more wrinkles than I remember. She looks older, and suddenly I feel a rush of some sort of feeling. It's like everything mixed together that I don't have the words for. Grown-up words, like pity and resentment and longing. I've heard those words before, and they somehow seem to fit exactly how I'm feeling right now.

"You can trust me", I say. Then Blue comes in and Mommy talks to her for a long time, using hospital words. I don't really hear what they're saying, because suddenly, I feel very tired. Before closing my eyes, I say a quick prayer to Holly. *Dear Holly, no dreams right now please. Love, your sister, Fern*

CHAPTER 15

When I wake up, Mommy and Brian are gone, and I am alone in my hospital room. All of a sudden, everything looks scary. The IV pole next to me looks like a skinny monster with two sharp teeth. The beeping machine in the corner has red lights that look like eyes. Everything, everything here is going to get me. I reach for Pox beside me, but he isn't there. Of course he isn't. I forgot to ask Mommy to bring him. Maybe she's right. Maybe I *am* too old to sleep with him. I clutch the sheet next to my face, but it isn't the same. There is something funny going on in my chest. It feels like I've forgotten how to breathe. I try to take deep breaths, but my body just won't let me, and soon I'm panting like a dog in the sun. My throat is dry, and there is a funny taste in my mouth that I can't seem to get rid of, no matter how many times I swallow.

It tastes like the time I licked a metal chair when I was two. I don't know *why* I licked the chair. I guess I wanted to find out what it tasted like. Maybe I really do have pica, because a chair isn't food. It's a bit weird how I was only two back then, and I can still remember it like it happened yesterday or even an hour ago. I remember things when I was even younger, too. But the time I licked the metal chair was the first time Mommy hit me. She said I was a bad girl, and stupid too. I cried for a long time, because I didn't want to be bad or stupid. Now when she says those things to me, I don't cry. Because she smiles when I cry, and I don't want to make her happy after she was just mean to me.

I hear familiar footsteps in the hallway. How can footsteps be familiar? But I spend so much time listening, I guess I can tell who people are by their footsteps. That's kind of a cool superpower. These footsteps are Raymond's, I think. And I am right.

"Hi, Fern", he says. "Feeling better this morning?"

My stomach rumbles in response. I wish I could have some breakfast, but it's in the trash now. I can't tell Raymond that, though.

"My throat hurts", I say. "And my mouth has a weird taste in it. Like a metal chair. And I think I've forgotten how to breathe."

"You've forgotten how to breathe?" Raymond's forehead crinkles up. "How?"

"I just can't take deep breaths like I used to."

"Let's see." Raymond's puts down the yellow notepad he is writing on and focuses on my chest. "Breathe in as deep as you can."

I do.

"Deeper, Fern. Can you?"

I try, and come up gasping. Raymond reaches for me.

"May I touch your chest?"

I nod, and he puts his warm hand right on my heart. "Now try."

My throat just can't do it. I am getting scared.

"Huh", Raymond says. "Your heart feels almost as if it's racing. And you're not breathing deeply at all."

My breathing is like waves now, the kind during a storm. Short and choppy. I can only say two words at a time before stopping to breathe again. "Why did...you...come?"

"I work here, remember?" He smiles at me. "And it's my job to take a blood sample right now. That means I'm just going to prick your arm and fill up this tube."

"Okay....go ahead."

"Hopefully the blood will tell us something", Raymond murmurs. "If not, I'll look further into this breathing thing."

He rubs my arm with a cold cloth and slides in the needle. I turn my head to watch my blood fill up the tube.

"You don't have to look, Fern", Raymond says gently.

"I...want to. Makes...me feel...in...control."

Raymond smiles at me, a secret smile. "I always watch the blood too. The other doctors think I'm crazy. They say they've seen enough blood to last them a lifetime, so why would they want to see more of it? But it's just one of my quirks, you know?"

"What is...a...quirk?" I ask.

"It's something that makes you unique. Special. It's not a bad thing."

Raymond pulls the needle out of my arm.

"They're very fast in the lab. We should get the blood results pretty soon."

It is getting harder to breath, even little breaths.

Raymond must notice, because he says "Who's your nurse, Fern? I want someone to take a look at you while I go to the lab with this blood."

"Blue", I gasp.

"There aren't any nurses named Blue here", Raymond tells me.

"I...call her...Blue...in my...head because...she...wears...blue...all...the time."

"Oh, Corinne? Yeah, blue's her favorite color. Everyone else wears green scrubs, but Corrine grabbed the last set of blue ones. Blue. I like that. See, that's one of your quirks."

"What...is?"

"Making up names for people like that. Hang in there, Fern. I'll go get Blue."

Raymond leaves. My throat burns and twists like it's trying to escape from my body. There is a knock at the door, and it's Blue.

"Dr. Ray told me you were having shortness of breath", she says. "Let's take a look.

She presses her hand on my chest and tells me to breathe deep. And then deeper. And deeper after that. She takes a things she calls a "stethoscope" from. Her neck and rests the cold metal on my skin. She puts the ends of the stethoscope in her ears.

"This will help me listen to your heartbeat", she says.

"Is it...bad?" I ask. "Is my... heartbeat... bad?"

"Not bad exactly, but it's a little fast. You may be nervous. That would explain the rapid heartbeat and difficulty breathing. Are you nervous?"

I am nervous, but not for the reasons she thinks. The hospital is scary, but Mommy and Brian are even scarier. "I..am a...little...scared", I breathe.

"I know."

Blue touches the top of my head. It tingles. "Lots of kids are scared to come to the hospital. But you're going to be just fine, you'll see. And your mommy and daddy are coming back to be with you. They wouldn't leave your bedside until visiting hours were over. Even though you were asleep. They care so much about you, Fern. A lot of kids don't have parents like that."

She is right in one way: most kids don't have parents like mine.

"Brian's...not my...Daddy", I say. "My...daddy...left".

"Oh. But Brian seems nice."

I am too tired to argue. I lay back and close my eyes.

"Try to relax, Fern", Blue says. "Think about something happy. How about a funny video? We've got a whole box of them."

I shake my head. "To relax...I need...Pox."

"Who's Pox?" Blue asks.

"Pox is her stuffed rabbit".

I hadn't even noticed Raymond come into the room. He is holding my blood sample and wearing a worried look.

"Dr. Ray! How did the blood sample turn out?"

Raymond hesitates. "You'll eavesdrop on us, won't you, Fern?"
I nod.

"I guess it's better to just say it, then", Raymond sighs. "If this upsets you, Fern, just tell us, and we'll go somewhere where you can't hear. But personally, I believe it's beneficial for children to hear the results of their exams."

"So what's the story?" asks Blue.

"Somehow, her sodium level has skyrocketed. It's in a very dangerous place right now, and if it's not treated right away, then...well, I don't want to go there. But we need to test the saline solution in her IV to make sure she's not getting too much salt. What puzzles me is that her blood sample was fine earlier. I have a theory, but it will get us in quite a situation if I'm wrong, and also if I'm right. For now, though, Corinne, you can get someone to test the solution in her IV. Call her mother and her mother's boyfriend, too. I have a few things to do."

He runs off, which I've never seen someone do in a hospital. I think they don't run because people are always being wheeled around on stretchers and no one wants to trip over them. But Raymond moves very fast, and Blue and I are left wondering where he is going. Blue tells me she is going to the phone to call Mommy and Brian, and then they need to test my IV.

"Try to relax", she says as she leaves, noticing my tight muscles.

I can't help it, though. My body is getting tight on its own. The memory of Mommy pouring salt in my IV is still fresh in my head. Could the salt be hurting me? Raymond said something about getting too much salt. Suddenly, like broken glass, something in my head shatters and I understand. I cram my fists in my mouth so I don't scream. It would hurt my throat anyway. Mommy isn't trying to help me. She's lied to everyone and told them I was sick. And now, she's *making* me sick. As soon as Raymond comes back, I will tell him. In the meantime, though, I have to lie here in bed, knowing that I am being hurt and I can't do anything to stop it.

My fingers drift toward the little box on the table next to me. The ladybug box. Why did Mommy give it to me? I pick it up. The box is very fancy. It is stained blue wood with gold clasps to keep it shut. I open it. The inside is lined with fuzzy blue velvet. I rub my finger across it. Then suddenly, my finger hits something else, something sharp that cuts and leaves a slit of blood. A paper cut. There's paper in the box. Tucked into the top with tape is a piece of paper. Could it be for me? I don't know if the box was ever used before. Either way, I'll see what the piece of paper is. I untape and unfold it. I recognize Mommy's handwriting. It's neat and cursive. She takes a lot of pride in her handwriting. She told me once that when most people get to be grown up, they forget cursive and their handwriting just looks bad. "Never me, though", she said. And I suppose that's a good thing, because I can always read everything she writes. Whenever Daddy writes anything for me, I have to squint like the letters are in a secret code.

"Fern", the letter says. *"I see you have found this note. I knew you would find it, because you often spy and sneak around, so it was only a matter of time. I have something to tell you, Fern. By now, you probably know that putting salt in your IV was not to help you. I don't think you ever believed that. But I have my reasons for doing it, Fern. You won't ever understand them, but I do have my reasons. You are probably thinking that you should tell someone that your mother is doing something she isn't supposed to. But you won't tell. What I'm about to say may sound shocking to you, but believe me, I will do it if I have to. Perhaps you have heard Brian tell you that you'll get hit if you tell anyone. Perhaps I've told you that. But it goes deeper than that, Fern, because if you tell anyone about anything I am doing, or if you mention this letter to anyone, I will kill you. You may want to tell your father. Well, let me tell you something. He is gone. He isn't coming back. Stop wondering, stop thinking about him, cut him right out of your life. This is serious now. No one can help you. Do not show this letter to anyone or I repeat, I will kill you. I never wanted another kid, anyway."*

I feel like my body just lifted right up out of me. I put the box back and fold the note inside it. So much is spinning through my head. I can't handle it all. This is grown-up stuff. It's not fair. I start going over the lines of the letter in my head. They were so horrible, they just stuck in my brain and I can't get them out. *"I have my reasons."* What reasons? Why would Mommy try to hurt me? *"You may want to tell your father."* I do. I want Daddy here now, right this second. I want him to put a Batman Band-Aid on my finger and tell me I'm a superhero. *"No one can help you."* If Mommy meant everything she wrote, then she's right. No one can help me. *"I never wanted another kid anyway."* I untangle these words like a ball of yarn. She never wanted me. I try to squeeze my eyelids shut to get rid of the tears that I feel building up. But there's something more. She never wanted *another kid*. Could that kid be Holly? And of course, the line that sticks in my head: *I will kill you.* As much as I want to believe that she's my mommy and she loves me and she would never do that, somewhere deep inside the back of my mind, I know she means it. And I can't take any chances.

I start to cry. Tears drip onto the note, smudging the black ink. A few minutes later, Brian and Mommy run into the room. It has been snowing again. Mommy has flakes on her coat and in her hair, and Brian has tracked muddy slush all over the floor.

"You got here fast", Blue observes. I didn't even realize she had come back. I hope she didn't see me crying.

"Beth was speeding the whole way", Brian says. "We got pulled over by the cops. Now I've gotta pay the damn ticket."

Mommy's eyes shoot little lasers at Brian. "I was speeding", she says, "because I heard my child was in grave danger." She rushes over to me and plants a kiss on my forehead. I stiffen.

I never wanted another kid anyway.

"Shhh, shhh", Mommy whispers in my ear, pretending to soothe me. "It'll be all right, Honey."

Then, when she thinks no one is listening: "Did you find the note?" I move my head up and down the slightest bit.

"Good", she whispers. "And Fern? *I mean it.*" She squeezes the back of my neck so hard it hurts, then turns to Blue.

"Well, what are you waiting for? Do something!"

As if he heard Mommy, Raymond knocks on the open door and comes in without waiting for someone to say "who is it?" or "enter".

"You wouldn't believe..." he pants. "All the doctors...not *one* available... gonna just do it myself...we really need more staff, Corinne."

He sounds like me. Only a few words at a time. But I think that's just 'cause he's been running. Running all over the hospital to find someone to help me. That makes me feel good inside, even though it's getting harder to breathe.

"Dr. Ray, slow down", says Blue. "Just slow down. You're saying no one was available to test the saline solution?"

"Not...a single...person."

"Deep breaths", Blue says, which is funny, because she was telling me the same thing, but Raymond can actually *do* it. He takes big gulps of air like he's choking down water.

"Damn it", Blue mutters. "We really need more staff on call at times like these. Did you get the testing equipment?"

"Yep." Raymond is talking normally again. "Got it from the storage room."

He snaps open my IV bag and dips a spoon in, taking some of the liquid. I see Mommy stiffen up like she's afraid, or like she's worried she'll get caught. Brian squeezes her hand.

"Remove the IV, please, Corinne", Raymond says.

Blue slips the needle out of my arm. I wonder if I can bend my elbow now, but my muscles feel tight, like a stretched rubber band. The IV sample leaves the room along with Blue and Raymond. Mommy and Brian's eyes look at me, squinty-like. Snake eyes. We don't talk. My chest is tight and bursting with a million thoughts and screams and tears, but I keep quiet and press my lips together so I won't cry. We wait for thirty-one minutes. I time it. I try to be still, but my body seems to be thinking something else. I twitch and shiver. I hold my arms down and squeeze my legs together to try to stay still, but my knees pop up and shake and my arms tighten and loosen like shaky screws.

Finally, finally, Raymond and Blue come back. They both look worried.

"In the hall, please", Blue says to Brian and Mommy. They follow her. Raymond stays with me. I twitch my way out of bed to listen at the door. Raymond moves to stop me, but halfway, he seems to give up. He sits down on my bed and shoves his face in his hands.

"Oh God, Fern", I hear him murmuring. "What has this mess become?"

Raymond is sad and I want to make him feel better. His brown hand sticks out of his white doctor's coat. I grab that hand and squeeze it. He squeezes back, and we both listen at the door, even though I don't think doctors are supposed to do that.

"We found-" It sounds like a Blue is struggling to get words out of her mouth. "We found high amounts of salt in her IV. Frankly, I have no idea how that could have happened. We give our patients saline based on their needs, and-".

"Wait a minute", Mommy snaps. "Are you saying that the hospital is responsible for making my daughter *sicker*?"

"Mrs. Kyros, it was an awful mistake, and we can assure you-".

"*You* must have done it, Corinne! When we visited and you were replacing the saline in her IV! You must have given her too much salt! You've poisoned my daughter!"

"We have a mind to sue!" Brian says.

"Not yet, Brian", Mommy mutters. "Corinne, how exactly was Fern harmed by the sodium found in her IV?"

"Well, it would certainly explain the shortness of breath. And it seems as though she's been having some muscle tightness. The salt could have caused that, too."

"So you make a dangerous mistake with my child's IV", Mommy hisses. "And you put her in severe danger, as if she hasn't already been through enough? Brian's right! We should sue!"

"Please, Mrs. Kyros", Blue begs. "I'm always so careful with the IV tubes-".

"Obviously NOT", Brian says. "I hope you've got a good lawyer."

"Please, let's just stay calm", Blue says. "I'm sure the hospital can provide compensation for the error."

I can imagine Brian's beady eyes squinting.

"What kind of compensation?" he asks.

"Well, the hospital can cover part of Fern's medical bills..."

"*Part* of them?" Mommy snaps. "Try *all* of them. And you have to feature her on your website page. Explain how sick she is, and ask for donations. And I want you to set up a box at the front desk too, for more donations. She'll need them after all the trouble *you've* caused."

I hear Blue gulp. "Of-of course, Mrs. Kyros. I'll need to talk to my boss, but I'm sure we can accommodate your needs. I'm just so sorry about this. I must have done it, there's no other possible way-".

"Cut the chatter", says Mommy. "Show us out."

As they walk down the hallway, I hear Brian mutter, "And Corinne, don't get so used to that blue uniform. You may not be wearing it for long."

Raymond and I listen to them leave.

"They're...going to...fire...Blue?" I whisper. "Like...Daddy...got fired?"

Raymond tugs at his mustache. "I don't know how your daddy got fired, Fern, but this is very serious. I suppose Corinne, or 'Blue' as you call her, could lose her job over something like this."

"But...that's...not fair. It...was a...mistake", I say, even though I know Blue didn't do it.

"I need to ask you something very important, Fern", Raymond says. "Did your mother or Brian put salt in your IV?"

I will kill you.

"No", I say.

Raymond sighs. "Are you sure, Fern? Are you absolutely positive? Because if it turns out that everyone thinks it was Blue, she *could* get fired. So it's very important for you to tell the truth."

I know it's important. Raymond doesn't have to tell me that. But he also doesn't know what will happen to me if I tell.

"I'm absolutely positive", I say, crossing my fingers behind my back.

That night, I can't sleep. The new IV they put in feels worse than the old one. More poky. But mostly, I'm worried about Blue. I don't want to be the reason she gets fired. What if she ends up with no place to live? What if she has to pay child-support, like Daddy does, but she gets fired like he did and she can't afford to pay anymore, so she can't see her kids again?

I tap at the thing over my mouth. They put it there before I went to bed, to help me breathe, and it's kind of working. It is clear plastic with a tube. It's weird to lie in bed with it on, and I really want to pull it off, but Blue told me that it will help me breathe. And even though it's uncomfortable, I'd rather deal with the funny mask than go back to gasping for breath like a fish out of water. I close my eyes and try not to dream. The doorknob rattles. I keep really still, but my eyes pop open, so I can see what's going on.

It is Raymond. I can tell from the hallway light that spills into my dark room. He is carrying a bunch of little machines. I can't tell what they are. I pinch my arm hard to make sure I'm not dreaming. It hurts. There will be a red mark there in the morning, but at least I know I'm wide awake. Raymond pulls a flashlight out of his pocket and shines it on one of the little machines, and I see they are actually video cameras. He shines the flashlight in each corner of the room. The beam of light passes right over me. I keep my eyes wide open and try not to breathe. Raymond pulls a stool over to the first corner of the room and fixes a video camera in place, so it's pointing right at my bed. He does the same with the other three corners of the room. Then he leaves, after sweeping the flashlight across the room to make sure everything is in place. Once he is out the door, I let my breath go in a puff of air. It makes the inside of the machine over my mouth and nose go all foggy.

So I am now being watched by video cameras. Why would Raymond do that? Is he trying to catch me doing something bad? Then it hits me. Raymond's not trying to catch *me* doing something bad. He's trying to catch Mommy and Brian. I feel a hot worry creep up my neck and tingle all over my body. How can I possibly sleep now? I turn over, trying not to imagine the video camera calculating every move I make.

I wake up staring at the cameras. They're pretty well hidden. I might not even notice them if I hadn't seen Raymond put them there last night.

Mommy and Brian come in, carrying red balloons that say "get well soon". Just like the cards that lined Holly's wall. I try to stay calm as Mommy flutters around me like a butterfly, putting on a show for Blue, who watches from the doorway. But my eyes keep darting up to the cameras. Blue doesn't notice, but Mommy does. When Blue goes to get my breakfast, Brian pulls the front of my pajamas tight with his hand and leans in close to me. His breath smells like cigarettes. I wonder if he smokes a lot. I always hold my breath when I see someone smoking, because Daddy told me that smoking is bad and if you breathe in smoke from someone else's cigarette, it's just as bad as smoking one yourself. I never want to smoke, so whenever I see someone else with a cigarette, I time how long it will take to pass them and hold my breath seven seconds before. I shouldn't ever have any smoke in my body if I keep doing that.

"What do you know?" Mommy asks.

"Huh?" I try to twist away from Brian's smelly breath. "What do you mean?"

"You're a good eavesdropper, Fern, but a bad liar", Mommy says.

"We saw you looking at something", Brian adds. I could swear he breathes extra hard, just to get his smell all over me.

"I wasn't looking at anything!" I protest.

"Really?" Mommy crosses her arms. "Then why were you paying so much attention to the corners of the room?"

"There's nothing there, I promise!" I can't tell on Raymond. The cameras are like my protectors.

"Brian." Mommy snaps her fingers, as if he's a dog. "Go look in every corner. And hurry! Corinne is coming any second with Fern's breakfast!"

Brian lets go of me and shuffles to the corner. He has that annoying way of walking, the kind where he doesn't pick up his feet, so his shoes make a scuff-scuff-scuff sound. My ears don't like it at all.

"Nothing here", Brian says, and I let my muscles relax because I am so relieved. I didn't even realize I was holding them tight.

"Check higher, you idiot! Not just at eye level! Use that stool! The stool", Mommy pauses, "that wasn't there yesterday."

Brian nods and climbs up onto the stool. I wonder if he'll break it. I hope it collapses under him and he goes crashing to the floor.

"Aha!" Brian's fat fingers grab the tiny video camera and tug it off the wall. "What have we here?" He smirks. His teeth are blinding white. How can that be, since his breath is so bad?

"A video camera?" Mommy gasps. "Fern, do you know anything about this?"

I shake my head.

"You do!" Brian grabs my shoulders and shakes me hard. "Tell us, kid!" He shakes harder, and I begin to feel sick.

"Brian, let her up", Mommy says, but she is smiling. "It doesn't matter if Fern knows anything or not. All we have to do is turn off the video camera and delete whatever it's already filmed. Don't be stupid."

Brian lets me go, and I fall back against my pillow. I was holding my breath the whole time. Brian must not know anything about electronics, because it takes him twenty-three minutes to turn off all the video cameras and delete what was already filmed.

Mommy whispers "Hurry! Someone could be coming any second!" at him the whole time.

"And remember, kid", Brian says as he steps off the stool. "Not a word of this to anyone."

"Or I'll do what I wrote I would do", Mommy says. I guess she doesn't want to say the word "kill" in a hospital.

"Okay", I whisper.

Blue brings my breakfast tray with French toast, maple syrup, and cranberry-raspberry juice. I try to stuff it in my mouth as quickly as I can, because once Blue leaves, Mommy will take the food away.

"Slow down, Fern. You'll make yourself sick." Mommy takes the plastic fork and knife and cuts my French toast into tiny pieces. Then she cuts those tiny pieces into even tinier pieces. I know she's taking a long time on purpose, so I won't get to eat anything.

I'm right, because once Blue leaves, Mommy stuffs my breakfast in a paper towel and throws it away. Brian whines that he wanted it.

"Drink this instead." Mommy hands him my cup of juice. I watch it leave the tray.

"Does it have her spit all over it?" Brian asks. "I don't want it if it has her spit all over it."

"Fine", Mommy snaps. "Don't drink it." She dumps it down the sink before I can say that I want it back. The juice looks like blood going down the drain. I watch the red disappear into the sink pipes, and think that I'll just wait until they're gone. I can get food then. I have to wait a long time, though. Mommy and Brian are allowed to stay until noon, and they stay every second they can. Noon is when we get lunch. Noon is when I get to eat. Blue must hear my stomach rumbling from a mile away, because she brings me my meal first. I eat every bite. I got lunch today. This is a good thing.

Another good thing is that before Mommy and Brian left, Brian whispered "Salt?", and Mommy said "No, better wait a day or so. If they've got video cameras, they suspect something. We'll do it tomorrow if nothing else happens." So that was good, because there is no extra salt in my IV today.

Raymond comes in after lunch to take another blood sample. The way they're taking blood from me, I'm surprised I even have any left. Raymond glances around my room.

"The blood", I remind him. Both of us always watch my blood as it fills up the tube, because he likes watching it, and I like watching it, and everyone else thinks we're weird for liking to watch it. So we decided that we would be weird together.

"Right." Raymond sounds distracted. "Keep your eyes on the blood, Fern." He pulls the needle out. "Keep watching." Then he stands up and wanders to the corner where one of the video cameras is stuck. Mommy erased everything and put them back, turned off, so it wouldn't look 'suspicious'. I keep one eye focused on the blood and one focused on Raymond as he takes the camera off the wall and presses the buttons.

"Damn! They malfunctioned!" He drops the camera on the floor.

"What's malfunctioned mean?" I ask.

He turns to find me staring at him. "Oh! I'm sorry, Fern, I didn't mean for you to hear that…I just…"

"It's okay." I shrug. "Mommy and Brian swear, too. So what's malfunctioned mean?"

I can tell Raymond is trying to decide whether or not to tell me about the cameras, even though it doesn't matter, because I already know. "It means something didn't work like it should have", Raymond says finally. He picks the camera up off the floor. "In this case, this camera didn't work. It isn't even on."

"What's the camera for?"

"You know what?" Raymond says, standing up. "I'm going to get you a snack. It's good to have a little sugar after you get blood taken. Keeps you from feeling weak. What would you like?"

I know he's changing the subject on purpose, but I decide not to ask anything more about the video cameras.

"A peanut butter sandwich, please", I say. "With grape jelly."

Raymond brings me a sandwich on a tray. "Might have good news", he says.

"They had grape jelly?"

"They did, but that's not the good news. I just talked to Blue, and she's coming up here now to talk to me about-".

"I'm here, Dr. Ray." Blue smiles at me. "Fern, you have jelly on your nose."

"I know." I'm not about to wipe it off, either. It makes me think of Daddy.

Just like Raymond said, Blue talks. A lot. I eat my sandwich and try to listen, but all I can understand are bits and pieces of the sentences floating around my ears.

"She's doing well."

"Blood was normal."

"Insurance is gonna make us let her go."

The word insurance sounds like a hospital word to me.

"Am I going home?" I ask.

"Yes, Fern", Blue says. "Yes, you are. Call Mrs. Kyros", she says to Raymond. "I have a feeling there'll be a scene."

There's a scene, all right. Twenty minutes later, Mommy and Brian are in the hospital room. Mommy is screaming that they're not taking good enough care of me by letting me go home.

"This is your fault!" she yells at Brian.

"How is this my fault?" he shouts.

"YOU KNOW EXACTLY WHY, BRIAN! YOU KNOW EXACTLY WHY I'M ANGRY!"

I know, too. I have to leave because I am better. If Mommy had put the salt in my IV last night, I would still be sick and they would have to keep me in the hospital. And Mommy wants me to be sick. I'm not sure why it's Brian's fault, though. I think Mommy is actually mad at herself, but she doesn't want to admit that.

"YOU PROMISED!" Mommy yells at Blue. "AFTER YOU SCREWED UP WITH THE SALT, YOU PROMISED YOU'D PAY HER MEDICAL BILLS! AND NOW YOU'RE BACKING OUT!"

"I'm not backing out, Mrs. Kyros. It's just that Fern has received the medical care she needs, and, well, there's nothing anyone can do except make sure she eats enough and drinks plenty. I'd recommend a therapist too. She doesn't *seem* to have pica, but sometimes behaviors will change in a new setting. And we don't offer psychiatric evaluation here. I'm sorry, Mrs. Kyros. We've done all we can do."

CHAPTER
16

W hen we get home, I ask Mommy if I can go back to school now that I'm better.

"Oh no, Fern", she says. "No, no, no. You're still sick."

"But I'm *not*", I protest. Mommy pinches the back of my neck.

"Yes", she says. "You are."

"School's overrated anyway", Brian sneers, chomping on a turkey leg.

The smell is making my stomach feel sick. Daddy took me to the fair once, when I was six. Mommy stayed home, because she said the fair had too many germs. Daddy took me on the scrambler and the zero-gravity spin and the upside-down roller coaster. But my favorite ride was the Ferris wheel. It stopped when the carriage Daddy and I were. In was just at the top, and we could see the whole entire fair. That's when Daddy first spotted someone eating a turkey leg. The person was just in the carriage below us, and the smell drifted into our noses like wind.

"Smell that?" Daddy said. "That's the reeking of the American public."

We watched as a fly landed on the guy's turkey leg. He shooed it away and kept eating with his mouth open.

"Gross" I said, but I said it quietly, so the guy couldn't hear us.

"Look over there", Daddy said, pointing. I followed his finger to a big yellow stand that said "Seth's Smokin' Turkey Legs!" There was a line of seventeen people. Even from the top of the Ferris wheel, I could see flies rising from the stand and buzzing into the air.

"Let's count the people we see eating them" I suggested.

"Okay." Daddy pointed to the guy below us. "One."

We counted thirty-four people eating turkey legs by the end of the day.

"Double the amount of people in the line that we saw from the Ferris wheel", I said.

"You're right", Daddy said. "Leave it to my girl to come up with a way to find math in turkey legs."

I smiled, happy that I was his girl. I snuggled up close to his brown jacket, the one that always smelled like his aftershave, and fell asleep as the car started home.

I stare at Brian's turkey leg.

"What?" he laughs. "You want some?"

He thrusts the drumstick toward me, then pulls it away. "Too bad."

"The reek of the American public", I mutter. Daddy was absolutely right.

"What's that?" Mommy snaps. "The what?"

"Nothing." I bow my head. "I'm going up to my room now. But can I have something to eat first?"

"Fine." Mommy tosses me a tube of saltines. "But that's it for today, because you're sick. If you behave, maybe you can have more tomorrow."

I hold the crackers to my chest like they're a trophy, and hurry up the stairs. I feel stronger from the food at the hospital, but I am still hungry. I decide to make the crackers last as long as I can, in case Mommy won't give me any more food. One an hour. I bite into my two 'o clock saltine and try to ignore the hunger rumbling in my stomach like lava. At least I have Holly's diary.

"I hate my wheelchair. I don't even need it. Last night, I had a dream that I was running free in a field. Mom wasn't there. The field had blue and silver clouds all around it, and there were other kids waiting for me. They hugged me and said "Good job, Holly, good job", and I was finally free from Mom.

I want to play with other kids so badly, but whenever Mom takes me out of the house, they always stare at me because I am in a wheelchair, and I want to tell them that I'm not really sick, but Mom won't let me do that. Sometimes, other kids point at me and whisper to their parents, and their parents say "Shhh, it's not nice to point". They say it like I can't hear them, but I can hear just fine."

I flip through the pages and find that Holly wrote in her diary exactly once a week. On Wednesdays. There are fifty-two weeks in a year, and two hundred pages in the diary, and every page is filled with exactly one entry. That means that Holly wrote in the same diary for almost four years. That's more than half the time I've been alive. Had Mommy pretended she was sick the whole time? And why isn't there another diary, if Holly liked writing so much? I decide I will read the whole diary from over to cover. Maybe that will give me some clues. I look at the first page. Then I look at the last page. The handwriting is a lot different, but it all still looks like Holly's. Little-kid writing in the front, grown-up writing in the back. Holly was eleven when she stopped writing. My age when she started, eleven when she stopped. What happened? Did she really die? I flip the next page of the diary, determined to find the answers.

The next morning, a package comes to Brian's house. Mommy didn't lock me in my room last night, so I run downstairs to see who the package is for. It's taller than me. In fact, there are two packages, one tall and one square and fat. I peer over the square, fat one to see who it's from.

"Is it for me? Is it from Daddy?"

"No and no", Brian smirks. "Your Daddy's not coming back, kid."

"He is." I look at Mommy. "He *is!*"

"Fern, listen to me", Mommy says, going to the drawer under the sink to get the scissors. Already, she's organized almost all of Brian's house, so she knows where everything is. She said she couldn't live in a "pigsty".

"He's not coming back." She slams the drawer to make her point. "He doesn't even know where you live."

I am quiet, because it's true. Daddy doesn't know where I live. But that doesn't mean he's not coming back.

"What's in the box?" I ask, anxious to change the subject.

"Stuff." Mommy tries to cover it with her hand, but the box is way too big to be hidden by her bony fingers.

"Is that a wheelchair?" I ask. It looks like one. It's all folded up inside the box.

"It's not a wheelchair", Brian says, slapping his hand over my eyes.

"Yes it is. I saw it."

"Geez, Brian, we talked about this. Fern's not going to tell. *Are you?*" Mommy glares at me.

"Does the note still count when we're not in the hospital?"

Mommy grabs my shoulders. "*It counts more than ever.*"

"So, are you going to tell?" Brian asks, even though he already knows the answer. I want to slap the smile right off his fat lips.

"No, I won't tell."

"Good. Then yes, it's a wheelchair. You're going to sit in it and be sick, got that?"

"Because you *are* sick", Mommy adds.

"I'm not sick! And I don't want to be in a wheelchair!"

I run upstairs. Holly was in a wheelchair. Holly is also dead. I clutch Pox and open up the diary.

"I'm scared. If I could have one wish, it would be to be brave. If I was brave, I would tell someone what Mom is doing to me. Then all the people who donated money to us would get their money back. And I could go to school. There is a company called Operation Hope that gives sick kids anything they want. Mom told them about me, and they said they would send a form for me to fill out about a wish. They said I could have anything I want. Could they give me bravery?"

"Fern!" I hear Mommy calling me from downstairs. "Fern!"

I don't answer. I'm not going down there.

"If you come down, I'll give you a glass of water!"

I run down the stairs, two at a time. The wheelchair is all set up. It's big and ugly. It has footrests and wheels with rubber along them so it won't skid. It has handles so I can be pushed around. I absolutely hate it with every ounce of my body.

"Can I have my water?" I ask. I haven't had anything to eat or drink today, and it's making my head feel light like a feather.

"If you sit in the wheelchair", Mommy says. "Then you can have some water."

Even though that wasn't part of the deal, I sit down. It's comfortable. I hate it even more for that. There are leg straps and a lap strap, which Brian ties tight around me.

"Hey, stop! I can't breathe!"

"Get used to not breathing", he says. "This is where you're staying."

"What?" I struggle to twist my body around, but the straps are too tight, cutting into my skin. "Mommy, let me out!"

"You're safer in there", she says, smiling like the crazy murderer in *The Shining*. I want to like that movie again, but after seeing Mommy like this, I don't know if it's possible.

"Let me out, Mommy!"

"It's 'Mother', remember?"

I eventually get my glass of water, and five crackers too, but I have to stay in the wheelchair as long as Mommy wants.

"What if I say no?" I say.

"Then I'll put you in the wheelchair and you won't get the crackers."

So I agree, because by this point, my stomach is rumbling like the sea after a tropical storm. I eat the crackers tiny bites to make them last as I sit in the wheelchair and watch Mommy and Brian unpack the second box. There are a bunch of shiny silver tubes that connect to form a pole that's taller than me. There's a clear plastic tube and a needle-like thing. I don't know what all the pieces are, but I know what they'll become once they're put together.

"An IV?" I ask.

"Close." Mommy pushes down on two pieces of the shiny metal to connect them. "A feeding tube."

"Do I need one?"

"Yes."

At first, I am excited, because a feeding tube means that I won't be hungry or thirsty anymore. Mommy attaches the plastic bag to the rolling pole, like the one I had in the hospital. Then she makes Brian hold my head still as she pushes the tube closer and closer to my nose.

"What are you doing?" I shriek.

"Putting your tube in", Mommy says calmly. "Now stay still. Brian, grab her by the hair. That'll make her stop moving."

So Brian grabs my hair, and when I try to twist away, I can feel my hair being ripped from my skull like Velcro, so I keep my head still. Mommy slowly pushes the tube up my nose. I am shaking. Everything turns double as I try to focus my eyes on the tube. At first, it feels like I have to sneeze. Then it tickles. Then it scrapes and hurts, and finally, it burns like there's fire coming out of my nose.

"Take it out!" I scream. "Please, Mommy, take it out! I'll do whatever you want! Just stop the burning!"

Then there is a little tickle in the back of my throat, and I feel something there. I try to swallow, but it doesn't go away.

"What's in my throat?" I cry, but the tube mangles my voice, so it comes out all gluey.

"Just the tube", Mommy says. "You'll get used to it."

"You sound weird", Brian says.

"But it hurts!"

"Didn't you get it, kid? I said you sound weird. That a clue to shut up. We know what's best for you."

"Aren't you going to put something for me to eat in that bag?" I ask. "So I won't get hungry?"

"Oh, Fern", Mommy coos. "That's not the point, not the point at all."

She fills the bag with water and puts in a few drops of yellow food coloring, so the water looks orangey-yellow. I start to feel a drip in the back of my throat. Water! I wish I could drink it normally, but it feels good to have it sliding down my throat like a tiny waterfall trickle. Then the trickle stops. Mommy plugs up the tube in my nose, so no water is coming out anymore. I understand now. I'm not getting water or food. I'm just getting hurt.

CHAPTER 17

"There."

Mommy stands back to admire her work. Brian does, too. He kisses her on the nose.

"Ready to go?" he asks.

"Yep." Mommy goes to the closet to get her coat.

"Wait, go where?" I ask. I'm still stick in the wheelchair.

"To the store", Mommy answers.

"Can you let me out of the wheelchair?"

Brian laughs. "Kid", he says, "that's the whole point."

"What?" I'm very confused. If I'm in a wheelchair, why are we going to the store all of a sudden?

"What Brian means", Mommy explains, "is that's we're going to the grocery store with you. In your wheelchair. And you're going to act sick. Just go along with everything I say."

"But I'm not sick!"

They ignore me. Brian grabs the wheelchair and roughly shoves it out the door. It's a big job to get it into the car. They have to put the seats down, and even then, the wheelchair is too tall to fit in the back.

"We could put her sideways", Brian suggests. "I think that's the only way."

Brian lifts me in the wheelchair and brings me crashing down on my side. One wheel of the chair spins helplessly like a stuck bug. My cheek is resting against the smelly fabric of the seat. We drive to the store like that, with me bouncing along in the backseat. It feels like my brains are about to spill out on one side. Brian stops the car way in the back of the parking lot, so they can get me out without people seeing that I'm basically stuck in the car like an extra piece of furniture. When I'm pushed upright again, all the blood rushes to the other side of my body. I shake around a little, trying to get balanced again.

"Stand still", Mommy snaps. She puts on a fake-worried look and wheels me into the store. They've attached my fake feeding tube so that the pole with the bag rolls right along with the wheelchair, like a little moving hospital. Mommy wheels me to the fruit-and-vegetable section of the store.

"Look through the aisles like you're shopping", she whispers to Brian. "Go slow, and act like you don't know me."

"Why do I have to act like I don't know you?"

"Brian, you idiot, *remember*? Single mother, more sympathy? Get going!"

She shoves him roughly toward the cereal aisle. My stomach feels funny, and not just from hunger. It feels like there's a million marbles in there, rolling around. And a voice whispering in my head. Holly. **"Tell, tell, tell. This isn't right. Tell. This is what she did to me. Tell, please tell."**

"Mommy, please don't do this", I beg. "Please."

I don't exactly know what she's planning, but whatever it is, it can't be good.

"Shut up." Mommy tugs a strand of my hair a little too hard. It comes out in her hand. "Hmmm..." she mutters, staring at it.

"Mommy!" I want to snap my fingers to bring her back into the real world, but I don't know how to snap. "Mommy, don't do this! Take me home, please!"

My words must be just as good as snapping, because Mommy crinkles the hair in her fingers and drops it to the shiny grocery store floor.

"What did you say?"

"I said don't do this! It's not right! Please, take me home! Please!"

"You're going to do two things for me", Mommy says, ignoring the fact that I'm begging. "First, you're going to be quiet. And second, you're not going to tell anyone anything except that you're sick, and you have cancer. Is that clear?"

"*Cancer*? I don't have cancer! People die from cancer!"

Mommy shrugs. "Well, you'll die if you tell anyone it's not true", she whispers.

"What about my hair? People with cancer are bald."

"You just haven't started chemotherapy yet", Mommy says. "Because... we can't afford it."

The idea sinks into her brain like a heavy weight being pressed on a loaf of bread.

"Yeah, we can't afford it", she repeats.

Before I can say anything, an old woman comes up to us. She's holding three cans of cat food, a bottle of multivitamins, and a box of Raisin Bran. She doesn't say anything at first, she just kind of stares at us while inching closer and closer, like she wants to pat my head. Old people like patting heads, I've noticed. Maybe they like the feel of hair.

"Is she your child?" the old woman asks Mommy.

Mommy pulls down the corners of her mouth into a frown and sighs, a sigh full of fake-sadness, but to the old woman, it's real. "Yes, Fern's mine. I'd give anything for her to be healthy again."

"Oh, dear." The old woman looks like she wants to ask more.

"Fern has leukemia, see", Mommy says loudly.

At first I thinks she's saying it loud so the old woman can hear, because sometimes old people can't hear very well, but then I see the heads of other shoppers turn, and I realize she's saying it loud to draw more attention.

"Yes, she has cancer", Mommy continues. "It's difficult being a single mother and raising a sick kid, you know."

The old woman pats Mommy's arm. "I know, dearie, I know. Does she have a father?"

Mommy gives a short little laugh, like a bark. "Lord knows where he is! As soon as she was born, he ran off. Hasn't sent any child support checks or anything. And we really need them at this point. Fern still has her hair, as you can see. She's happy about that, aren't you, Fern?"

Mommy nods at me, so I say "Yes, I'm happy to have hair."

The old woman smiles, full of pity. "I wish I could be happy about it, too", Mommy says. "But the truth is, she's still got hair because we just can't afford chemotherapy. I work two jobs, but it isn't enough."

The old woman looks as if she could cry. "Let me pay for your groceries, dearie. Any way I can help."

"Oh!" Mommy blushes. "No, no, that's all right, I couldn't accept that."

"Then at least let me chip in." The old woman digs into her purse and pulls out a crumpled fifty-dollar bill. Her hands are shaking as she hands it to Mommy, who snatches it, a greedy glint in her eye.

"Thank you", Mommy says. "This will help pay for her feeding tube liquid. It's not enough for chemotherapy, but it's a start."

I look at the old woman's wrinkled face and try to send out a message with my eyes.

"Please, help me. I'm not sick, I'm trapped. Please help me."

But I must look pathetic, because the old woman smiles at me, pats me on the head, and hurries away.

"Mommy!" I whisper when I see the old woman disappear behind a row of oatmeal packets. "We can't keep that money!"

"Of course we can!" Mommy snaps. "She *gave* it to us, Fern! Now shut up!"

She stuffs the fifty dollars into the pocket of my wheelchair. If my stomach hurt before, it's absolutely screaming now. Mommy pushes me through the aisles, stealthily avoiding Brian when she sees him. Other people look at us for a few seconds, but no one's gaze lingers long enough for them to say anything. A little boy who looks like he's about four years old says loudly, "Why is she in a wheelchair, Daddy?", but his daddy hugs him close and tells him that it's not polite to ask questions like that.

I feel tears behind my eyes as I watch the boy pick out a tub of mint ice cream with his daddy. Mint ice cream is my favorite kind. Daddy and I used to get it when Mommy was working late at The Happy Hour Casino. We never bought it from the store, because Daddy said it tasted like freezer. Instead, Daddy drove me to our favorite ice cream shop, the one with the red wooden picnic tables and the tree that was perfect for climbing. The tree gave us lots of shade, and we always laughed at the people huddled inside on the beautiful days, but we were secretly glad they were in there, because it meant we had the whole outside to ourselves. Daddy ordered pistachio with chocolate sprinkles every time, and I ordered mint chocolate chip with rainbow sprinkles every time. The ice cream from Astro's always melted really quickly, so by the time my spoon scraped the bottom of the cup, there was ice cream all over my face and my hands and my arms and my hair. The table was a soupy mess too. Daddy always got a cone, the kind that tastes like Styrofoam, and he licked his ice cream in perfect circles so there was never any mess.

I feel sad now, watching this little boy and his Daddy pick out mint chocolate chip ice cream. I wonder if the boy's Mommy is working late tonight, or if she's waiting at home with spoons and bowls out, ready to share the ice cream with her family, like Mommy never did. A tear trickles its way down my left cheek.

"A little more", Mommy tells me.

"What?"

"Cry a little more. No one is noticing us."

I decide to push all the tears back into my eyes and let them out when I'm alone. I won't cry for Mommy. She scans the aisles up and down. No one is looking at us. Mommy lets out a sob then, a really loud sob that breaks into smaller cries like a wave that breaks into foam. But she's not really crying. I'm an expert on knowing that. Other people aren't, though, because they turn to stare at us.

"What's the matter?" a man asks.

"Nothing, nothing." Mommy waves him off. "It's just..."

"Just what?" says a woman.

A crowd is starting to gather around us. I scratch at my arms. Crowds make me itchy.

"I was just thinking", Mommy sobs, "how much I want to have a healthy child again. I keep looking at that man and his son over there."

She points to the little boy and his father with the mint chocolate chip ice cream. "And I was just wishing that I could share ice cream with *my* child. But she can't even eat solid food! She needs a feeding tube!"

Nervously, a young woman steps forward. "What's her diagnosis?" she asks.

Diagnosis. There's that word again. I wonder if the young woman works in a hospital.

"Fern has leukemia", Mommy says. "She still has her hair because we can't afford chemotherapy. She doesn't have a father. He walked out on me as soon as she was born, and we've never gotten child-support checks or anything. Without the chemotherapy, she's likely to die."

Everyone is the aisle is quiet. I hear the normal sounds of the grocery store around me: the buzzing of cash registers, the crying of babies, the chatter of other shoppers. But the aisle that we are in is absolutely silent, like someone hit the pause button and froze time right in this one spot. Then, slowly, the man with the ice cream pulls a twenty-dollar bill out of his wallet.

"Go give this to the lady", he says to his son. "The least we can do is help."

The boy toddles over and presses the money into Mommy's hand.

"Thank you." Mommy smiles. "This won't do much, but it's a start."

The crowd murmurs as the little boy slips back to his father, who picks him up and hugs him.

"It's a *start*", Mommy repeats. My face turns red.

A man standing by the Froot Loops says, "I'll donate a hundred dollars, ma'am. My son has a wheelchair like your little girl, so I can understand how hard it is."

A hundred dollars? My mouth drops open.

"I'll give some money, too", says a woman.

Suddenly, people all around the aisle are crowding around Mommy as she fake-cries. They're patting her on the back and handing her money and saying "it must be so hard, I just can't imagine..." and "don't worry, it'll be all right".

Mommy is fake-crying, but there are real tears coming out of her eyes. I think she uses the same trick I do, thinking about something sad. I wonder what happened that's sad enough to make tears on her face. I see a glint in her eye, though, like a lost sparkle. She loves this.

It makes my stomach hurt so badly I forget about being hungry. I want to shout to everyone "I'm not really sick! Help me, please help me!" My eyes search the crowd, and I pretend I get to choose any person, any person. At all, to take me home. I lock eyes with the man by the Froot Loops, the one who has a son in a wheelchair. I want him to take care of me. I want to meet his son and tell him about Holly. Please, I beg silently. Please take me home with you. But if he has mind-reading powers, they must be turned off, because he takes out another twenty dollars and hands it to Mommy. She stuffs all the money in my wheelchair pocket. By now, she is positively glowing. I have read that expression in books before, but I never knew what it meant until right now. Everything about her seems so happy, but all the people in the aisle can see is sadness.

"Listen, everyone", Mommy shouts. "Please listen."

As people start hearing her, they quiet down until there is that weird silence in only one aisle again.

"This is", Mommy sniffles, "very thoughtful. I can't even *tell* you how many nights I've stayed up and prayed for something like this to happen.

You all have been very generous, but unfortunately, it isn't enough to pay for chemotherapy. We just moved here, and we don't know a lot of people. I can't send Fern to school, so she doesn't know any other kids. I don't have the money to buy her the special treats she deserves for being so brave during this hard time. We live on Hammond Street, house number 666. If anyone would like to send a little something-anything at all- please don't hesitate to do so. It would be a great help."

People start nodding, and one woman starts crying. Then I hear a loud voice.

"What's going on here? Ma'am, are you asking for *money* from these people?"

The man who's talking is wearing a name tag with the words "PATRICK- SUPERSHOP MANAGER" on it. Underneath are smaller words: "How may I help you?" I know how he can help me, but Mommy doesn't give me a chance to say anything.

"God, blame everything on the single mother with the sick kid, why don't you?" she says. "Just because we can't afford medical treatment doesn't mean we'll ask for *charity*."

She breezes by him and walks straight out of the store. No one follows us. Maybe Patrick believed Mommy. Maybe he just didn't care. Mommy flips open her cell phone and presses her nails into the buttons to call Brian.

"We're done here", she says. "Meet us at the car. I need help loading the wheelchair back in."

Brian takes his time coming out. Mommy gets cold, so she sits in the front seat of the car and leaves me outside, staring around the parking lot. I'm cold too, but I can't even wrap my arms around my chest to keep warm, because my arms are strapped to the wheelchair. I count the minutes that pass. After twenty-nine minutes and thirty-one seconds, I see Brian, pushing a cart that's piled high with bags. They load me into the car on my side, and I feel my insides spill to one side again. They stack the bags around me. Brian drives home, with him and Mommy in the front seat and me on my side, surrounded by groceries, staring at a bag of chips that I know Mommy won't let me have.

CHAPTER
18

One tube of Saltines, one glass of cranberry juice, and one bowl of dry oatmeal. That's what I get to eat each day. Every morning, Mommy brings it up to my room and says "That's your food for the day. Don't eat too fast, 'cause you're not getting any more." I can't eat too fast anyway, because the tube in my throat tickles when I swallow. It's very boring food. I try mixing the dry oatmeal with cranberry juice, but that turns out to be absolutely disgusting.

Since the food is so boring, I read Holly's diary every day while I eat. I'm already halfway through. I feel like I know Holly, and I realize that I'm actually part of her, because we share the same mother. I spend days wondering what she looks like. I know what she looks like in my dreams and in the picture that fell out of Mommy's album so long ago, but I can't help thinking that the girl in the picture was really just a shell of Holly. Mommy took her and drained all her happiness out through a straw. I wonder what Holly looks like when she's smiling or laughing. What she looks like when she's not wearing a school uniform or appearing in my dreams in a stained bloody nightgown. What she looks like when she's happy. I learn about her, too. Every week, she wrote in this diary no matter what. She took it to the hospital with her when she had to, which was a lot. I know her favorite color, red, and her favorite song, "Fireflies" by Owl City. One of the people who thought she had epilepsy because Mommy told them she did sent her an iPod and headphones, and she listened to "Fireflies" every single day. I spend so long thinking about Holly and reading her diary, I don't even notice all the days passing by.

In a movie I saw with Daddy once, there was a prisoner who kept track of the time by drawing marks on his wall, one for every day. I decide to do that too. I draw a tally mark every day at three 'o clock. The tally marks are all in the corner, so Mommy won't see. Before I know it, I have tallied a week. I am getting more tired and thirsty and hungry with every day, and sometimes I wonder if Mommy is giving me sleeping pills again. Every night, Mommy helps me out of my wheelchair and into bed, and every morning, when she brings me my food for the day, she puts me back in the wheelchair and won't let me out all day. But at night, I am free. I try to sleep during the day, so I am awake at night, but it's getting harder. When Mommy lets me out of my wheelchair at ten o'clock at night, she goes to bed with Brian and I have the whole house to myself. Mommy doesn't bother locking my door anymore, since I pretend to be asleep when she checks on me at ten fifteen. Then at ten thirty, I sneak downstairs and hope that maybe the cupboards will be unlocked, but they never are. I take a pen, though, to keep writing the marks on my wall, and a flashlight so I can read Holly's diary. Then I sneak back upstairs.

I now keep Holly's diary in my wheelchair pocket. "I am reading seventh-grade books. A man delivered them from the library for me and he told Mom they were seventh-grade books then. He said "Aren't you proud of her?" and Mom told him "I just hope she lives another day." Along with reading and science and math and history, I have taught myself to block my mind when Mom says things like that, because she says them all the time. Mostly, I want to go to school, but Mom says that will never happen."

The morning after I read this in Holly's diary, I ask Mommy if I can go to school when she brings my food and straps me in the wheelchair. "No", she says. "That will never happen." Just like she said to Holly.

"Why not?"

"Because you're *sick*, Fern. You have *cancer*."

"No I don't!"

"Oh, really?" says Brian, appearing at the door. "How do you know?"

That question throws my brain off its tracks. How *do* I know? I suppose I don't know any more than I did before Mommy started saying I was sick. But will I ever be really *sure* I don't have cancer? Or something else?

Brian notices my silence and laughs. "You'll never go to school, kid. But cheer up. Being dumb isn't so bad. I hated school. All cool kids do."

My hands try to clench into fists, but they're so shaky and weak that they just hang limply where they're strapped.

"I want to go to school."

"No."

"Yes."

"No, damn it!" Mommy yells. "No!"

"Yes."

We go back and forth for a few minutes. Mommy must have done this with Holly, because she isn't backing down. I need to change my strategy.

"No!" she snaps.

"Yes", I say.

"No!" she yells again.

"No", I agree.

"Yes!" she barks, before clapping her hand over her mouth when she realizes what she said.

"Yes, Mommy?"

I make my eyes big and round like I didn't know I was tricking her.

"You said yes?"

For the tiniest fraction of a second, I see the corners of her mouth quirk up, like she's going to laugh.

"Yes?" I beg, smiling.

"Fine", she says. "You got me this time, Fern. But not when it counts, you won't get me. Not when it counts. I'll get you some books, if you'll just shut up about it."

"Thank you, Mother."

"Spoiled kid", Brian mutters.

The next day, Mommy dumps a stack of books on my lap as I'm sitting in my wheelchair. I look at the covers. "Elementary Algebra", "A History of the World For Kids", "Junior Astronomy", "Grammar & Spelling."

I spend the afternoon leafing through the books, too excited to even do any of the work in them. I line them up, favorite to least favorite. "Junior Astronomy", "Elementary Algebra", "A History of the World For Kids", and "Grammar & Spelling" last. I open them to the middle and smell them. I run my fingers along the spines. Then I read another page of Holly's diary.

"Mom is taking me to a doctor tomorrow. She says this will really determine what's wrong with me, but I know that no matter what the doctor says, she'll still go around telling everyone I have life-threatening epilepsy. She's been taking me out to stores when I'm in my wheelchair so everyone can see how sick she claims I am. She tells me to drool and partly close my eyes, and if I don't, she gives me pills that make me do that stuff anyway. People are sending us money. I know because I hear Mom tearing open envelopes late at night and shouting "Yes! Yes!" When I ask her what she's so happy about, she just smiles and says "oh, nothing" but the next week she'll have a new purse or new shoes."

My excitement over the books has drained completely out of my head. I sit in silence, thinking about what Mommy has been doing to me the past few weeks. Every other day, we go to a new store and Mommy tells Brian to stay in the car. Then she pushes me around in my wheelchair and tells people that I have cancer but she can't afford chemotherapy.

And people have been giving her money. Whenever they do, there's a little voice in my head that keeps saying "Do something! Do something!" Maybe it's Holly.

I have already eaten my food for the day, and it's only six 'o clock at night. Mommy and Brian haven't even made dinner yet. I hear pots and pans clanging downstairs, and a bit later, Brian comes to my door.

"We're making dinner, kid. Buttery spaghetti with cheese. And garlic bread. Mmm, can't you smell it?"

I can. I think Mommy has been making dinners that smell extra good recently, just to make me mad when she won't let me have any. Or it could be just my mind playing tricks with me because I'm so hungry. I'll never know.

"Want to come down and join us?" Brian asks. Then he laughs. "Oh, wait, you can't."

I don't see what's particularly funny, so I sit with my lips pressed together, wanting to punch him.

Instead, I open Junior Astronomy and vow to send Brian to Pluto if I'm ever let out of this stupid wheelchair. The Junior Astronomy book is interesting, so interesting that it keeps me from thinking about the dinner that I'm not having. At the end of each chapter, there are three questions in a little blue box that says "Things To Consider". I consider the things it tells me to, but what I like best is at the bottom of the blue box. Right under the questions, it says in bold letters, "WHAT'S OUT THERE?" I think about that as Mommy takes me out of my wheelchair. What's out there? And will I ever get to see it?

It seems like my question is answered the next morning. When Mommy lifts me into my wheelchair, she says, "We're going to a store today, Fern. Someplace new." That isn't a surprise, because we always go to someplace new. The surprise is waiting for me at the store. Mommy pushes me through the aisles. My cheek stings from pressing against the seat of Brian's car. I had to lie sideways again, like I do whenever we go out. We are in a toy store. My eyes sweep over the colorful plastic things on the shelves. We're in the girls aisle. I hate it. All the pink gives me a headache. It gives Daddy a headache, too.

When I was five, he took me to the toy store to buy me a birthday present. Mommy had been in a bad mood, so she'd forgotten to buy a present, but Daddy told me we would go to the toy store and I could pick out anything.

"But nothing pink", he warned.

"Nothing pink", I agreed. I knew what I wanted, anyway: a superhero. Daddy was all too happy to buy me one.

"Superman?" he asked, smashing the plastic figures into each other and making ka-pow sounds. "Or Batman?"

"Neither."

"Not Wonder Woman, I hope", he said, making a face.

"Nope. Green Arrow."

"Who?" Daddy looked confused.

"Green Arrow", I explained, pointing to the action figure on the bottom shelf. "I want him."

"Don't you want one of the real guys, Fern? A real superhero?"

"Green Arrow is a real superhero."

"Why not Batman, Fern? C'mon, Batman's awesome! No one's even heard of Green Arrow before."

"That's why I want him. He's a superhero too, only no one really knows it."

"Ah, a secret superhero. We'll get you that one, Fern. We'll get you Green Arrow."

I hugged Green Arrow tight to my chest and slept with him clutched in my hand every night until Mommy said superheroes were "for boys", and she threw Green Arrow away.

Mommy can't stop me from liking superheroes, though. No one can. And that's what I want to be when I grow up. A superhero. My eyes drift over to the boy's aisle, where a huge figure of Superman stands tall above all the mini figures below him. I wonder if Green Arrow is still there.

A man is talking to Mommy now, and she is telling him that I have cancer. I would tune him out, like I do with everyone else, but he says something that makes Mommy say "Oh, thank you! That's a wonderful idea!" I listen close, because Mommy's version of a wonderful idea and my version of a wonderful idea are two very different things.

"Fern!" Mommy snaps. "Are you listening?"

"Yes!" I exclaim. "Yes, I'm listening."

"I'm sorry", Mommy says to the man. "It's her medicine."

I'm not taking any medicine, but the look on Mommy's face says "keep quiet".

"Mr. Seapy was telling me about a convention for cancer patients", Mommy says.

Convention. I don't know that word.

"Who's Mr. Seapy?" I ask.

"The man standing right in front of you", Mommy says, exasperated. "Sorry Mr. Seapy, her medicine makes her a little confused, too."

"What's a convention?" I ask.

"It's like a giant meeting", Mr. Seapy says. "A fun meeting. There will be lots of activities and workshops and other kids to meet."

He hands Mommy a colorful brochure.

"The date and location is on there, as well as a list of things they have. It might be a good thing for your daughter. It helps for kids to know they're not alone."

But I am alone. Very alone, only I'm the only one who knows it. Mr. Seapy gives Mommy a fifty-dollar bill.

"For your daughter's chemotherapy treatment", he says. He leans down close to me. He has a nice smile and smells like mango hand lotion.

"Take care, Fern."

I feel sick. When we get home, Mommy tells Brian about the convention.

"It's in three weeks", Mommy says. "That's pretty short notice. We've got a lot to do, and not a lot of time to do it."

I'm afraid to ask what we need to do.

CHAPTER 19

"I am a wimp. A chicken. Why do they call scared people chickens, anyway? Do chickens get scared a lot? I don't think they do. If they're going to compare a scared person to an animal, they should say 'rabbit' instead, because in my dreams when I am running in a field, the rabbits always jump away from me, and there are no chickens anywhere. I suppose I have a habit of getting off track, but it's very boring being almost ten years old and being stuck in bed all day with only my books. I want to tell someone what Mom is doing, but she says if I do, she'll hurt me. So I'm a chicken. Or maybe a rabbit."

I sigh and close Holly's diary, switching off the flashlight that I keep hidden under my covers. Holly feels the same way I do. I stroke Pox and decide that I'm thirsty. There is still something lucky in my life. Mommy and Brian locked the cabinets so I can't get food, but they can't stop me from getting tap water. About a week ago, I decided that since Mommy and Brian lie so much about other stuff, Brian might be lying about the water being bad, too. So I tried the water, and it was just fine. Now I drink as much as I want at night.

A week passes, and I can see myself getting thinner and thinner by the size of my wrists. They look too little to even hold up my hands at the end. I am scared. I eat every bite of the food Mommy brings me, but when I ask for more, she shakes her head and says I'll get sick of I eat anything else. We both know this is a lie. Sometimes, I am too tired to struggle, so I just sit in my wheelchair and read my school books without complaining. It's getting harder to focus. Whenever I see a picture of food in my textbook, I turn the page right away, because looking at it just makes my stomach cry.

Holly is not doing so good either.

"The doctor says there is nothing wrong with me except for the fact that I'm pale and I don't get enough food or water. He said "What this girl needs is a day at the beach with plenty of fried dough and juice boxes!" Mom smiled and nodded her head, but when we got home, she said, "That's never going to happen, Holly, so don't go getting any ideas, do you hear me?" Mom also said we would be going to another doctor, one farther away in the city, because this one couldn't find anything wrong with me. I told Mom that maybe the doctors are right and she is wrong, since they've all gone to medical school and she just works at The Happy Hour Casino. I got slapped for that. Now I have some color in my cheeks, in the shape of a red handprint."

I imagine Mommy slapping Holly across the face just like she did to me. I can almost feel the stinging in my cheek.

That night, I am too tired to go downstairs and get water, or even to read Holly's diary. The door cracks open, and light spills through my room. A small figure enters, holding something circular and letting it sway from side to side. It's Holly, with her dark braids and blood-stained nightgown. I look at her skin, and then at mine. I'm almost as pale as she is, now. Does that mean I'm dead, too? Holly is swinging a clock. "Not much time left, Fern", she whispers. "Not much time left."

"Not much time for what?" I ask.

She doesn't seem to hear me. She drops the clock and it shatters on the floor. Stepping over the broken glass, she hugs me. He bony fingers press into my back, and she rests her pointed chin on my shoulder.

"Please don't be like me, Fern", she whispers. "Please."

"Why not?" I ask. "What happened, Holly? Why won't you tell me what happened?"

I see her eyes flash past me to the pillow on my mattress, which I got two days ago from the Salvation Army. Holly screams and grabs it, tearing into the cloth with her teeth and ripping it apart with her bare hands.

"What, Holly? What is it?"

She keeps screaming and tearing the pillow apart, like it's a live animal that she's trying to kill. When all the feathers have floated to the floor and settled in with the broken glass, Holly suddenly becomes calm. She drops the shredded pillow case, walks over to me, and presses her cold, dead lips against the top of my head.

"Now, you're safe, Fern", she whispers. "Now you're safe."

"What do you mean?" I ask, but there is nothing in my room but me and a whole mess of glass and feathers on the floor. I know I should get out of bed and clean the mess up so Mommy and Brian don't see, but Holly's visit leaves me feeling cold all over. I pull the blanket up to my chin and shiver. Someone is shaking me. Gently at first, then roughly when I don't open my eyes.

"Fern! Fern!"

It's Mommy. I wait for her to say "How in the world to you explain this mess here on the floor?", but she doesn't. I peek my eyes open and look over the side of my mattress. The floor is clean.

"Is there any glass there, Mommy?"

"Call me 'Mother'. And what are you talking about? What glass?"

My eyes dart around the room for signs of last night's visit with Holly, but everything is just as it was when I went to bed. I have a pillow under me, even though I saw Holly tear it up and scream. How could the scream not have caused Mommy and Brian to wake up? Then I remember the slow feeling of drifting off to sleep, right before the door opened. Oh.

"What glass?" Mommy repeats. "Is there something you're not telling me, Fern?"

"No", I say. "Never mind."

"Good", Mommy says, handing me a tube of crackers, glass of juice, and a bowl of dry oats. "We have a plan today."

"Another store?" I ask, hoping the answer is no.

"Not today", Mommy says. "We have something...different."

I hear a buzzing sound from the bathroom downstairs.

"Hey, Beth!" Brian yells. "It works!"

"What works?" I'm scared now. "*What* works?"

"The electric razor".

"Why does Brian have an electric razor?"

Mommy takes a deep breath.

"Fern, we need to shave your head."

"My...you need to...what?" I touch my fingers to my blond hair. I can't even remember the last time it's been washed. Suddenly, I imagine all of it falling to the floor. I'll be bald, like Leah. And I don't have a grandmother who will make me knitted hats. I don't even have a grandmother at all.

"Come on", Mommy says. "To the bathroom. Brian's got the razor all set up. It won't hurt, if that's what you're worried about."

"You can't do this!" I beg.

"Please!" Mommy sighs. She is obviously not feeling very patient today, but then again, she's never very patient. "We can do this the easy way", she tells me. "Or we can do it the hard way." I didn't know there *was* an easy way and a hard way to get my head shaved.

"I won't do it."

"I see you choose the hard way, then." Mommy lunges for me, grabbing me by the ankle.

"Let go, Mommy! I'll call Raymond! I will!"

Mommy lets go of my ankle in surprise. "You'll do *what*?"

"Nothing", I say quickly, pulling down my sleeve a little to cover the numbers written on my arm.

"You'll call Raymond?" Mommy demands. "Is that what you said?"

"No!" I cry. I can't believe I was stupid enough to tell Mommy that I could call Raymond. I wrote his number on my arm and didn't even bother to memorize it, because I thought it would always be there. Stupid, stupid, stupid.

"That *is* what you said!" Mommy yells. "Do you have Raymond's number?"

"No!" I pull my sleeve down farther, just to be sure.

"Yes, you do", Mommy hisses. "Why do you keep pulling on your sleeve like that, then?"

I feel her bony fingers grab all the way around my arm and lift up my sleeve. There's Raymond's phone number, written in smudged black ink. I stare at the numbers, trying to imprint them in my head, but Mommy is too quick. Her grip on me gets tighter as she leads me down the hall. I stumble behind her like a zombie.

"Too slow", she snaps, and jerks me forward. I lose my footing, and now she's completely dragging me by the arms. My feet scramble to stand up, but Mommy is going too fast, and we are coming to the staircase. My skin screeches along the splintery wood, burning and rubbing. Help me, Holly, help me. Did she do this to you too? Mommy gets to the stairs, but she doesn't slow down. I thump along behind her, my knees scraping the stairs with every step. I imagine there's a fire lighting under me, one that will get me if I don't move faster. Or maybe it'll get Mommy. A blaze of red and orange spilling from my hair, my hair that's about to be gone. Mommy reaches the bottom of the stairs and lets go of me so I fall into a heap. The fire has gone out now, and I am nothing but smoke.

"Get up!" Mommy pulls me to my feet.

I want to say "See, I can walk just fine without a wheelchair", but I don't. Mommy is already mad enough.

"Brian!" Mommy screeches, dragging me into the bathroom. "Get a wet washcloth!"

"Why?" Brian has a razor with a big blade plugged into the wall. He's trimming the hair under his arms with a pair of tiny scissors. It's disgusting.

"A wet washcloth!" Mommy shouts again. "Hurry!"

"Geez, Beth." Brian brushes his pile of armpit hair to the tile floor.

"Just get me the damn washcloth! I'll explain later!"

Brian tosses the washcloth to Mommy like a fat, dripping jellyfish. Mommy presses the washcloth against my skin. Then she starts scrubbing. Hard. I can feel the burning of my skin under the cool towel material.

"Stop, Mommy! It burns!"

Mommy grins, a smile that splits her face into two evil halves. "Oh, it hurts, does it? Well, you should have thought of that before you wrote on yourself."

She scrubs harder and faster. "Do you know the number? Tell me!"

"No!" I say.

"That's right", Mommy agrees. "So if I ever catch you on the phone, it means you lied to me. And the consequences for lying are very, very severe."

I don't want to ask what exactly "very, very severe consequences" are. I have a pretty good idea, and in my head, they look like what was done to Holly. Tell me, Holly. Did they give you very, very severe consequences? What were they? Did they make you die?

"Time to shave", Brian says, holding up the razor and grinning like a crazy hairdresser.

"I'll do it." Mommy takes the razor from Brian. "You hold Fern down."

There is nowhere to run. I smell a mixture of sweat and grease in the air near my body, and I curl myself up so I become even smaller. Brian's odor is big enough to fill the entire room.

"Make her stand up straight", Mommy tells Brian. "And hold her head still."

Brian grabs behind my ears and squeezes, giving me a headache. Maybe some brains will pop out my nose. I try to squirm loose, but his hands slap my chest back against the cool tile floor.

"Do it, Beth", he growls. "Just do it."

I close my eyes. Unlike blood, losing hair is *not* fun to watch. The razor feels smooth against my head, not rough like I expected. I jerk my head away and feel the blade dig into my scalp, spraying tiny droplets of blood around the bathroom.

"If you'd stayed still, that wouldn't have happened", Mommy says.

I feel hair falling from my head. I am losing part of me. It feels weird, like I am being thrown away somehow.

"Get around the ears", Brian tells Mommy. "And the back of the neck."

"I *know*, Brian."

A single tear slides down my cheek as Mommy shaves my head.

"She's crying!" Brian announces.

He's happy. But why? Why does he like to see me upset?

"My God, Fern, grow up", Mommy says. "There, you're done. That wasn't so bad, was it? Don't be a baby."

I don't answer her. I tear away from the bathroom, almost slipping on the blonde hair that rests on the tile floor. *My* hair. They even took my hair from me. What else is left? I run to my room and slam the door. No footsteps follow me. Tears stain and smudge the pages of Holly's diary as I read. I need her now. I need to hear her voice, not just read the things she writes. I need my sister Holly to hug me and tell me I'll be okay. I squeeze the diary to my chest and rub my newly bald head.

My days change a little bit after I get my head shaved. Every day, Mommy drags me into the bathroom and makes sure no hair grew on my head overnight. Each time I wake up, I brush my hand to my scalp, but it's always the same: bald head, shiny as an egg. It makes my ears stick out. Mommy comes into my room an hour before she goes to bed each night, and we practice for the convention. I don't know if I really need practice for that sort of thing, but Mommy insists that I know what to say. She writes a list of phrases and answers for me in case people ask me about my illness. I'm not allowed to say that I don't have cancer. I'm not allowed to say anything except for the words on the list. "Yes sir, I was diagnosed when I was three." "No, I don't have a father. He left when I was born." "Yes, my mother is very nice. It's hard for her to take care of me all by herself." Since I don't plan on saying any of these lies, I guess I will be very silent at the convention.

We are supposed to leave very early tomorrow morning. The convention starts at eleven 'o clock, but Mommy says she's putting me and my wheelchair and feeding tube in the car and four in the morning. I can't believe I have to spend six hours with my face pressed against the seat of Brian's car. Mommy dresses me up nice for the convention, in the only dress I have, the blue one. She scrubs my face until it's shiny and pink. She even sprays her perfume all over my body so I will smell nice.

"Can I have a hat?" I ask. "Absolutely not. Everyone there has cancer, Fern. It's nothing to be ashamed of."

At this point, I don't even bother saying that I don't have cancer. I let Mommy keep my head shiny and smooth, bald for everyone to see. Just before Mommy puts me in my wheelchair, I sneak upstairs and slip Holly's diary into the Grammar & Spelling book.

"What's that?" Brian sneers when he sees me. "You think you can bring a book?"

"Just in case I'm bored in the car", I say, hoping that I hid Holly's diary well enough.

"You think a book will make you smarter?" Brian says, his voice mocking me.

I turn to Mommy. "It'll keep me quiet", I beg. "I won't say a single word until we're at the convention. I promise."

"Not a single word?"

"Not a single word. Can I have some breakfast?"

Mommy tosses me a tube of crackers. "Don't push your luck."

I lie in the backseat of Brian's car, on my side like always. It's kind of hard to read like that. I keep seeing double. For the first hour, I read the Grammar & Spelling book, in case Mommy is watching. It's boring. I know everything in it already, and I'm anxious to read Holly's diary, but I make myself wait until Mommy flips open The National Enquirer and puts in her earbuds.

"Mom has been seeing a man. His name is David. At first, she didn't want to tell him she had a kid, because she thought he wouldn't like her if he knew about me. So she kept me in my room whenever he came over. Then one day, I was writing in this diary and I needed my pencil sharpened. I forgot David was over, and Mom won't let me out of bed, so I yelled "Mom! Can I have the pencil sharpener, please?" And David heard me. Mom explained to him that I was very sick and I would probably die soon. He asked why she didn't tell him earlier, and she said because she was afraid he wouldn't love her. Then David said, "I'll always love you, Beth", and Mommy fake-cried into his shoulder for a long time."

I let the diary fall to the floor of the car with a thump and stare wide-eyed at the window.

Daddy knew Holly. He *knew* her. And all this time, he never told me about her. And then he left me alone with Mommy and all these secrets. Holly was his little girl too. Maybe he knows what happened to her. And he didn't even tell me. I feel something boiling inside my stomach. Not hunger, but anger. I let the feeling flow through my body until I am clenched up tight with rage at Daddy. How *could* he? I thought when he left, it was just *him* leaving, but a whole other part left, too. All the secrets and history and pain that I never knew about are gone. Mommy and I are a blank slate, and she's scribbling all over us with permanent marker. A thought pops into my mind like the soap bubbles Daddy and I used to blow in the backyard from little plastic wands. *I hate Daddy.* I let the thought float through my mind and I absorb it, soaking every word into my blood. *I. Hate. Daddy.* He didn't tell me anything. Not one word. I have never felt so mad in my entire life.

Soon, though, the anger turns into sadness, and I am sobbing, wishing that Daddy would come hold me again and call me his little superhero.

"What are you crying for?" Mommy asks, not looking up from The National Enquirer.

"I'm...hungry", I sniff. "Really hungry. Can we get something to eat?"

"Fat chance", Mommy snaps. "You've already had your crackers."

"I could use a snack", Brian offers.

Mommy rolls her eyes. "You *always* need a snack, Brian."

"There's a gas station up ahead", Brian says. "I'm stopping. We're not getting anything for the kid, are we?"

"Nope." Mommy steps out of the car and opens the backseat.

"What are you doing, Beth?"

"Brian, we can't just leave her here. The police would be all over us. Every day, you hear stories about kids who die in locked cars. We don't need that kind of trouble."

"We don't need *this* kind of trouble, either", Brian mutters as he lifts my wheelchair out of the car. Mommy wheels me into the convenience store with my feeding tube. Food is organized neatly in rows like colorful little toys. I want more than anything to jump out if my wheelchair and grab some candy and a soda from the rainbow color-coded soft drinks display. As Brian pays for his cheddar pork rinds, a girl stares at me. She's older, maybe ten or eleven.

"What's wrong with you?" she asks.

"Brea, shhh!" her mother scolds. "You know better than that!"

"It's all right", Mommy says. She explains about how sick I am, and how I don't have a father, and how medical bills are just too expensive. She knows this speech of lies so well, I wonder if she practices it in front of a mirror.

"So...she's dying?" the girl named Brea confirms.

"Brea! You don't just *ask* someone that!"

"Whatever." Brea grabs a pack of skittles, my favorite, and heads to the cash register.

"I'm so sorry ", Brea's mother apologizes. "We've been in the car for nearly four hours, and Brea's in a mood...still, it doesn't give her the right to be so rude to your daughter."

"It's all right", Mommy says. "We're used to comments like that. But in answer to your daughter's question, yes, Fern is dying."

Brea comes back with her bag of skittles, and her mother whispers something to her. Brea rolls her eyes and heads back down the candy aisle. Mommy goes to the refrigerator in the back of the store and picks up a bottle of diet Pepsi. Brea returns, carrying another package of skittles. She tosses them into my lap.

"Mom wanted me to give these to you."

"I thought you might be hungry", Brea's mother says. "You're so little...can you eat skittles? With your feeding tube and all?"

I glance back to the refrigerator. Mommy has put the diet Pepsi back and is examining the back of a coke bottle. Brian is paying for a case of beer.

"Yes", I whisper. "I can eat skittles. Thank you."

I tear open the red package. Daddy used to buy me skittles at the store that was next to The Happy Hour Casino. On summer nights, we would surprise Mommy by waiting by the door for her, but first, me and Daddy always shared a package of skittles from the drugstore. We sat on the warm sidewalk and divided them by color into neat little piles. Daddy always let me have all the green ones. But I'm mad at Daddy, so when Brea gives me the package of skittles, I press all the green ones back into the package, even though they really are the best.

"Thank you", I say again, swallowing the last of my skittles.

"You're welcome." Brea's mom smiles. "Don't eat too fast, honey, or you'll choke."

I nod. Brea takes the packet from me and puts it in the trash, but not before dumping all the green skittles into her hand and popping them into her mouth one by one. I guess green skittles don't remind her of a Daddy who lied to her.

"Let's *go*, Fern", Mommy snaps from behind me. As she wheels me back into the car, I hope I don't have skittle-breath. The rest if the drive is quiet except for Brian's burps that make the whole car smell like beer.

CHAPTER
20

"David is nice. I like him. Mom says they might get married. That would be good, because then I would have a dad again. Sometimes, in my dreams, I see my dad hugging me and pushing away Mom. Then I get out of my wheelchair and we jump on the clouds, which are even bouncier than trampolines. I usually have these dreams after David comes to visit. I think that means something."

I close the diary, because I don't really feel like reading good things about Daddy. He didn't tell me. If he loved me, he would have told me everything.

The convention is in a huge hotel building. Mommy says we will get a room there and stay for the night. I've never stayed in a hotel before. And Brian isn't even going to be there. Mommy told him that 'single mothers' get more sympathy, so he shouldn't come to the convention with us. He wasn't happy after she told him that, so he smashed a plate on the floor, and for once, I was glad I was in a wheelchair, because otherwise I would have stepped on the glass and cut my foot.

Mommy and I watch Brian drive off. Mommy has a huge suitcase with her. She even brought her hair dryer, because she said the hotel might not have one. I don't get a change of clothes because there wasn't room in the suitcase, but I don't care. I have the two things that are most important to me. Pox, and Holly's diary. The hotel is so fancy, there's a man in a suit who opens the door for us. He has a funny-looking hat.

"Thank you", I say, and he bows to me. Wow.

"Don't thank the help", Mommy says.

"What's the help?"

"The people who work here."

"But if they're called the help, then they help us, so we should thank them, right? We should thank people who help us."

Mommy tells me to be quiet about things I don't know anything about. The room we go into is absolutely huge. I have never seen such a high ceiling. It's almost like the ceiling isn't even there at all, just a spiraling sky, up and up.

"Put your head down", Mommy snaps. I stop staring at the ceiling and look around. There is a staircase that's twists around the corner and pictures all over the walls. There's a desk that's shiny wood, and people in uniform are pushing around things made of golden bars that have suitcases riding on them. I wonder if they're sort of like fancy feeding tubes, since this is a convention for sick people. Everywhere in the room, there are parents and bald kids. Some of them have wigs, but they're so shiny and perfect, you can tell right away that they're wigs. Some kids are wearing hats. I'm not the only one in a wheelchair either, or the only one with a feeding tube. Some older kids smile at me. The younger ones look kind of scared and excited at the same time. On the desk, there's a sign that says "Kids Cancer Convention Check-In Here".

"That's where we need to be", Mommy says. She starts pushing through the crowd without saying "excuse me", so I say it for her. "Excuse me, sorry, I'm sorry, watch out please!"

Some people give me dirty looks, but a lot of them smile at me.

"We're here for the convention", Mommy tells the lady at the desk.

"Wonderful!" she says, looking a little sad. I guess being in a room with a bunch of sick kids could make anyone a little sad.

"I'm Martha", the lady says. I decide to call her sparkle because her nails are painted with sparkly polish, and she doesn't look like she should be named Martha anyway. Martha sound like somebody's grandmother, and Sparkle is young and pretty.

"I like your nail polish", I say.

"Thank you." Sparkle smiles.

I'll bet Mommy is jealous because I never said I like *her* nail polish that she always wears. Sparkle pushes a bunch of papers and a pen that says "Springfield Getaway Hotel" at Mommy. Mommy tells Sparkle all about me while she fills out the papers. The entire speech of lies. I've memorized the pattern by now. First she explains how sick I am, then how I don't have a father, then how we can't afford treatment. She ends with saying that I might die. Sparkle looks at Mommy with her mouth slightly open. A piece of gum is wedged between her teeth. Mommy writes "Beth Kyros" at the bottom of the last form with a flourish. She really does love signing her name.

Sparkle takes the papers and Mommy looks around the room. I imagine that she's an eagle and everyone else is a field mouse. Eagles eat field mice. I read that in "A History of the World For Kids". Mommy is looking at all these people like an eagle looks at field mice. Which one should she lie to next? Which one should be the eagle's next meal? I could use a meal right now, or at least a snack. Mommy has drifted off to talk to a lady who's holding a bald toddler wearing a pink knitted hat. In the corner of the room, there's a big table with lots of snacks and drinks and a sign that says that they're for people at the Kids Cancer Convention.

I haven't used my wheelchair on my own before. I'm dying to get out of it and just walk over, but I'm strapped in too tight and there is no way that I can reach to untie myself. I put my hand on the wheels and push forward, my feeding tube thumping along next to me. The wheelchair glides along the smooth floor to the snack table. My shaky hands grip a juice box as a boy with glasses and a bald head smiles at me. He looks older. Nine, maybe. Or ten.

"Hi", he says.

"Hi." I stick the straw into the juice box and let the sweet juice flow down my throat.

"I'm Antonio", the boy says. "I'm here for the convention. With my parents. Did you know they have classes and activities for us here? It's grouped by age. How old are you? Four? I'm ten."

"I'm seven", I say when Antonio pauses to shove a cookie in his mouth. "Oh. Sorry."

"That's okay. What do you mean about groups and classes?"

Antonio reaches into his pocket and pulls out a sheet of paper. "You have to fill out a form. To let them know what you want to do. Wait here, I'll get you one."

I watch Antonio's skinny legs dart through the crowd. Why does he want to talk to me?

Antonio reappears with a form and spreads it out on the table. "Okay. I'll help you fill this out. Hey, wait. I didn't even ask your name. What's your name?"

"Fern."

"That's cool. I was named after my grandfather. I'm Italian. You know, a lot of people say I talk too much. Do you think I talk too much?"

I consider this. "Yes", I say. "But it's alright, because I don't talk a lot. I like to listen."

"You're smart for a little kid", Antonio says. "Did you know that?"

I feel my face get hot. "I don't know", I say. "How about we fill out the form?"

"Right. So you pick an activity for each block. Any activity, as long as you're in the age range. The adults have activities too. Or groups, I guess. Meetings about what it's like to have a kid with cancer."

Mommy will like that. I bend over the table and fill out the form. I choose "What Is Cancer?", "Hospital Survival Skills", and "Dance

Therapy" for the first day, and "Relieving Anger", "Therapeutic Writing ", and a class called "Courage" for the second day.

"Dance therapy, huh?" Antonio says. "How are you gonna do that in a wheelchair?"

My eyes fall to my lap. I didn't think of that.

"Just kidding!" Antonio flicks my ear. "You can do *any* of the activities. I asked them about it. They have special accommodations."

Just then, a woman comes over to the snack table. "Not eating too many cookies, are you, Antonio?" she says.

"No, Mom." Antonio turns to me. "Fern, this is my mother. Mom, this is my friend Fern."

My friend. A smile creeps into the corners of my mouth. I have a friend.

"Well, aren't you just the cutest little girl!" Antonio's mother exclaims. "Call me Jean, honey. It's so good to see that Antonio has a friend. We weren't really sure what to expect when we came here, but it seems like a wonderful convention. What classes did you sign up for?"

I glance down at my form.

"You haven't passed that in?" Jean says. "Fern, honey, you were supposed to give that to Martha at the front desk. Here, let me take it for you."

"You can take mine too, Mom", Antonio says, trying to smooth out his crumpled form.

"Antonio! I told you to pass that in as soon as you were done filling it out!" Jean shakes her head at me and smiles. "My boy, he's so disorganized."

The first class I am in, "What Is Cancer?", is in a big meeting room with two long tables that are pushed together. I am in the seven-to-twelve age group, but it seems like all the other seven and eight and nine year olds went to the other class, "Bandanna Tie-Dye", so I am with the older kids. The teacher is a man with a beard who looks like Santa Claus, if Santa Claus was a real person and not just a made-up story for little kids. The teacher's name tag says "Howard". He passes out paper and pens in case we want to take notes, but he says we don't have to.

"You don't have to do *anything* you don't want to", he tells us. But when he starts talking about what causes cancer, I write everything he says on my paper. Five other kids in the class take notes, and their handwriting is neat and perfect, with little bullet points for each different thing Howard talks about. They also dot their i's with little hearts. I try to do that, but it ends up a smudgy mess, so I go back to writing normally.

After the class, a girl wearing a purple baseball cap comes up to me.

"I saw you taking notes", she says. "Aren't you a little young for this group?"

"I'm seven."

"Oh. Why aren't you making bandannas with all the other little kids, then?"

I shrug. "I wanted more information about cancer."

The girl scrunches up her face. "Really?"

"The information might help me someday."

She laughs, and it sounds like little fairy bells. "You're funny. What's your name?"

"Fern."

"I'm Rachel. Are you scared to be here?"

I smile a little. I'm terrified, but not for the reasons Rachel thinks.

"Yeah, a little."

"Well, you can stick by me if you ever need anyone", Rachel says. "It was good to meet you, Fern."

"Nice meeting you too", I tell her, and stick out my hand for a shake.

She takes it and laughs again. "You're a weird little kid. I like it", she says before skipping away. I stuff my notes in my wheelchair pocket and go to find Mommy. She said she would be waiting for me right outside the class, and I had better be there or else. I find her leaning against a glass window, talking to a man and batting her eyelashes. But I happen to know they're not *real* eyelashes. I saw her stick the on this morning before we left. I wonder for a moment what would happen if they just came off in her fingers. I bet the man she is talking to would scream.

Mommy sees me out of the corner of her eye and waves goodbye to the man, that annoying kind of wave where you scrunch up your hand and wiggle your fingers.

"Fern!" She rushes over to my wheelchair. "I saw you talking to someone. Who was it?"

"Just a girl I met. Her name is Rachel. She's nice. She says I can stick by her if I need anyone."

"Well, you won't be doing that." Mommy grips my wheelchair and takes me down the hallway, away from all the people. "I don't want you talking to anyone, Fern. We're not here to make friends."

"Why *are* we here, Mommy? I'm not sick."

Mommy claps her hand over my mouth, and I can taste her perfume. "Don't you *ever* say that here, Fern. Got it? *Ever.*"

"But why are we here?"

"I'm an adult, Fern. I don't need to explain myself to you. Now, do you know where your next class is?"

"Yes. Conference room number seven. Hospital Survival Skills."

"Huh", Mommy grunts. "If it were up to me, you wouldn't be going to all these useless classes.

"Where did *you* go, Mommy?"

"To a meeting."

"What meeting?"

"For God's sake, Fern, you don't need to know *everything*!" She storms off, leaving me in the hallway to find conference room number seven all by myself.

CHAPTER
21

Hospital Survival Skills takes place in a big room with lots of windows. Everyone sits cross-legged on the floor, even the teacher. Except for the kids in wheelchairs, of course. Antonio sits next to me, and it feels good to have someone I know close by. I don't see Rachel anywhere.

"Okay", the teacher claps her hands. "Let's get started. We'll go in a circle, and I want you to say your name and a fun fact about yourself. I'll start. My name is Linda, and my favorite food is corn quesadillas with spicy salsa. Next?"

Linda points to the girl sitting next to her.

"My name is Emily, and I'm eight years old. And I like horses."

Linda's directions go around the circle, and I hear some kids struggle to come up with something to say. Some turn red, like they're shy and don't want to talk. After Antonio tells everyone he's Italian, it's my turn.

I can't think of anything special to say. Am I boring? I must be, or else I would be bursting with information.

"My name is Fern", I say slowly. "And I have an older sister named Holly." I expect everyone to turn and stare at me, but words keep moving around the circle until they end up back with Linda, who claps her hands again.

"Wonderful! Now we're going to talk a little about hospitals. Who here has been to a hospital?"

A giggle ripples through the room, and it takes me a minutes to realize what's funny. *Everyone* here has been to the hospital. They all have cancer. Every hand in the room shoots up. Mine does too.

"So you've all been to the hospital", Linda says. "How many of you have been scared?"

All the hands in the room, including mine, go up again, but more slowly. I think that people don't like to admit it when they're scared.

"It's okay to be scared", Linda tells us. "I've never had cancer, but I had my tonsils out when I was younger. I was petrified."

"What's petrified?" Emily asks.

"It means very, very scared. Do you ever feel very, very scared?"

"Yes", Emily nods. "When the doctors poke me with needles."

"I was scared the first time I had chemotherapy", Antonio says.

"And I was scared when I had to go to school for the first time after I lost my hair", a boy calls out.

Linda doesn't seem to mind that's he doesn't even raise her hand.

"I was scared when I had to stay in the hospital all by myself", another kid says.

Suddenly, everyone is calling out what scares the about the hospital.

"I was scared when I didn't get any food to eat", I say.

Everyone stops talking and looks at me.

"You *what?*" Antonio asks. "You didn't get any food? Who didn't give you any food? Everyone in my family is always giving me food. It's an Italian thing, I guess. We get pizza after chemotherapy. Real pizza that my mom makes, not the fake stuff from the pizza parlor. And sometimes we have-".

"Antonio, hang on a second", says Linda. "Fern, what do you mean you didn't get any food to eat?"

I wish I could take my words back. I don't like all the eyes that are looking at me. They want to know what's going on, but if I tell, Mommy will do what she said she'd do. *I will kill you.*

"I just mean it's hard to eat sometimes", I say quietly. "With my feeding tube. It hurts my throat."

"Oh", Linda laughs. "I thought you meant your parents didn't feed you."

That's what I did mean, Linda. Please listen to my eyes, not my voice. Please listen and hear me, but don't make me tell.

"Feeding tubes absolutely suck", says an older girl. "I used to have one, and it felt like there was something jammed in my throat all the time."

They talk about feeding tubes and getting poked with needles and losing their hair and chemotherapy, but I can't focus anymore. My mind wanders from place to place.

"What about you, Fern?" Lydia asks.

"Huh?" I focus my eyes back on the group.

"Does having your blood taken scare you? Do the needles?"

"No", I say. "I'm used to them. Raymond and I like to look at the blood as it fills the tube. We're both weird about that, I guess."

"That's gross", says the girl who said that feeding tubes suck. "That's really gross."

"Who's Raymond?" asks Antonio.

"My friend", I say. Antonio scrunches up his face but doesn't say anything.

"My Mommy holds my hand when they take my blood", says a little boy in a fisherman's hat, and just like that, words start buzzing around the circle again, and I can sit in silence and just think.

After the class, I am so focused on thinking about Holly and why Daddy didn't tell me about her that I don't even notice everyone else leave.

Linda is the only person left. She's moving tables back to the center of the room. She has to say my name three times before I answer.

"Fern, are you okay?" she asks.

I nod, shaking my head out of the dazed, dreamlike feeling it gets into so much these days.

"Well, come on. It's lunch time. I'll walk you there."

"Do you need help with the tables?" I ask, because it's polite to offer to help someone. Mommy would be proud, but like a little electric zap, I suddenly realize I don't care about making her happy anymore. Still, the tables look very heavy for one person to push. Then I remember I can't get out of my wheelchair, so I can't help anyway.

"No thanks, the tables are set", says Linda. "Is there anything you want to tell me, Fern? You were pretty quiet in class."

I focus on her eyes, bright green masked by rhinestone-rimmed glasses. I squint and look at her, thinking "please hear me" as hard as I can. Please hear my eyes, not my mouth. My mouth lies, but eyes never lie.

"I'm okay", I say.

"Good." Linda grasps the handles of my wheelchair. "Let's get lunch."

Lunch is happening in the big room with the high ceiling. There is a table with lots of turkey and ham and cheese slices and jars of peanut butter and jam and jelly. There are more loaves of bread than I've ever seen in one place. Then there's a table with chips and granola bars and juice boxes and sodas. The last table has every kind of dessert I can think of. It seems like a lot of people brought homemade brownies or cakes or something. I wish we had done that.

"Do you see your mom?" Linda asks. My eyes scan the room. Mommy is in a corner, talking to a crowd of people who are nodding their heads sympathetically.

"No", I say. "I don't see her anywhere."

Antonio waves at me from a table in the back.

"I'm all set", I tell Linda. "Thanks for your help."

Mommy doesn't see me as I take a plate with a peanut butter and jelly sandwich, two cherry juice boxes, and a cup of green Jell-O. My favorite lunch ever. I try to squeeze behind everyone as I wheel myself to the table where Antonio is sitting. Mommy doesn't see me. If she did, I wouldn't get anything to eat. Not even a cracker.

"What was up with you in class?" Antonio asks, biting into a sandwich. "You just got all quiet. You okay?"

"Yes", I say, stabbing my juice box with the flimsy straw. "I'm fine."

"Good, because I have to show you something. Have you ever heard of Operation Hope?"

"No."

"Well, it's this organization that lets sick kids have one wish. Whatever they want. Seriously, *anything*. You can meet anybody famous or go anywhere or do anything.'"

"Anything?"

"*Anything*", he confirms, nodding hard.

"What kind of things do kids get?"

"Well, I know one girl who got to swim with dolphins", Antonio says. "And a boy who went to Disney World. A lot of kids go to Disney World. But that's not what I would want to do. I want to drive a real race car. Hey, did you know that race car is spelled the same both forwards and backwards? What's that called? A metaphor?"

"A palindrome," I say. I read that in Spelling & Grammar.

"Yeah, a palindrome. Is your mom a teacher, Fern?"

"No. She works at The Happy Hour Casino."

"How come you know so many big words, then?"

I shrug. "From books, I guess."

"And you're smart, huh?" asks Antonio. "You've gotta be smart to know that kind of stuff."

Being called smart makes me feel weird, so I change the subject.

"What did you want to show me?"

"Oh, yeah." Antonio grabs two slips of paper and two pencils resting in the pile at the end of the table. "Put your name on this piece of paper", he says.

"Why?"

"Because all the kids at the convention are supposed to put their name on a piece of paper. And then they're going to pick twenty of us to get wishes from Operation Hope. And we don't even have to go through a process and do a bunch more paperwork like if we were normally applying for a wish. It's all taken care of."

"And this wish is just for sick kids?"

Antonio grins. "Yep. We're lucky in that way, I guess."

I push the pencil and paper back at him. "I can't. I mean, I don't want to."

"Why not? You can have *anything*, Fern."

"I don't want anything." Again, I'm lying. I want plenty of things. To see Holly. To get rid of Brian and Mommy. For Daddy to tell me the truth. To call Raymond. But Operation Hope can't give me any of those things.

"I just can't think of anything, Antonio."

"Well, you don't have to decide what you want *now*. You just have to put your name in. That's all. Come on, what are you afraid of?"

"Nothing." Another lie.

"So write your name down." I take a deep breath and carefully write "Fern Kyros" on the piece of paper. Antonio squints at it.

"You're smart, but your handwriting's not that good."

"Neither is yours", I point out.

He's written "Antonio Ranalli" in messy scrawl on his paper. At least, that's what I think it says. It's kind of hard to tell.

"Seconds!" calls a man in a white apron. "Anyone want seconds?"

Suddenly, I get an idea.

"I'll be back", I tell Antonio, and wheel over to the tables as fast as I can. I grab every packaged food that can fit into the large pocket of my wheelchair: granola bars, snack cakes, pretzels, chips, peanuts, popcorn, and even a few juice boxes. The pocket bulges, and I hope no one saw me taking anything. Mommy can refuse to give me food all she wants, but now I've got a secret stash. I find my way back to where Antonio is sitting.

"They're just about to call the names", he says.

"What?"

"For Operation Hope. They just came around and collected all the names. I put yours in for you. One of us could get chosen. Or both of us!"

The Jell-O I ate starts bouncing around in my stomach. I twist my fingers together. Please not me, please not me. I would love to have any wish I wanted, but Operation Hope is for sick kids, and I'm not sick.

"Did everyone put their name in?" Sparkle yells from a platform in the front of the room. She has a microphone clipped to her shirt, so she doesn't even need to be so loud. But I think she just likes hearing her own voice, like Antonio. I see Mommy standing in the corner with a group of other parents. She has that glitter in her eyes again. What is she up to? I feel my body start to shake.

"Fern." Antonio puts his brown arm on my pale one. It feels warm against my cold skin. I'm so chilled with fear, I'm probably sweating snow.

"Fern", Antonio says again. "You're all shaky. Are you okay?"

"Yes." I force the corners of my mouth to lift up into a smile. "Just excited."

"Are you ready?" Sparkle shouts.

Everyone cheers and claps, including Mommy. I give her a weird look, and she glares back at me with a glare that says "Don't mess this up." I don't even want to know what she's done, but I can tell it's something awful by the way she's smiling at me. Sparkle shakes a big cardboard box decorated with snowflake wrapping paper.

"We've got all the names in here. The twenty children that are picked will receive a wish from Operation Hope. Please remember, even if you don't get chosen, you can still apply for a wish. Just visit the table by the door on your way out tomorrow. The point of this is to make the wishes easier on the parents- no paperwork to fill out, except one form that the child does, stating what they would like their wish to be. Everything else is all taken care of by the organization."

"Pick the names!" a boy yells from the table in the front of the room. "Please! I gotta see if I'm going to Hershey Park!"

Sparkle laughs and dips her nail-polished hand into the box. "Okay, here goes."

I cross my finger, and my toes too.

"Bella Porter!"

A mother screams from the back of the room, matching the scream of a four-year old girl in a tutu.

"I'm going to meet Snow White!" Bella screams. "At Disney World!"

Bella's mother hugs her and kisses the top of Bella's bald head. They're both crying. One down, nineteen to go. Nineteen chances I might get picked. I will cross my fingers and toes and hope it's not me with every slip of paper that's taken out of that box. Five more names are called, then Sparkle squints at a piece of paper.

"I can't quite read this. The first name starts with A. Last name Ranalli? Someone needs to work on their handwriting..."

"That's me!" Antonio jumps up. "Antonio Ranalli! That's my name! Did I get picked? Did I?"

Sparkle smiles at him. "Yes, Antonio. You got picked."

He jumps my hand and squeezes it, trying to hold in the excitement that seems to almost be bursting out of him.

"I got it, Fern! I got it! I'm going to wish to drive a real race car! An orange one. That's my favorite color. I wonder where they have race cars. I'm not old enough to get my driver's license yet, but since it's a wish, I bet they'd let me drive for a day. I'd wear a helmet if my mom made me, I guess. How fast can race cars go? Do you know, Fern? Do you?"

He says all this without even pausing to take a breath.

"I'm glad you got picked", I say. "I'm not sure how fast race cars can go, though. Faster than normal cars, definitely."

Antonio starts talking again, this time about how he wants to be a race car driver when he grows up, and wouldn't the rush of air feel so cool on his bald head? I'm half listening, nodding when he takes a breath, but keeping count of the names that are being called.

"Jerry Ford!" Sixteen.

"Miles Gardner!" Seventeen.

"Fern Kyros!" Eighteen.

Fern Kyros.

Oh no. I try to shrink down inside my wheelchair as everyone claps and yells. Mommy runs toward me, hugging me and squeezing too tight like she always does.

"Don't question it", she whispers.

"You got picked, Fern!" Antonio yells. "What are you gonna wish for?"

At the mention of a wish, Mommy smiles.

"Leave that to me", she murmurs into my ear.

Mommy leads me way from the table as the last two names are announced. She brings me into the hallway where no one can hear us.

"You got chosen."

She doesn't sound surprised.

"You don't sound surprised", I tell her.

"I'm not." She smiles. "Let's just say you had...an edge over the other kids."

I feel like a salty wave just crashed over me, stinging and pounding and spraying.

"What edge? Mommy, what did you do?"

"If you promise not to tell", she says, "this can be our little secret. I did it because I love you, Fern. I wanted you to get that wish."

No, she didn't. She wanted it for herself. I swallow hard and close my eyes.

"Just tell me what you did."

"Well, they came around to collect the slips", Mommy says. "And you wouldn't believe it, but those idiots didn't even bother reading them to make sure a kid's name wasn't written more than once! I had about twenty of those slips with your name on them. I folded them all over so you couldn't see the writing. Said I'd been collecting them from the other kids so they wouldn't have to get up. So you should really be thanking me, Fern. *I* was the one who got you that wish. Not that ridiculous woman with the awful nail polish."

"You mean my name went into the box *twenty times?*"

Mommy nods. "You're welcome."

I spin my wheelchair around. "Lunch is over. I've got to get to my next class."

"Aren't you going to thank me?" Mommy snaps. "Don't be ungrateful, Fern."

My stomach feels like a pretzel, all twisted up in knots.

"I hate you", I whisper. The pretzel untwists.

"What was that?" Mommy grabs the back of my wheelchair. "What did you say?"

"Nothing." I try to push on the wheels of my wheelchair to move, but Mommy isn't letting go. The wheels spin helplessly.

"I thought I heard you say you hated me", she whispers.

"I didn't say that!" Please, Holly help me.

"I think you did. I also think that we can't have rude little girls here. Do you understand what I'm getting at?"

I'm shaking too hard to even nod yes or no. Mommy leads me farther down the hall. She unstraps me from my wheelchair and holds my chest tight so I can't run.

"Did you say you hated me?" She pulls me close by the collar of my shirt. Coffee-breath again, hot in my face.

"I didn't say anything." My fingers are crossed behind my back.

"You're a liar, Fern. You know what gives it away? Your eyes. Those big, bright blue eyes that dart everywhere. You have your father's eyes. I hate them." I use my big, bright blue eyes to stare her down.

"Let me go please, Mommy. I didn't say anything."

"Liar!" she yells. "Liar, liar, liar!" With each "liar, she hits me on the arm, harder each time.

"Stop!" I yell, and she presses her hand over my mouth.

"Shut up! No one can hear you!" She's not making any sense, she's just hitting and swearing and yelling "Liar! Liar!" A shadow appears at the end of the hallway.

"Everything okay?" calls a janitor.

Mommy shoves me back into my wheelchair, straps me in, and sashays down the hall like she's on a runway. I follow. The janitor has a grayish-brown beard and deep, dark eyes.

"Everything okay?" he asks again.

"Oh, yes", Mommy coos. "Fern here was just crying because her feeding tube was hurting her while I was trying to adjust it. I did it out here in case we had a scene. And as you can see, we did. She throws a tantrum whenever something hurts her. Swearing, hitting, screaming- you know, she's just full of anger at her whole situation. And I can't blame her."

As Mommy launches into her speech of lies, the janitor looks at me. I am shaken and exhausted.

"I can understand", the janitor says softly. "I've seen a lot of sick kids here, and I just can't imagine what all these parents go through."

"Oh, yes". Mommy sinks onto the floor. I am surprised, because normally, she wouldn't get near a floor that might get dirt or germs on her clothes. Mommy starts fake-crying, little choking sobs that catch in the back of her throat. Minnow sobs, instead of big goldfish gulps.

"Want me to take her to her last class?" the janitor offers.

Mommy nods, not lifting her head.

"Dance Therapy", I say helpfully. The janitor nods and leads me away.

"Do you know where it is?" I ask.

"The ballroom", he says.

"This place has a ballroom? For dancing and stuff?"

"Yes, it's quite fancy. I've worked here for years, and I've seen a lot of fancy dances. People all dressed up, delicious food, live music..."

"Did you ever go to a dance?"

He shakes his head. "Only to clean up afterwards."

I feel sorry for him, but I've never been to a dance either.

"What's your name?"

"Dave."

"Are you the help?"

"I suppose so", he says flatly. "They sure treat me like it."

"What do you mean? Who does?"

Dave shifts his eyes down the hallway. "Don't worry about it, kid."

"My name is Fern. And *who* does?"

"Mostly everyone who works here. Everyone thinks being a janitor is a pretty dirty job."

"Why's it dirty?"

"You sure ask a lot of questions, you know that?" Dave says. "Why do you care, anyway? You gonna be a janitor when you get big?"

"Not in my wheelchair", I say.

"Oh", he says. "Sorry."

"It's okay. It's not your fault. Why did you ask if I was the help, Fern? It's kind of a snobby term, and you don't seem like a very snobby girl."

"My Mommy calls people who work here "the help". And you work here. She said I'm not supposed to thank the help. But I did. I thanked the man at the door with the funny hat."

"The bellhop."

"Yes. He held the door open for us, and isn't it polite to thank people when they do that?"

"Don't know where you got your manners from, Fern. From what you say, your mommy sure doesn't seem to have any."

"She thinks she does."

I see the door to the ballroom. Double doors, with little gold-rimmed windows. Dave parks my chair right in front of the door and swings it open.

"Think you can manage it from here?" Without waiting for an answer, he turns and walks away.

"Dave! Wait!" He spins on his heel, making a squeaky noise.

"Yeah?"

"Thanks for taking me here." He smiles, although you can't see it because his beard is sort of hiding his lips. But his dark eyes twinkle, that's how I know he's smiling.

"Thank *you*, Fern", he says, and turns back down the hallway.

I can tell his walk is a little lighter.

CHAPTER 22

The Dance Therapy class is so big that there are four teachers there to teach it. I expected it to be mostly girls, but about half of the kids are boys. The girls stay on one side of the room, and the boys on the other. I wonder if they'll make us dance together.

"Okay!" Sparkle shouts. She's one of the teachers. "As you all know, at the end of the convention, we hold a party in the lobby. A party where there will probably be dancing. So you're probably here to work on your skills, or maybe you're here to just have a good time and see what this is all about, right?"

A boy calls out "I didn't know there was a party! Will there be food?"

"Yes", Sparkle says. "And a real disco ball too."

The girls start gasping and chattering like a forest full of tree frogs. I'm not really sure what a disco ball is. I've never seen one. Sparkle and two other teachers take the kids without wheelchairs to the bigger part of the room, and a teacher named Jackson takes the wheelchair kids-there are about seven of us-into a small huddle.

"Now then", Jackson says, "you guys were pretty darn brave to come here, right? Who says kids in wheelchairs can't dance?"

"Yeah, who?" a girl shouts.

Jackson throws his fists into the air. "No one, that's who! Anyone can dance! And you guys are gonna *rock it*!"

I'm not really sure what Jackson means, but I like him. He shows us how to move our arms in a fancy way so it looks like we're swaying. Then he shows us how to count along to a beat and snap along to music and wiggle around in out wheelchairs.

"Y'all learning something?" he keeps saying.

I'm learning that I can't count along to music very well, but that's not what Jackson is talking about.

"Y'all are learning that anyone can dance!" Jackson shouts so loud that the other group stares at us. "That's right, anyone can dance!" he shouts at them. "And these kids in wheelchairs got some pretty good moves!"

Sparkle checks her watch. "We've got fifteen minutes", she says. "Want to mix the groups up?"

The other teachers nod.

"Go get 'em!" Jackson tells us. He flips a switch on a machine he calls a "boom box", and music fills the air, loud and zippy. The ballroom is suddenly moving all at once. Little groups start to form, and I start to panic. Where do I fit?

"Fern?" someone calls. "Fern? Is that you?"

I would recognize her voice anywhere. Twisting around in my wheelchair, I see her. Missing front teeth, IV pole attached to her arm, and a knit hat from her grandmother, the kind she gets every time she has chemotherapy.

"Leah!"

Leah smiles. She looks better than when I last saw her. A few pounds heavier, and a whole lot happier. When she gets a good look at me, though, her face drops.

"Fern! You've got *cancer*?"

Hating myself for having to lie, I nod.

"Oh my gosh!" she drags her IV pole over and wraps her arms around me. "Are you okay?"

"I guess so."

"You're well enough to be at the convention, right? What *happened*?"

"A lot", I say. That's true, at least.

Leah hugs me again. "I'm just glad I got to see you again."

"Me too."

"You don't look too good", Leah says. "Are you sure you're okay?"

I nod, even though I'm not sure of anything anymore.

"I'm sorry, that was stupid of me to say. I've had people ask me the same thing, and it's really annoying. I don't want to be like them."

"Don't worry, you're not", I say, hugging her back. "You will never, ever be like anyone else."

Leah tells me we should hang out tonight, and I say yes, we should, but I know that Mommy would never allow it. She'll want to parade me around the hotel to talk to people about how sick I am. Or lock me in the hotel room without dinner.

"Me and a few other girls are going to the movies and then out to dinner. Can you come?"

"I don't know", I say.

"Your mom won't let you? Is she kinda strict?"

"Very", I whisper.

Leah touches me lightly on the shoulder. "Don't worry. I'll make sure you can come with us."

Mommy told me to meet her right after Dance Therapy, right outside the ballroom. I find her talking to a man wearing the hotel uniform. "I barely make enough money to cover the medical bills", Mommy is saying. "It's just *so* hard."

The man in the uniform looks concerned. As I sit beside Mommy in my wheelchair and wait for her to notice me, Leah comes up to us, dragging a man and a woman behind her. Her parents, probably. Leah stands right in front of Mommy, so Mommy can't help but look down at Leah's purple and green knit hat.

"Hi! I'm Fern's friend!" Leah says. "Are you Fern's mommy?"

I can tell that Mommy doesn't really know what to say.

"Um...yes", she finally replies.

"I'm Leah. Me and Fern were at the same hospital before. Can Fern come with us to the movies tonight? And dinner? Please?"

"Fern will be staying in the hotel room tonight", Mommy says, pulling me closer to her, which isn't easy in my wheelchair. "She can't risk any germs."

Leah turns to her mommy, who seems every bit as soft and warm as I'd imagined when I first met Leah.

"Beth, isn't it?" she says to Mommy. "I'm Geraldine. I'm so glad our girls have become friends. It's hard for Leah to get to know other kids, so this is a big thing for her. Is it hard for Fern, too?"

Mommy lets out a short bark of a laugh. "Fern's too shy. She doesn't fit in."

"All kids can fit in", Geraldine says. "And I think Fern and Leah have hit upon a really special friendship. The other girls we're taking out are nice, too. I can understand your hesitation. These girls are older, after all, and Fern is just five."

"I'm seven", I say.

"Mom!" Leah covers her face with her hands. "I told you she was older than she looked!"

"The movie theater is completely clean, with a special row for wheelchairs", Geraldine continues. "One of the others girl, Sammy, is also in a wheelchair, so Fern won't be the only one."

"That's not what I'm worried about!" Mommy snaps.

"The restaurant we're eating at already knows our situation. We'll get something that's easy for Fern to swallow, with her feeding tube. Again, she's not the only one with that, either. Celia has a feeding tube, too. And we take her out to eat all the time. We're very careful, Beth."

"Please, please, please!" Leah sings, dancing around Mommy.

"No." Mommy stays firm.

Leah stops dancing around. Her face grows low and sad. "Okay, Fern's Mommy. I understand. But don't you feel sorry for Fern? Doesn't she deserve to have some fun? I mean, she's sick, so she deserves fun, right?"

"Leah!" Geraldine looks cross, but behind her cross mask is a little glimmer of victory.

They are winning.

"Leah, don't pester", says Geraldine. "Try to understand why Beth is reluctant to let us take Fern out. There *are* some risks, I suppose. I can find someone else to give the bar coupons to."

She puts her hand on Leah's shoulder, and they sadly walk off, Leah's IV pole going thunk-clink, thunk-clink.

"Wait!" Mommy shouts after them. "Did you say bar coupons?"

Geraldine walks back to Mommy, a huge smile on her face. "I sure did. I got these coupons so my husband and I could get some martinis, but Leah really wanted us both to come with her and her friends to dinner and the movies. So we've just got these coupons. It's okay, though. If you didn't want them, I thought I'd offer them to one of the other girls' moms."

"No, no!" Mommy snatches the colorful coupons from Geraldine's hand so fast I'm sure she got a paper cut. "I'll take those."

"Does this mean she can go?" asks Geraldine.

Mommy is busy examining the coupons. "Yeah, yeah, go ahead, Fern."

Leah grabs my hand and pushes my wheelchair away without a second look.

"That was awesome", I tell her.

"Well, mom and I had kind of a plan", she says modestly. Then she breaks into a gap-toothed grin. "It's really *was* awesome, wasn't it?"

Geraldine comes jogging over. She's kind of a round woman who bounces like a kickball when she runs. "How did you like that, girls?" she says, panting.

"Brilliant", Leah says. "Just brilliant."

"What about you, Fern? You doing okay?"

"Yes, thank you, Mrs....um..."

"Call me Geraldine", she says.

"Or mom", Leah adds.

"We're gonna be late for the movie if we don't hurry", Geraldine says.

We ride the elevator to the floors where each girl is staying. Leah gets to knock and peer through the keyhole. There are five of us. Katie is a little bit older than me and Leah. She's twelve, and I recognize her from Dance Therapy. Celia, the girl with the feeding tube, is freckled and smiling at everything. Sammy is in a wheelchair, like me, only hers is so whole lot nicer looking. She's decorated it with dragon stickers. She and Celia are both nine. And then there's Leah and me. Geraldine's cell phone buzzes.

"Jake's waiting for us in the car", she says. "Katie, will you push Sammy's wheelchair? I'll get Fern's."

It is a warm night, so warm I don't even need a jacket. Mommy didn't bring me one anyway. I like being with these people. When the bellhop opens the door for Geraldine, she thanks him, and so do we. I guess not everyone here treats "the help" badly. Jake turns out to be Leah's daddy. He's tall and bald on the top of his head.

"Shave your head to support Leah?" Katie asks.

Jake smiles. "Don't even have to. It shaves itself!"

They laugh and slap palms. Even though I don't really understand what's going on, I smile. I soak up all the happiness around me like a sponge. Holly would have loved this. When we get to the theater, Sammy pokes me and says the movie we're going to see is about fairy houses.

"What's a fairy house?" I ask.

"Well, you know the tooth fairy?"

"No. That's a made-up story."

She laughs, and the dragon stickers on her wheelchair seem to rear their heads back and laugh right along with her.

"You'll see", she says. "I've seen this before. Sit next to me, okay? I'll explain it to you."

I end up sandwiched in the front row if the theater between Sammy and Leah. Sammy doesn't get a chance to explain the movie like she said she would, because every time she opens her mouth, the people in the row behind us hiss "Shhh!" Eventually, they kick the back of our seats and say "What's *wrong* with you kids? Can't you little brats just shut up for five seconds?"

"Haven't you ever seen five little bald girls at a movie theater before?" Katie asks. "We've all lost our hair 'cause of a radioactive disease that will spread and make you bald too if you kick our seats."

"Yeah!" Celia says, throwing a piece of popcorn at the row behind us.

Geraldine tells everyone to stop it, but I can see she's proud of Katie for standing up for us. She squeezes Katie's arm and says "That's my girl." I want her to squeeze my arm and call me her girl too.

For dinner, we go to an Italian restaurant. The whole place reminds me of Antonio. All the waiters talk loud, and fast too. And a lot. I hear yells of "Pasta, pasta!" And "Order for table twelve, and hurry up! They can't wait all night!" I wonder if this is what Antonio's kitchen is like. We get to sit at a big table that's has cushiony booth seats on one side and normal chairs on the other. I absolutely love booth seats, but Sammy and I can't sit in them because of our wheelchairs.

I look around the restaurant. There are lots of pictures on the wall. I recognize the Leaning Tower of Pisa. "A History Of The World For Kids" had a chapter on Italy, and the Leaning Tower of Pisa was mentioned all over that chapter. I told Mommy and Brian about it, only I called it The Leaning Tower of *Pizza*. It sounded like that, and besides, it's in Italy, and pizza is Italian, so it just makes sense. Brian asked me if I knew how stupid I sounded, and Mommy said it was pronounced "pee-za", not "pizza". There are also pictures of cheese and bread and colorful vegetables. The lights are hanging low from the ceiling, in shades that make the tables speckled with yellow and green and red light. Everywhere I look, I see something else I want to stare at. I've only been to a restaurant a few times in my life.

When I was three, Mommy burned the turkey in the oven for thanksgiving and we went out for Chinese food. Mommy sniffled and moaned through the entire dinner, and Daddy kept patting her on the back saying "It's okay, Beth, it's okay. I don't even like turkey that much anyhow."

And when Mommy got her bonus check one year from The Happy Hour Casino, she took me and Daddy out for dinner at a place that served a lot of fancy drinks that I wasn't allowed to have, because they had alcohol in them. I didn't mind, because they smelled funny anyway.

And right before Daddy left, he took me to a fancy restaurant, just the two of us. The napkins were folded like fans, and the waiter called Daddy "sir" and me "miss." I even got to have a fizzy red drink in a tall glass with sweet-tasting cherries. Daddy said the drink was called a Shirley Temple. He said it was named after a famous actress.

Geraldine passes around menus. "Order whatever you like, kids. This is your special night. But nothing hard to swallow, Fern and Celia. I don't want to have to explain to your parents if food gets all caught in your throat because of your feeding tube." The waiter comes to take our order, and he hands us all little Italian flags. I decide I'll give mine to Antonio later.

I order pizza with olives on it. "And what to drink?" the waiter asks, his pen hovering above a notepad. "We've got coke, sprite, lemonade, milk, Shirley Temples..."

"Can I have a Shirley Temple? Can I?" Leah asks Geraldine. "Sure, honey." Everyone else chimes in that they want one too, except for me. Shirley Temples make me think of Daddy, and I don't want to think about Daddy tonight, because I'm still mad at him.

"I'll have a sprite, please", I say.

CHAPTER
23

On the ride back to the hotel, I can't help noticing how nice it is to be in a car without my cheek squished sideways against the seat. Leah's parents help me and Sammy stand up, and they lift us into the seats. Then they take out wheelchairs and fold them right up. Katie and Sammy and Celia are sleeping over at Leah's hotel room.

"Can you come, Fern?" Leah asks. I hesitate. If I ask Mommy, she might get mad at me, and I don't think Geraldine and Leah have a plan this time for getting me to go with them.

"I'll have to ask", I say.

I've never had a sleepover before. When we're back in the hotel, Geraldine says, "Now we'll take the elevator up to Fern's room to ask her mommy if a sleepover is okay. Is that alright, Fern? Would you like to sleep over?"

I nod my head, happy and full from pizza and olives and sprite. The elevator bursts open and Mommy comes tumbling out.

"Fern!" she cries when she sees me.

She trips, stumbling on her dress and high heels.

"Oh, my", Geraldine says when she sees Mommy.

Mommy smells like alcohol. She has stains on her clothes, and Mommy *never* gets stains on her clothes. Her eyes are wild and crazy, not the sort of piercing, glittering scary gaze I'm used to.

"Fernhowyoudoing?" she says, and her words sound scrambled together, like they were thrown in a blender and mixed on high speed.

"She's fine, Beth", says Geraldine. "We all had a very nice time."

Leah steps in front of Geraldine.

"Can Fern sleep over, Mrs. Fern's Mommy? Please? She's my friend."

Mommy throws her hands into the hair. "Sure, sure. Sleepovers are good for Fern. She doesn't got any friends, you know."

Then she pats Leah's head. "You're baaaaalllld."

Geraldine quickly pulls Leah away. "We'll take Fern for the night, okay? I'll bring her right back to your hotel room tomorrow morning, safe and sound."

Mommy wobbles a little bit. "Safeandsound", she repeats, and stumbles off.

"Geez, Geraldine", mutters Jake. "How many free drink coupons did you *give* that woman!"

"Two!" Geraldine says defensively. "Just two. She must have bought the other drinks on her own! And we're not having this conversation in front of the children. Come on, let's get them upstairs."

There are four beds in Leah's hotel room. Her parents get one, Sammy and I get one, Leah and Celia get one, and Katie gets one to herself, since she's the oldest.

Geraldine offers to help me out of my wheelchair so I can change into my pajamas.

"That's okay", I say. "I forgot to bring any."

She gives me her extra t-shirt, and it's so big on me, it hangs down in front of my knees, just like a nightgown.

"Thank you", I say.

The shirt smells like lavender.

Once we're all settled in bed, Jake turns out the light and Geraldine comes around and kisses us each on our bald heads. When she comes to me, I sink down a little, not knowing what to expect. Mommy has never kissed me goodnight. Daddy never did, either, because he wasn't really the type of person to do that sort of thing. We had a secret handshake instead. Clap, clap, slap one-together, slap two-together, touch fingers, fist bump, and pull our hands away and make a claw. Me and Daddy did our secret handshake every night before he left. I clutch Pox tight to me, thankful that I remembered to bring him, as Geraldine leans down and kisses me gently on the top of my head. It makes my scalp tingle. I wonder if she's wears lipstick and if there's a red or pink lipstick smudge on top of my head now. After Jake and Geraldine leave the room, Sammy says we have to wait for five minutes before we start talking.

"Otherwise, Leah's parents will hear and tell us to go to sleep. Parents always wait about five minutes after their kids go to bed, and then they go do whatever parents do at night.", she says.

"Oh, please", scoffs Katie. "They know we're gonna talk all night. It's a *sleepover*. I've been to tons of them, and trust me, no one sleeps."

"My parents won't mind if we talk", says Leah.

So Katie teaches us to play Truth or Dare. No one says they're tired, but at about one o'clock, when we ask Katie "Truth or dare? Truth or dare?", she doesn't answer us.

"She's asleep", Celia says, peering over her side of the bed.

Ten minutes later, Sammy and Celia are both asleep too, so it's just me and Leah lying there in the darkness.

"Did you have fun today?" she asks me.

"Yes", I say. "Your parents are really nice."

She's quiet for a minute, then says, "Fern? Can I ask you something?"

My stomach jumps a little.

"Okay. What?"

"Do you believe in fairies? Like in the movie we saw?"

"I want to", I sigh, "but I know they're not real."

"I know too", Leah says. "But I want them to be real. I want them to be real so badly."

"I want a lot of things to be real so badly."

"Like what?"

I don't feel like telling her, so I say, "What would you do if fairies *were* real?"

Leah answers right away. "I would go to the Fairy House Palace and try to meet one. The Fairy House Palace is this place in California where all these artists have made fairy houses. Actually, they're more then fairy houses. They're incredible!"

"Fairy mansions."

"Yeah. Or fairy castles. I've seen the pictures online, but we don't have the money to go."

"Maybe you will when you're grown up."

"I guess. But that's a long time to wait." I can tell thinking about how she can't go to the Fairy House Palace makes her sad, so I try to change the subject.

"Do you think genies are real? Genies with bottles and wishes?"

"If they were, I'd find one. And I'd wish for us both to be better."

I feel tight inside. *But I'm not sick.*

"What about Santa Claus, Fern?" Leah asks. "Do you believe in him?"

"Not since I was two. Mommy told me he was a big fat lie."

"The Easter Bunny?"

"No. I had a nightmare about a big rabbit coming into my room when I was younger. I screamed for twenty minutes straight. Daddy came into my room and told me the Easter Bunny wasn't real, and Mommy went to take aspirin because she said I was a damn brat who couldn't even give her one night of peace."

"Wow. That's mean. Why would your mom say that?"

I roll over into my side, away from Leah. The pillow hurts my neck. "I don't know."

"Wait, Fern! I'm sorry. I shouldn't have asked."

"It's okay. I shouldn't have told you. Mommy doesn't like it when I tell people that she's done mean stuff to me."

I can tell that Leah wants to ask what kind of mean stuff, but she doesn't want to upset me, so she changes the subject.

"So do you believe in zombies?"

"No. Zombies are just dead people, and dead people aren't like zombies. So zombies aren't real."

"What about vampires?"

"Nope."

"Do you believe in werewolves, then?"

"No."

Leah is quiet for a minute. Then she asks, "What *do* you believe in, Fern?"

Now I'm the one who's quiet for a minute.

"Fern?" Leah asks, to make sure I'm not asleep.

"Angels", I tell her. "I believe in angels."

I start to tell her about the Bald Guy at the church and how Heaven is probably green with lots of glitter, but she doesn't answer. After I realize that she's fallen asleep, I sneak out of bed and to my wheelchair. I pull out a flashlight and the diary and read under the covers about Holly, my personal angel.

I can sense that the sun has already come up and is shedding light through the room when I am shaken awake. Mommy. She's come to bring me my crackers. I wonder how long I can make them last today. Another day, another tally mark on the wall. Then I realize that the hands that are shaking me awake are not Mommy's hands. These hands are softer and warmer. I hear the chattering of excited voices in the room. Who do the voices belong to? Then I realize where I am, in a hotel room, and the chattering voices are my friends. *My friends*. I'm safe for now.

"Fern", Geraldine says gently. "You want some breakfast?"

I roll over. My hair is plastered to the side of my face.

"Yes, please."

"We got room service!" shouts Celia, bouncing on the bed.

"What's room service?"

"You don't know what room service is?" Katie's eyes widen. "Girl, you gotta get out more."

"This is my first time in a hotel", I say, rubbing my eyes so hard they sting.

"Room service is when people bring food right to your bed!" Sammy says.

"You were asleep when we ordered. We didn't know what you wanted, but we have a little of everything", Jake tells me. He's wearing blue pajama pants with pictures of yellow iguanas on them.

My eyes search the trays on front of the beds. Every breakfast food I can imagine is there. It feels a little scary being able to have whatever I want. I guess I am just too used to crackers, oatmeal, and juice. After deciding which pastries have the most frosting, Leah and I both choose carrot cake muffins.

"Those are really more like cupcakes", sighs Geraldine. "I don't even know why they bother to slap the muffin label on them. You girls will be bouncing off the walls all day."

Leah giggles at me. She has white frosting on her nose, but I don't tell her that.

Right after breakfast, Geraldine tells us that she promised our parents we'd be back at our hotel rooms to get ready for our first class. I'm the last one to get dropped off. I watch the other girls go before me. Their parents hug them and thank Geraldine. I know Mommy won't do that. She opens the door when Geraldine knocks, swings it open so hard I'm afraid it might come right off its hinges. I wonder if we'd have to pay for it.

"Where have you been?" Mommy growls.

"Fern was having a sleepover with Leah and some other friends", Geraldine explains. "Remember?"

Mommy's eyes narrow. They still look funny, but she's not wobbling and talking weird anymore, so I guess she's back to normal.

"Get in here", she growls, yanking my wheelchair inside the hotel room. She slams the door in Geraldine and Leah's faces. Just before it clicks shut, I see Leah give me a tiny wave and a look that is so full of sadness I just want to cry and run into Geraldine's arms so she can kiss my bald head again and order me breakfast cupcakes. Mommy listens at the door for Geraldine and Leah's footsteps to be gone. Then she turns on me, swearing under her breath, hitting me but not slapping, because that would make too much noise. She grabs my neck and pumps quickly, so it feels like I'm choking. I gag, and her smile twists into a glare.

"Shut up! You tricked me, you little bitch! You are never, and I mean NEVER, going to see that woman and her ugly little girl again! NEVER!"

My body hurts all over, like it was pounded with the meat tenderizer that Daddy used to use to crush Oreos for ice cream toppings. Tears run down my face. When Mommy has finished hitting, she sinks down on the bed.

"I *knew* I shouldn't have let you talk to that girl! You weren't supposed to eat anything last night, and I'll bet you did! I'll bet you did!"

I remember Holly's diary entry that I read last night.

"Today I said NO. It wasn't anything major, and it definitely won't stop Mom, but at least I said it. She told me I had to pretend to have a seizure in front of David to show him how sick I am. She showed me everything to do. Slump over, flail arms, hang tongue out, drop eyelids, roll around, tense up. But I said NO. If David really loves Mom, he doesn't need to feel sorry for her. I told her this, and then I said I wouldn't fake a seizure. She took off her high heel and hit me right in the back. The pain was blinding at first, but then it was over, and I had said NO. There's a funny-looking bruise on my back now, but I don't mind, because it reminds me to say NO. It's the best bruise I've ever gotten."

After I read that, I had closed the diary and imagined the word NO dancing around my head in sparkly green and purple letters. What would Holly want me to say right now? Instead of crumbling into myself and giving in to the hurt that feels so real it tears my chest apart, I sit up and cross my arms, trying to ignore my throbbing heart. The hurt will go away. The hurt will go away. Please, Holly, make the hurt go away.

"Why wasn't I supposed to have anything to eat?" I ask.

"Because you're a bad girl, and bad girls don't deserve any food", Mommy snaps.

"I'll starve if I don't eat."

"Then maybe you deserve to starve."

There is a knock at the door.

"Stay here", Mommy says as she goes to answer it. It's Jackson.

"Fern here?" he asks.

"Why?"

Mommy doesn't invite him in.

"Because it's past time for her class. We just wanted to make sure she's okay."

"She already went down in the elevator." Mommy starts to close the door.

"Wait!" I yell. "I'm still here! I'm coming!"

As Jackson leads me out the door, Mommy gives me a look that makes me sure I'll get in trouble for this later. Jackson doesn't stop talking the entire way to the ballroom.

"You're in Relieving Anger, right? I teach that class. I'm looking forward to working with you."

He explains all the things we'll be doing. Punches, kicks, meditation, using our hands as weapons- all to get our anger out.

"But don't worry", he says. "You can still do all of it in your wheelchair. Except the kicking."

CHAPTER 24

The Relieving Anger class is almost as full as the Dance Therapy class was. I don't see Leah or Antonio, but Katie is talking to an older group of kids on the far side of the room. There are ropes hanging from the beams, and a funny-looking bag at the end of each rope. Jackson tells me the bags are there for punching and kicking. The first thing we're supposed to do is draw a picture. I don't really know what that has to do with Relieving Anger, but I roll my wheelchair over to where Katie is sitting anyway.

"Any idea why we're doing this?" she asks. "I want to get to the punching and kicking."

"Draw your cancer", says Jackson. "That's what I want everyone to do."

A boy raises his hand. "So...you want us to draw a picture of ourselves?"

"Not *you*", says Jackson. "Your *cancer*. Your cancer is not *you*. *You* are special and unique and talented. Your cancer is horrible and destructive and awful. So draw a picture of whatever you think your cancer looks like. Like if your cancer was a person."

"My cancer has lots of hair, because it took mine", says a girl next to me.

"Technically, chemotherapy took your hair", says Katie. "But it's still a good idea."

The girl sticks her tongue out at Katie. "Whatever."

"Girl, where are your manners?" Katie says. "Introduce yourself to Fern here. She's my little buddy."

I decide I like that term a whole lot better than 'kid'.

"I'm Abby", says the girl. Abby was Katie's roommate at Orlando Children's Hospital. She tells me this while we draw. Her picture sure does have a lot of hair, all piled up in mounds and curls.

"Ugly hair", she tells me. "Because cancer doesn't deserve anything cute."

Katie's drawing looks like a giant snake with fangs and three eyes.

"Why three?" I ask.

"That's the number of years I've had cancer", she tells me.

"Katie's scared of snakes," says Abby. "That's why her picture looks like a snake. When we were at the hospital, some zoo people came to visit us, and they brought all these animals in cages."

"And I thought they were going to be *nice* animals, like rabbits and mice and ferrets", says Katie.

"But they weren't", Abby says. "They asked for volunteers, and Katie's hand shot straight up because she thought she was gonna get to pet the flying squirrel they showed us. So they picked her and a bunch of other kids, and they had them all stand in a line and hold out their hands."

"Don't forget they told us to close our eyes!" adds Katie.

"That's right", says Abby. "They told everyone to close their eyes. And so Katie and all these other kids were just standing at the front of the room, and they put a giant snake right in their hands. It was so big, it took seven kids to hold it. When we all opened our eyes and saw it, it was so gross. Parts of it were sagging everywhere in the places kids weren't holding it."

"It was terrifying", Katie shudders. "And when Katie saw it, she just screamed so loud I thought the snake would even cover its ears. She dropped the snake and ran out of the room. They found her hiding somewhere."

A grin crawls up Abby's mouth. "You'll never guess where!"

"Don't you dare tell her, Abby!"

"You tell her then. But this is something your little buddy needs to hear."

"Fine. I was so scared, I didn't even know where I was going, so I just kept running up the staircase. And then there was this hallway of rooms, so I ran into one of the rooms."

"And who was in the room?" asks Abby, even though it's pretty obvious she already knows the answer.

"A woman", answers Katie, turning red all over.

"And what was she doing?" Abby smiles wider.

Katie buries her head in her hands and starts giggling. "Giving birth."

All three of us explode with laughter.

"I didn't know where I was!" Katie protests. "I was hiding behind the door when the woman in the bed starting moaning, and a bunch of doctors cam rushing in yelling "It's coming, it's coming!" And I couldn't just *leave,* or they'd know I was there!"

"So you got to see a baby being born", I say. "Wow."

"It was disgusting", Katie says.

"More disgusting than the snake?" Abby teases.

Katie pauses to think about that. "Well, no. Not more disgusting than the snake, I guess."

I try to imagine hiding behind a door while a woman was having a baby. It sounds scary and gross, but kind of magic at the same time. Like I would be seeing someone come into the world for the first time, all brand-new without even a name.

"What happened next?" I ask.

"Well, after the baby...you know, *came out*, they started screaming "It's a boy!" And the baby started crying. And the mother started crying too. And the father. And I think maybe even one of the nurses. I had never seen so many people cry happy tears at one time. Then I felt something weird in my nose, and it knew I was gonna sneeze. I tried to hold it in. You know, covering my face, plugging my nose, the whole deal. But you can't cover up a sneeze."

"Sneezes ruin everything", Abby decides.

"So anyway", continues Katie, "I sneezed, and they all turned and looked at me. They were kind of shocked at first. Just staring at me. I felt like I had to say something, so I was like "Hi. Congratulations on the baby."

The doctor asked me what in the world I was doing, and I figured I couldn't get more embarrassed than I already was, so I explained the whole thing. They looked at me funny for a second, and then the woman who had just had the baby starting laughing.

"What was the baby named?" Abby asks.

"I asked them the same thing! And the mother said "I don't know", and the father said, "Well, we're not naming him after anyone in the family, unless we want him to be teased for his entire life."

I said "What about Stephen?" because that's my favorite boy's name."

"Like Stephen King?" I ask.

"No, like Stephen Hawking", Katie replies. "He's a famous scientist and mathematician. And he's in a wheelchair. I read a book on him in third grade, and ever since then, he's been my favorite famous person."

"Did the parents end up naming the baby Stephen?" I wonder.

"Almost", says Katie. "After I suggested the name, the mother and the father were quiet for a long time. And I was just standing there, wondering if I had offended them or something, but then mother said "Stephen is a beautiful name. Don't you think so, Phil?"

And the father said "I love it. But let's call him Steven with a V. I can't stand names with "ph" in them." The mother said "Me neither. Steven it is. Welcome to the world, Steven Judith'."

"Wow", I say. "You named a baby!"

"I guess I did", Katie smiles.

"Hey", Abby says to me. "You haven't drawn anything yet."

I look down at my paper. It's blank. The thing is, I don't have cancer. So how can I draw what mine looks like?

"Five minutes!" Jackson yells, and his words come flooding back to me like bits of shells in the sea. *"You are special and unique and talented. Your cancer is horrible and destructive and awful."* Well, I may not have cancer, but I *do* know what's horrible and destructive and awful. I start to draw.

"It has two heads!" Abby says when I'm done. It does. On the giant body of a monster, there is a head of Mommy and a head of Brian.

"It's creepy", Abby tells me.

"It's...weird", Katie says, tilting her head to see my picture from a different angle.

Jackson tell us to choose a partner and a punching bag. Katie and Abby are partners with each other, so I end up with a boy named Tyler.

"I don't wanna be with her!" Tyler complains. "She's a baby! We can't share a punching bag. I'm so strong, the bag will swing back and knock her down in two seconds flat. Besides, she's not even supposed to be in this group! She's not seven!"

"Yes, I am", I say. "I'm actually seven and a half. And if you want to find another partner, go ahead. I don't care."

Tyler's bald head turns pink, and he looks down at the floor. "She's even got a stuffed *rabbit*", he says, like "rabbit" is a bad word.

Today I said NO.

"Yes, Tyler." I hold Pox up for everyone to see. "I *do* have a stuffed rabbit. His name is Pox, because I got him when I had the chicken pox. And he makes me a million times stronger than I look. So I won't get knocked down by the bag. But maybe you will."

"That's my little buddy!" yells Katie. "Tell him, Fern!"

"Okay, okay!" Jackson shouts. "That's enough. Tyler, you and Fern will be partners. I assure you she can handle it."

He winks at me.

"Stuffed *rabbit*", Tyler mutters, but I pretend I don't hear him.

Jackson passes around tape and tells us to stick our pictures to the punching bag. Tyler's picture looks like a giant egg with claws.

"Now on the count of three, I want one of you to punch your cancer picture as hard as you can. Imagine you're punching cancer itself. Then the next person punches. Remember to stay on opposite sides of the bag, and never punch at the same time."

He shows us how to punch so our knuckles won't bleed. Then he says "Now let's go beat up some cancer!"

I let Tyler go first, because he's been making jabbing motions the entire time Jackson was talking. Tyler punches his cancer right in the center, swinging the bag a little. If his cancer is an egg like I think it is, the shell would crack and there'd be drippy goo everywhere.

"Your turn", Tyler says to me. "Hurry up."

I study the picture I taped onto the bag. Mommy and Brian's faces glare back at me. I close my eyes and picture their words running through my mind in red letters, like blood. Brian. Teasing me with descriptions of food he won't let me have. Laughing at me. His disgusting, twisted smirk. His greasy hands. I punch him square in his big fat nose. The bag swings back and hits Tyler in the stomach.

"Wow", he says.

I smile, promising myself I will hit even harder the next time.

"Your turn."

After Tyler swings and misses, I look at my drawing of Mommy. Her words are the worst. The sharpest knives. She told me Daddy didn't love me. She made me sick. She lied to everyone. *"I never wanted another kid, anyway." "You're pretty stupid, you know that?" "You'll get send to an orphanage where they'll whip you."* The slap in the face, leaving her red signature of hurt. And most of all, *"I will kill you." "I will kill you."* I swing my fist and pound the picture of Mommy so hard my knuckles rip the paper. I keep punching and punching, not hearing any thing around me, not hearing Jackson yelling "Fern! Fern, slow down!" and Tyler whining "Hey, no fair! It's my turn now! It's my turn!" I stop attacking the punching bag, tears streaming down my face. I'd didn't even realize I was crying. Kids turn and stare at me.

"You okay?" Katie asks quietly.

I shake my head no, no, I'm not okay. What does okay even mean anymore? Jackson leads me to the corner of the ballroom, where yoga mats are set up in rows.

"You got pretty out of control", he tells me. "What's up?"

I shrug. "I was mad, I guess."

I know this is a bad excuse, because Daddy once told me "Being mad doesn't give you the right to throw a fit." Actually, he said that to Mommy after they were fighting and she threw a lamp that smashed on the ground and fizzed and sparked all over, till it went out completely. Their argument fizzed out then too, and Mommy started crying. Real tears, not fake ones.

To my surprise, Jackson doesn't get mad. Instead, he hold his hand out for double high-fives.

"That's my girl!" he exclaims. "You're mad! Say it with me: 'I'm MAD!'"

"I'm mad", I whisper.

"Louder!" Jackson says. "I'm mad!" "Louder, Fern! Come on, imagine like your words are hitting the drawing you made!"

I close my eyes and smile. Mommy hurt me with her words. Now it's time to turn it around.

"I'M MAD!"

"Good job! Now I want you to relax, okay? Try some breathing and meditation."

"What's meditation?"

Jackson calls over a woman named Stephanie. "Show our girl Fern some mediation, would you?" he says. "I've gotta get back to the bags. Two little guys have just abandoned their drawings and started beating the crap out of each other."

"I'll take it from here", Stephanie says.

Her lips are smiling and soft. I wonder if she wears lip gloss. Not sharp red lipstick like Mommy, but fruit-flavored shiny stuff, the kind I see at the drugstore. Stephanie shows me how to breathe in and out really deep. She feels my chest like she's a doctor and says I've been breathing all wrong. I didn't know it was possible to breathe wrong.

"Breathe as deep as you can and hold it for five seconds", she says. "Then let it out."

She does it with me, her breathing as smooth and deep as glass marbles, and me gasping for air. After that, we learn wrist grabs and finger locks to defend ourselves, only Tyler doesn't want to be my partner after what happened at the bag, so I get to work with Jackson.

"Try it", he says holding his wrist out. It's double the size of mine. Using both hands, I twist his hand like it's the lid on a hard-to-open pickle jar. He starts tapping his leg, so I twist harder.

"Stop!" he yells. "I tapped out! I tapped out!"

I drop his wrist. "What's tapping out?"

"When you hit your leg like that, it means don't go any harder. It hurts enough."

"Oh. Sorry".

"No problem", he says, shaking out his wrist.

"So if you tap out, I have to stop?" I ask.

"That's the idea", Jackson replies.

"I wish it was like that in real life", I say.

"Huh?"

"Tapping out. If someone is hurting me, I could just tap my leg, and they would stop, no matter what."

"Has anyone been hurting you?" Jackson asks curiously.

I've said too much. "No!" I say quickly. I was just saying it as an example. Can we try the finger locks now?"

Jackson examines the red mark where I twisted his wrist too hard.

"Yeah", he says. "But do the other hand this time."

CHAPTER
25

After Relieving Anger, I roll my wheelchair along the hallway to catch up with Katie and Abby.

"My little buddy's a killer!" says Katie. "Honestly, Fern, you just went *wild*. I've never seen a little kid punch so hard.

"It was kinda creepy", Abby admits. "Like you were possessed or something."

"Girl, you been watching *The Exorcist* again?" Katie demands.

"Maybe", Abby replies. "But it was just sitting there on my dad's computer. I figured I might as well watch it."

"Well, it's made you deranged."

They talk about *The Exorcist* until I stop in front of a door leading to a small room. A sign on the door says "Therapeutic Writing.

"I'll see you guys later", I say.

"You're doing Therapeutic Writing?" Abby asks. "Not Friendship Bracelets 101?"

"Friendship Bracelets 101?"

Abby shrugs. "You gotta have something to do in the hospital. Gets boring, you know? It's useful to know how to make cool bracelets."

The Therapeutic Writing room is small with a blue walls and white tables and bookshelves where the books are organized by size, biggest to smallest. If calm was a room, this would be it. There are a few other kids sitting at the white tables, already writing. My eyes travel to a desk at the front of the room, where an old gray-haired lady sits. She has glasses on a chain, the kind that sit low on her nose. Her eyes are watery blue. She is sitting so quietly, she could almost be another piece of furniture in the room, until she speaks.

"Fern", she says. "Come on in."

She moves a chair away from an empty white table so I'll have a place to park my wheelchair. The wheels almost get stuck on the fuzzy white carpet. I wish I wasn't strapped into this wheelchair. If I got out and walked around on that rug, I bet it would feel just like walking on a cloud. The woman hands me a stack of paper and a pen.

"I'm Delilah. Write whatever you want, okay? Anything."

"Okay."

I take the pen, and it feels right in my hand. I'm glad she gave me a pen and not one of those scratchy pencils that make so much noise I can't think. I like writing in pen because it can't be erased, so you need to be careful. You can't fix mistakes in pen, but you can't get rid of good stuff, either. I look around. Everyone else has their heads bent down close to their paper, and in wonder what they're writing. I know for sure what I'm going to say on the paper. Holly's let me read her writing. Now I'll give something back. I cup my hand over my paper and lower my head so no one can see what I'm writing.

"Dear Holly, This is your sister Fern. I have a question. Are you dead? When I read your diary, I thought you must be. Do you have a diary hidden somewhere else that I don't know about? Every page is filled in the one I'm reading, but I haven't read it all yet. I'm getting close, though. And when I finish, where will I be? Will you still be with me in my dreams? What

happened, Holly? Are you in Heaven? Is it beautiful and filled with sparkles in your favorite color? I wish I could meet you. I think about you all the time. You wrote that you knew David. He's my Daddy, but he left me and Mommy. I'm mad at him, because he knew you were my sister and he didn't even tell me! I don't know where he is now. I live with Brian, who is Mommy's boyfriend. I hate him. Can you see me, Holly? Can you hear my thoughts? It seems like everything that happened to you is happening to me. But I don't want to die. I want to save myself. Can you help me? Love, your sister, Fern."

I fold the letter in half, then in half again. I guess I was focusing so hard, I didn't even realize that the minutes were ticking by like a steady drip of water from a tap. As everyone leaves, I wheel myself up to the desk where Delilah is sitting, staring at a picture on her desk, except she's not really looking at it. Her eyes are pointed in that direction, but they have a faraway star to them, like the thing she's really staring at is somewhere else.

"Um...Delilah?" I ask.

She jerks her head toward me. "Fern! I'm sorry, I was just..."

"I have two questions", I say.

"And I've got two answers."

"Do you have any envelopes?"

She rummages in her desk drawer, which is surprisingly messy. Delilah and her desk drawer are like a little messy island in a big ocean of clean. Delilah gives me an envelope, and I put the letter in it, but I don't write Holly's name on the outside, because then someone might notice.

"What's the second question?" Delilah asks.

"Who were you looking at a picture of?"

I can see that I've scared her. Her eyes dart around the room, like there might be an escape somewhere.

"That's quite a question", she finally says.

"You said you had two answers", I remind her.

"I did." She sighs. "I did."

She tilts the picture toward me so I can see it. It's a little girl, probably not much older than I am, dressed in a puffy white gown and holding flowers. Her light brown hair is done up in curls and bows.

"Who's that?" I ask.

"My daughter Camilla", Delilah says. "On the day of her first communion."

"How come you're sad looking at Camilla?" I ask. "Wasn't her first communion a happy time? She's smiling."

"I wasn't sad", Delilah protests. "I was just...thinking."

"You were sad. Your eyes told me so. They were looking for something you couldn't find in the picture."

Delilah raises her glasses-on-a-chain to get a better look at me, and for a moment it's just her and I in the clean, empty white of the writing room.

"Camilla is dead," Delilah says softly. "She got into a car accident with her boyfriend when she was sixteen. He had been drinking, and... they hit the side of the curb."

"That's awful", I say.

"Every time I look at that picture-" Delilah starts. She sounds like she's about to cry. "Every time I look at that picture, all I can think about is how I wish Camilla was that little again. She was seven in that picture. Seven! Not old enough to drive or have a boyfriend."

Delilah stares out the window, and she looks so sad that I feel like crying too.

"Don't worry", I say. "I think Camilla is in Heaven with my sister."

Delilah looks back at me. "Your sister?"

I hadn't planned on telling her about Holly, but something about her sad eyes made me feel safe.

"Holly's my sister", I say. "And she's in Heaven with Camilla."

I expect Delilah to get that "I'm-so-sorry-for-you-poor-child" look on her face, but she doesn't. I've been seeing that look a lot ever since Mommy started pretending I was sick.

"How did she...I mean, what happened?"

"I'm not really sure. Mommy doesn't talk about it." Which is true.

"I'm so sorry", Delilah says.

"For what?" I ask. "You didn't do anything wrong."

"Yes, but your poor mother..."

I don't want to talk about Mommy, so I change the subject.

"What do you think Heaven looks like?"

"I'm not sure. I've wondered that quite a bit. I suppose it looks like whatever you want it to."

"I think Camilla and Holly are very happy there", I say.

"Me too. But I miss Camilla so much. I wish she was still here."

"And I wish Holly was still here."

We are both quiet for a while, missing Camilla and Holly. Then Delilah says, "We'd better get you to the final party, Fern. Everyone will be wondering where you are. If I'm not mistaken, if started fifteen minutes ago."

"Okay." I strain my wheelchair forward over the cloud carpet.

"Wait, take a tissue to wipe your face. You've been crying", Delilah says.

As I scrub my face hard, Delilah looks me over and smiles. "If you don't mind being a few more minutes late, I think we can do a little something for you."

"What?"

"Come here", she says mischievously.

I struggle over and look where she is pointing. In her messy desk drawer, there is a little make-up pouch.

"Would your mother mind?" Delilah asks.

"No."

I don't care what Mommy thinks. She'll punish me even if I didn't do anything wrong anyway. Delilah rummages through the bag and pulls out make-up that looks familiar. Mascara, eye shadow, lip gloss, blush.

"I never wear lipstick. It's too strong", Delilah tells me.

"Like a stab of blood", I agree.

Delilah dabs a little bit of blush of each of my cheeks and lip gloss on my lips. It feels weird, like I've just drank a bucket of grease. I see Delilah slip the mascara back into the bag, and I know why. She feels bad, because I can't wear it anyway. I don't have eyelashes. A day after Mommy shaved my head, she plucked my eyelashes out with tweezers, one by one.

"You're a bit young for eye shadow", Delilah says. "So we'll skip that."

She holds a pocket mirror in front of my face. "How's it look?"

I stare at the girl in the mirror. Am I really that pale and thin? My ears stick out, and my eyes suddenly seem way too big now that I don't have hair.

"Thank you", I say. "It's great."

"I used to do Camilla's makeup all the time", Delilah tells me.

Mommy's never put make-up on me, even though she's got bags and bags of it, probably even more than CVS. I wouldn't want to wear make-up every day, but on rainy weekend afternoons, it would be nice to play dress-up in her clothes and smear her make-up on my face instead of staying in my wheelchair. Not that she's ever let me near her clothes or makeup. Delilah seems like the kind of mother who'd do that, though. I'm wearing the same dress I wore yesterday, my only fancy one. The one that's light blue with a white ribbon. Delilah says I look absolutely beautiful, and she wheels me down to the ballroom.

The last time I saw the ballroom, there were punching bags hanging from ropes and yoga mats in the corner. But now it looks like a whole different world. There are tables and chairs in the corners and sides of the room, covered with a red tablecloths and glitter. A huge banner hangs from one side of the doorway to the other. It says "Kids Cancer Convention". There are tables with food and paper plates and cups. The middle of the room is cleared out so that people can dance there. At the top of the room is the disco ball. I've never seen anything quite like it. It's a huge ball with what looks like tiny mirror squares all around it. It's spinning, and when the light hits it, it makes patterns and glowing spots on the ballroom floor. Like millions of tiny fireflies in that one glittering ball. There are red and blue balloons all around the room. And everywhere, everywhere, there are people. I feel like I'm inside a giant kaleidoscope.

"Where are all the parents?" I ask.

The room is entirely full of kids and teachers.

"They're at a final meeting", replies Delilah. "They'll be joining you in a while. Right now, it's kids only."

I smile. I like that, kids only.

"You okay?" asks Delilah.

"Yes", I say. "I'm okay. Thank you for everything."

"You're welcome, Fern", she smiles.

Delilah leaves, and I am left alone in this big, colorful, spinning mass of life. I decide to get food first, because when Mommy comes, she won't let me have any. Leah, Celia, Katie, Abby and Sammy are sitting at a glitter covered table by the punch bowl. I wonder if we'll all end up eating a pound of glitter in our food by the time this is over.

"Fern!" Leah calls.

It's hard to get over to that table with everything that's going on. I take a plate of waffles with maple syrup from the food table, and roll my wheelchair up to Leah's table. Who knows, this could be my last meal for a long time. The convention is over after the party, so Brian is picking me and Mommy up to take us back to his house, where I will probably go back to eating crackers and juice and oatmeal.

"Let's give each other our addresses!" suggests Sammy.

So we take the red and blue napkins from the table and write out our addresses and pass them around. It feels weird, like the sort of thing you would do with a group of friends. Then it hits me: I have a group of friends, and I am lying to them. If they knew I wasn't really sick, would they still like me? I keep quiet and write my address in careful letters on my blue napkin. I know that Mommy always gets the mail before I do, to see if anyone she met at the store sent us any money for chemotherapy, but there's always a chance she could let me have a letter, right? Just like the time the edges of her mouth almost smiled when I tricked her by saying yes-no-yes-no-no-yes. Just like the times when I was little and she made me a cake on my birthday. Just like all the times we went to the beach and I was so proud to have her as my Mommy because she was so beautiful that when she lay on her back to get a suntan, people would stop and stare and try to talk to her. I'm not proud of my Mommy anymore.

I try to erase these thoughts right out of my mind as I pass around my address and we eat and talk. Time seems to speed up. Why do good things have to move so fast, but when I'm with Mommy and Brian, everything seems slow, like it's caught in a puddle of honey? Before I know it, I see Mommy and all the other parents come in. Geraldine hugs Leah, and then me.

"Don't touch my daughter!" Mommy snaps. She's wearing more makeup than usual. I smell Irresistible Iris, her perfume. Mommy brings me to the side if the room, patting my bald head all the way so everyone can see what a good mother she is.

"We're going to have a long discussion, Fern", she says. "And you won't like it one damn little bit." Her voice gets lower, more growly, when I am saved by Sparkle.

"All right, everyone!" she shouts from the front of the room. Sparkle sure is loud. "Twenty of you were chosen for Operation Hope. If you are one of those children, please come to the table at the front of the room to fill out your wish form. Parents, please let your children do this on their own. It's *their* wish."

I love the last thing Sparkle says. Mommy can't come with me, but that doesn't stop her from yanking my head downward and whispering "Listen up. I talked to Brian last night, and we've decided on a cruise."

"Huh?"

"A cruise, you stupid child. In the Bahamas. So on your form, you need to write that you want a cruise in the Bahamas for you, your mother, and her boyfriend. Got it?"

I get it, but I'm not doing it.

"But we cheated!" I whisper. "It's like stealing!"

Mommy slits her sharp fingernail along my back, and I feel droplets of blood forming there in a tiny line. Soon, they'll fall down the back of my dress like red rain.

Today, I said NO.

"Is Fern here?" Sparkle calls. "We're waiting for Fern."

Leah, Celia, Sammy, Abby, and Katie start cheering.

"You know what you have to do", Mommy hisses at me.

For once, she's right. I *do* know. I make my way up to the table next to Antonio. He grins at me and whispers "race car". I give him a weak smile in return. Sparkle passes out twenty wish forms, one for each of us. Antonio grabs his pen and starts scribbling out what looks like "race car". I wonder if the Operation Hope people will be able to read his handwriting.

I focus on my own form. Suddenly, the lights in the ballroom seem too bright and the disco ball is spinning too fast. I'm caught in a maze of lights and colors and spinning and lies, and I can't get out. I wipe my sweaty palms on the paper. It leaves grayish marks.

You know what you have to do.

But this time, it's not Mommy's voice echoing those words in my head. It's Holly's voice.

Come on, Fern. You know what you have to do. Remember, today you're saying NO.

The first part of the form is easy enough. Name, date, address, phone number. I fill in the address and phone number of my old house, so Operation Hope will never find me. That way, Mommy won't be able to lie to them anymore. The bottom part of the form us the hard part. It just has one question: What is your wish?

What is your wish, Fern? What is your wish?

I look at Leah sitting with her friends. Leah, who wants fairies and genies to be real so much. Leah, who I heard crying in the middle of the night. My friend Leah.

I write: "I wish for Leah to be able to go to California with her family to the Fairy House Palace." I remember that I should probably write Leah's last name, but I don't know it, so I write the address she gave me, and "Leah is nine and not in a wheelchair and her mother's name is Geraldine and her father's name is Jake and she gets a new knitted hat from her grandmother every time she has chemotherapy." That should do it.

Underneath that, I write "This is a SECRET wish, so don't tell Leah or my mom about it please. I mean it. Please." Just in case. I add a few more "pleases" and fold the form over. I drop it in the basket. *That's* what I needed to do.

Good girl, Fern. I'm proud of you.

Thank you, Holly. Today I said NO. I can't help smiling as I go back to Mommy.

"Did you do what you needed to do?" she asks me, eyebrows raised. I stare right at her mean, squinty eyes.

"Oh, yes."

CHAPTER 26

After we fill out our Operation Hope forms, music starts playing. Mommy drifts off to a group of other parents to tell them her speech of lies. Katie and Celia and Leah and Abby dance together in a group, and Sammy and I wave our arms and snap our fingers like I learned in Dance Therapy. I can feel the floor spinning under me and the music changing from loud and fast to slow and soft when I feel a tap on the shoulder. It's Antonio. He's wearing a suit and tie smudged with chocolate.

"Wanna dance, Fern?" he asks.

"Oh, um, no thanks", I say. He doesn't leave.

"How come?"

"Yeah, how come?" asks Sammy. "Dance with him!"

The freedom I felt just moments before zips away, and I feel like crying. If I dance with Antonio, he might decide he wants to be my boyfriend. And boyfriends are bad, because Brian is Mommy's boyfriend.

And he's plenty bad. Besides, if Antonio wants to be my boyfriend, does that make me like Mommy? Will I grow up to lie and hurt and make people sick?

"I'm too young", I say, looking at the floor.

"Fern, I don't have to be your *boyfriend*", Antonio says, the tips of his ears turning pink. "That stuff is gross. I just want to dance as your friend."

"Do it!" Sammy says.

"In my wheelchair?"

"Why not?" Antonio grips the handles of my wheelchair and pushes me out into the middle of the dance floor. He grabs both my hands. Mine are cold, his are sweaty. He swings my arms around, and we dance. The music turns loud again, but Antonio and I don't care. Celia and Abby and Leah and Katie and Sammy join us, and soon we're all dancing in one big circle, just being happy. I dig deep into my brain, but only a little bit of fear is left.

The party ends at five o' clock. Mommy has already packed up her huge bag, and Brian is sitting in the car, honking the horn to get us going. My friends and I are sitting together, one last time, when Mommy marches up and grabs me by the arm.

"Come on, Brian's waiting."

I say goodbye to Katie and Antonio and Celia and Abby and Sammy. Leah and I lock eyes. I move my wheelchair closer to her for a hug, but Mommy jerks me back.

"These your friends?"

"Yes." I am terrified.

"Why'd you bother making friends?" Mommy asks, her arms crossed.

"Because...because..."

Of course, it's Antonio who speaks up. "Because we like Fern, Mrs. Fern's Mom. I'm Antonio. Nice to meet you. I'm Italian. I want to drive race cars when I grow up, and I even got picked to-".

Mommy silences him with one wave of her hand. "You realize this won't last?" she says to no one in particular. "Every one of you is going to die. Get it through your heads, kids. You all have *cancer*. Cancer doesn't wait for you to make friends. It kills you. I don't know who'll be first, or who'll be last. But there's no use hanging on each other if you all know the end is pretty damn close."

Leah looks away, and I can see a tear roll out of her dark eyes and splatter onto the front of her dress.

"And Fern", Mommy continues, "you and I have something *major* to discuss. So say goodbye to the other cancer kids. Look, that one's even crying. What you do, Fern? Tell her how ugly her knit hat is?"

"It's not ugly!" I say. "Her grandma made it and it's beautiful and she's my friend!"

I scoot over and wrap my around Leah, who is shaking with sobs. I feel hot anger bubbling up inside me, like I'm a volcano.

Katie probably does too, only her mountain explodes. She stands up and yells at Mommy.

"LOOK, LADY. I DON'T CARE WHO YOU ARE, BUT YOU CAN'T TREAT MY FRIENDS LIKE THAT! YOU WOULDN'T LAST THIRTY SECONDS IF YOU HAD CANCER! YOU KNOW WHY? 'CAUSE YOU'RE MEAN AND RUDE AND *WRONG*! WE ARE DAMN WELL NOT DYING! AND IF NO ONE'S EVER TOLD YOU THIS BEFORE, IT'S TIME YOU KNOW! YOU'RE A TOTAL ASSHOLE! AND BELIEVE ME, I WOULD USE A HELL OF A LOT STRONGER LANGUAGE IF MY MOTHER WASN'T IN THE ROOM!"

While Katie is yelling, I hug Leah tight.

"Remember the fairies", I whisper. "I lied. They're absolutely, positively real. But I was telling the truth about your hat. It *is* beautiful. ".

Leah hugs me back without saying anything. That's when we hear the smack.

Katie doubles over, clutching her nose. Already, I can see drops of blood splattering the floor. Mommy takes a deep breath, crossing to Antonio, and puts her hand on her hips.

"YOUNG MAN!" she screams. "WHY DID YOU JUST HIT THAT POOR GIRL?"

"Huh?" For once, Antonio doesn't seem to have anything to say. "I didn't-".

"OH, YES YOU DID!" Mommy roars. "I SAW YOU!"

She turns to the crowd. "CAN WE GET SOME HELP OVER HERE? THIS BOY JUST HIT THAT GIRL!"

My blood boils. I know who really hit Katie, and it wasn't Antonio. It was Mommy.

As people begin to swarm around Antonio, Mommy grabs my wheelchair and bolts away. No one notices.

"Drive!" she screams at Brian the minute I'm loaded into the car on my side and she's in the passenger seat. "Drive!"

Brian drives, all right. Over every pothole and speed bump. I close my eyes and pretend I'm on a roller coaster and that's why everything is bouncing and turning. When the road flattens out, Mommy twists in her seat and says, "Fern, we have something to talk about." I am too mad at her to answer, but she doesn't seem to notice.

"That old lady- Delilah, I think her name was- came up to me at the party. And do you know what she said?"

My stomach clenches like a fist. I have a pretty good idea.

"What?" I choke out.

"She told me she was sorry for my loss. So I asked her what the hell she was talking about, and she said 'I know, it's hard to talk about. I lost a child, too.' I said "What are you getting at?" and she said she was talking about Holly. Now, Fern, how would she know about Holly?"

My voice comes out as a little squeak. "Um...I don't know?"

"Stop!" Mommy yells at Brian.

He slams on the brakes. Mommy's head jerks forward, then back.

"My GOD, Brian!" she yells.

"Hey, don't yell at me", he protests. "It's the kid who's causing trouble, remember?"

Mommy's eyes narrow into slits. "Of *course* I remember", she says. "Fern. How do you know about Holly?"

I realize I have a few choices. I could tell her everything, about the diary and my dreams and the picture in her blue album, or I could pretend I don't know what she's talking about. Or I could say that Daddy told me, but even though I'm mad at Daddy, he doesn't deserve what Mommy would do to him if I said that. I settle for a grain of the truth, not the full serving.

"I saw a picture", I say. "When we were packing up our things to move to Brian's house. It was on the floor. A school picture, and a form with it. A form with Holly's name and your name. So I thought Holly must be my sister."

I try to play back in my mind what I just said. It seems true enough.

"Mmm-hmm. And what led you to believe Holly is dead?" asks Mommy.

She's being way too calm about this. I'm scared. When Mommy's calm, it's like she's a lion waiting to pounce.

"I just thought..." I stammer. "Since you never told me about her... and she's not here...I just thought..." I don't get to tell Mommy what I just thought, because she moves so quickly, she could be a lightning bolt.

One minute, her hand are clicking the car window up and down, up and down, and the next minute, they're on my throat, squeezing into my neck. I can't breathe. My mouth forms the words "help" and "stop", but Mommy squeezes harder. I am running out of breath. All of my body begins to feel numb and fuzzy. Mommy shakes me while she squeezes. I close my eyes and feel myself floating. Is this what it's like, Holly? Is this what it's like to die? I am floating higher and higher into purple indigo sky. Why did I think Heaven would be all light when dark is just as beautiful? I can almost see you now, Holly. The tips of your fingers, reaching for my hand. I lift my arm, and...crash. I am back in Brian's car, smelling grease and beer and Irresistible Iris perfume. So close, Holly. So close.

At Brian's house, we settle back into our routine. Mommy gives me crackers, juice, and oatmeal. She takes me out to a store every other day to get people to pay attention to her, and also to get money, because she has started going to fancy shops every Saturday and coming back with perfume, shoes, and handbags. Before she started pretending I was sick, she never went to shops like those, because she said she couldn't afford them. It makes me wonder just how much money she is getting in the mail. We also get packages sometimes, of stuffed animals and toys and books. Brian likes to open them in front of me and wave the stuff around, watching my eyes follow it back and forth, back and forth, before stuffing it in garbage bags and dumping it in the attic. I don't care about the toys and stuffed animals, but I really do want the books. I have finished all the books Mommy got me from the library, and done all the work in them too.

Mommy shaves my head once a week. Sometimes she forgets to be gentle, or she just doesn't care, because my head gets bloody lines on it and Mommy says "Oh, shit", and scrubs my head too hard with sour-smelling bars of soap.

Did she do this to you too, Holly? Did she chop off your dark braids? I don't know if people with epilepsy are supposed to be bald, but I don't think so, because every time I see you in my dreams, those braids are streaming from your head, thick and beautiful.

I draw a tally mark on the wall for each day, surprised at how quickly they're adding up.

"Something that bothers me a lot is how often people take windows for granted. They can be sitting in a room with a beautiful view, but their eyes are glued somewhere else. Now that I'm in a hospital room with no windows, I think about these things. It's a special hospital for people with severe epilepsy. Mom says I'll be here a long time, so I should get used to it. If they think we're doing well, the hospital staff take us outside every day. Mom convinced them I'm nowhere near well enough, so I have to stay in bed. My roommate, Molly, goes outside every day. Every night, I ask her about what it's like outside, and I write down what she says. I'm going to write a poem called "Outside My Room". But how can I write a good poem about somewhere I've never been?"

After reading that in Holly's diary, I try to look out the window every day. I see the world change from drizzly April to flower-scented May to sunbeam June. It's getting harder and harder to stay awake, because I'm so tired. Sometimes I even fall asleep when Mommy takes me out to the store.

One morning, we are at Walmart when an old woman says "My goodness! That child is wasting away!"

"Yes", Mommy says. "It's tragic. Soon, she'll be gone."

That night, I hear her talking to Brian when I'm out of my wheelchair after Mommy put me to bed. I'm listening at the vents.

"She's almost dead", Mommy is saying. "It's getting more attention, but she can't just *die* yet. Not yet."

For a moment, I don't know who they're talking about, but when I feel my stomach growling and clawing at my insides, I realize that *I'm* the one they're talking about. Am I almost dead? I don't feel myself dying. What does dying feel like? Maybe it's just like being alive, except you eventually just get more and more tired until you stop, like one of those wind-up toys that buzzes and spins around a table when you turn the little plastic knob, but then it gets slower and slower until it stops altogether, hard plastic toppling over. My breath comes in short little bursts. I see color behind my eyes, red and blue. I climb onto my mattress and hold the pillow over my head. I cry.

I heard a prayer once, when I was younger and Mommy and I were at the grocery store. There was a woman with a tiny baby all wrapped in her arms. She was rocking him right over by the soup aisle, whispering a prayer to him until he closed his tiny baby eyes.

Now I lay me down to sleep, I pray The Lord my soul to keep. If I should die before I wake, I pray The Lord my soul to take. Amen.

She said in over and over in a soft chanting, and I listened like I was under a spell until Mommy pulled me away and said it was time to go.

If I should die before I wake...

I remember the man in the ambulance squeezing my hand tight and telling me not to go to sleep. The blue and red behind my eyes blurs together until it becomes sleepy purple. I blink open-shut, open-shut.

If I should die before I wake...

Don't fall asleep. I keep my eyes wide open all night, which is not easy, because I really need Holly's help right now, and when I'm asleep, it's easier to see her.

The next morning, Mommy creates The Game. She wakes me up early to explain it, because she says we have a new store to go to and we need to leave sooner. Mommy doesn't call it The Game, but I do in my head, because that's what it seems like. A game, one that I can't win.

"You've been getting thin", Mommy says.

"I need more food."

"And you'll get it", Mommy smiles, "*if* you cooperate."

"What do you mean?" I ask.

"Shut up and listen up!" Brian snarls. He's leaning against the door frame, like he always does. I'm surprised he doesn't leave grease marks there.

"As of right now, you get no food or water for the day", Mommy says. "But if you do well when we go shopping, I will give you five percent of the money we make to buy food for yourself until the next shopping trip. That's two days to plan for. No exceptions. Got it?"

Why can't she just give me food like a normal mother, Holly? Why? Why The Game?

"Got it?" Mommy hisses again.

A little blob of spit flies out of her mouth and lands on my chin. I nod weakly.

"Got it."

Brian drives us to a new store, one that's two hours and twelve minutes away.

"We've exhausted all the local stores", says Mommy. "People are getting suspicious. It's time to branch out."

I wonder if Mommy played The Game with Holly. I wonder if Holly ever won.

The car pulls into a parking lot that's so full, it takes Brian seventeen minutes to find a place to park.

"Remember", Mommy says as Brian swerves into a parking spot, almost hitting the car beside us, "the better you do, the more money you'll have to buy food. So what does that mean?"

"Wide eyes, slumped head, drool, and tears", I recite.

"Good girl", Mommy says, but my heart doesn't pause like it used to when she called me a good girl. I don't want to be a good girl if it means lying and stealing money.

"Have fun", Brian smirks.

He gets back into the car and crackles open a bag of chips. The barbecue smell tunnels itself into my nose and rests there, teasing me.

We get a lot of money from people at the store, mostly from a man in a business suit who thinks Mommy is "charming". It must be the perfume, because if people knew what Mommy was really like, no one would think "charming". They would think "liar." I get five dollars and eighty cents out of the one hundred and thirteen dollars that we collect. Mommy stuffs it in in my wheelchair pocket, which I'm glad I emptied out after the convention. The packaged snack wrapper are zipped inside my mattress, in the same place I first found Holly's diary. The snacks themselves are long gone. After we're done at the store, Mommy drives to a 7-11 and lets me go in by myself.

"You earned it", she says. "This is what you get for two days, so make it last."

"I didn't even think she'd make a buck", Brian says.

I pretend not to hear him as I yank the door open and pull my wheelchair inside the air-conditioned store. I guess the math book I read was useful, because I'm able to calculate that five dollars and fifty cents equals a jar of peanut butter, a two-pack of orange Hostess cupcakes, a big jug of water, and two single-serving packages of dry Raman noodles. Thirty cents left over, which I dump into the can at the checkout that says "EVERY PENNY HELPS FIGHT LEUKEMIA!" There's a picture of a smiling bald kid, and it make my heart hurt a little, because that kid could be someone I know, maybe someone I saw at the convention but didn't talk to. The cashier, who is big and wears bright pink lipstick, makes an "awww" sound when she sees me dump my change in the can.

"One cancer patient helping another", she whispers. "Beautiful. Where's your Mommy, little girl?"

I say she's in the bathroom, and the cashier offers to give me my food and water for free, but I push the money at her anyway, because that would be like stealing, and Mommy and I have already stolen enough. That night, I eat peanut butter with my fingers and read Holly's diary. Just like a normal kid. Peanut butter fingers in the jar, eyes locked on older sister's private life. But the peanut butter is one of the only things I get to eat, and my sister is dead. So I guess it's not so normal after all.

CHAPTER
27

"My eleventh birthday is in exactly one week, July third. I am still in the special hospital for people with epilepsy. I hope I won't be here on my birthday, but Mom says I probably will. She says a lot of things that's aren't true, though, so I try not to listen to her. Molly says the hospital staff will throw me a little party and give us balloons and slices of cake. She asks my favorite kind. Vanilla cake and chocolate frosting. Hers is the opposite. David told me to make a birthday list, but the only things I want are a new diary, art supplies, and to get out of the hospital. Of course, I can't have that last thing. Mom is crystal-clear about that."

I decide I will celebrate Holly's birthday. After I'm sure Mommy and Brian are asleep, I sneak downstairs to look at the calendar. July third is sixteen days away.

If I should die before I wake, Holly...happy birthday.

I fall asleep with my fingers in the peanut butter jar.

The next morning, Mommy doesn't come to wake me up. Instead it's Brian who bangs the door open and yells "Get up, you little brat!" I lick the peanut butter off my finger.

"Where's Mommy?"

Brian rubs his forehead. "My God, kid, you're killing me. I just got up, and you expect me to give you every freaking detail of your mother's life? Fine, she in the bathroom puking."

"Why?" I ask.

Brian doesn't answer. He helps me into my wheelchair, only he's very rough about it. Probably on purpose. But Brian forgets to strap me in, and I don't remind him. He leaves the door open because he says he is going to make bacon. He wants the smell to drift upstairs and tease me. But Brian is stupid, because I don't even like bacon, and he knows it. I told him that last time he decided to play *his* Game. He goes around town collecting fast food menus, and at night, he comes into my room and reads them out loud to see if he can make me cry because he and Mommy would never buy me any extra food. Three nights ago, he read me a McDonald's menu. He practically shouted "BACON DOUBLE CHEESEBURGER" and licked his lips. After telling him I hated bacon, he started to describe the breakfast sausage. Normally, I don't like that either, but when you're hungry, everything starts to sound good. My stomach growled, and he heard it and laughed.

Now, here he is, thinking about bacon, and he didn't even remember to strap me in my wheelchair. I wait until he leaves and I hear sizzling in a pan downstairs. I may not like bacon, but it smells really good. I hear Mommy shouting from the bathroom "For God's *sake*, Brian, I'm in here vomiting and you think this is a good time to make *bacon?*"

Brian yells something back that I can't understand, and they start to argue. I know I'm safe to leave my room, but I can't make any noise. I slip like a snake out of my wheelchair, hoping I don't make a thump on the floor. I crawl out the door and stop at the top of the stairs. The third one from the top is creaky. I learned that the first night I snuck out of bed. I go down the stairs on my bottom, stopping every seven seconds to listen for angry footsteps or voices yelling "Where the hell do you think you're going?"

Where *am* I going? It only takes me a second to know. I'm going to find the picture of Holly that I saw in Mommy's blue album. I want that picture, and I'm going to get it. I'm not sure where Mommy keeps her blue album, but the best place to start looking is probably in her bedroom. I lay flat on my stomach and use my hands to scoot along the floor like an inchworm. My bones feel like stretched rubber bands, snapped forward and back, twisted and wrapped again and again until all that's left is a saggy, rubber snake. The only time I get to move is at night, when I'm sneaking around the house, but I don't even do that very much anymore because I'm too weak.

The door to Mommy and Brian's bedroom is open, so I slip right in. The first thing I notice is the mixture of smells. It's like a rose met a Big Mac and decided to share a room. A rose. That's actually what Mommy would be, if she had a plant name like me and Holly. Sweet-smelling when you first look at her, but reach a little deeper, and her lies pop up like thorns.

Mommy and Brian's clothes lie in piles around the bed. Brian has tracked mud all through the room with his big, expensive boots. I know they're expensive because the price tag is still on them. They rest like two big smelly boats next to the bed. All of Mommy's clothes are soft and silky and lacy, how I wish Mommy was herself. I don't like those *things* she buys, though. Some kind of fancy underwear that's more lace than cloth, and a thing I've heard of called a "bra" that looks like a barely-there bikini top. I've seen Mommy buy these pairs of underwear and "bras", and they're expensive. I wonder why you have to pay so much money for one tiny little piece of lace. Maybe it's rare lace from a faraway country that is so expensive, they can only use a little bit on the underwear and bras. I wish I had the kind of Mommy who would tell me these things.

There are bottles and bottles of perfume on the dresser, and pictures hanging on the walls, but none of me or Daddy. They're just pictures of Mommy and Brian, which makes me a little bit sad. Remembering why I am there, I sit in a pile of Mommy's silky clothes and think. Where would the blue album be? I hear a funny pounding, but it's just my heart, I think. Maybe Mommy and Brian can hear it. I squeeze my fist over my chest. Stop, heart, please stop. *Holly, please make my heart stop.*

Oh, no, Fern. You don't want that. Once your heart stops, you're like me: dead. You have to keep fighting.

A chill passes through my ribs. Did Holly just answer me in my own head? Am I crazy? **Look where you did before.**

I whip my head around, but no one is in the room. No one but me and my crazy, crazy head. Look where I did before? What does Holly mean? Where did I look before?

I remember back when I was in first grade, Mrs. Petchonka taught us how to solve a math problem. First, say what you know. Next, say what you need to know. Then say what might be true. Then you will know what *is* true. It sounded weird when she had said it, because I didn't think any of the math problems she gave us were hard at all, but here it makes perfect sense.

First, say what you know.

I am looking for a blue album with Holly's school picture. She told me to look where I did before.

Next, say what you need to know.

I need to know where the blue album is. I need to know if Holly is really talking to me. I need to know why Mommy is making me sick. I need to know so many things in this world, I can't even list them all.

Then say what might be true.

Holly might be telling me where the blue album is. But where? And why?

Then you will know what is true.

And suddenly, I do. Crawling to the bed, I finger the zipper on the mattress. Carefully, I unzip it, and stuffing peeks out. I stick my hand inside and feel something hard. Mommy hid her secret in the mattress, just like Holly! I pull out the blue album and wipe dust off the cover. It's plain, with a little gold trim on the edges. I let the spine fall open and the first thing I see is Holly, frowning up at me from that school picture. I lift the picture from the album and place it on the bed. I should leave now. I have the picture, and that's what I came for. But the blue album draws my eye. It's not a photo album of Mommy and Daddy's wedding at all! It's a diary! Mommy's handwriting fills the pages, slanted and loopy. She kept a diary, just like Holly! I scan the first page, dated all the way back to when Mommy must have been in high school. My breath sucks in, and I look quickly around to make sure I'm still not seen. This is a piece of Mommy in my hands. A *real* piece of her, not a lie. I trace the writing with my hand. Finding something like this is like finding a map right into Mommy's mind.

I flip through the pages, too excited to read anything, and a piece of paper falls out. It's a note, but not from Mommy. The handwriting is spiky and a little bit messy. And it's signed "Colin". Who's Colin? I look back to the photo of Holly.

Read it, Fern.

"Dearest Beth, I'm sorry I can't say this to you face-to-face. You'll probably hate me, and I can't blame you. But I'm not ready to be a father, Beth. We took things too quickly. I'm only seventeen, and you're only eighteen. I have my whole life ahead of me. You do too. You're a wonderful, beautiful girl who will make someone very happy someday. But I'm just not ready. I'm leaving, and I wish I could tell you where, but I just need to be out of this whole situation. Please don't try to contact me. I've changed my email and phone number. I just need to start over. I'm so sorry, Beth. If it weren't for the baby, I would stay. It is what it is, though. You'll always be my girl and hold a special place in my heart. Love, Colin."

I read the note once, twice, three times. I can't exactly understand what all of it means, but I'm pretty sure the baby is Holly. I read the last line again.

"You'll always be my girl and hold a special place in my heart."

I can't imagine someone thinking about Mommy while writing those words. I may not understand a mushy grown-up note, but I understand that Colin *loved* her. Like Daddy loved me. And he left her. Like Daddy left me. I feel an aching hole right in my chest where my heart is, and suddenly I'm crying so hard I can barely breathe. The ache gets bigger and bigger. I'm not making a sound, just letting tears stream down my face and drip onto Mommy silky clothes. I hug the blue album tight and pick up Holly's picture and the note from Colin. Then I sneak back to my room.

Mommy stops throwing up around noon. I have Holly's diary under the covers, and Mommy's diary open on my lap. The picture of Holly and the note from Colin are zipped into my mattress. So many secrets in one place. I'm surprised the room doesn't explode. Mommy's diary is fat and yellowed. The first entry says "January 1ˢᵗ, 1983", and the last one was just a few days ago. I don't know where to look. My excited fingers skip from one page to another until I'm sucking on three paper cuts. Finally, I let the diary fall open to the last page, the one that was written a few days ago. Below the date, there are just two words. "She knows." It doesn't take long to figure out the "she" Mommy's talking about is me. Questions begin to take shape in my head and beep their way in and out of my brain. I decide I will finish reading Holly's diary before I start Mommy's. Because my older sister always comes first.

I stop asking for library books, since I have plenty to read. Mommy throws up almost every morning, but she's always better by the afternoon. We still play The Game, and I'm getting better at it. I end up with six or even seven dollars to buy food. I always drop exactly seventy-five cents in the Cancer Kids donation can. It helps the sick feeling in my stomach go away faster after Mommy talks people into giving us money. And I help. Now I cover my eyes whenever I see a mirror, because I can't stand to look at the face of a liar.

As I roll my wheelchair along the aisles of 7-11 one morning, I notice packages of balloons, and I remember Holly's birthday, which is today. I count my money. After donating my seventy-five cents at the checkout and convincing Pink Lipstick Lady that Mommy is just in the car and I'm not wandering the store alone, I have six dollars left, and eighty cents. I divide the money into two piles on my lap. Two dollars for food, and three dollars and eighty cents for Holly. She's my older sister, so it's only fair that she gets a little bit more money. I can only afford small bag of pretzels and a single bottle of fruit punch with my two dollars, but Holly's birthday only comes once a year. With the three dollars and eighty cents, I buy two balloons, one red and one green, a tiny notebook that the label says is "travel-sized", a single birthday candle from a huge bin that says "Stock up- only ten cents each!", and the last carrot-cake cupcake from a glass display case of pastries. I stuff the birthday things in the bottom of the 7-11 bag so Mommy won't see. She's waiting for me outside.

When she sees my pretzels and fruit punch carefully covering the other things, she eyes me suspiciously.

"That's all you could afford?"

I shrug. "Nothing was on sale."

"Well", she says, "don't come asking for more food. You know the deal. If you blew all your money on expensive crap, that's your problem."

At home, Mommy shaves my head and leaves me in my room strapped to my wheelchair, because she says her back is absolutely killing her and she needs to take a hot bath.

"If I didn't have a kid", she says, "I could afford the spa."

Brian is at work, so I'm stuck here alone again. I hear the bathroom lock click and smell bath perfumes that float upstairs.

I pull out Holly's diary. Only twenty-nine pages left.

"Today is my birthday. I am still in the hospital. This morning, the nurses all came in and sang "Happy Birthday" to me, and Molly joined in. She gave me a friendship bracelet. The nurses gave me an extra hour of computer time in the computer room, which we visit once a day. I researched epilepsy, like I always do.

Mom got here late morning, carrying a big, wrapped box. The nurses and doctors said I was lucky to have such a caring mother who spoiled me, but later, when I was alone, I tore off the fancy ribbon, and the box was empty, except for a note, which said. "I've already spent enough on you with all your medical bills. But if anyone asks, I got you an expensive pair of slippers."

Molly and I ate cupcakes from the hospital kitchen with red sprinkles and a birthday candle stuck in mine. Everyone sang again, and Doctor Palmer said "Make a wish, but don't tell anyone!" I wished that I could be brave enough to tell everyone what Mom us doing to me. As they were clearing away our cupcake plates, I saw David standing in the doorway holding a bag. He kissed Mom on the cheek and came in to sit on my bed and wish me a happy birthday. Then he said "Sorry it's not wrapped", and gave me the bag. Inside was a brand-new journal and a set of colored pens. Exactly what I wanted. I hugged David tight and he winked at me and whispered "Liking those expensive new slippers?" I think David understands me a lot better than Mom does. I flipped open the journal and sniffed the very center, because I love the smell of new paper.

Mom kissed David again and said "You shouldn't have, Honey. Holly's spoiled enough as it is." David had to leave then to go to work, but Mom stayed, and after dinner, she said "Let me see the journal, Holly." Before I could say anything, she took it into another room. An hour later, she gave it back, with big black scribbles across every single page."

I sit in silence, feeling sorry for Holly.

Tonight, after Mommy puts me in bed, I will throw her the best birthday party ever, much better than the one she had in the hospital. I close my eyes and hear the sounds of my little world. My stomach growling. The bathtub draining, then Mommy's blow dryer. Brian coming home from work. Fried chicken sizzling in a pan. Wine corks being popped, and the clinking of glasses. I imagine Mommy and Brian touching their wine glasses together to make the thing that is called a "toast" or "cheers", when people touch their wine glasses together because they are happy about something. I nibble on a pretzel. It's going to be a long night. Mommy's acting a little bit funny when she puts me to bed. I don't think she's had too much wine like she did at the hotel, but her eyes keep flickering away from me and she seems the tiniest bit sad.

"What's wrong?" I ask.

She snaps back into herself again. "Nothing's wrong!"

But I'm not giving up. "Something's wrong. What?"

"*Nothing*, Fern. Mind your own business."

Mommy tucks and untucks my sheet so she doesn't have to look at me. I take a deep breath.

"Is it about Holly?"

Mommy freezes up like a statue.

"Is it?" I ask again.

When Mommy speaks, her voice shakes and rattles. "I'm not sure what you know, Fern, or how you even found out, but I'll tell you one thing. You will *never* mention Holly again. She's done. Over. I don't want to hear that name out of your mouth one more time, is that clear?"

Her voice gets stronger when she says "Is that clear?", like she's a normal Mommy just telling me to do something that all kids do. "I want you to pick up your room, Fern, is that clear?" "Your backpack should be in the closet, Fern, is that clear?"

Instead, I'm being told never to say my sister's name again.

"Is that clear?" Mommy says louder, like I didn't hear her the first time.

I remember how Holly said that Mommy scribbled black in her new journal and didn't even give her a birthday present and kept her in the hospital on the day she turned eleven. *Don't worry, Holly, I'm not giving up on you.*

"Why?" I ask. "Why can't I talk about Holly?"

I tilt my head and open my eyes really wide, so I'll look like what grown-ups call "innocent". Mommy doesn't fall for it, though.

"You can't", Mommy snaps. "You just can't."

I've done something, something big. I've made Mommy afraid. She knows I know about Holly, but she doesn't know how much. And I'm not about to tell her. For the first time, I have the power and she will listen to *me*. I cross my arms across my chest.

"Why can't I, Mommy? She's my sister." I feel my face getting red and mad. "It's not fair! She's my sister, and I want to know what happened to her!" I'm afraid Mommy is going to slap me, so I put my head down in my lap.

Mommy grabs my head and forces me up. "Listen here. If you say *anything* to anyone about Holly, I'll have to take drastic measures."

She lets go of my head, and for the first time, I'm glad I'm bald, because if I had hair, she'd be grabbing and pulling it.

"What's drastic measures?" I ask.

"Remember the note in the box, Fern? Do you still have it?"

I do. The box is sitting in the corner of my room. I put it there so I don't have to look at it. Mommy picks it up and unfolds the note inside. She takes a pen out of her pocket and pulls off the cap. When Mommy writes, she sticks the pen cap between her teeth and it hangs there like a cigarette. Brian says that the pen cap in her mouth is "sexy", but I think it's just gross. Who wants their pen cap covered in spit?

"We're going to make a change to this note."

In big but still cursive-neat letters, Mommy writes *"Also, if you mention Holly to me or anyone else, I will kill you."* Mommy thinks she's smart, but I am too now, after reading the section of Grammar & Spelling that talked about "literally" or "figuratively". "Literally" is real and "figuratively" is not. Mommy must be talking about *figuratively* killing me. Which means she wouldn't really do it. She never would. I feel stupid for not realizing it before. Had I really been afraid of my own Mommy?"

I smile with relief. I feel like I've solved a thousand-piece puzzle.

"You mean figuratively!" I tell Mommy. "You will figuratively kill me, right?"

Mommy looks startled, and then she sneers at me. *"Figuratively?* All right, Miss Dictionary, where'd you learn that one?"

"Not the dictionary, Mommy. Grammar & Spelling. The book you got me from the library."

"Damn it", Mommy mutters. "I didn't think you were actually going to *read* the whole thing. You're only seven."

She's avoiding something. I feel my heart start beating a little faster.

"Figuratively, Mommy, right?"

"Call me Mother, Fern. How many times do I have to remind you?"

Yes, definitely avoiding something.

"Mother, fine! I'll call you Mother! *Figuratively*, right, Mother?" The word echoes through my mind in a chant.

Figuratively, figuratively, figuratively.

"No, Fern. Literally."

I stare up at Mommy, who suddenly looks like a monster. She looks like the Mommy who hurt Holly and now she wants to hurt me.

"Literally", she repeats. Her voice sounds like the clunk of a rock.

"But you're my mommy", I whisper, terrified.

"That doesn't mean I have to love you", she says, before closing the door.

CHAPTER 28

I suppose I knew it all along, or at least I had little hints of it all my life, but now it's right out there in the open, like a thick fog filling the room. *She doesn't love me.* I don't bother to count the minutes like I usually do before I get out of bed. I just put my head down and cry. I don't know quite how long I lie face down on my pillow, but when I lift my head to look around, the pillow is soggy with tears. My face feels wet and sticky, and my stomach is growling.

You still have me, Fern.

Holly! It's still her birthday, at least I think it is. I don't have a clock, so I can't tell if it's after midnight or not. Mommy may have said I can't talk about Holly, but she can't hear me now. And she never said I couldn't throw a birthday party.

I crawl off my mattress and ruffle through the bag from 7-11, which I have hidden so Mommy wouldn't see it. I take out the balloons, notepad, cupcake, and candle. I take the sheet from my bed and lay it on the floor like a picnic blanket. That will be the tablecloth. I wrap the notebook in the 7-11 bag, since I don't have any wrapping paper. That's Holly's present. A new notebook, since Mommy scribbled all over hers. I carefully unwrap the cupcake and stick the candle in it. This will be the birthday cake. I wish I had some matches to light the candle. Daddy taught me not to be afraid of fire.

I pretend that Holly is sitting right next to me on the sheet.

"Happy birthday", I tell her. I hold out the notebook in the 7-11 bag. "This is for you. Since Mommy scribbled all over yours." I take the notebook out of the bag and open it. "See, I wrote in here "I love you, Holly. Happy Birthday". I'm going to zip the notebook into my mattress, where I found your diary. I got two balloons, one for me and one for you. You get the red one, because your favorite color is red and your name is Holly and holly berries are red. I get the green one because my favorite color is green and my name is Fern and ferns are green."

I put the red balloon between my lips and blow, but I'm too dizzy and tired and hungry to make the balloon puff up like it's supposed to. It hangs from my lips, saggy and limp. I feel like the balloon, deflated and tired.

Come on, Fern. You can do it.

But I can't, Holly. I'm not strong enough.

You *are* strong enough. Do you realize that with everything you've been through, you've never said 'can't'? Don't let a balloon be your first 'can't'."

Holly's right, of course, because older sisters are always right. It takes me half an hour to blow up both balloons, and when I'm done, I lie on my back, panting and red-faced. The balloons rest nearby, barely touching the ground, they are so light. But they don't have helium in them, so they can't fly away. I learned that in Astronomy For Beginners. To fly, balloons need helium. I wish I was full of helium right now, so I could just drift right up and crash through Brian's ceiling. I would lie on my back as the helium carried me up, up, up to Holly, who would be waiting for me on a silver-soft cloud. We would look at the stars together, the stars that don't twinkle, they just shine on and on, because they don't give up. Just like me.

"Time for cake!" I say, like Holly is here. I'm afraid to sing in case Mommy hears me, so I lean over the candle and hum "Happy Birthday". "Make a wish, Holly." What would she wish for? To be alive again?

I want to give my wish to you, Fern. Like you gave your wish to Leah. Make a wish, Fern. Anything you want.

I close my eyes and pretend the candle is burning bright in front of me.

"I wish I could be brave enough to stand up to Mommy." I open my eyes and blow.

After I eat the carrot cake cupcake, which is a little stale and has weird crunchy things in it, I clean up from the secret birthday party and fall asleep with the balloons blowing gently around the room.

Mommy throws up again the next morning, and the morning after that, and the morning after that. I get used to Brian coming into my room to wake me up. At least he's too dumb to notice the balloons, which still bounce around the room, even though the air has gone out of them a little bit. I am getting closer to the end of Holly's diary.

"I am not out of the hospital yet. I've been here for exactly a year. Mom tells me every day how expensive it is, and how she's wasting all her money on me, but I happen to know she's not, because she's always collecting donations to pay for my medical bills, so she's really getting the money from other people. I got so every big news today that makes the entire hospital room look brighter, like the sun just grew a thousand times. David came to visit me today, and he was carrying a little white box with a red bow. He sat down on my bed and said "I have to tell you something? You know how much I love your mother, right?" I told him I knew. David stared at my bedspread. "Ever notice how boring hospital beds are?" he asked.

"All the time", I said. "What did you come to tell me?"

"Well", he said. He looked out the window. "Isn't it a nice day, Holly?"

"It's *raining*", I told him. "What did you come to tell me?"

He smiled. "I guess there's no use beating around the bush. I love your mother a lot, Holly, and I want to be with her for the rest of my life."

My heart started pounding with excitement, and the monitor they had hooked up to me started beeping and a bunch of nurses came running into the room.

"She's okay!" David said. "She's just excited." I nodded. The nurses didn't say anything, but they didn't leave, either.

"You want to marry my mom?" I asked David.

He looked embarrassed and said "If...if it's okay with you."

I couldn't believe he was actually asking my permission, because Mom has never asked my permission on anything, let alone something as important as marrying someone. I told David that it was absolutely, one hundred percent okay with me, and I hugged him tight, and the nurses started clapping and one of them even started crying. Then I opened the box with the ribbon, and inside was a silver necklace with red holly berries that had green leaves. David said it was fir me, and he put it around my neck. It felt cold against my chest.

"Just a little something special for you", he said when I thanked him. "Like an engagement ring?" I asked, and he said yes, it was kind of like that.

"But you're not marrying *me*", I told him, and he laughed. That night, David asked Mom to marry him, and she said yes."

I really do think Daddy forgot about me. There are no letters and no phone calls, just memories. Does he even remember me? Maybe he has a new family with another little girl who loves him. I hope he doesn't leave *her*. Actually, I hope he does, even though that sounds mean. Then he can come back to me. I read the next five entries of Holly's diary, but they're all short and written kind of messy, like Holly was so excited she just couldn't form the letters quick enough. How long does it take to plan a wedding, anyway? On the last page I read before I fall asleep, I find the answer.

"Mom and David's wedding is in nine weeks! Nine weeks until I'll finally have a dad! In all the books I've read, the kid is really mad about their parent getting remarried, but I just don't understand that. Maybe it's because I never knew my real dad. Either way, I'm really glad Mom is marrying David. But there's a big problem. I'm still in the hospital. I'm meeting with a doctor tomorrow to talk about maybe going home, but I know that Mommy will do anything she can to make sure I stay. When Molly's asleep and no doctors are around, she's been forcing my mouth open and giving me little blue pills. She holds my nose and mouth closed until I swallow them. I told her I'd tell, but she said I'd be sorry, so I'm keeping quiet. But I always feel a little weird after I have the pills. Kind of tired and numb. And they make me drool, which is gross. I'm scared about this, but I'm excited about the wedding. My heart is beating fast all the time, so much that my heart monitor has recently been beeping more than usual. It's annoying, because whenever it beeps, everyone comes rushing in. I tell them I'm fine. But am I?"

I close the diary and hold it under my chest, so I can feel my heart pounding against the hard cover. That's a good question, Holly. *Am I okay?* How do I know? Is it too late? I press the book harder against my chest, so I feel like there's a little weight there, and a little cold, just like the necklace that my Daddy gave to Holly.

It's on August fourteenth that it happens. After I get my bag of groceries from 7-11, a box of granola bars, a jar of peanut butter, and a bottle of water, I sit in my wheelchair in my room and flip open Holly's diary. As I unwrap a granola bar and pick the chocolate chips out to save for later, I notice that there are only two pages left in the diary. Just two pages, and then...nothing. No trace of Holly. Will she still be real to me? Leaning over the diary, I squint at the handwriting on the second-to-last page.

"Great news! I'm going home in two days! I talked to the doctors, and they said I don't seem to be getting better, but I'm not getting worse. They said there was nothing more they could do for me and that I would probably be more comfortable at home. Of course, Mom threw a fit and insisted that they could be doing something more for me. She told them I was dying, but Doctor Briggs (who's my favorite), actually stood up and said "Mrs. Kyros, Holly is *not* dying. You need to trust our judgment about what's best for her!"

Mom yelled "Fine! I'm done with you people, anyway! You can't even help a sick kid!"

When I got back to my room, Doctor Malden told me to start getting my things ready, because I was going home on Wednesday. She said the doctors need two days to take out all my tubes and monitors and do a few last tests to make sure I'm safe. Molly cried when I told her I was leaving. I gave her a friendship bracelet I made out of red and blue string. It was kind of a tangled mess, but she tied it around her wrist and said she would never take it off. I feel like I've been stuck in a time warp, and I'm finally stepping out of it. Maybe living with David, things will be better."

I am scared to turn the page. One last glimpse into Holly's world, and I want a happy ending. Instead, there are only six words written on the page.

"Mom is pregnant."

And under that,

"Save yourself, baby."

I let the diary fall to the floor with a thump.

Mom is pregnant. Save yourself, baby.

A message to me. I was the baby. I was the one in Mommy's belly after Holly stopped writing. Mommy told me once that I was born ten weeks early.

"You were a c-section", she had said. "Made my life harder right from the start. They had to cut me open because of you." I was scared, so I had asked Daddy what Mommy meant.

"Sometimes when babies are born early, the mother has to get surgery", he said. "It happens a lot. But Mommy's okay, and you're okay now. It's no one's fault."

"Is it bad to be born ten weeks early?" I asked.

"Not bad", Daddy said, "but not common. It just means you were ready to face the world earlier. You were a fighter. You still are."

I wonder if he would still say I'm a fighter now. I pound my fists against my forehead. I was ready to face the world earlier, but not early enough. Not early enough to meet Holly. I came so close to having a big sister. We were only separated by Mommy's stupid belly.

Suddenly, I feel red-hot mad. I dig my fingernails into my palms, leaving half-moon marks. My fingernails are very long, because no one's ever trimmed them. If I want them cut, I have to do it with my teeth, which I don't like to do. I dig deeper, feeling my nails hard against my shaky hands. That's all I can do. I can't kick my legs or wave my arms, because my head is spinning and I'm so tired. I can't even be mad like a normal kid, which somehow makes me even madder. I jerk my head back and forth until my brains feel scrambled. I reach my hands out in claws for something, anything, to scratch, but my hands close around air and I open my mouth in a silent scream.

Yell, Fern.

I close my ears to block out Holly's voice, but she's still there.

I'm not going anywhere, Fern. You may be done with the diary, but I won't leave you. I promise.

But what now, Holly? What now?

You know what now. Don't stop reading.

But I don't have any other books!

Yes you do, Fern. Come on, think.

My eyes rest on my mattress.

That's it.

I pull the zipper, dig through the soft fluff, and open Mommy's diary.

CHAPTER 29

The next morning, after Mommy puts me in my wheelchair, I unwrap a granola bar, open my jar of peanut butter, and sit bent over Mommy's diary. Her handwriting is kind of hard to read. The first few pages are about Mommy's school. She went to Saint John's Prep and had a boyfriend named Colin. The same Colin who left her, but when Mommy wrote the beginning of her diary, she didn't know that yet. She said Colin was "dazzling, with sparkling brown eyes and sexy abs." I hate the word sexy. It's what Brian calls Mommy when she's in her work uniform, the one with the short skirt. And what's an ab? Is that like the short version of adverb? I learned about adverbs in the book Grammar & Spelling, but I've never heard them called "abs" before. And why would Colin have adverbs, anyway? Mommy's diary is very confusing.

She writes more about school and how she and Colin kissed with their tongues. Besides being absolutely disgusting, that doesn't even make sense, because people are supposed to kiss with their lips. Just the idea of my tongue in someone else's mouth makes me shiver. I bet it's like a worm in my throat, a slimy worm, the way my feeding tube feels. I don't skip any pages of the diary, though. I don't want to miss anything. I can read fast if something's boring, and Mommy's diary is very boring at the beginning. So I read fast. I dip my granola bar in the jar of peanut butter and take a bite.

Mommy's diary is boring for exactly thirteen more pages, and then there's a scribbled note in the middle of page 37.

"Dear Diary, I don't have time to write anymore. Colin and I are getting serious, like, really and truly serious. Writing's not my thing, anyway. This diary actually started out as a homework assignment for English class, and I just kept writing in it. But now I'm going to stop. Maybe I'll pick it up again someday, but probably not."

But she obviously *did* start writing again. One year later. That's what the next diary entry says. The page is stained and wrinkled a little, with tiny blotches, and when I look closer, I realize that the blotches are splatters of tears. Mommy was crying when she wrote this.

"He's gone. Just gone. He left a note. But he's gone. I haven't eaten or slept in two days. I've never loved another person like I've loved him. He wrote that he wouldn't have left if it weren't for the baby. I know it's selfish and immature, but right now I feel this hate inside me. Like, I want to hurt the baby, but I also want to keep it, because it's the only part of him I have left. I have his notes and gifts he gave me, but here's a chance for me to have a real, living part of him. That's why I'm not getting an abortion. Mom and Dad are furious. They said we'll talk later tonight, but I don't care what they have to say. Nothing in the world matters now that Colin is gone."

The next page was written three weeks later.

"Things just keeping going from bad to worse. A few days ago, Mom and Dad told me that they were "very disappointed with my life choices". "If you're old enough to get pregnant", they said, "you're old enough to take care of yourself." Then they told me that unless I got an abortion, they expected me to move out within a week. I screamed. I cried. I told them that the baby was the one thing Colin had left for me, and no way was I giving that up. "Fine." Dad said. "Would you like me to help you pack?" I screamed at him and ran to my room. This baby had damn well better be worth it."

Mommy told me that Grandma and Grandpa died before I was born, but reading Mommy's diary makes me wonder if they're really dead. Maybe she just doesn't want to ever talk about them. And honestly, I can't blame her. What they did was very mean. I always thought that families were supposed to take care of each other no matter what, but I guess not. Thinking about that makes tears slide down my face and land in the same spots that Mommy's tears landed years ago. I touch the pages. How could anyone be so mean?

"When I woke up this morning, there were boxes in my room. Dad had put them there after I fell asleep clutching Colin's note. When he saw I was awake, he and Mom came into my room. Mom looked like she hadn't slept. Her eyes were red and puffy. And she was holding a mug of coffee, which is quite unusual for her, since she claims to hate coffee.

"Do you know where you're going?" she asked.

"'Cause you're leaving today", Dad added.

I glared at them both. I actually had no idea where I was going to go, but I sure as hell wasn't staying with them. They didn't want me, anyway. And I didn't want them.

"I know where I'm going", I lied.

"Do you want me to drive you there?" Mom asked softly.

"Like hell I do!" I spat.

Her face crumpled, and she started sobbing. Dad put his arms around her and said "See what you've done now, Beth? Out! I don't care where you go! Just get out!" He slammed my door. I was too mad to cry. I stuffed a few pairs of clothes and my wallet into a suitcase. Mom was waiting for me at the bottom of the stairs, crying. She tried to hug me, but I pushed past her. As I saw Dad pop open a can of beer, the anger inside me suddenly exploded, like the fizz when he cracked open that can and let the beer stench seep into my pores.

Sitting on the counter was a ceramic heart I painted for Mom when I was six. It was pink, messy, and said "I love you in a thousand ways." I picked it up and smashed it.

"I love you in *zero* ways now!" I yelled.

Mom knelt by the broken, pieces, holding the chip that said "love" in one hand and the chip that said "you" in the other. I grabbed them from her and ground them under my foot.

"You little bitch!" Dad shouted. "Get out!"

I ran to the dining room and swept my hand across the crystal wineglass collection, the wineglasses that my parents had gotten for their wedding, birthdays, anniversaries, and even from me when I saved up my allowance for a month to buy them a nice gift. Glass shattered on the floor, like a thousand minuscule diamonds.

"Damn you! *Damn you!*" Dad yelled. "Get your ass outta this house before I call the cops!"

I ran for the front door, crunching over broken glass.

"Beth, wait!" Mom called. She pressed her hands against the glass of the window, and for a moment, I was reminded of myself at four years old, pressed against the glass, waiting for Dad to come home and swing me around in his arms. As I walked across the frozen ground, she started to cry, her breath fogging up the window. I raised my middle finger at her for one last goodbye."

I drop my granola bar in the jar of peanut butter and put my head between my knees. Mommy opens the door to find me like that, four hours later. "What's the matter with you?" she asks. "I lift my head. I know I've been crying, and she can tell.

"Nothing", I say.

"Good", she says. "Because I need to tell you something. Come into the bathroom, I'll tell you there. It's time to shave your head again."

As Mommy runs the razor over my head, making it shiny-smooth, she tells me "the deal", as she calls it, only it's not really a deal at all, since a deal has to have both people agreeing, and I haven't agreed to anything yet.

"We're leaving early tomorrow morning", she says. "To go see a special doctor at the hospital we went to before. This doctor will help us. He's going to give you some cancer tests."

"But I don't have cancer!" I say.

"Look, Fern." Mommy sounds tired, and I wonder if she got enough sleep last night. I didn't. "If you're really so stupid that you need this spelled out to you, fine. Do you feel dizzy?"

"Yes", I say, because I do.

"Headache?"

"Yes."

"Do you feel weak?"

"Yes." I am starting to get a little bit worried.

"And you've lost weight, haven't you?"

"I don't know", I say. "I don't have a scale."

"You don't need a scale to tell", says Mommy. "You're wasting away. And do you know what all of the things I just asked you mean?"

I shake my head, and the razor scrapes along my scalp and hurts. I decide I'll have to remember not to move my head anymore when there's a razor near it.

"The things I asked you- dizziness, headache, weakness, weight loss- those are all signs of cancer. And you have all those signs. You don't want to believe me, Fern. I know you don't. But the fact is, you're very sick. And you might die soon."

"No, I won't", I say. "I'm not dying."

"Can you prove that I'm wrong?" Mommy asks.

I keep quiet, because I *can't* prove that's she's wrong. And if I open my mouth, it might just spill out that I'm scared she's actually *right*.

"Mother knows best", Mommy says, shaving one last bit of hair off my head. Then she clutches her stomach and mutters "Oh, God", and throws up in the toilet and I run from the bathroom.

It feels weird to run, like my legs are brand-new. Like baby birds with wings that aren't quite ready yet. Maybe my legs aren't quite ready yet to be out of a wheelchair. But then, I don't think they ever needed to be in it in the first place. I don't run because I'm scared, though. I run because it's a chance to escape. Mommy will probably be in the bathroom for a long time. She throws up most mornings. So this means now I get the whole house to myself for a while. Brian left early to go work at The Happy Hour Casino. I sneak downstairs, making sure to skip the third step, because it still creaks. Now my legs feel tired, like they're rubber bands that have just been snapped.

I hear Mommy groaning upstairs as I make my way to Brian's computer and climb into the spinning chair. I type "cancer" into the search bar. About a million results come up, so I just click on the first one. And Mommy is right. Weakness, weight loss, aching. I don't see dizziness or headaches on the list, but from what I've learned so far, I don't want to know. I crawl back upstairs, listening for Mommy, who is still in the bathroom.

Tears slide down my face as I bury myself in my sheets. I'm dying. I'm really dying.

You're not.

Holly's voice rings clear through my head, so loud I can't help but listen.

Don't you think Mom researches this stuff too? She knows what cancer looks like. And if you really did have it, she'd have gotten you to the hospital already. Stop crying. Crying won't get you anywhere.

Holly's right. Still, there's a nagging little storm cloud in the back of my mind as I open Mommy's diary and start to read.

"I'm sitting on a smelly cot in a homeless shelter. I really don't have anywhere else to go. There's a woman with a baby sitting next to me, and the baby is screaming its freaking head off. My kid had better not do that, because let me tell you, I won't be even a fraction as patient as the woman next to me. She's been trying to quiet the little beast for half an hour. I wish I had some earplugs."

Mommy doesn't write as often as Holly does. The next page in her diary is a year after she last wrote.

"Oh my God, I can't stand it one more second. This stupid baby is driving me insane! I'm renting an apartment, and the neighbors already stopped by twice to bitch about all the crying. I told them if I had a good roll of duct tape, I'd use it. They didn't laugh. When the baby isn't crying, she glaring at me. I swear, she *glares* at me, like it's my fault she was born! I went into labor seven weeks early, and let me tell you, it was hell. By hour five, I didn't even care if the damn baby survived being a "preemie" or whatever stupid thing they call it. Her name is Holly. I didn't name her. The nurse that cleaned her did. She asked for a name for the birth certificate. "I don't give a crap", I said, so all the doctors and nurses started suggesting names like it was their freaking *job*, and one of them finally came up with Holly, after their pet ferret. I actually laughed at that, so the baby was named Holly. Holly looks a lot like Colin. I despise her."

I shudder as I close the diary. *No more today, Holly. Please. It's too awful.* I flip through the remaining pages. The next entry is two years later than the one before it. Before I can stop myself, my eyes are darting across the page.

"I don't know what the developmental milestones are for kids, and I don't care. But Holly is literally tearing the apartment to pieces. She spoke her first word before she started walking, but she does both now. From the single baby book I've read, I guess the first word is supposed to be a big thing. Holly's didn't even make any sense. We were out for a walk one day, and she just pointed at a plant and said "Fuh-ern." I mean, how random is that? All she does is sit on the floor and stare at the newspaper. Sometimes she scribbles all over it with pencils, but I don't care because I don't read it anyway. She's almost two now, and she's got these huge green eyes that look just like Colin's. I miss him so much. I thought having a kid would keep him a part of me, but it's really the opposite. It just reminds me how he left, and I'm stick taking care of a little piece of garbage I didn't even want in the first place. I cry every night when I go to bed, missing the feeling of his body next to mine."

My eyes are getting fuzzy from reading so much. But so many thoughts are swirling around in my head that they just can't settle down, no matter how many times I close my eyes and try to organize them into neat little boxes. Because I *need* all of this information. It's even more important than school learning because I'm finally, finally getting a tiny peek into Mommy's life. Her real life, not her Lie Life. And Holly...what happened? It's all one big question mark pounding at my brain.

"Holly is sick. Strep throat. You wouldn't believe how loud a little kid can cough. My neighbors (the ones who aren't assholes) heard her coughing and rang my doorbell. When I opened it, they were standing there, an old man, an old woman, a plate of cookies, and a very sexy-looking guy. His name was Tim, and after Mr. And Mrs. Fielding (his parents) left, he leaned on the doorframe and said "sick kid, huh?" I suddenly felt shy."

At this point, I start skimming the diary, because all it's talking about is how "sexy" Tim is and a bunch of other stuff I don't really understand and I don't think I even *want* to understand. But toward the next page, something catches my eye.

"I went to the grocery store with Holly, who was still coughing, and an old lady came up to me and cooed over Holly.

"She's sick", I said. "Contagious, probably. I wouldn't touch her if I were you."

But the old lady laughed and said she had grandkids of her own, so she was used to lots of toddler germs.

"What's she have?" she asked.

"I don't know. Strep throat?" I answered.

"Poor baby", the woman said. "You're a single mom, right?"

I said I was, and she asked me how I was getting along. I answered her honestly- not well. Right before she left for the cat food aisle, she slipped me a fifty dollar bill.

"Take her to the doctor", she said. "It's on me."

I really didn't know what to say, so I stood with my mouth gaping open. No way was I spending the day in the doctor's office with a bunch of screaming, sick kids, so I went to the nearest liquor store and got the nicest bottle of wine that fifty dollars could buy. I deserved it."

She deserved it? *She deserved it?*

My stomach feels funny. I don't want to know what's on the next page, but I read it anyway. Two years later.

"I was thinking to myself the other day: How did I let it get this far? After that day at the grocery store when Holly had strep throat and the old lady gave me some money, I felt...weird. Like this could really help me. So after Holly got better, I took her back to the store a week later and told everyone that she had a seizure, even though she hadn't. They grouped around me and patted my back and offered suggestions of what it might be- everything from diabetes to epilepsy. For some reason, the word epilepsy really latched onto me, and as a man was paying for my groceries ("It's on me- you've got enough to worry about", he said), I found myself telling him "Yes. Holly has epilepsy." The words sounded right on my tongue.

"They don't know how long she'll live", I said. "The seizures are destroying her brain."

I clapped my hand over my mouth. I didn't know why I had said that. But the man and the cashier both looked at me, and then at Holly, who was grabbing at the newspapers displayed by the candy. She could be screaming about wanting a chocolate bar, but instead she was leaning out of the cart so her fingers could touch the New York Times. I'll never understand that kid.

"Epilepsy?" the cashier asked. "Isn't that the disease that gives you those out of control seizures?"

"Yes", I whispered, tearful at the mess I was creating. "That's what she has."

Then I fled the store before they could ask me anything else.

Once I was outside, I breathed the November air deep into my chest. But I didn't feel *bad*. I felt...energized. I liked the attention. It made me feel like I was worth something, not just another single mother with a baby. If it makes me feel better, what's the harm?"

So this is how it started. I think about Holly reaching for those newspapers. Was she trying to read? Did Mommy know that? It seems like a mother should know it if her kid wants something to read. And why did Mommy say Holly had epilepsy? I sound the word out. Ep-Ih-Lep-See. Why did that word stick in Mommy's head? Then I realize it wasn't the word epilepsy that got Mommy all hyper like she had drunk a million cups of coffee. It was the word attention. A-Ten-Shun. *That* sounds more like the Mommy I know. The next entry of her diary is six months later. Holly would have been three.

"It was Holly's third birthday yesterday. I feel slightly guilty, since we spent it in the doctor's office. But the kid won't know the difference. If I remember, I'll pick up a treat for her on the way home. I try not to let myself love Holly, because to me, she is Colin, and Colin is gone. But when she looks at me with those big brown eyes and says "Mom, I want pineapple juice, please", I sometimes feel a little twinge of something inside me, something I don't want to feel. So I tell her "Get it yourself, Holly. You know where it is", and she does. I keep little cans of pineapple juice on the bottom shelf of the refrigerator, even though I can't stand the stuff. It's too sweet. But Holly loves it. So when I finally think I've gotten rid of her for a while, she'll come up to me, grasping a can of juice in both hands, and says "Open, please." I don't know much about how kids learn to talk, but I think there's something different about Holly. She speaks almost like a little adult. Very serious. I've never seen her laugh. She always says "please", and "thank you". Everyone tells me how well-mannered she is, but I think it's just confusing.

So anyway, we're at the doctor's office so Holly can get some tests to see if she has epilepsy. *I* know she doesn't have the symptoms I'm describing to the doctor. But he doesn't know that. They prick her with needles and stick loud machines right next to her and prod her and stick her with wires. And she doesn't even blink.

"She's so brave", the doctor said to me. I nodded, grateful that she wasn't crying and trying to resist the tests. We're in the waiting room now, and I'm frantically searching my phone for the symptoms of epilepsy and how doctors test for it. Because Holly has epilepsy. Or, at least, everyone will *think* she does."

I feel my eyelids pressing down. If they could talk, they'd be begging to go to sleep. I close my eyes.

CHAPTER
30

"She has it! She has it!"

That's what I hear five minutes later. Mommy is screaming. "She has it! Please believe me! She has epilepsy! The test results are *right there*! Do more tests if you have to, but I'm not leaving until we get a clear diagnosis!"

I step out of bed, feeling light and floaty. I am in a room that's all red, no other color. It makes me think of blood. I need to get out of here, but the screaming is right outside the door, which is cracked open. I can't stand this blood-cranberry juice-sick-blood room for one more second. I stop at the door and look out. Mommy is in the hallway, screaming to nothing. I am scared.

"You're okay", says a voice next to me.

I whirl around, grabbing for my feeding tube pole so it doesn't fall over like it does all the time. But I don't have a feeding tube pole anymore. It's just gone. And I don't feel the scratchy tube in my throat, either.

"You're okay", the voice says again.

Holly. She is standing next to me.

"Look", she says pointing.

The room around me has melted away, and Holly and I are standing in a field. Blue skies, green grass. Not a speck of red anywhere. The field is so big I can't see anything beyond it but the point where the green blades of grass blur against the blueness of the sky and the whiteness of the clouds. I follow Holly's finger where she is pointing to a rushing steam. "Pineapple juice river", Holly says.

"It looks like water", I tell her.

"It does", she agrees. "But when you dip your hands in it and drink, it becomes anything you want. It's always pineapple juice for me, because that's my favorite."

"I know", I say. "Mommy used to buy cans of it to keep on the bottom shelf of the refrigerator."

Her green eyes squint in the sunlight.

"How do you know that?"

"Mommy's diary. She wrote about you."

Holly smiles, but she doesn't say anything. Cupping her hands, she kneels by the stream and drinks.

"Delicious", she says, wiping her mouth with the back of her hand. "Even better than the kind Mom used to buy."

I join her and she shows me how to cup my hands so water won't leak out.

"But it's not water", she warns me. "Remember that."

"Then what is it?"

"Whatever you want. Drink, Fern."

So I dip my hands into the cool water, and when I drink the liquid from the stream, it tastes exactly like grape juice.

As I lean over the stream, the sun warms my back. I haven't felt sun for a long time.

"Is this Heaven?" I ask Holly.

She shakes her head.

"Not yet."

"Not yet? What do you mean, not yet?"

I turn around, expecting to find Holly there, but all I see is the never-ending field.

"Holly!" I yell. "Come back! What do you mean? Please tell me what you mean!"

I sink to my knees as the sky turns dark. I don't feel the sun on my back anymore. Far, far off into the distance, I hear screaming. Fat raindrops land on my back, soaking through my clothes.

No, Holly, you were right. This certainly isn't Heaven.

I run. I run towards the screaming, but the closer I get, the farther away it sounds. I don't get tired as I run, but I wish did, because then it would give me a reason to stop. I could keep going forever, and who knows if I'd ever get anywhere? I let myself fall to the ground, expecting to land on the soft, billowy green grass that grew almost as tall as my waist just a few minutes ago. Instead, I hear a hard crunch as I land on crabgrass. The sky isn't blue anymore. Was it ever, really? Or was it like that stream, just as blue as I ever wanted it? I taste a raindrop on my tongue, and it is salty. Tears. It is raining tears. In fact, tears are what I taste when I wake up, still shivering from the chill of those raindrops pelting my back. But I'm not wet.

I lie in bed, feeling nothing at all, which I suppose is okay, after feeling so many things in my dream.

My feeding tube is back, of course, hurting my throat. And I'm sure if I got up and ran right now, I'd feel tired. Not Heaven, Holly. But for a few minutes, almost. I don't know how long I lie there, but Mommy comes to get me when it's still dark out. I pretend to be asleep, and she pulls me out of bed by my arm.

"Get up."

I stand, knees shaky. Mommy wrinkles her nose. "Your clothes stink." I don't point out that my clothes aren't clean because she didn't wash them.

"Here, put these on", Mommy says. "They came with the donations. You've got to make a good impression today. Show them I take good care of you." She tosses me a pair of overalls and a light blue shirt.

"Thank you", I say.

"You don't get to keep them", Mommy replies.

She closes the door. The overalls feel right on my body, not weird like a hospital gown or a dress. But what I like best about them is the two big pockets. Mommy's diary fits in one, and Holly's diary fits in the other. I sit in my wheelchair and wait with Pox. When Mommy comes back to get me, she looks sick.

"Did you throw up?" I ask.

She scowls. "Yes."

"Is Brian coming?"

"No. They've been getting on his case at The Happy Hour Casino about not showing up for work. So he had to go today."

I smile.

"Wipe that grin off your face", Mommy snaps. "You and I have a bit of talking to do about your behavior. You're tired. You're dizzy. You've lost weight. You feel achy and weak. That's true, right?"

I nod.

"So that's what you're going to tell the doctor. But you're also going to tell him that you have no appetite, got it?"

"But that isn't true", I say. "That would be lying. And it's not good to lie."

"Is it better to be killed?" Mommy asks. "Literally. Not figuratively."

I shake my head. "This isn't fair."

"It's not about what's fair", Mommy snaps. "I'm the adult, and you're the child. You do what I say. Now, are you going to cooperate?"

"Yes", I say miserably.

"Good." Mommy wheels me out to the car, but she's not strong enough to lift my wheelchair.

"I could get out", I say, "and just sit in the backseat. The wheelchair folds up. When I was with Leah, her mommy folded up two wheelchairs and put them in the trunk."

Mommy is out of breath. She is panting, which is not like her, because Mommy normally doesn't do anything that might lead to big, gasping breaths because she says they are "very unattractive".

"I guess there's no other way", she says. "Can you stand up?"

"I'm okay", I say, wiggling out of her grasp. I don't tell her I've been sneaking out of bed most nights and stretching my legs, so I can walk just fine. But she expects me to lean on her and limp to the car, so that's what I do. I sit in the backseat, positioned behind Mommy so that she can't see me. Mommy sits in the front. Her car is a lot different than Brian's. There's not a speck of dirt or dust anywhere. I want to put my feet up on the seat so I'm more comfortable, but I'm afraid to do that. There are no wrappers or magazines or paper scattered on the floor. Mommy's car smells, too. Not greasy, like Brian's car, but like a mixture of Floral Tropics air freshened and that leathery, new-car smell, even though she's had her car for as long as I can remember. I guess she keeps her car so clean, the new-car smell never wore out. I don't like that smell. It makes me feel sick to my stomach.

As we drive off, Mommy turns on the radio, which has a silver button so shiny I can see myself in it. I bet Mommy polishes that button every day, so there's never fingerprints on it. She turns on the Pop Radio, and a horrible, horrible sound fills the car. It sounds like whining at high volume, and I wonder how Mommy can like it, because she's always telling *me* not to whine. The voice that's singing doesn't even sound like a human. And the words are very, very inappropriate. I try not to listen, which I am very good at, because I do it all the time when Mommy yells at me or Brian teases me.

Mommy clicks open a water bottle, and a strong alcohol smell mixes with the air freshener and new-car smell. I think it's gin or wine, but I'm not sure. Mommy told me once that she mostly drinks gin, because beer and scotch are for slobs. Brian drinks a lot of beer and scotch. I wonder if Mommy thinks he's a slob.

After a while, I decide the noise from the radio isn't so bad, because Mommy is singing along, so she doesn't notice me reach into my huge pocket and pull out her diary.

"I ordered Holly a wheelchair online.

"I'm spending a lot of money on you", I told her. "So you'd better be good."

"Okay, Mom", she replied, bowing her head. She's looking more and more like Colin.

She's five now, old enough to go to kindergarten. But I called up the public school in our town and told them that I would be homeschooling Holly, because she was very sick. They said they understood, and promised to send over some kindergarten-level materials for her. I couldn't believe it was that easy, but then again, all of my life has been hard. Don't I deserve a break?"

I glare at the back of Mommy's seat headrest. She's gotten all the breaks in the world. And it's her choice. She didn't have to do this to Holly. But when I read the next page, it says,

"Sometimes I feel a little nagging inside me, wondering why I doing this. Like, maybe it's wrong. I know in a way that it is, but I can't stop doing it. It's like smoking. It just feels good. Today, a package came in the mail from Tim, the hot grandson of Mr. and Mrs. Fielding. I didn't know he still remembered me. But he did, because of Holly. The package included a note that said, "I hope your little girl is feeling better. My grandparents told me how sick she was. I hope you won't be offended by this, but I just received a bonus from work and wanted to pay for a bit of Holly's medical treatments. My grandparents told me how hard you work to take care of her, and I thought I could just help out a little bit. Sincerely, Tim."

Inside the package was a stuffed tiger and a check for one thousand, five hundred dollars. I tossed the tiger to Holly and clutched the check. One thousand, five hundred dollars! I could do *anything* with one thousand, five hundred dollars! That evening, I wrote Tim a long letter, thanking him for the check. I told him that it would be well spent. And it will be. Just not on Holly."

I want to find out what Mommy spent the money on, but the date at the top of the next page is six months later.

"I've been doing countless hours of research. And I've decided to say that Holly has epilepsy. She doesn't really, but if I teach her to act the right way and keep her in a wheelchair, people will believe me. People are so stupid. They see a sick kid and just seem to melt. I've called everyone who's sent Holly money and gifts and told them about the epilepsy. With each phone call I made, I got more and more excited, until I was breathless when I announced the news, pretending to sniffle. I can't explain it, but I feel calmer now. In control."

Mommy swerves into a gas station, making my stomach leap.

"Are we almost there?" I ask.

"No", Mommy growls. "Not even halfway. The damn traffic is backed up about two miles."

"Do we need gas? Is that why we stopped?"

Mommy glares at me.

"Just stay here."

She goes into the convenience store. Maybe she's getting me some food. I haven't been allowed to eat today because Mommy said she didn't want me throwing up in her car if I got carsick. Trying to ignore my stomach, I take Mommy's diary out from my overalls. I hid it in my pocket when Mommy stopped the car.

"Holly is six now. And she's started asking questions about her illness. I tell her that she's very sick so she can't go to school and she needs to stay in her wheelchair and see doctors. But Holly gets this look on her face like she doesn't believe me. She looks at me with those huge eyes and blinks a lot, and it makes me uneasy, because I think she's smarter than I realize.

She's a mysterious little girl. She doesn't like people touching her, unless she approaches them first. Sometimes I find her staring at nothing, and sometimes she'll just say something so strange, I wonder if she's really a six year old. The other day, I was setting up her wheelchair, and she said "We are the new versions of old ideas." I didn't even bother to ask her what she meant.

Holly has started wanting books. She takes my People, Vogue, and National Enquirer magazines and studies them. I thought she just liked looking at the pictures, but then she started asking questions about the words in the magazines. Like, "Why are these people famous? Why is it called the red carpet? Is red a special color for movie stars? Why is that woman wearing such a short dress? Why is that woman naked? Why do those men never have shirts on? Why did Brad and Angelina have to announce their divorce to everyone? Why did they get married if they didn't like each other anyway? Why would I want to have a flat stomach? Why are these women happy because they lost weight?" When she asked, "Why is it called Play*boy* if there are no boys in the magazine? There's just naked girls", I realized I had better find her something else to read, and fast. The last thing I needed was for her to start asking those questions in the wrong place.

So tomorrow, I'm taking her to the library on the way back from the doctor's office. I asked them to run some tests on her. To make her tired, I stopped at the drugstore and bought children's Benadryl. I'm going to tell her it's candy."

I glance toward the convenience store where Mommy went in. I don't see her. I rub my eyes and turn the page, which Mommy wrote just a day later.

CHAPTER
31

"Holly refused to take the Benadryl.

"That's medicine", she said. "Not candy."

So for lunch, I made her a smoothie and slipped the Benadryl in. She drank the entire thing, and by the time we got to the doctor's office, she was asleep. I told them Holly's story, but not her real one. Her fake-sick story. I actually have it hidden in a document on my computer labelled "Medical", where I keep documents of questions doctors might ask, symptoms of epilepsy, lists of hospitals, and more. I am well prepared.

They took Holly into an examining room and tried to wake her up.

"She always tired", I said. "That's one of the things that worries me." Holly wouldn't wake up, but they decided it was just better to do the tests while she was asleep, because then she wouldn't throw a fit.

The doctor was absolutely sexy, I swear. While he was testing Holly's blood pressure, I touched his arm like it was an accident, and I got this tingly feeling all through my veins, like an electric surge. When he sat me down and told me that nothing seemed to be wrong, I asked him question after question. Was he *sure*? Would he test for this disease quickly? Or that one?

"She's very sick", I told him. We had been in the office for two hours. He rubbed his forehead, which somehow made him look even sexier.

"Tell me her symptoms again."

I had the list floating around in my brain, inspired by my research on Google.

"Fever every night, aches, spasms, difficulty breathing, and exhaustion", I recited.

"How high?" he asked about the fever.

I racked my brain for a suitable number, not low, but not ridiculously high. It had to be believable.

"Sometimes up to 102 degrees", I said.

"Hmmm. Describe these 'spasms'", he replied.

"Well...they're kind of like seizures, I guess, but I can't be sure since no one will give us a definite diagnosis. But they're very scary. They happen at least twice a day. She just goes all rigid, or sometimes limp. Lots of drooling. I do what I should, you know. Turn her over so she won't choke. Don't try to touch her. Just let it run its course."

"Mmm-hmmm. And how do you know to do all this? Has another doctor recommended it?"

Shit. I was completely focused on convincing him I took good care of Holly that I hadn't even considered that he might ask me how I knew it all. Of course, I had looked it up online.

"We've been to loads of other doctors that told me those things", I said. "But none of them could really help us. That's why we came to you. You *will* help us, won't you?"

I gave him a simpering smile.

"Won't you?"

"I'll try", he said.

"Holly's test results will be available next week", he said. "Come back then."

Holly woke up a few hours later, but she was sort of out of it for a while. She spent hours staring at the ceiling, muttering senseless phrases like "Get me out onto a silver cloud", and "Don't sleep with the shadow nearby." I watched her for a while, trying not to worry. But I did.

I had essentially drugged her, and here I was, leaning over her, perhaps seeing her for the first time. She looked so tiny and pale lying there. Her lips fluttered as more bizarre words leaked from her mouth, and I was reminded if the first time Colin and I kissed. God, she looked like him.

A sudden bout of rage filled me, and I wanted to hurt her. Like, really and truly hurt her. I ran to the bathroom and splashed cold water on my face. Why would I want to hurt my own child? Why did I hate her? I answered the question while looking at my bloodshot eyes in the mirror.

Because she is like Colin, thoughtful, pensive, intelligent, and serious. And Colin left me. I want no part of him. And Holly is part of him. Therefore, I want no part of her. It was a clear, concise reason, like the math proofs I did in tenth grade geometry. I was always good at math, especially those proofs. There was a right, and there was a wrong. No in-between. You either had the answer, or you didn't. Now, as I tell people that Holly has epilepsy, I think to myself: am I on the right side of that proof? Or worse, am I in-between?"

I carefully fold over the corner of the page and think for a while. Am I a part of Daddy? Is that why Mommy doesn't like me?

I see Mommy coming out of the store, carrying a big bag. She gets back into the car and drives, without saying a word to me or even looking in the backseat to make sure I'm still there. I sigh loudly, just to let her know I'm hungry.

"No", she says, like she's reading my mind. She tears open a bag of pretzels. "No, you can't have any."

I open the diary again. My eyes are blurry, but there's nothing else to do. Mommy doesn't write about her feelings anymore or what she's thinking. She just writes about how she's making Holly sick. Each diary page has a chart drawn on it, with categories. "Doctors visited", "symptoms", "Holly's reaction" "doctor's advice", and "money made". The first page with the chart looks like this:

Doctors Visited	Symptoms	Holly's Reaction	Doctor's Advice	Money Made
Dr. Benedict at Salem Children's Hospital	I slipped Holly a few sleeping pills so she would be tired, I also told Dr. Benedict that Holly had a seizure. Looked up seizures in order to describe one accurately	She's been asking for books, so I've had someone at the library deliver them to her. After telling them about her epilepsy, they were happy to do it. The library even started a collection of money for Holly's treatment	Dr. Benedict recommended us to a specialist in Springfield for more tests	$152 dollars (from the library collection)

Library collection? Words start to spin through my head as I turn the pages, skimming each one. Doctor. Hurt. Money. Earn. Sick. Epilepsy. Medicine. Holly. Holly. Holly.

I must be moaning, because Mommy turns around and snaps "What's wrong with you?" I quickly hide the diary.

"Nothing", I say. "Nothing at all."

"Good. Keep it that way." She curses at the car in front of us, slamming her palm on the horn. A loud noise fills the car, and she sticks up her middle finger at the woman who comes to the window and says "What the hell are you doing?"

I open the dirt and flip past the pages with the charts on them, because I don't want any more words circling through my head right now. I am going so fast, my eyes almost miss the note scribbled on one of the pages.

"I met someone today. This is it."

This is it.

My fingers curl around the next page, but I am afraid to turn it.

This is it.

Why are you scared, Fern? It's just a diary. It can't hurt you. I was the one who got the hurt from that diary. It's over now. Turn the page, there's something I want you to see.

"His name is David. I was at the doctor's office with Holly yesterday for a brain scan (they still say nothing's wrong, but I tell them they aren't trying hard enough). He was there to get his ankle looked at. He had fractured it on the ice the day before. We struck up a conversation. I told him all about Holly, making sure to emphasize how sick she was. And it worked. I told him how Holly needs to be in a special hospital (I've admitted her to The Epilepsy Center in Whipple), and the only times she's allowed out are for her other medical appointments. I told him she's not getting any better.

"I'm sorry", he said. "That must be hard."

His name was David and he smelled like aftershave. I was glad I had worn my Irresistible Iris perfume. I always wear it to the doctor's office. It makes them pay more attention. I told David about Holly's seizures.

"I try to do everything right", I said. "But it still seems like I'm failing. I just can't win!"

I had taught myself to cry years ago, when I was in ninth grade and wanted to make some asshole feel guilty about not going to the spring dance with me. It's really all in the eyes. You've got to open them wide, and then narrow them so they start producing tears. Obviously, I had researched this.

So I started crying for David, and he put his arm around me, right there in the office. Dr. Hershey came out of the examining room to report the results of Holly's brain scan, but I brushed him off. I let David hold me for a long time, and I called him that very night."

"We'll be there soon", Mommy says. "Remember what I told you."

"Yes", I say. "I will." I don't bother to look up from the diary.

"What's got you so entranced back there?" Mommy asks.

"Oh...I'm carsick", I say, trying to sound weak.

It isn't hard, because my legs are shaking so much from hunger I'm surprised I don't pop right out of the seat. I guess this is why seat belts were invented.

"Hmmm..." Mommy mutters. "I'm glad I didn't let you have anything to eat."

I bet she was just looking for a reason to say that.

I cup my hand over my mouth and pretend to sneeze. As I make the "ah-choo" noise, I turn the page of the diary so Mommy won't hear, because she's listening now, I can tell.

"David is the one. I just know it. He called and asked if I wanted to go out to dinner tonight. I made a big show of acting like I couldn't leave Holly, who is still at The Epilepsy Center.

"How about this?" he said. "You and I will go out for an early dinner and get takeout for Holly. Then we'll both go visit her in the hospital. You haven't introduced me to her yet."

So that's what we did. Holly seemed to really like David. I saw that spark in her brown eyes that had been lost when I started making her sick. That little spark made me angry. I wanted to extinguish it."

I'm not sure what the word "extinguish" means. It kind of sounds like "distinguished", which I know means fancy, because Mommy used the word to describe Brian's habit of eating an entire sausage pizza. "He has very distinguished eating habits", she said. I told that Brian and his sausage pizza were disgusting, and Brian waved a slice in front of me and said "But at least I can *have* pizza, kid." I want to ask Mommy what the word "extinguished" means, but if I do, she'll ask why. And I can't tell her why.

So I turn the page of the diary, because maybe the answer is somewhere there. But the pages are full of mushy details about David, lots of kissing and dinners and dates. I look for Holly's name on the pages, but I don't see it. I look closer, like maybe it's hidden somewhere like a secret code, but I can't find anything. Mommy wouldn't be the type of person to invent a secret code anyway. I am getting bored here in the backseat. My head hurts from reading so much.

"Almost there?" I ask.

"Not quite", Mommy says. "We're behind some idiot who's doing sixty-five on a highway. What do you expect?"

I don't answer that because I don't know what "sixty-five on a highway" means, so I guess I *don't* know what to expect.

"Which hospital are we going to?" I say.

"Same one as before", Mommy answers.

"I didn't remember taking this long", I tell her.

"It's a different branch, stupid", she answers.

"What's a different branch?"

"It means it's the same hospital, only in a different place." The hope I've been holding tight in my chest bursts.

"So Raymond won't be there?" I ask, trying not to let Mommy hear how disappointed I am.

Mommy sighs, slowing the car down.

"Raymond works at multiple locations. Including this one. But listen, Fern. I don't want you talking to Raymond if you see him. I don't want you having *anything* to do with him. Got that?"

"Why?" I ask. "I thought you liked Raymond."

Mommy cringes. "He's a loser", she says. "A good-for-nothing loser. I don't want you hanging around anyone like that."

"But *why*?"

"For God's sake, Fern, can't you see I'm just trying to protect you?"

But she's not trying to protect me, and she knows it. Besides, I like Raymond. The car stops in front of a huge brick building. Mommy unfold my wheelchair and lifts me into it. She straps my arms and legs.

"Don't", I tell her.

She looks at me. "What?"

"I don't want those straps. I want to be able to move."

She lets out a pitch of laughter, like a teakettle. "Too bad!"

I decide not to say anything else, because it don't think this is a good time to make Mommy mad. I'm glad that at least in my pockets, I have Mommy's diary and Holly's diary. And I'm holding Pox as tight as I can.

"Let go of that stupid rabbit and hang onto your feeding tube pole", Mommy says.

I move Pox to the other side of me and grasp the cold metal pole. But the road up to the hospital is very bumpy, so the feeding tube pole almost goes skittering away from me like a water bug. The hospital doors open for us, which it think is very cool.

When I wasn't in a wheelchair, I liked holding doors for people, especially women because they would pat me on the head. I could even tell which of them were mothers, because mothers have that special touch to their hands that's just a little bit warmer than other people's hands. Only good mothers have that, though. Mommy doesn't.

I used to savor those pats on the head or sometimes touches on the shoulder like they were the last, best piece of a Halloween candy.

About a month ago, I decided I really wanted the feeling of those warm pats again, so when Mommy took me out to the store to talk to people so they would feel sorry for me, I tried to tug open the door for an old lady, but my wheelchair spun around and I ended up crashing into a display of oranges. Mommy grabbed me by the neck and said in so very low voice, so other people couldn't hear, "Don't do that, you clumsy little idiot. You'll break something."

I told her that you can't break oranges. She grabbed my neck again and whispered "Shut up".

Then because people were staring, she said really loudly, "Oh, Fern, sweetie, it's okay! I know you didn't mean to! I'm sorry, everyone. It was just a little seizure. They've been happening at least ten times a day, so...I get used to them."

The store manager rushed to clean up the mess. "I'm so sorry", he told Mommy. "That must be very difficult." Then he offered me an orange, and I took it, even though Mommy was shaking her head at me. I wasn't sure how to peel it because my hands were so shaky and weak. So I just bit into the orange like it was an apple, and I ate the whole thing, even though the peel was bitter.

As I am thinking about oranges, I start to smell them for some reason, which is weird because we are at the front desk of the hospital. Then I realize the orange smell is coming from the lady behind the desk, who Mommy is talking to.

"We're here for the cancer tests", Mommy is saying. "Yes. Fern Kyros."

Orange Lady smiles and says "Right in here, ma'am. The waiting room off to your right. The doctors will be with you shortly."

Mommy wheels me into the waiting room, which is very cold, like they've hit the air conditioning on as high as it will go. The whole room smells like hand sanitizer. There are only two other people in the room, a man and a little boy. The man is sitting on one of the metal chairs with his head in his hands. The little boy is lying down with his jacket over him. The whole side of his face is bruised up and bloody. I see Mommy twitch back a little bit because she thinks the boy looks disgusting. But that doesn't stop her from walking up to the man.

Mommy has this funny way of walking when there are men around. She twists her hips and holds her fingers out at her sides and tosses her hair. I watch her from across the waiting room. She sits down next to the man with his head in his hands. She says something, but I can't hear what. Then she sits down and puts her arm around the man. He looks up, and I see that his face is stained with tears, which surprises me because I thought men never cried.

301

But then I remember the day that Daddy told me he was leaving. I was in my room, listening at the vent when he came in.

"Were you eavesdropping?" he asked.

"Yes", I said.

I didn't think there was any point in lying, since the only thing I could really be doing was eavesdropping if I was lying on the floor with my ear up to the vent.

"So you already know." Daddy's voice sounded thick like syrup. "I'll tell you anyway, because it's important."

"Tell me what? What's important?" I asked, because I actually hadn't heard any information through the vent. Just yelling and bad, hurting words, most of them from Mommy.

Daddy sat down on my bed. It sank a little bit lower to the floor. I pulled my knees up to my chest and hugged them tight.

"Mommy and I have been having some problems", Daddy began.

"I know that", I said. "You fight all the time. I hear."

"I know you do", Daddy said. "But this is about a little bit more than fighting all the time. See, when people fight, they usually forgive each other and move on. But Mommy and I have fought so much, so many times, that we can't really forgive each other anymore."

I covered my ears and rocked back and forth, because I knew he was about to tell me something I didn't want to hear. Daddy gently took my hands off my ears and held them tight in his big, rough palms.

"Fern, Mommy and I are getting a divorce."

He watched my eyes to see if I was going to cry, but I didn't.

"What's a divorce?" I asked.

"It means that Mommy and I won't be living together anymore", Daddy said.

"Can I live with you?" I asked.

Daddy hugged me.

"Fern, honey, Mommy and I decided it's better for you to live with her."

I started to cry then, because I didn't even want to think about Daddy being gone and just living with Mommy.

"No", I said.

"I know." Daddy brushed the hair off my forehead. "I know."

"I can't", I cried, burrowing into his shirt.

"You can", Daddy said. "I know it's hard, but things will really be better this way."

His voice cracked like the dishes that Mommy threw to the floor when she was mad. I looked up and saw a tear rolling down his cheek. He wiped it away with his shirtsleeve.

"You were crying", I said.

"Yes", he sighed. "Because I'm very sad."

"Me too", I said. "I want to be alone now, please."

"Okay. Is there anything I can get you?" Daddy asked.

"No." I buried my head under my sheets and stroked Pox's ear.

"You want a grape Popsicle?" Daddy asked. "I could have one too."

"No more grape Popsicles", I told him, and he left me alone after that, but I heard him go to his room and cry, like heavy stones hitting the floor and smashing into my whole world.

It was hot and stuffy under the covers. I thought about all the "no mores" that were coming. No more trips to the park. No more frosting in my hair on my birthday. No more Stephen King. No more Sandalwood Summers aftershave. No more superheroes. No more, no more, no more.

CHAPTER
32

I look at the man with the tear stains on his cheeks. I wonder if the boy lying down is his son. The boy's eyes are puffed up and almost swollen shut. Mommy is talking to the man, but I can't hear what they're saying. She has her back to me. Quietly, very quietly, I reach into my pocket and pull out Mommy's diary.

The page I open to, after skipping all the gross kissing and dating parts, is written six months later than the page before it. This is kind of confusing.

"Today, David asked me to marry him. We were at dinner, and right there in the middle of the restaurant, he got down on one knee and opened a pretty little box with a ring inside it. The ring had a ruby on top.

"A precious gemstone", David said. "Because you're precious to me. Beth, would you do me the honor of making me the happiest man in the world? Would you marry me?" I didn't know what to say at first. My brain was flooded with thoughts. If I marry David, would that mean I make less money off of Holly? More? Will I still be able to flirt with the doctors at Holly's appointments? What about the Epilepsy Center? What about Holly? What about *me*?

"I talked to Holly this afternoon", David said.

"You went to see her without me? What did she say?"

"She was very happy. She seems to be doing well, Beth. I'm no doctor, but it looks to me like she might be feeling a bit better. I gave her a necklace."

"Huh", I snorted. "Bribery."

"Oh, come on", David said playfully. "She loved it. And she seemed really happy, Beth. This will be good for her. So what do you say?"

The nosy couple at the next table, who had apparently been listening, shouted "Marry him!", and a group of others joined in, until what seemed like the whole restaurant was shouting "Marry him! Marry him!"

I basked in their attention.

"I don't know", I said loudly. "My daughter has epilepsy, and this might be too much for her."

"It won't be!" David pleaded. "Holly really likes me!"

By now, a group of waiters had gathered at our table.

"I just don't know…" I said. "I already can't afford Holly's medical bills. She's going to die soon, and I just…" I forced myself to cry.

"I'll help pay your daughter's bills!" shouted a man.

"And the dinner's on the house!" a waiter added. A woman waved a hundred dollar bill in the air.

"Here, ma'am, take this! Don't let epilepsy get in the way of marriage! If this will make you and your daughter happy, do it!"

"Well…" I fingered the money, loving way the crisp bill felt in my hands.

"We'll help!" said a family of four seated behind us. "Come on, everyone, let's help this lady! Marry him, ma'am! Don't worry about the cost! We'll help!"

Their teenage son took off his baseball cap and passed it around. I heard the clinking of coins, the crunch of bills, the scribbling of checks being written.

When the baseball cap full of donations was in my hands, I surveyed the crowd. A few were crying.

"How old is your little girl?" someone asked. "What's her name?"

"Her name is Holly, and she's eleven", I answered.

"So young", a waitress murmured.

David was still on one knee, with the ring box held out to me.

"Well, Beth? What do you say? All these people just offered to help Holly. And I'll help too, of course. I've got a steady paycheck. You won't have to worry about her medical bills anymore.

"Marry him!" yelled the teenage boy who had given his baseball cap. I looked at the donations. I could probably get a little more, but I thought it was better not to push it.

"Okay", I said. "Yes, David, I'll marry you." We hugged, and I folded the money into my pocket and thanked everyone.

Then I ordered another drink, the most expensive martini the restaurant carried, because like the waiter said, dinner was on the house."

I look over at Mommy. The man's head is on her shoulder now, and she's patting his hair, which looks greasy, like maybe he hasn't washed it for a while. Is she really trying to comfort him?

Then the door opens, and a man in a white coat says "Fern Kyros?"

"That's us", Mommy says, getting up.

I slip the diary back into my pocket.

"Remember your symptoms", Mommy whispers as she wheels me down the hallway behind the doctor. "Tell him what's wrong with you."

"Nothing's wrong with me!"

"Shut your mouth", Mommy snaps. "You have cancer. Lean your head to one side. Drool a little bit. Close your eyes halfway. And twitch a little. Good, very good."

I do what I'm told, and it feels weird, like I really *am* sick, and that makes me scared. We come to the door of a little room that is dark inside with afternoon shadows. There is a bed with that type of uncomfortable plastic covering that's always cold. I see machines with red lights flashing.

"We're just going to do a quick evaluation and then some tests", the doctor in the white coat says.

"Okay", Mommy winks at him. "Let's get started. It's time to find out what's wrong with this kid once and for all."

"Actually, Mrs. Kyros, I won't be doing the tests", says the doctor. "We have a very nice man, Dr. Raymond, who will be working with you and Fern today. He's wonderful. Transfers from different branches of this hospital. Very smart, I can tell. And all the kids love him."

Mommy jumps to her feet. "No!" she practically shouts. "Not Dr. Ray!"

"Why not?" The doctor in the white coat looks confused.

"Because...because..." Mommy stammers. "We've seen him before, and he was just awful to us! Just awful! I won't have him near my child!"

"Okay." The doctor in the white coat rubs the bald spot on his scalp, like he's getting a headache. "Why don't you come with me, Mrs. Kyros, and we'll sort this out."

Mommy looks at him with a smile that's too big.

"Oh, thank you, doctor. This really does mean a lot to me, this accommodation."

She walks out of the room with the doctor after telling me to "stay put". Her hips are doing that twisting thing and she's swishing her hair like she always does when there's a man around.

Once I can't see them anymore, I open Mommy's diary.

"I threw up this morning. Thank God David stayed over last night. He brought me toast and ginger ale in bed. I swear, the man is just perfect. I felt better around noon, so I'm not sure what it was. Food poisoning, maybe? We went out to eat last night, me and David. I'll call the restaurant later today and threaten to sue because their food made me sick. Of course, I don't have a lawyer or anything, but one thing I've learned is that if you threaten to sue, people will do almost anything for you. I can get a good sum of money out of this if I'm convincing enough.

Later, David and I went to visit Holly at The Epilepsy Center. Holly gave David a picture she drew. It was actually quite good, but I didn't tell her that. She had drawn a scene of birds resting on a fountain in the summertime. That's what she called it, too, "Birds Resting On A Fountain In The Summertime."

I snorted. "How original", I said.

"It may not be original", she replied, narrowing her eyes, "but at least it's not a *lie.*"

I glared at her and mouthed "shut up".

David looked uncomfortable. "It's very good, Holly", he said. "How did you get the idea?"

"From outside", she replied, fingering her holly berry necklace.

"You can't go outside. I'll be very angry if the nurses disobeyed me", I said.

At The Epilepsy Center, patients are allowed outside every day if a parent approves. I told the nurses that Holly wouldn't be going outside, no matter what. Her face twisted into a grimace, and for a flash of a second, I felt a kind of joy inside me. A joy about seeing her sad like that. So again I stated firmly that Holly was not to go outside. It would make her seem sicker that way.

"Why can't you go outside?" David asked.

"David, are you crazy?" I exclaimed. "It could kill her! She's too sick to go outside. My God, don't I have enough to worry about already?"

"I'm sorry, Beth. I know. I'm sorry. You're just trying to do what's best for her", David said, rubbing my back.

Holly was staring out the window.

"I get the ideas from out there", she said. "No one can stop me from looking out the window. I also get my ideas from Molly. *She's* allowed outside. She tells me everything she sees, so it's almost like I'm out there with her."

I took a long, hard look at Holly. Her fingers were still toying with the necklace that David had given her. Her dark eyes darted around the room, like Colin's did when he was nervous. But Colin is over. History. Out of my life. And therefore, Holly should be too."

I feel sick to my stomach.

What did Mommy mean when she wrote that Holly should be out of her life too? I'm not sure. I think I would definitely have liked to see Holly's drawing. I bet she was a good drawer.

Mommy is still gone, so that probably means that she is arguing with the doctors. I sigh to myself and shake my head and turn to the next page of the diary.

There are only three sentences written there in careful letters, like Mommy wanted to get the words just perfect, because they were so important.

"I am pregnant. I do not need Holly anymore to remind me of Colin, because now I have a piece of David. I must plan carefully."

A shiver scrambles down my spine and rests in my stomach. What would Mommy have to plan carefully? In the very back of my mind, I know, but the thought is too awful to float to the top of my head. I don't want to turn the page, but I do.

It is written three months later, according to the date at the top of the page.

"Last night, Holly died. I took her out of the hospital for what I told the doctors was another medical appointment. She seemed to be doing better. So excited about me and David getting married. She was wearing a white nightgown and her holly berry necklace. Bare feet. I put her in the car, and we just drove and drove without saying a single word.

It was beginning to get dark when Holly asked me, "Mom, where are we going?" I pulled over and looked at her, huddled in the backseat. Her wheelchair was folded up beside her. She looked so small and scared, certainly not eleven years old. Her brown eyes seemed to grow larger as she blinked at me, wondering what was going on.

I put a hand to my swollen stomach. There was new life in there. Holly was no use to me anymore. All she did was give me painful reminders of how Colin loved me and left me. Soon, I would have a new baby. And

I wondered to myself, would I fall into the same pattern that I did with Holly? Would I make the baby sick?

I made a decision that night, sitting on the side of the road. If David stayed with me, then I would treat the baby as well as I could, since the baby would be a part of David, and David would still love me. But if things didn't work out between the two of us...I wouldn't get angry. Not at myself, anyway. I would get angry at the baby. The baby would become my little punching bag, but unless I got pregnant again, I wouldn't kill the child, just keep her sick. If David ever left, I would need the support and attention, the kind I got when I told everyone that Holly had epilepsy. The money I got. That would be useful, too.

I didn't want to admit that I was thinking this way, but that night, as I stared up through the sunroof at the stars that made their patterns in the sky, I thought to myself, in a rare moment of self-realization just reserved for this diary, "This is the way I am. This is the way things will be."

"Mom?" Holly asked again in a small voice. "Where are we going?"

The sound assaulted my ears. I couldn't stand to hear her one more second. But I stayed on control, speeding the car away from the side of the road and further into the night.

"Shut up", I told Holly. "Not another word."

I didn't hear anything from the backseat for a while, and then my ears picked up the sound of wind rushing into the car.

Holly was opening the door.

"Stop that!" I yelled. "Close the damn door!"

Tears were running down Holly's cheeks, from the cold wind or just plain crying, I wasn't sure.

"Stop it!" she screamed.

"Stop what? You're the one opening the door! Don't you know how dangerous that is?"

"No, I mean stop the whole thing!" Holly cried. "You're making me sick, Mom! I know it! I don't have epilepsy! I'm not dying! I've never had a seizure in my life! I'm going to get help! You need it!"

"No!" I grabbed Holly and slammed the door, clutching her warm little body to my chest. "Don't move!"

"I'm not sick!" she screamed. "I'm not! I'm not! Please stop it, Mom! I know what you're doing!"

The last sentence she spoke sent me over the edge. I accelerated the car to eighty miles an hour.

"You're going to kill me!" she wailed.

I slammed on the brakes. The car stopped by the side of a field. All was silent. No houses around. We were in the middle of nowhere. As I opened the car door and lifted Holly out, she began to panic.

"Mom? What are you doing? Why are we out here?" I cupped my hand over her mouth and opened the trunk, taking out a pillow that I had stolen from her hospital bed.

She kicked and struggled, but I carried her to the middle of the field and pinned her down. She was shaking in her nightgown. I glanced up at the sky. I didn't see the constellations anymore, just star after star, like shining lights beaming themselves down on me and Holly. For a moment, I stared up at them and down at her, just absorbing the whole scene. This was it. I let out a crazy laugh.

"Am I insane?" I yelled to the night sky. "Am I insane?"

The silence after I spoke seemed louder than ever. I felt tears in my eyes.

"Goodbye, Holly", I whispered. Then I laughed, shoving the pillow over her face.

She struggled at first, but she was so weak, it didn't last long. Three minutes later, she was limp. I waited a while, then removed the pillow. Her skin was milk-white, her eyes closed. For the first time, I noticed how long her lashes were. I put my hand to her chest. No heartbeat. I checked her forehead, like a mother does when they think their child has a fever. Stone cold. She was dead.

A numbness took over my body. I had done it. My heart was pounding in my chest, and my breath came in gasps. I touched Holly's skin. I had never touched a dead person before, but here I was, putting my hands on one. And it was my own daughter. I tried not to feel. I really did. All the memories of Colin were gone now. Erased. No more pain. Even so, I couldn't help the tears that formed behind my eyes and spilled out onto my cheeks. Holly was gone. And I was finally free.

I picked up her limp body and placed in gently in the back on the car. My hands were shaking as I gripped the steering wheel and drove back to The Epilepsy Center. At times, I thought I heard Holly's voice in the background, whimpering, asking why. Why, Mom? But when I looked back, she was lying still, her dark braids splayed across the seat.

I reached the Epilepsy Center an hour later, and realization suddenly dawned on me. I had a dead child in my car. I picked her up and carried her into the front office. At least I didn't have to pretend I was crying, because tears had been streaming down my cheeks for the entire drive. Over what, I wasn't sure.

A nurse spied me from her desk and rushed over. "Beth! What happened? Is Holly okay?"

This was it. I steeled my courage and burst into a fresh bout of sobs.

"She...she had an awful seizure on the way to the doctor's office! I tried to do everything I'm supposed to when it happens, but she was failing around, worse than ever. Finally, she just stopped moving. I don't think she's breathing!"

The nurse felt Holly's chest. She spoke rapidly into a walkie-talkie.

"Emergency! Patient seems unresponsive! At the front desk! We need doctors, ASAP! Let's go, people!"

Everything seemed to happen in a whirlwind after that. I continued crying as the action happened around me. Doctors rushed into the room, carrying stretchers. They took Holly away, and a nurse led me down the hallway, patting my shoulder. I saw her clasp her hands in a prayer.

"Dear Jesus, please save this child", she murmured. It seemed like the type of thing a good mother would to, so I prayed too.

Ten minutes later, a doctor came out of the examination room where they took Holly.

"Beth", he said gently, "Holly is dead."

"Oh, God!" The nurse gripped me in a hug, but I stood stock-still, the questions of the doctors swirling around me.

"What happened?"

"When did the seizure start?"

"How long did it last?"

"What did you do?"

"Were there any warning signs?"

I fired off the answers to each question. I had them prepared and written down for days before I smothered Holly. That was the key factor. No one could tell that I did it.

According to the doctors, it was a seizure. And I couldn't be responsible for that. I cried the appropriate amount, maybe a little more. I sat in Holly's room and listened to her roommate, Molly, sob beside me. This irritated me. I wanted to be alone with my thoughts and newfound freedom.

"Shut up", I told Molly. "She was *my* daughter."

Molly was quiet, but still, I couldn't settle. I told the doctors that I was taking a drive.

"Do you need company?" they asked. "You're so upset, Beth, are you sure it's safe?"

I burst out the door, crying in response. I drove a long time, clutching my pregnant stomach, which had started to hurt. It's just you and me now, baby. You and me."

CHAPTER
33

I can't move. Something inside me has finally broken. I am crying, crying harder than I've ever cried before. Harder even than when Daddy left. Somehow, in the very back of my mind, I knew that Holly had died, but just seeing all the details on paper puts me in a kind of numbness. I can't feel. I am not hungry anymore. Not thirsty. I just *am*. And when the numb feeling starts to go away a tiny bit, the only thing I feel is terror.

In my brain, I work through what I've learned. Mommy killed Holly because Colin left her. And Holly reminded her of Colin. She said that if things didn't work out between her and Daddy, she would hurt the baby. And the baby is me.

When scientists find put all their facts together, they call it a conclusion. I learned that in the Beginning Astronomy book. And I have come to a conclusion. Mommy is going to kill me because Daddy left, and so now she doesn't want any part of Daddy. And I am a part of Daddy.

The diary is not over, though. I count. There are twenty-seven pages left. But the story is over. It's all over. Holly is dead. What could be in those twenty-seven pages?

Mom's not back yet, Fern. You have time.

Holly!

But you're dead.

I was dead the entire time. Nothing's changed except you. You've always been smart, Fern. But now you're wise, too.

What's the difference?

You know things, but you also *understand* them. So turn the page of the diary. You need to read it.

Is it about your funeral, Holly? Because I'm already sad, so I don't want to read about your funeral.

It's not about my funeral, I promise. Read it. I'll be right here.

I look at the date at the top of the page. "Seven years later!" I say out loud to Holly. **Right. Seven years after Mom was pregnant with you. And when did she start making you sick?**

I feel hot all of a sudden, hot and cold at the same time, because I know the answer. Maybe this is what Holly means about being wise.

I understand what might be in those twenty-seven pages now. And I am right.

"David left today. We decided on a divorce a long time ago, but somehow it didn't seem real until I saw all his bags at the staircase. Then, suddenly, I wanted him out of my life more than anything in the world. Fern was crying upstairs. She really loved David. I don't know why. I hated that man. And now, a part of me hates Fern, too, because she is like him. Why is it that children are always like their fathers? She doesn't look like David, but she has his curiosity. I've caught her eavesdropping multiple times. I think she already knew about the divorce. She's a smart little kid.

I've been lonely for quite some time now. I've tried going out to bars to get some shred of attention, but no one seems to notice me, the sad woman in the corner sipping a martini, paid for by the money that people donated for Holly. I still have a bit left. When I sent out letters telling everyone that Holly was dead, I got an outpouring of sympathy, the best yet.

Anyway, I've see so many attractive men in The Happy Hour Casino (where I work), but one of them especially catches my eye. He's a bouncer there. I've seen him chatting up other women, but once his brown eyes fixed on me, I knew I had to get the courage to talk to him. But how? Now that Holly is gone, I don't know how to talk to people anymore. But there's one thing that I know will get anyone's attention: a sick kid. And I have a kid. I just have to make sure she's sick."

So Mommy made me sick to get *Brian* to like her? I want to rip up the diary, tear it into shreds.

Don't, Fern. Just keep reading. Please. You'll find what you need to know.

The next page is dated a month later.

"I've been planning, researching, and spending hours online looking up illnesses to tell people that Fern has. There is a poison called Ethanol Glycol that's in antifreeze. It's colorful and sweet-tasting, like Gatorade. And Fern loves Gatorade. All I have to do is mix in the slightest amount of antifreeze, and see what happens. I won't put in enough to kill her, but just enough to make her sick. I know the drill by now. And I have a plan."

What was Mommy's plan, Holly?

You know. Her plan was *you*. Everything she's done to you. You'll see.

On the next pages of the diary are charts, like the charts Mommy wrote about Holly. It makes me feel sick to see those charts with my name on them. There is one chart on each page, one chart each day. On the seventeenth chart, the word "Cancer" is written in all capital letters.

"It's taken a while, but I've finally settled on a plan. Cancer. That's what Fern has. People get lots of sympathy from cancer. I've already got Brian as a boyfriend, but somehow, I just can't stop faking, lying, and hurting Fern. The addiction is back. Every time someone says "I'm so sorry" or "It must be hard", I get a little rush of happiness inside, a warm feeling. Like people care about me for something other than my looks, which is all Brian cares about. I'm getting attention for something else, for once. And I don't want to give that up."

The charts stop when there are only three pages left of the diary.
Will I want to read them?
No.
Do I need *to read them?*
Yes.

Okay, then. The next page is almost like a timeline, everything that's happened. Ethanol. Gatorade. Brian. Pox. Fern. Hurt. Cancer. Bald. Leah. Convention. Make-A-Wish. Cruise. Doctor. These are *my* words. My story. I decide I don't like these words anymore.
These are bad words, Holly. Sick words. Why do I need to read them?
Not that page, Fern. There are only two pages left. Read those. And hurry, I don't know how much longer Mom will be gone. She can argue with doctors for ages, but even this is a long time for her.

The next page is written in smudged ink, with reddish-purple fingerprints on it. I sniff the fingerprints, and they smell like wine.

"It's happening again. I'm pregnant. Brian and I got busy a while ago, and I suppose that it was inevitable that a baby should come out of all of it. I've been experiencing morning sickness, like I did with Holly. It's hard, because I have to keep Fern controlled at the same time. I strap her into her wheelchair every day so she can't move or escape. But she's more daring than Holly. I've got to watch out with her. Actually, I'm giving up with diaries. They're too much to think about. They pick my thoughts apart, force me to analyze them. And I can't do that anymore. I just can't. So I'm never looking at this diary again after I finish it. I'm hiding it in my mattress and letting it rot away. This stupid thing was making me feel guilty about the way I was living. And, like Fern, guilt is one thing I don't need anymore.

Speaking of Fern, I haven't told her yet that I'm pregnant. It's not noticeable. I went to the doctor the other day while Fern was locked on her room doing who-knows-what, and they confirmed it. If I was to be completely honest with Fern, I would tell her this.

I had Holly as a piece of Colin. Colin left. And I killed Holly. I have you as a piece of David. And David left. And now, I will have a new baby as a piece of Brian, who hasn't left. Yet, you're still here. What does that tell you? You're smarter than you let on. Don't pretend you don't know this, Fern. It means you're done for. I have no need for you anymore. As much as this may hurt you, I do not love you. You were just a vehicle to get attention. Not my little girl. I'm not sure exactly when, or how, but you are going to die. Soon. And I can get away with it, because I'm your mother. And mother knows best."

Stop crying, Fern. It's okay. That's why I showed it to you, so you can stop it.

How?

Read the last page.

I already did. The first time I found it in Mommy's room, when I was sitting in all her lacy underwear and bras that were thrown across the floor. And Brian's boots. I remember Brian's boots, too.

The last page has changed, though.

Did Mommy write something new in it? I thought she had given up writing.

She didn't write anything new, Fern. The page has only changed for *you.*

For me? I turn to the very last page of Mommy's diary, and there are the two words, the same ones that I saw there before.

"She knows".

But Holly is right. Those words aren't the same anymore. They look the same. But only me and Holly can tell that they're not. When I first read the words "*she knows*", I thought that Mommy meant I knew about Holly. She did, but that's not all. When I look at "*she knows*" again, I see everything, all that I know. All that Mommy meant. I know about Holly. I know the truth about how she died. I know that Mommy is making me sick. I know all of these things, and a lot more. And Mommy knows that I know. That's why she wrote that.

I close the diary. It's done. Over. I let all the pages and thoughts sink into my head and worm into my brain! Then suddenly, I realize something.

"Oh, my gosh!" I yell. "Mommy's pregnant!"

"Congratulations!" says a voice across the hall. I think it's the woman in the room across from mine, the one with stitches over her eyebrow. I saw her when we came in.

I cry quietly to myself for a while so the woman won't hear, because then she might ask why I'm sad that Mommy is having a baby. And I really don't want to explain how if there is a new baby, I'm going to die like Holly. And the baby will be hurt like we were.

I hear the click-click-click of Mommy's high heels in the hallway, and the heavy thump of shoes landing beside her. Doctor's footsteps. I have noticed they all walk the same, without a pattern, except for the few times when I've heard Raymond walking, and then it sounds like CLUNK-step, CLUNK-step, CLUNK-step. Sort of like the beat of a drum. The word "baby" keeps flowing through my mind like a poison river. Baby, Father, leaving, lies, sick, hospital, dead. It's another pattern, like Raymond's footsteps, but it's not a good pattern. Mommy comes into the room. A doctor who is not Raymond follows her. Mommy smirks at me. The Doctor Who Is Not Raymond sit on a wooden chair next to me.

"We're all set, Fern", he says. "You don't have to see anyone you're not comfortable with, okay?"

"*I'm* comfortable with Raymond", I say. "But Mommy doesn't like him."

Mommy gives The Doctor Who Is Not Raymond a tight smile and glares at me at the same time. I wonder how she does that.

"Anyway", he says, "we're just going to run a few tests. You might have to stay overnight, depending on the results, but it won't be scary. We'll make it as un-scary as possible, okay?"

I'm tired of doctors treating me like a little kid.

"Un-scary isn't a word", I say.

"Fern!" Mommy exclaims. "That was extremely rude! I'm sorry, doctor, she's not usually like this. I don't know what's gotten into her."

The truth. That what's gotten into me. And being able to finally say NO.

"Don't worry about it, Mrs. Kyros. I'm sure Fern is just a little nervous. Are you, Fern?"

"Yes", I say.

But not because I'm here.

"See!" The Doctor Who Is Not Raymond smiles at Mommy. "See, Mrs. Kyros? Perfectly normal!"

"Call me Beth", Mommy says, smiling so hard her teeth show and she looks like a really creepy clown. I shiver, imagining the really creepy clown in the middle of a field at night, shoving a pillow over Holly's face.

"First things first", The Doctor Who Is Not Raymond says. "I assume you've gotten chemotherapy treatment for her before? That's why Fern's bald? And in a wheelchair? And the feeding tube? Did another doctor prescribe that?"

I see Mommy's eyes flicker from creepy-mean to a little bit nervous.

"Yes!" she says quickly. "Yes, we had a specialist who gave her chemotherapy and the feeding tube and the wheelchair. But that specialist recently moved to Florida without any advance notice. That's why we're here."

The Doctor Who Is Not Raymond nods.

"But the feeding tube can't be touched", Mommy says. "That was the main thing we were told. Fern doesn't get enough nutrients, see, so it's very important that the feeding tube stays in her. At all times."

I know why Mommy is saying that. She doesn't want them to find out it's not a *real* feeding tube. It still hurts my throat, worse than ever now. Sometimes I feel food getting caked on it, and then I just want to throw up, because that's really gross.

I look at Mommy's stomach. Maybe it's just my imagination, but it looks a *little* bit bigger. Enough for the tiniest part of a baby to start, I guess.

I know all about how babies are made, because when I was four and Mommy took me and Daddy to the Christmas party at The Happy Hour Casino, a group of the bigger girls were talking about something called sex. They were all turning red and laughing a lot, so I stood close by and listened. And now I know everything, even though I don't really want to.

The Doctor Who Is Not Raymond tells me to take off my clothes. He hands me a weird-looking piece of paper and tells me to put it on.

"What is it?" I ask.

"Fern, sweetheart, that's a hospital gown, okay?" Mommy says. "I'm going to help you put it on so you won't be scared. I'm right here, don't worry."

She smiles at The Doctor Who Is Not Raymond and he closes the door, leaving me alone in the room with Mommy.

"Why are you being nice to me?" I ask.

"Silly!" Mommy lets out a tinkling laugh. "Aren't I always nice to you?"

"No", I say. Mommy's eyes narrow.

"Quiet", she hisses. "I won't have you saying things like that with other people nearby. That doctor could be just outside the door."

I clutch Pox tight.

"Put on the hospital gown", snaps Mommy.

I don't move.

"I said, put it on!"

Mommy unwraps the slippery paper gown and holds it up to me.

"Take off your clothes", she says.

But I am afraid to take off my clothes, because I have just remembered the diaries in my pockets, and if I take my clothes off now, Mommy might see them and know I was reading them.

So I tell her "I'm grown-up enough to get changed by myself. Can you please stand in the hallway? Please?"

"What?" Mommy snickers. "You don't even trust your own mother?"

No, I don't. Not at all.

"That's kinda pathetic, Fern."

Mommy grabs at me, but I jump away. She almost touched the edge of Holly's diary.

"Let me do it myself."

"Stubborn brat", Mommy says. "Just take your damn clothes off already."

"I'll scream", I say. "And then The Doctor Who Is Not Raymond will know something's wrong."

Mommy tilts her head. "The Doctor Who Is...what? Never mind, Fern. If you're grown-up enough to change by yourself, you're grown-up enough to live without *this!*"

She grabs Pox from my arms so quick, I'm not even sure if she moved at all. Maybe Mommy is like The Flash. Mommy looks at me for three seconds, which I count in my head. On her face is the scariest clown grin I've ever seen. She holds Pox right in front of me and rips his head off. Stuffing rains down on my lap. Pox, now torn apart, lies on the floor like a dead, limp rag. At first I feel sadness, but it is shoved out of the way by anger. I blink back my tears.

"I'll get you for that", I say.

I don't know what makes me say it. Actually, I do. Pox was the only piece of Daddy that I had left. Mommy is destroying me, her last piece of Daddy, and now she's destroying mine.

A smile passes though Mommy's face. It's still a clown smile. "You'll get me?" she teases. "How, Fern? How will you get me?"

I keep quiet because I don't know. I cross my arms and glare at her.

"Oooh, tough", Mommy mocks.

"Everything alright?" The Doctor Who Is Not Raymond calls, knocking on the door.

"Yes, yes!" Mommy's voice changes to sweetness and light. All lies.

"We're fine!" She turns back to me. "Just put on the damn gown, Fern."

She leaves, making sure not to slam the door, even though I knew she wants to. But the Doctor Who Is Not Raymond is standing right there, and Mommy doesn't want him to know she's mad. I open the paper gown. It rips, but I don't care.

I put on the gown as fast as I can, ripping it a little more. It's huge. I think about six of me could fit in here. I wrap it around myself and it looks like I'm a mummy. I am about to open the door to tell Mommy and The Doctor Who is Not Raymond that I'm ready to just get this over with, but I hear something, so I stay very quiet and listen.

"I think she's near death", Mommy is saying. "It just tears me up inside, you know? She's so *young.*"

"Fern seems like a fighter", replies The Doctor Who Is Not Raymond. "I can't guarantee that her cancer will go away-no one can, for any child-, but I can tell you that I see hope."

"You don't understand!" sobs Mommy. "Every time I look at the poor kid, I think about how it could be her last day on this earth! You doctors always *say* you understand, but you have no idea! Have *you* ever had a child as sick as Fern?"

Mommy is a very good actress. She should go on Broadway if she ever gets fired from The Happy Hour Casino for sneaking drinks without paying for them. I know she does that, because I heard her tell Brian.

The Doctor Who Is Not Raymond clears his throat.

"Beth, I've never had kids of my own, but I can tell you, I see a lot of children in this Hospital who are much worse off than Fern. I know it's not easy to accept that your child has cancer. I know. But things are going to be all right. Shall we go back in now? Fern's had long enough to change."

"Wait!" Mommy begs. "Stay with me out here, doctor. Just for I few moments. I need...I need a shoulder to cry on."

So Mommy does her fake-crying that could possibly get her on Broadway, and I get bored, so I look out the window because that's what Holly used to do. And when I look out the window, I see a man walking toward a car. I smile, because I know who that man is. Raymond. He's wearing his white doctor's coat. He walks to a red pickup truck with a dent in the side and opens the door. He takes out a bunch of papers from the front seat, closes the door, and walks back into the building.

I guess my powers of observation are really working today, because I notice something very important. Raymond did not have any keys to his car. That means he left it open. So anything could get inside. Or any*one*.

CHAPTER
34

An idea starts to trickle into my head like a leaky faucet, but before the basin is all filled up, the door opens, and Mommy and The Doctor Who Is Not Raymond come in and catch me staring out the window.

"What are you looking at?" The Doctor Who Is Not Raymond asks gently.

"The trees", I say quickly. "The trees outside are very pretty". I don't actually like the trees. I think they're very boring.

"Well", The Doctor Who Is Not Raymond says, "I just have a few question for you and your mom, Fern, and then we can start, okay?"

I want to ask "start what?", but I can't because Mommy says "That's fine, Connor. That sounds very good." He must have told her his name when she "needed a shoulder to cry on."

The Doctor Who Is Not Raymond takes out a clipboard, and I squeeze in my breath, because the drawer he takes it out of is only one above The drawer where I've hidden Mommy and Holly's diaries. He asks Mommy a lot of questions about something called "insurance".

I sort of know what insurance is because before Mommy started making me sick, she was on the phone a lot with insurance companies, swearing at them and saying "Yeah? Then I'll take my business somewhere else! You've just lost a customer!"

But after she told everyone I was dying, her voice got so sweet it was like syrup, and no more swears came out of her mouth. Instead, it was "Oh, yes. Yes, my little girl is very sick. The doctors...well, they don't know how long she has left. Your company may just save her life."

Then The Doctor Who Is Not Raymond asks about my cancer. I know he's asking *me,* because he looks right at me. But maybe Mommy doesn't know that, because *she* answers and explains everything that's happened. Only, it's not true. She's definitely not making it up as she goes along, though. She had this planned. Thinking about that makes my stomach hurt.

Tune her out, Fern.

"How old are you, Fern?" The Doctor Who Is Not Raymond asks me. I finger the ripped up pieces of Pox that are still clutched in my hand. Mommy has already told him that I got mad and ripped up Pox. She said I destroy toys all the time.

"I think it's the anger about her illness", she said.

"Fern?" Connor asks again. "How old are you?"

"Seven", I say automatically.

Think about that for a minute, Fern. How old are you? "Seven", I say again, trying to quiet Holly's voice in my head. What would she say that? I've been seven for more than a year.

Wait a minute.

"What's the date?" I ask Connor.

"November tenth", he says. My mouth hangs open, which must look very weird, but I don't care. I'm not seven anymore. My birthday, October third, was a five weeks ago! I forgot all about it! *Mommy* forgot all about it!

She didn't even get you a present. Or say Happy Birthday. Or do anything.

"I'm eight", I tell Connor.

"Eight." He chuckles. "Forgot your own age? Didn't you have a party?"

No.

"Oh, yes", Mommy jumps in. "I threw her a huge party this year. We picked up a dozen of her friends, went to the movies and out to ice cream, and spent the night opening presents and roasting marshmallows in the backyard. And you should have seen the presents! I got her a canopy bed with frills and lace all over! A little extensive, I know, but after all she's been through…"

At least she got one part right, the part about "after all I've been through." But I didn't get a canopy bed. I didn't even get a hug. Or anything at all.

I remember one time when I was in kindergarten and a girl named Brooke came up to me and said "My mommy told me I have to invite every girl in the class to my birthday party."

She didn't like me, so before she gave me the invitation, she squashed in in her fist. I didn't like Brooke, either. She was a very confusing person. For example, she had a new best friend every day! How is that even possible? Every morning, she would pick a girl in our class and say "You're my friend", and "you're not my friend" to the girl she had been friends with the day before. Trying to put Brooke into words made my head spin. Thankfully, I was never one of her "friends". And every day at recess, she chased Toby Remberson and Josh Tremont around the playground and yelled "I'm gonna kiss you!" I brought a book outside and watched this day after day.

One recess, Toby fell while Brooke was chasing him and skinned his knee. He started to cry, and I felt sorry for him, and I wanted to say something, but Mrs. Jett was already taking him to the nurse while Brooke watched, giggling, which I thought was very mean of her.

Anyway, Brooke's party was the only one I ever went to. I spent an hour in the toy store with Daddy, picking out a present. We both agreed that a Batman figure with a Batmobile would be just perfect, but a sales lady suggested that we might want to look for a present for a little girl in the aisle with girls toys.

Daddy and I hated all of the pink in that aisle because it gave us both headaches, so we grabbed the first thing we saw and left the store to get grape slushies from Dairy Queen so our headaches would go away. We didn't even look to see what the present was until we were in the car.

I opened the bag, and found a doll with shiny blond hair and big blue eyes in a white dress with a veil. The label said "Wedding Doll! So Every Girl Can Find Her Prince Charming!" I tossed it back into the bag, because I thought it was awful looking, but when we got home and I gave it to Mommy to wrap, she said that it was absolutely beautiful and that all girls should have a doll like it and how did me and Daddy, who are obsessed with superheroes, manage to find such a thing?

Brooke thought the same thing as Mommy, because when she opened the present, she squealed like a puppy and all the girls gathered around the doll to brush its silky hair. It was a very good party. Brooke's mommy had paid for a man to bring a pony for us to ride. She bought pink and purple foam princess crowns for us to decorate. But I didn't do any of that stuff, because I don't like ponies at all, and the glue they were using to stick fake jewels on the princess crowns made my fingers feel funny. I hate glue because when it dries and flakes, it feels like my skin is peeling off.

Instead, I sat under the big dining room table with Brooke's eight year old brother, Cole, and played with superhero figures while we both ate pieces of the pink cake with white frosting that Brooke's mommy had given us. He had all the superheroes, every single one.

"Batman's the best", he said. "I've got two of him."

He handed me one.

"Can we fight them against the bad guys?" I asked.

"No, only one Batman can fight, he had replied. "Not two. But you can be Sinestro if you want."

"Do you have a Green Arrow?"

"Yeah, but I don't ever play with him. He's not that strong."

"Yes he is!" I insisted. "I want to be Green Arrow."

Cole shrugged. "Okay", he said.

So we peeked above the table and found that all the girls were off playing "Pin the crown on the princess".

"The coast is clear", Cole whispered. "Ready, captain?"

"Ready", I whispered back. The table was still full of cake plates with smears of frosting and half-melted ice cream, but Cole said it didn't matter. We leaned the bad guys against the cake box and collected our armies. Batman was the leader of his, Green Arrow was the leader of mine.

"Ready, set, GO!" Cole yelled, and Green Arrow smashed right into the Joker, landing him in a puddle of vanilla ice cream.

"Great work, Green Arrow", Cole exclaimed. "I guess you're a pretty good fighter after all."

I grinned. "Thanks, Batman."

We played attack the bad guys on the cake table for an hour until Brooke's mommy found us and yelled about the mess we had made. I think she was mad at me, because she sent me home without a goody bag, but I didn't care because all the stuff in them were things I absolutely hated. Strawberry lip gloss, a candy necklace, a gold paper princess crown, a purple hairbrush, and a Cinderella doll. But I still had the best time ever, because right before Daddy picked me up, Cole came over and pressed Green Arrow into my hand.

"You can have him", he said. "You played real good with him, anyway."

It was the best birthday party ever.

I guess I kind of spaced out for a little bit, because Mommy and The Doctor Who Is Not Raymond are staring at me.

"Fern?" The Doctor Who Is Not Raymond says. "I asked you if there was anything you wanted to tell me."

Tell him, Fern. Tell him.

Tell him what? About you, *Holly?*

Yes. He might be able to help. You don't have much time left, Fern. Mom needs to be stopped.

I can't.

You can. Think about all the things she's done to you.

I start to list them in my head. Killing Holly. Making me sick. Killing Holly. Lying. Killing Holly. I know what I need to say.

"Fern, listen to Doctor Connor!" Mommy snaps. "He's asking you a question!" The Doctor Who Is Not Raymond leans down to my level and speaks very slowly, and very loudly too, like I'm deaf or maybe just stupid.

"IS THERE...ANYTHING...YOU WANT...TO TELL ME?"

"Yes", I say, looking at a Mommy. "She killed Holly."

I have never seen a room get so quiet before, not in my entire life. The only thing I hear is the tick-tick-tick of The Doctor Who Is Not Raymond's watch.

Finally, he asks, "Who is Holly?"

I am about to tell him, but Mommy's been lying in wait again like a lion, waiting to jump.

"Oh, Connor! I didn't kill anyone! You see, Holly is an imaginary friend that Fern made up. The doctors are her last hospital told us it was a way of coping with her cancer. So she made up a friend named Holly and told everyone they were sisters. Then one day, we were driving home from another medical appointment, And Fern suddenly lets out this scream and wails "Wait, Mommy! We forgot Holly!" I told her Holly was just fine, but there was no calming her, so we had to drive all the way back to the hospital to get Holly. Fern kept yelling at me "Go faster, go faster!", and I drove as fast as was legal, because I knew this was important to her. But when we got in the parking lot, she started crying even harder because she said that Holly was dead because I didn't drive fast enough. I tried to ask her how that made sense, but Connor, she was just inconsolable. So now she tells everyone we meet that I've killed Holly. I'm sorry, I know it's ridiculous. We must be the biggest wastes of time..."

The Doctor Who Is Not Raymond writes something on his clipboard.

"Not at all", he says. "The doctors at Fern's hospital were absolutely correct. It was a way of coping for her. And blaming you for "killing" Holly is her way of expressing anger that just happens to be taken out on you. You don't deserve it, but it happens to many children with cancer. They get angry, and need someone to blame. I see it all the time."

My mouth is hanging open. How in the world could Mommy lie like that right to someone's face? She must have practiced it, when she could have been taking care of me like a mother should. I hate her, I absolutely hate her. But then I remember my not-quite-fully-formed plan and I feel a little bit better. Mommy apologizes to The Doctor Who Is Not Raymond again and puts on hand on his shoulder, and the other on her stomach where the tiniest bit of a baby is.

Save yourself, baby. Mommy might like The Doctor Who Is Not Raymond now, and that means Brian might leave. And if Brian leaves, you're just an extra piece of Brian, something Mommy wants to get rid of.

I stay quiet as The Doctor Who Is Not Raymond does the cancer tests on me. Some of them hurt. Some of them don't. But I stare straight ahead through each one. I am numb. I don't dare look at Mommy.

He finally screws the cap onto a test tube of blood and says "I'll be right back. Fern, you need to have snack after those test, especially the ones where I took blood. Losing blood and not eating afterward isn't good for your body. Is she allergic to anything, Beth? Nuts? Dairy?"

No matter what Mommy says, The Doctor Who Is Not Raymond is going to get me a snack, so she might as well tell the truth. She figures that out too.

"No", she growls. "No allergies."

"Good." He leaves the room, and I am alone with Mommy again. I try not to look at her, but she grabs me by the neck and squeezes. I feel the feeding tube in my throat.

"What the hell is wrong with you?" she sputters. "How could you?"

I cross my arms, even though they're shaking like one of those vibrating massage chairs that Mommy always likes to test out at stores.

"I told the truth", I say.

"Shut up!" Mommy hisses. "How could you know that about Holly? How could you know I killed her?"

She covers her mouth, because she knows she's said something that will give me fighting power, like how Green Arrow gains super-health after he shoots with one-hundred percent accuracy.

"So you *did* kill Holly", I say.

Mommy doesn't answer. "You'll pay for this", she whispers. "My God, you'll pay."

"For what?" I ask. I feel very brave for some reason. "*I* wasn't the one who killed Holly. You did it. In a field. With a pillow."

Mommy's mouth hangs open. "How...?"

I realize I've said too much. Will she guess that I read her diary?

"There's something going on here", Mommy says slowly. "And I don't like it. I have a suspicion, Fern, and I'm not going to tell you what it is right now, but no matter what, you will be *severely* punished when we get home. *Severely*."

But I don't care, because I have a plan. I just hope it works. The Doctor Who Is Not Raymond comes back into the room, and Mommy and I pretend that everything is normal.

He gives me a tray with a glass of orange juice, and two protein bars. "I want every bit of that gone, Fern", he says. "You most likely have very low blood sugar right now, so I need you to finish all of that food, okay?"

He doesn't have to tell me twice. I dig in, watching Mommy.

"There's coffee downstairs in the cafeteria, Beth", The Doctor Who Is Not Raymond says. "Would you...would you like me to bring you some?" The tips of his ears turn pink. That happens sometimes when Mommy is around men who like her. She says it's the cost of being beautiful.

"When will the test results be back?" Mommy snaps, ignoring The Doctor Who Is Not Raymond's question about coffee and tea.

"In about an hour", he answers. "In the meantime, are you sure there nothing I can do to make you guys more comfortable? Fern, we have a bunch of movies you can watch while you're waiting. What's your favorite?"

I can't tell him my favorite, because Mommy is sitting right there, and she would get very mad at me if I told her that my favorite movie was "The Shining", so I say, "Any movie is fine, thank you."

"She's so polite", says The Doctor Who Is Not Raymond.

He brings me "Charlotte's Web", which I pretend to watch. Mommy is staring at me the whole hour, and it's very hard to focus on something when someone is staring at you. Finally, The Doctor Who Is Not Raymond comes back after an hour and twelve minutes. He is smiling.

"Oh, Beth! You'll be glad to hear this!" he exclaims. "Fern's tests results are completely normal! No sign of cancer whatsoever! She's completely fine!"

"What?" Mommy snaps.

"It's a miracle!" The Doctor Who Is Not Raymond says. He tries to hug Mommy, but she pushes him away.

"What?" she snaps again. "Are you sure? Are you absolutely *sure*?"

"Positive", he answers. "Fern is cancer-free."

He looks at me.

He wants you to do something.

What?

Anything. Show him you're happy you don't have cancer.

"So...I'm fine?" I ask The Doctor Who Is Not Raymond.

"Yep." He's still grinning.

"I can't believe this!" Mommy shouts. "I absolutely cannot believe this! She's been sick for years, and you have the gall to tell me she's *fine,* you idiot? What kind of doctor are you?"

The Doctor Who Is Not Raymond looks stunned, like Mommy just shot him with a laser.

"Beth, I-"

"Save it", Mommy snaps. "I want those tests done again. She's not okay. Just look at her! She's near death!"

"Beth, please!" The Doctor Who Is Not Raymond says. "Please don't say those things here! I'll tell you what. All patients need to have a follow-up exam in a month. We'll redo the tests then if that's what you really want. But I can guarantee you that Fern is fine."

"A month?" Mommy asks.

"A month", The Doctor Who Is Not Raymond confirms.

"Fine", Mommy growls. "But I want these tests done with extra care, got it?"

"Right", The Doctor Who Is Not Raymond answers. He turns to me, still smiling. "And guess what, Fern. You're free to go! You don't have to spend the night!"

"She doesn't?" Mommy says. "Why not? She should! What if there's a problem?"

"We only have patients spend the night if their tests showed there was anything wrong", The Doctor Who Is Not Raymond says. "And since Fern's tests were clear, she can go home."

Mommy opens her mouth, probably to yell some more, but her cell phone starts playing "Single Ladies" at that exact moment. She picks it up.

"Hello? What? Oh shit, I completely forgot! Yeah, I'll be there as soon as possible." She snaps the phone shut. "I've gotta run. I actually have an appointment of my own now."

"Because you're pregnant?" I blurt out. There's that weird bravery again, coming whether I like it or not. Mommy's face turns the color of a tomato, which is gross, because I hate tomatoes.

"How did you know?" she whispers. "Am I fat? Or did you find...never mind, this isn't the place to discuss it."

"You're pregnant?" The Doctor Who Is Not Raymond exclaims. "Congratulations, Beth! That's wonderful! When are you expecting?"

"That's what I'm going to find out", Mommy snaps. "That, and a bunch of other things. Like if the baby's a boy or a girl. Personally, I hope it's a boy. I can't stand little girls." She gives me a nasty grin.

"Well, I think both genders are wonderful", says The Doctor Who Is Not Raymond.

Poor man. He just doesn't get it. No one does, Fern. But you have to try and make them understand. I didn't try, and look where that got me. Dead. Keep going, Fern. Stick with the plan.

How? If we have to leave right now, the plan will be ruined!

No it won't. You'll see. This is actually better than I thought. Just listen to your head.

You mean listen to you.

Same thing, Fern. Same thing.

CHAPTER
35

"Let's go, Fern", Mommy says. She helps me back into the wheelchair.

"She probably won't be needing that for long", The Doctor Who Is Not Raymond says.

"Oh, cancer's not her only issue", Mommy replies. "She's be in this wheelchair for life. I *told* you it wasn't a miracle."

The Doctor Who Is Not Raymond looks like he doesn't know what to say, so Mommy ignores him and pushes me out of the room.

As we're going down the hallway, I remember that I've left Holly and Mommy's diaries in the drawer in the office. I twist around in my wheelchair and watch as I'm pushed further and further away from them.

Holly, help me. What do I do?

You need to get those back.

Why?

They'll come in handy, trust me. But you've got time. Remember the plan, and just add an extra step. You can get the diaries then.

Mommy leaves me in the waiting room. The nurse at the front desk looks at me like I'm not supposed to be there.

"The doctor said it was fine", Mommy tells her. "She just needs to stay here for a little bit. I'll come get her."

"Why?" I ask. "Why are you leaving me here?"

Mommy bends down and uses her hissy-rattlesnake voice so the nurse can't hear. "I don't want you coming to my appointment. Just stay." I feel like a dog. *Just stay.*

"It's okay, right?" Mommy asks the nurse.

The nurse sighs. "Is she in medical danger?"

I can almost hear the wheels in Mommy's brain squeaking. She can lie and get attention. But the she won't be able to leave, at least, I don't think so. They'd probably want her to stay if I was really sick. If she says no, she's admitting that I'm okay for now, and then she can leave.

"She's okay", Mommy says finally. "She'll just wait here."

"Alright", she nurse says. "But don't expect me to entertain her. This isn't a daycare center."

"She can entertain herself", Mommy says, walking out the automatic doors that open for her. I sit in my wheelchair, waiting, waiting, waiting.

How much longer, Holly? I don't like waiting, waiting, waiting.

You've got to wait at least an hour, or else people will get suspicious.

So I listen to Holly, because she's my big sister and she knows best, so I wait for exactly an hour. I watch the clock change from number to number. I watch the seconds click by in the silent room, like the ticks of the heart monitor they just used on me. I count the minutes, sixty in all. Subtract one every time the clock hits the twelve. If you really think about it, clocks can be kind of entertaining if you're very, very bored like I am.

Finally, an hour has gone by. I look at the nurse at the front desk. She's got a cup of coffee next to her, and I know it's coffee because I can smell it. It's kind of funny, I love the smell of coffee, but I hate the taste of it. Daddy let me try his coffee once, and I spit it right out, all over the floor. Mommy yelled at me for making a mess, but Daddy just laughed.

The nurse at the front desk looks tired. Her head is resting on one of her hands, and she doesn't really seem like she's working. Maybe she'll get fired for that, like Daddy got fired from his job. Was it for not working? I hope he's found a new job, a good one, like at a candy store or a butterfly garden and not at a bad place like the zoo or a boring office.

I take a deep breath and pretend to look out the window. "My mom's waiting outside", I tell the nurse, even though I don't see Mommy anywhere. "I have to go now."

"Fine by me", she replies. "Need any help with your wheelchair?"

She looks up from her coffee cup, and I see that her eyes are very blue and very, very tired.

"Those feeding tubes can be hard to maneuver when paired with a wheelchair", she reminds me.

"No thanks, I'm all set", I say, making sure she knows that I'm absolutely fine. If she insists on helping me, the whole plan will be ruined.

I wheel down the hallway to the door that goes outside, but I don't open it. I wait until the nurse looks down again, and then I wheel the other way, back toward The Doctor Who Is Not Raymond's office. I am very lucky, because the door is open. I go right to the drawer where I hid the diaries. I take them and put them in the pockets of the wheelchair.

Don't stop, Fern. Keep going. Don't hesitate.

But someone might be coming!

Don't worry, I'll warn you. Haven't I warned you about everything else?

I have to admit that this is true.

After I get the diaries, I peer down one side of the hallway, and then the other. It's getting close to winter, so it's almost dark out. I have to hurry. On one end of the hallway, there is another door that leads to the outside. I speed toward it, pushing my wheelchair as my feeding tube clanks beside me.

Take it out.

Take what out?

The feeding tube. It makes too much noise. Go back to Connor's office and find a pair of scissors. Take them outside with you, and get rid of your feeding tube there. Don't risk doing it in the building.

I don't even want to think about what I would do without Holly.

I go back to Connor's office, quietly, quietly, and find a pair of scissors in a cabinet that I. Have to stretch way up to reach, because my arms are still strapped into the wheelchair, so my hands are like tiny t-Rex claws. I look around the office. Maybe there's something else I can use to help my plan.

Stop stalling, Fern. Be brave. You know what you have to do.

I think that just like living older sisters, Holly can be a little bit bossy. I don't realize how much my hands are shaking until they are clutching the scissors. I hold them out in front of me, like a weapon. Like I'm Green Arrow. A superhero wouldn't be scared right now, but I'm terrified, so guess I'm not a superhero.

Don't be so sure of that, Fern.

Huh?

I'll explain it later! Hurry!

I open the door, and a cold blast of air hits me in the face. I should have remembered to look for a blanket or coat or something. But like Green Arrow, I have to be brave. I also need to get out of this wheelchair.

I wheel myself to the side of the hospital building, so no one would be able to see me unless they were looking right out the window and straight down. I grasp the scissors with my T-Rex bound arms. My stomach growls and I realize that I feel very tired and dizzy.

Look at your tiny little wrists, Fern. You've lost weight, too.

At first, I don't understand why Holly says that, but as her words flash around my head like flashlight beams, I realize what she means.

Look at your tiny little wrists...

So tiny I can wiggle right out of the strap that holds me. So that's what I do. My legs have gotten thinner, too, and the straps aren't holding me back anymore.

I slip out of the wheelchair, stumbling a little bit. I feel like a baby taking their very first steps. I take the pair of scissors and saw through the feeding tube. It's still in my nose and throat, but at least I don't have to drag around the metal pole anymore. And finally, as I step out of the wheelchair for the last time, clutching Holly and Mommy's diaries with arms I can now use, I am finally free.

No one knows where I am, and I can do whatever I want. I need to find Raymond's car. I remember the color if the car from the window. Red. I'm not sure what kind it is, because I don't really know anything about cars, because I think that is boring stuff. But right now, it would definitely be useful information. I think that I'm learning that everything can be useful information.

I run across the empty parking lot, leaving my wheelchair and feeding tube behind, only I'm not really running, because I stumble around and shift from side to side, like Mommy walked that night at the convention when she had too much to drink. Raymond's car is all the way on the other side. I know which car is his because I look in all the windows of the red cars for clues. Raymond doesn't have a pair of fuzzy blue dice hanging from that mirror-thing in the front of the car. Or a baby seat with little whales on it. Or a bumper sticker that says "Happy Hookers". I'm not sure what a hooker is, but I think it has to do with fishing. And Raymond doesn't really seem like the type of person who'd fish. But he *does* seem like the type of person who's have a bunch of papers in the front seat. The paper of top says "RAYMOND BEACON- Confidential." I've found it. I reach out my finger to the car. The sky above me is turning to twilight. I don't have much time left, but what if there's a car alarm?

I press my finger against the red car. It's smooth, but not shiny. I wonder how long it's been since Raymond's been to a car wash. Mommy goes every other day, and I've never seen Brian go.

You don't have much time. Hurry! There's no car alarm, because he didn't lock the car.

Of course. I open the backseat and crawl in. Raymond's doesn't smell like Mommy's or Brian's. It smells like cinnamon sugar, and I don't know why until I see the air freshener. The seats are dirty, but not with gross stuff like food and spilled beer. It's a good kind of dirty, stained with mud and leaves that mixes the cinnamon smells with a forest smell. I climb over the backseat and into the trunk, where I lie flat on my back, like a mummy. I put the diaries under my head like a very hard pillow.

He's coming, Fern. Stay brave.

I hear footsteps outside the car, and Raymond opens the door. I wish I could sit up and see him, tell him that it's me, it's Fern, and I need help because Mommy is going to hurt me because she is pregnant again and Raymond, I have so much to tell you but I'm so scared and I'm lying here like a mummy trying to escape. But I don't think Raymond has the power to read my thoughts, because all I hear in my head is Holly's voice.

Stay quiet, stay quiet. No matter what, stay quiet.

I hold my breath, and Raymond starts driving. He turns on the radio, which makes me relieved because the radio makes no much noise that it will cover up my breathing. I imagine I must be turning purple or blue. I let out a big gulp of air, and clench my body, because what if Raymond heard? But I don't think he did, because he keeps singing along with the Beatles. He actually has a good voice, the kind that makes me want to sing along, but of course I can't do that.

I don't know how long it is from the hospital to Raymond's house, but after about half an hour, I have to go to the bathroom. I am very good at holding it, though, since when I was two, Mommy made me wait forty-five minutes after I told her I had to use the bathroom. She said it was to "train" me, but now that I think about it, I think she was just being mean.

After another fifteen minutes, the car slows down. I can't tell where we are or what's outside, because I am still lying down. Raymond turns off the radio and I hear him sigh as he steps out of the car.

"Long day", he says to himself.

What do I do now, Holly? What if I'm left in the car forever?

You won't be left in the car forever, Fern. Wait until you hear Raymond go into his house. Then come out.

And then what?

You decide, Fern. This is your story. Your life. Mine is over.

I guess I'm on my own for now. I hear the heavy slam of a front door. I wait five more minutes, but only five, because I really have to go to the bathroom. Then I sit up and look around.

Like Brian's house, Raymond's house is in what people call "the middle of nowhere". There is a deep forest off to one side, and a dirt road leading up to a red brick house. There are lots of trees in Raymond's yard that are perfect for climbing.

I feel a little bit sad, because Daddy used to climb trees with me, only he'd sit on the lowest branch and I'd climb up, up, up. There was a special tree I'd climb, but it was near our old house, the one we lived in before Daddy left. It was at a park about five minutes away. Mommy always hated it when Daddy took me to the park, because she said "I don't want Fern bringing home any nasty germs that those other little kids carry. God knows she's carrying enough of them by herself. That all little kids are, David. Walking germ factories."

But Daddy would take my germ-filled hand anyway and walk with me to the park. He didn't even mind that I stopped a lot to look at interesting bugs on the ground. In fact, he even got me a jar with air holes to put them in, so soon I had a pet spider, a pet moth, a pet salamander, and a pet frog. I didn't have them for long, though, because after I was asleep, Mommy let them all outside.

Anyway, I wasn't actually getting any germs from other little kids, because Daddy and I never went on the playground equipment. We went right to the tree, and trees don't have any germs. The tree had a branch that was almost like a seat, and Daddy sat there and read Stephen King books out loud while I scrambled up the trunk, grasping the branches and pulling myself higher and higher until the tree swayed and Daddy called "That's high enough!" Then I would find a branch to sit on, one where I could stare up at the clear blue sky and pick out cloud shapes.

"Ready!" I called to Daddy, and he would stand up and read Stephen King novels louder, so I could hear them all the way up in the tree. But after we finished Pet Sematary, a bunch of parents came over and asked us not to read "those kind of books" out loud anymore because we were "scaring the children."

"I'm not scared", I said from my branch high up in the tree.

"Not *you*", a mother wearing a fanny pack snapped. "*Our* kids. And your father shouldn't be letting you climb that high in that tree, anyway."

Daddy asked me the next day if I wanted to go to the library and find something else to read instead. "Something that those parents would think is 'appropriate'?" I asked.

Daddy sighed. "I guess so. When we were leaving, one of them suggested a series called "The Friendship Fairies." I'm guessing you don't want to read that."

"No", I said. So the next time we went to the park and I climbed up the tree and Daddy sat at the bottom, a bunch of parents crowded around him. Daddy told me later that they were just looking for something to complain about.

"A dragon!" I called down to Daddy. "Green, with blue fire coming out of its mouth!"

Daddy was very smart, because he knew what I was doing.

"What else do you see, Fern?" he asked me.

I squinted at the sky. "A stingray", I told him.

"What's she doing?" I heard someone say. "There aren't stingrays or dragons in the sky."

"She's seeing the clouds", a woman replied. "Hey, Janie, come here! Look at the clouds!"

"Stop licking the slide!" a father scolded his son. "Come over here and listen to this girl in the tree."

I looked down and found that there were a bunch of kids at the bottom of the tree too, asking me to tell them what was in the clouds. I think they thought I was magic.

This worked for a few weeks, but then the kids started telling me what they wanted to see. A baseball bat, a princess crown, a dollar sign, a TV. But those weren't things you can see in the clouds.

When Timmy Kincaid said "Hey, tree girl, do you ever see letters in the clouds? Like "I AM A FREAK?"

I decided that it was time to shut down my cloud-announcing, so I told Timmy, "No, right now I see blood pouring out of an elevator." Daddy and I had watched "The Shining" again just two days before.

After I told Timmy that I saw blood pouring out of the elevator, nobody brought their kids over anymore because they thought I was "disturbed". They told Daddy I needed "professional help".

"Help with what?" I asked.

"Never mind", Daddy said. "They're just being mean. But we should probably find a different park."

But I liked the park we had been going to, so I came up with a very good idea. The next time he asked me "Fern, you wanna go to the park?" I said, "Yes, the one we always go to."

He frowned. "I'm not sure if that's a good idea", he said.

"We have to", I told him. "Please. You said to never mind the mean people. But you're minding them now. You're minding them a whole lot."

Finally, he smiled and ruffled my hair, which I only liked when he did it. "And you're right, Fern. I *was* minding what other people thought, which isn't a very good example to set."

"Yeah, like you *ever* cared about setting a good example" Mommy called from the kitchen, where she was cleaning the silverware drawer.

"Ignore her", Daddy whispered. "And get your coat."

So I got my coat, but I also got a notebook and a pen, and Daddy and I went to the park.

When we got there, the other parents muttered to each other and whispered. I think it was about us, but Daddy and I marched on to our tree, because we didn't care.

I climbed up, up, up the branches until Daddy told me to stop. And when I lay back and found shapes in the clouds, I took the pen and wrote down what I found on the pages of the notebook. Then I folded it into a paper airplane and sent it flying down to Daddy. That was how I told him all the shapes I saw in the sky. And no one ever knew.

CHAPTER
36

I want to climb one of the trees in Raymond's yard now, but I *really* have to go to the bathroom.

Be brave, Fern. Knock on the door.

So I walk up the front steps, but not because I'm brave. Because I have to go to the bathroom.

No, Fern. It's because you're brave. Knock on the door now. Stop stalling.

Sometimes I think it's a good thing that Holly can be a little bit bossy. I knock on the door and count the seconds that pass before it opens. Thirteen, fourteen, fifteen, sixteen. The door swings open and Raymond is standing there, still wearing his doctor's coat.

"Fern?" he asks.

I swallow hard.

"Can I use your bathroom please?"

He rubs his eyes, maybe to make sure I'm still there and not just a ghost.

"My...what?"

"Your bathroom. I don't want to go in the trees like people have to do when they're camping because it's cold out and it would probably be very uncomfortable and I don't have any toilet paper."

"Fern, what are you...how did...where are...?"

I am amazed that he can ask three questions in just one sentence.

"The bathroom?" I remind him.

"Right." He lets me in. "But when you're done, Fern, we need to have a talk."

After I'm done in the bathroom, I don't open the door, because I need time to think. What will I tell Raymond?

The truth, that's what you'll tell him.

Holly is right. No more lies. Ever. So now it's time to tell, the truth to myself. I'm terrified. I don't want to come out of the bathroom, because what if Raymond throws me out of the house? I wouldn't have anywhere to go. I put my head in my lap. I feel dizzy. Why is the truth so hard?

Raymond knocks on the door.

"Fern? You okay?"

I realize I have been sitting on the floor for a while now.

"Yes!" I call back.

I flush the toilet again so he won't know I was sitting on the floor because I was scared to come out. Raymond has changed out of his white doctor's coat. He is wearing a sweatshirt and jeans now. As soon as I see him, I start to cry. Tears stream down my face and I can't even speak. Raymond wraps me in a hug, warmer than any blanket.

"It's okay, Fern. You're safe."

I am still crying as he guides me to his living room and sits me down on the couch.

"You don't have any shoes on", he says, touching my bare feet, which are cold and muddy.

He gets me a pair on clean white socks. They come up to my knees. I sit on the couch, shaking and crying.

"Fern, please", Raymond begs. "Tell me what you're doing here. Tell me what's wrong."

But when I try to tell him, more and more tears spill out. He gets up and wraps a warm blue blanket around me.

"Want some tea?" he asks. I am crying too hard to speak, so I just nod, even though I don't really like tea because I think it's boring. Raymond must know I need a while alone, because he stays in the kitchen while the tea is brewing.

For the next few minutes, I look around his living room. There are lots of bookcases in here. In the corner is a desk with papers piled so high, I doubt Raymond can even work there.

The walls are painted blue, which makes me feel calm, because it's like looking into the blue sky when I was lying in the tree and sending down cloud-shape messages in paper airplanes. I take deep breaths. One, two, three.

Raymond comes back, holding two cups of steaming tea.

"Peppermint", he says. "Do you like sugar or milk?"

For the first time, I can speak.

"S-sugar", I stammer. "N-not milk."

He sets a box of sugar cubes in front of me. I've always liked sugar cubes because they are perfect cubes. No clumps, no circles, no mistakes in sugar cubes. I drop five of them into my tea.

"Now can you tell me what you're doing here?" Raymond asks.

The truth, Fern.

I look out the window at the gray sky.

"I needed to escape."

"Escape what?" Raymond asks. "Who brought you here?"

I squirm a little bit, because this part of the truth is hard. Then Raymond gets a look on his face, something like dread scrambled with anger mixed with relief blended with shock.

"You didn't...not in...oh God, Fern, does your mom know you're here?"

"No", I whisper.

He leans forward and puts his hands over his face. "You snuck into my car, didn't you? Tell me the truth."

"Yes", I say. "I snuck into your car."

"Oh my God, Fern", he mutters. "You have no *idea* how much trouble I'm going to be in with your parents. Why didn't you just *call*? You had my number."

"Mommy scrubbed it off", I told him. "And she won't let me use the phone so I haven't been able to call any of my friends from the Cancer Convention, either."

More, tell him more.

"Mommy tells everyone I have cancer", I say. "That's why I'm bald."

Suddenly, Raymond seems to forget that I snuck into his car. He is very interested in what I'm saying. "Fern, did you say that your mother... *tells* everyone you have cancer?"

"Yes."

"Why would she do that?"

I blink back tears. "She gets money from it. And...and Holly is dead now and I will be too because Mommy's pregnant and she doesn't need a piece of David anymore because that's what she said in her diary!"

The tears spill over. Raymond hands me a box of tissues. They smell like lavender.

"Why don't you start from the beginning", he says. "Tell me everything." So I do. The truth, the whole truth, and nothing but the truth, like they say on "Judging Amy", which was a show that they played at the hospital.

The entire time I'm talking, Raymond's face does not change, which scares me a little. Is he mad at me? Is he scared? What will he do? Finally, I pull out the diaries, which I've been holding onto the entire time.

Shyly, I tiptoe over to where Raymond is on the couch and sit next to him. I show him the diaries, one by one, page by page. We read them together, quietly, not speaking. The only sound in the room is our breath. When we turn the very last page of Holly's diary, Raymond's eyes widen a little is surprise.

"The baby was me", I tell him. "Holly was trying to warn me. She talks to me sometimes. In my head. Do you think I'm crazy?"

Raymond strokes my hair, just like Daddy used to. "No, Fern. I don't think you're crazy at all."

"Can I hold your hand while we read Mommy's diary?" I ask.

He doesn't answer, but he grabs my hand anyway. We go page by page through the diary. I try to skip the boring pages about love and kissing and boyfriends, but Raymond reads every word. I am bored, so I pick up the box of sugar cubes and examine one, rolling it around in my hands.

"I've always liked sugar cubes", Raymond says, not looking up from the diary.

"They're perfect", I agree. "No mistakes ever. Just square, all put together perfectly. All the little pieces connect."

"I wish life was like that", Raymond says. He frowns at the diary.

"You're almost done", I say. He reads faster, like there's something he has to do, but he wants to finish the diary first. When he gets to the last page, he lets the diary fall to the floor and stares blankly ahead.

"Raymond?" I ask. "Raymond?"

Suddenly, Raymond grabs me and hugs me tight. He smells like Winter Cranberry aftershave.

"Fern", he murmurs. "Oh, Fern, I'm so sorry. I had no idea. I mean, suspected there was something going on, that's why I installed the video cameras, but no one believed me when I said that you might be being abused. I'm sorry. I'm so sorry."

"Why did no one believe you?" I ask. "Why did you put in the video cameras?"

Raymond sighs. "I put in the video camera because I thought your mother might...well, I'll get to that in a minute. No one believed me because they knew I had been, um...seeing your mother and that we had sort of broken up. Stopped dating, if we ever actually *were* dating. They said I was just trying to get back at her by making her look bad. But I wasn't, Fern. I was doing it to protect you."

He leans back and sips his tea, which is probably ice-cold by now.

"The cameras?" I remind him.

"Yes", he says. "The cameras. Fern, you mother has, well, this is kind of hard to explain, so I'll say it right out. I think you mother has Munchausen Syndrome by Proxy."

CHAPTER
37

"What's that?" I ask. It sounds like a big word, a scary word. A hospital word.

"She's making you sick", Raymond says simply.

His words hang in the air like pea-soup fog.

"How do you know?"

"I don't know for sure", Raymond answers. "But I have a few clues. Some things she told me about you just didn't add up. And now, I'm positive, because of the diaries. I put a camera in your hospital room to see if I could catch your mother in the act. Doing something she wasn't supposed to, like maybe putting something in your IV. Did she ever do something like that?"

"Salt", I say. "She put salt in my IV. And made me drink Gatorade that made me sick. And lied to everyone at all the stores we went to just so she could get money. And she took me to a cancer convention because she told everyone I had cancer."

I explain again about the cancer convention, and all the stuff Mommy did to me. I tell Raymond about The Game. I tell him about Operation Hope. I tell him about how Pox was ripped apart on the cold hospital floor. Then I tell him my *real* symptoms, how I feel dizzy all the times and how my stomach is always growling and how my wrists and legs look like matchsticks because I'm so little.

"She's starving you", Raymond whispers. "My God, she's starving you!"

I shrug, even though he's right.

"Listen to me, Fern", Raymond says. "Listen to me very carefully. I want an honest answer. Are you hungry?"

"I'm always hungry", I say. "And thirsty too."

"I'm going to get you something to eat", he says, standing up and heading to the kitchen. "Plain food. No, she needs carbohydrates. And her blood sugar! It's got to be way too low. Maybe I still have that jelly in the cabinet..."

As soon as he's gone, I reach for the box of sugar cubes and take one out. Perfect, like a shining little snowflake. I pop it on my mouth.

"My sugar is okay!' I call to Raymond. "I'm eating the perfect sparkly cubes!"

I hear laughter from the kitchen, but it's kind of sad laughter.

Seven sugar cubes later, I start to smell something being fried on a stove. I lay back in the warm blanket. I feel lighter now that I've told someone everything. But it's already black outside, and the weight of the darkness and worry is pressing down on my chest like a cold metal brick. Four minutes and twelve seconds later, Raymond comes back into the room, carrying a tray.

"Do you like grilled cheese?" he asks.

"Is the cheese orange?" I ask.

He nods.

"Then I love it", I say, even though at this point, I would eat a cardboard box, I'm so hungry.

He sets the grilled cheese in front of me with a glass of grape juice and a brownie.

351

"The brownie was made by one of my coworkers", he tells me. "The one you call "Blue." She brings me homemade desserts a lot, which is good, because grilled cheese is about the only thing I can cook. I'll tell you, Fern, I think she *likes* me."

I smile, thinking about Blue and Raymond sitting together, holding hands. It doesn't seem as gross as Mommy and Brian sitting together holding hands.

"And the grape juice", Raymond goes on. "I've always had a weakness for grape juice. Drank it every day when I was a kid, and as you can see, I'm still quite fond of it."

"What's a weakness for grape juice?" I ask.

"It means you really, really like it", Raymond says.

"Oh. I have a weakness for grape juice too, then."

I bend the straw he gave me and stick it between my teeth. The grape juice feels good on my throat, which still hurts from the feeding tube. It's still stuck in there. Just because I cut part of it off with scissors doesn't mean it's not dangling in my throat and sticking out my nose.

I guess Raymond notices this, because as I am biting into the grilled cheese, he asks, "What's that in your nose, Fern?"

"My feeding tube", I answer. "Mommy put it in. She got it online. It's not a real feeding tube, though. She pinned a part of it together do the liquid in the IV bag would never get to me."

"Where's the IV bag?" Raymond asks.

"Behind the hospital building", I say. "With the IV pole and the wheelchair. Don't worry, I hid them pretty well. So no one will find out."

Raymond doesn't answer. He tells me to lie down and wait. Then he leaves. At first, I am worried he is going to call Mommy, but he comes back carrying a doctor's bag. Immediately, the warm feeling I have dissolves like the sugar cubes in my tea.

"It's okay", Raymond says. "I'm just going to get the feeding tube out. It's not good to have it in your throat for that long. I'm assuming your mother never cleaned it? Replaced it? Took care of it?"

"No, no, and no."

"Thought so", he mutters.

He takes out a tool.

"Close your eyes", he tells me.

"No, I like to watch, remember?" I say. "Remember the blood."

He smiles, a half smile like a half-moon. "Right."

He tugs the feeding tube out through my nose. At first it tickles, then it feels like someone's pulling my nose out, then it feels like I'm going to throw up, and finally, it burns. I rub my nose as Raymond rubs my back to make me feel better.

"When you're feeling like you can, sit up please", he says. "I have something important to tell you."

I sit up right away, because I hardly ever hear important stuff that I'm actually *supposed* to hear.

"This- what your mother is doing, I mean- is very dangerous. It needs to stop."

I nibble on the brownie. Blue is a very good cook because the brownie is delicious.

"How?" I ask.

Raymond looks very tired.

"I need to make two phone calls", he says. "One to Child Protective Services, and one to your mother."

Don't let him call Mom, Fern. You know what she'll do to you.

"No", I say. "Please don't call anyone. Please."

"I have to", Raymond says. "First of all, it's my duty to report child abuse. Second of all, if I don't contact someone to let them know where you are, I'll be charged with kidnapping."

"But you didn't kidnap me", I say. "I got into your car and you didn't even know. That's not kidnapping."

As I am telling Raymond this, he is taking out his cellphone and dialing a number. I watch in horror.

"Please, Raymond, don't call Mommy", I beg. "Please. She'll make me go home. And I don't want to go home. She'll hurt me, I know she will!"

"Okay." Raymond puts the phone down. "What do *you* suggest we do? You have to go home, Fern, and we need to contact someone about the abuse."

"Can't I just live here? Please?"

Raymond looks sad and he says he wishes it could be that way.

"But maybe you can stay here for the night", he tells me. "It's already nine o'clock, and it's raining. And it's a long trip back to your house."

"Yeah!" I say.

"I'll call", Raymond says. "But we have to do what's best for you, Fern. I know it's not what you might want, but no arguing, okay?" \

I consider this. I don't want to go back to Mommy, but Raymond said he would do what's best for me.

"Okay?" Raymond asks again. "I'll call, but you have to go along with what I decide in the end."

Agree, Fern. Raymond won't hurt you. You know that.

"Okay", I say miserably. I bury my head in the blanket that smells like cinnamon. Raymond opens his cell phone and pauses.

"You know, Fern", he says softly, "I really do wish you could stay with me."

I try to keep my tears quiet under the blanket.

"Hello?" Raymond says. Then, "Who is this, please? Brian Kingsley? I think I remember you, sir. From the hospital....well, you see, I have Fern here with me. It seems she really wanted to see me, so she climbed into the back of my car. What? No, I'm sorry, I don't know where your wife was when it happened. It just realized Fern was here when she knocked on my front door....I assume you want me to bring her home now? What? Well, yes, I see your point. The thing is, she's at least two hours away....and the roads might not be safe, with the rain and all. I could keep her here overnight and bring her back first thing in the morning. I would need a guardian's permission, though. Can you give me that?"

I know it's Brian on the other end of the phone, and I know Brian hates me. He'll do anything to keep me away.

"It'll work", I whisper, lifting my head up a little bit.

Raymond nods, but he doesn't look like he believes me. Brian must say yes, though, because then Raymond smiles and says "Are you sure?" and then, "Well, *you* may feel that way, but I happen to think she's a wonderful child. Okay, thank you. Goodbye."

Then Raymond puts down his phone and lifts up the blanket I've burrowed back under.

"You're safe now", he whispers. "They're not gonna hurt you."

You did it, Fern. Didn't you hear Raymond? He's not going to let anyone hurt you.

Yes, but what happens when I get home? What happens now?

These are questions that even Holly can't answer, so I ask Raymond. We sit in the living room on the couches with fresh cups of tea.

"What's going to happen?" I ask, dumping nine sugar cubes into my cup.

"Have a little tea with your sugar?" Raymond says.

"Huh?" I ask. "I'm having tea *and* sugar."

"Never mind", Raymond says. "It was a joke."

"What's going to happen?" I ask again. "I need to know. Please."

Raymond leans back and smiles, but it's a tight smile.

"You can stay the night, thank God. It's the safest option right now."

"Why is it the safest?" I ask. "Will Mommy hurt me if I go back? Will Brian hurt me?"

"Let's just say you're safe with me, Fern. Your mother has done some pretty awful things. I'm calling Child Protective Services tomorrow, and they'll help you. You don't have to be scared. They're very nice."

"I've met them", I say. "They came to my old house."

Raymond seems surprised, so I tell him all about Mole and Frog.

"They were a little weird", I say. "But I liked them. Weird isn't bad."

"No", Raymond agrees, "it's not."

Suddenly, I have an idea.

"Raymond, I..."

"What's up, Fern?"

"I had an idea..."

"What's your idea?"

Tell him, Fern. I want to go back, too.

I take a deep breath.

"I want to go back and see my old house."

I have to explain to Raymond all about moving to Brian's house and leaving everything behind.

"Well, this certainly comes as a surprise", Raymond says. "When did you want to go back?"

"Tonight? It has to be soon, Raymond. I don't have very much time left."

"Whoa, whoa, whoa", Raymond says. "No one is going anywhere tonight. And what's this about not having much time left? What do you mean?"

"I might die soon", I say. "Mommy will kill me now that she is having a new baby. Just like she killed Holly. I want to see my old house again before that happens."

Raymond takes both of my hands in his.

"Fern, you're not going to die. I won't let that happen."

"I still want to see my old house." For some funny reason, that's all I can think about now, it's all I want. I want to go back to the place where I was happy once. Where Daddy used to live with me and Mommy and even though everything wasn't perfect, it was still good enough. "I don't even know your address", Raymond says.

"I know it!" I exclaim, and suddenly, I *do* know it. It pops into my head, clattering as it lands in my brain. 45 Bachelor Street. I guess I saw it so many times on our mailbox that it got smashed into my head and popped out just now.

"It's too late tonight", Raymond says. "But I'll tell you what. If you're feeling up to it in the morning, and if we can get going early enough, then we can go before I bring you home. How's that?"

I hug Raymond tight.

"Perfect", I whisper.

Raymond tells me that he doesn't have an extra bedroom, but I can sleep on the couch. I'm happy about that, because it's a very comfortable couch. He brings me way more blankets and pillows than I need.

"I only get a mattress at home!" I exclaim.

Raymond's forehead crinkles in concern.

"Are you sure you're warm enough?" he asks for what must be the millionth time.

"Yes, thank you", I say, for what also must be the millionth time.

"Do you mind taking an Ensure?" he asks.

I tell him I don't know if I mind, because I don't know what an Ensure is.

"It's like a protein milkshake", he tells me. "I think it would be good for you. Just one. I'm worried, Fern. You're too thin. You need some calories, and an Ensure is an easy way to get them. It's just a drink. You can even pick the flavor."

"Are there sleeping pills hidden in it?" I ask. "Or any other kind of pills that will make me sick?"

"Now, why would I give you pills that would make you sick?" Raymond asks.

I shrug. "Mommy did."

He hugs me again, and I can tell that he is very sad and also very worried, so I say "Okay, I'll have the Ensure."

"Thank you", he smiles. "There's chocolate, vanilla, butter pecan, strawberry, and mocha. Wait, I'm not giving you the mocha, you'll be up all night."

I don't tell him that I usually stay up most of the night anyway.

"Pick another flavor", he says, so I pick chocolate. It looks like melted ice cream. I stir it with a straw.

"Try it", Raymond urges.

"I'm scared", I admit. "What if there's something bad hidden in it?"

"Fern", Raymond says softly, "I *promise* I would never hide anything in your drink. I promise. I have this stuff because I give it to a lot of my patients, and you don't see me trying to hurt *them.*"

But I'm still scared, so Raymond goes to the kitchen and dumps the Ensure down the drain in the sink. He lets me open a new bottle and pour it myself, so I can see there's nothing bad hidden in it. Then I can drink it. It's gross and it tastes like chalk and I feel sick afterwards, but since Raymond is letting me stay at his house and giving me blankets and pillows and tea and food, I can at least drink some chalk for him.

At eleven o'clock, Raymond tells me I should try to sleep.

"If you want to visit your old house in the morning, we should leave by seven", he says.

"What about your work?" I ask. "Don't you have to work? If you don't work, you can get fired. Daddy got fired, and now he doesn't call me anymore."

"I can take a sick day", Raymond says.

"But you're not sick. That would be lying."

"True, you're more important than work right now."

We are both quiet for a while.

"Why do you want to see your old house?" Raymond asks finally.

Why *do* you, Fern?

I want to remember how I used to be happy there.

I know. And you're on the very edge of figuring something out.

"What?" I say out loud. Raymond looks at me.

"It's Holly", I explain. "She is talking to me."

Raymond smiles and puts a finger to his lips to show that he will be quiet.

What am I figuring out, Holly?

Think about it. Go over the facts. Where is David?

I don't know.

Where are you?

At Raymond's house.

Not *now*. I mean, where do you *live*?

Brian's house.

Does David know where you are?

No.

And he hasn't called you at Brian's house or sent letters to Brian's house. But he knows your old address. Do you think...

CHAPTER
38

"It's at my old house!" I yell. "Something from Daddy must be at my old house! *That's* why I wanted to go, but I just didn't know it! But *you* knew it, Holly! And you made me know it, too!"

No, I didn't. You figured it out on your own.

"I thought Daddy had forgotten me", I say.

How could he forget his own daughter?

I start crying then, but I'm not completely sad. Happy tears plus sad tears equals what? Just okay tears? I don't know. Raymond watches me cry for a while. He passes me tissue after tissue, but he stays quiet. I think he knows that this is between me and Holly.

When I finally stop crying and lie down, he asks, "Do you want me to stay with you until you fall asleep?"

"No thanks", I say. "I can do it."

"You're a brave, brave little girl. A survivor", he says.

Then he goes to bed. Of course, I can't fall asleep. Even though the day has made me very tired, I feel like a hummingbird, buzzing with excitement and anxiety. A million "what-ifs" are running through my mind, marching in a straight line that seems like it will never stop.

What if there aren't any letters from Daddy? What if the letters got thrown away? What if he completely forgot about me? What if he doesn't care anymore?

I sit up. The living room isn't quite dark. Raymond left the kitchen light on.

"In case you get scared", he said. "Sleeping in new places will do that to you."

But I'm not scared of the dark. Actually, I like it better than the light. But now I am glad the kitchen light is on, because I can get up without banging into the coffee table. I hear Raymond's grandfather clock chime twelve. At home, I would be just sneaking off my mattress now. I would go to the bathroom and get some water to drink. I would walk around the house to stretch my legs, skipping any creaky floorboards. I would read Holly's diary. Or Mommy's. But both diaries are finished, so I just stand up and tiptoe to the kitchen. I feel trapped, like I always do at night.

Get some food, Fern.

What?

Get some food. You know that when you get home you won't be allowed to eat. So get some food. I bet Raymond's cabinets aren't locked.

They're not. I drag a chair across the floor and open the doors to find boxes and boxes and boxes of cereal. The sugary, colorful kind. Fruit cups, too. The kind with fake fruit in syrup. And peanut butter and jelly and everything else sweet in the world I can think of. Raymond kind of eats like a little kid. My hand reaches toward a box of chocolate lucky charms, but I stop inches away. Do I really want to steal from Raymond after he's been so nice to me?

It's a tough world, Fern. You gotta do what you gotta do.

I grasp the cereal box as the chair tips backwards, sending me sprawling in a pile of chocolate cereal pieces and sticky marshmallows. I hear footsteps. Terrified, I scramble away from the mess. I need to find somewhere to hide. My mind is racing, not really even thinking. I dive behind the counter as Raymond comes into the kitchen, calling "Fern? Are you alright?"

He must see the cereal mess and the open cabinet and the tipped-over chair, because he says "What the...?"

Then he stops. I can't see him, so I imagine he's thinking. My heart is pounding like a buzz in my chest. He won't want to take me to my old house now, that's for sure. In fact, he'll probably punish me. Hit me, maybe, like Mommy and Brian do when I spill something. Or maybe this was all a trap. Maybe he really still loves Mommy and wants to make her happy by hurting me. Maybe he'll kill me, so Mommy won't have to. I let out a choked sob, and before I know it, Raymond is kneeling on the floor next to me, patting my back and whispering "Shhh, shhh, it's okay. I'm not mad. It's okay."

"I'm...s-sorry", I stammer. I curl myself into a ball in case he hits me. If you bring your knees up to your chest and stuff your arms inside your shirt and put your head down, it hurts less. This is one thing I have learned from Mommy and Brian. I feel a warm finger on the back of my neck.

"I'm not going to hit you", says Raymond. "I'm not going to punish you. I'm not mad. I just want to know what happened."

I lift my head up and look at him. His eyes tell me he's not lying. "I was getting food", I say. "When I go home, I'm going to get punished by getting no food. So I needed some. And Holly told me I should get some of yours and that you didn't lock the cabinets at night like Mommy does."

"Your mother locks the cabinets at night?" Raymond asks.

I nod.

"That's not okay", he says. "That is absolutely not okay. You deserve to eat. If you're hungry, I'd be happy to send some food home with you. Just ask me, okay? You don't have to be afraid."

"Okay", I say. "Thank you. Um, do you have a broom?"

"I'll take care of the cereal", Raymond says. "I spill it all the time myself. Accidents happen. You try to go back to bed, okay? We have to get up early tomorrow."

So I go back to couch and lie down, and after Raymond sweeps up the cereal, he comes on and stays with me until I fall asleep. I don't see Holly that night. I hear her voice, but it's through a cloud that sparkles and rains.

Be careful, Fern. Be careful. You might not find what you want. Be ready.

She says things like that all night through that cloud. I am standing on the other side of the cloud. It is raining Lucky Charms marshmallows.

At six-thirty, Raymond wakes me up.

"I put an extra toothbrush and a sweater in the bathroom", he says. "And a fresh pair of socks." I don't even remember how long it's been since I've brushed my teeth, so I brush them for five minutes straight. The toothbrush lights up and has the batman symbol on it. Raymond says I can keep it.

I pull on Raymond's sweater, which hangs down to my knees like a dress. I roll up the sleeve and put the long socks on. I glimpse myself in the mirror and gasp. There's hair on my head! Mommy hasn't shaved it in a while, so my light blond hair is growing back. It's still short, but it's there, like baby bird feathers. I like it.

When I come out of the bathroom, Raymond is already dressed in jeans and a green sweater.

"In honor of you", he says. "Green's your favorite color, right?"

"Yes. Like Green Arrow. I think you're like him, Raymond, except you don't shoot people with arrows."

"That's true", Raymond replies. "Shall we have breakfast?"

He takes two bowls out and hands me one. He opens the cabinet full of cereal boxes.

"Anything you want", he tells me. "I never run out of cereal. It's my favorite food."

I mix together every single cereal Raymond has.

"Very interesting", he says. "You want milk?"

"No thanks", I say. "Eww."

"Right. I don't like milk on cereal either", Raymond says, so we both have grape juice.

Raymond also makes me drink an Ensure, because he says that it will keep me from being hungry later.

By seven-thirty, we are ready to go. My knees shake as I stand by the door, clutching the diaries.

"Are you nervous?" Raymond asks.

"A little", I answer, trying to stop my knees from shaking.

"Did you, um...did you hear anything from Holly last night?" Raymond asks when we're in the car. Since I'm telling the truth, the whole truth, and nothing but the truth, I answer him.

"Yes, she was telling me I might not find what I want. At my old house, I guess."

Raymond scratches his head.

"She's right. You may not find what you're looking for. What *are* you looking for, exactly?"

"I'm not sure", I say. "A letter, maybe. At least a letter. Since Daddy doesn't know that we moved, he probably sent letters to my old house. *If* he sent letters, I mean. I'm kind of worried he forgot."

"Well, I can't be sure", Raymond says, "but know this, Fern. Even if you have no one else in the world, I'll always be here, okay? I'll be there for you anytime you need me."

"Thank you", I say. I want to stop talking about Daddy now because it's making me nervous. Raymond must know that, because he puts in a Beatles CD.

"Do you like the Beatles?" he asks.

"I don't know", I say. "But I like their name, because I like beetles. I like all kinds of bugs. Except for ticks, because they bite."

We listen to the Beatles for a while, and Raymond songs along quietly. I sit in the backseat, rereading pages from Holly's diary.

"Want to hear my favorite Beatles song?" Raymond asks. He switches to track five. "It's called 'Lucy In The Sky With Diamonds'."

"That's a funny name for a song."

"Well, it's a funny type of song" Raymond says. "Listen to the words."

I do.

"It sounds like one of my dreams with Holly", I say. "Kind of unreal. One night, I had a dream that we were in a field next to a river that turned into anything you wanted to drink. Pineapple juice for her, grape juice for me. That could fit into the song really well."

"It could", Raymond agrees.

"What's it *about?*" I ask. "The words are like dreams, kind of. But why does it keep saying "kaleidoscope eyes?" And who's Lucy?"

"Well, to be honest", Raymond says, "a lot of people think this song is about drugs. Do you know what drugs are?"

"Medicine?" I say, because I know the word "drugstore", and that's where you buy medicine, so "drug" must be another word for medicine.

"Well, yes and no", Raymond replies. "Technically, drugs are medicine. But the word usually means a bad type of medicine. One that can hurt you."

"Like what Mommy gave me?"

"In a way, I suppose."

I listen to the song a little more.

"I don't think it's about bad medicine", I say. "I think it's about dreams."

"Me too", Raymond sighs. "Now if only the rest of the world thought that way."

"What do you mean?"

"You see, Fern, people in this world always have to think everything's about something bad. They just can't appreciate the beautiful dreamlike simplicity of the Beatles."

We are both quiet for exactly twenty-three minutes.

Then Raymond says "I've always been partial to the Beatles."

"What's partial?"

"It means they're one of my favorites."

"I'm partial to Simple Plan", I say.

"What kind of songs do they sing?" Raymond asks. "Could you sing one for me?"

"My voice is very bad", I say. "Mommy told me never to sing. And she wasn't kidding, either."

"Well, I'm telling you it's fine. Not everyone can be John Lennon." "Who?" "A member of the Beatles. Come on, try it!"

Try it, Fern. If you can survive the abuse Mom's put you through, then you can definitely sing your favorite song.

So I sing "I'm Just A Kid", and Raymond claps and whistles, even though my voice hasn't gotten any better since the time I sang in the kindergarten chorus at school and Mommy pulled me aside and told me if I didn't stop singing, I would embarrass her and get a spanking.

Raymond doesn't seem embarrassed at all, but maybe that's just because it's only the two of us in the car.

"Again!" Raymond says. "This time I'll sing too."

So we both sing *"I'm just a kid, and life is a nightmare, I'm just a kid, I know that it's not fair"*, until Raymond stops and says "This song really speaks to you, doesn't it?"

"Speaks to me?"

"It means you understand it", he says. "You feel like the singer is singing right to you."

I smile, because that's exactly what it feels like.

"Tell me again what your address is", Raymond says. "I think we're close."

"45 Bachelor Street", I reply nervously.

It is a foggy morning, so I can't really see what's ahead on the road, making everything scarier.

I'm just a kid, and life is a nightmare...

"Raymond", I ask. "What if Mommy really is going to kill me because she's having a baby and doesn't need me anymore? What if nobody needs me?"

Raymond pulls the car over and touches my hand. "Then I must be nobody", he says, "because I need you an awful lot."

We are quiet for a few minutes. The car is warm and comfortable and it smells good too.

"What about Mommy killing me?" I ask.

"I won't let her", Raymond says. He starts driving again. "I absolutely will not let her. I'm going to take you to the police station, and they'll know what to do about your mother and Brian."

"Are the police nice?"

"Most of them. I'll stay with you though, in case you get scared."

I don't think anything can scare me if I'm away from Mommy and Brian. I stare out the window. I still can't see anything. Raymond slows the car down until it stops, like a ship gently coming to land.

CHAPTER
39

"W e're here", he says softly.

"Oh." I don't move, because for some reason, I am afraid to get out of the car.

"Do you...do you want to go look in the mailbox?" Raymond asks.

I nod, still not getting up. "Do you need me to come with you?" I shake my head.

"I think I need to do this on my own."

Raymond smiles.

"You're a strong kid, Fern. I admire that."

I slip out of the car. The fog swirls around my ankles. It feels like I'm in a dream, and I half-expect to see Holly. Our old house looks exactly the same. I walk slowly, partly because I'm tired and partly because I'm nervous.

Sitting next to the mailbox is a box, wet from the rain and mist. I open the mailbox. It's stuffed full. The letters are soggy and crumpled a little. The mailman was probably careless after the twentieth letter came. There's got to be at least twenty, I think, plus the box, which is addressed to me with no return address. It just says "From Daddy". So do all the letters, and I know this because I look at each one as I count them. Fifty-seven. I don't open any, though. I'm afraid.

It's cold out, and I can feel the wind whip through Raymond's sweater, chilling my bones. I hear the honk of a car horn. Raymond rolls down the window.

"Come on back, Fern. It's cold."

I take one last look at the house, and everything comes flooding back to me. The birthday cakes, the park, mint chocolate chip ice cream, Stephen King novels, superhero backpack, grape Popsicles, paper airplanes, the tree. All with Daddy. Never again.

I realize I am crying, and soon Raymond comes out of the car and wraps his big warm arms around me and carries me to the front seat.

"I shouldn't be letting you sit here", he mutters. "You're not even half of the required weight."

He takes a blanket from the trunk and wraps it around me. He carries in the box and all twenty-six letters, setting them, at my feet.

"Look at them when you're ready. I've got to start driving to the police station. Don't worry, you've got plenty of time."

I start to sort the letters by date. Daddy sent me the first one a week after we moved. It says:

"Dear Fern, I'm sorry I can't see you this week, but I've been having some problems at work. Nothing for you to worry about. I'll see if next week we can spend double the time together, since I've missed the past few weeks. See you soon! Love, Daddy."

The next letter, a week later, says:

"Dear Fern, I have something I need to tell you. I know I didn't come this week, and I promised I would. But I got fired from my job yesterday. I'm going to be okay, but things might be tight for a little while. I promise I'll call as soon as I can. Be strong, my little superhero. Love, Daddy."

I wonder if Daddy came to pick me up and found out I was gone. I imagine him standing on the doorstep, ringing the bell over and over and over. I hope he didn't think Mommy and I were just ignoring him.

"Dear Fern, Why won't you answer the phone? I've been calling and calling, but the answering machine picks up every time. Is your mother giving you trouble? If she is, just write me a letter and we can get it sorted out. Love, Daddy."

Is your mother giving you trouble?

I laugh a little at this.

Oh, if only he knew, Fern. If only he knew.

I have read three letters so far, so I find the next one. I want to read them in order, like a diary. Then I realize something. If Daddy's letters are like a diary, then that means I've read a diary written by every single person in my family. Mommy, Daddy, and Holly.

The next ten letters basically say the same thing. Daddy's in a tough spot, he doesn't know when he'll be able to visit me, and "be strong, my little superhero." Thirteen letters down, thirteen to go. Plus the box. I look at Raymond.

"You okay?" he asks.

"Yeah", I answer. "How much time do we have left?" Raymond says we've got plenty of time, and then he gives me a red and white peppermint to keep me from getting carsick while I read the letters. I don't get carsick, but I take the mint because it's candy and I like candy. The fourteenth letter is different.

"Dear Fern, I wish I could be there to tell you this. I'm very sorry, but I can't come to visit you anymore. I can't exactly explain why right now, but it doesn't have to do with you. It has to do with money. Money's a villain, my little superhero. Never grow up. Love, Daddy."

I turn to Raymond. My eyes are shining with tears that make everything in the car sparkle like Christmas lights.

"He couldn't visit anymore. Because money was a villain. I hate money, Raymond."

Raymond doesn't exactly know what I'm talking about, but he puts his arms around me. Then he digs into his wallet and gives me a one-dollar bill.

"If money's a villain", he says, "then destroy it, Green Arrow."

"You mean rip it up?" I ask. "But it's *your* money!"

"It's worth it", Raymond says. "Take out your anger on the money. Your Daddy said that money was a villain. Believe him. He sounds like a smart man."

So I rip the dollar bill to shreds, letting the green wisps of paper float onto the floor of Raymond's car. He waves his hand at it.

"Don't bother cleaning it up", he says. "My car's always a mess."

"Not like Brian's", I say. "His is gross-dirty. Yours is just...earthy."

Raymond laughs. "I guess I'll take that as a compliment", he says.

I tear open the fifteenth letter, okay for now because I, Green Arrow, have destroyed the villain. Then I stop unfolding the fifteenth letter and I tear open the sixteenth, seventeenth, eighteenth, nineteenth, twentieth. Twenty-first, twenty-second, twenty-third, twenty-fourth, twenty-fifth, until there's only one left. The envelopes litter Raymond's car like big ripped snowflakes. I read the letters with super-speed, like The Flash. The words blur together in my head.

"Dear Fern...I'm sorry...money...fired...little superhero...stay strong... tough spot...call me...if Mommy gives you trouble...can't visit...it will get better...remember...I love you...Love, Daddy."

I take a deep breath and peel open the last envelope.

"Dear Fern, I wish you were here. I miss you so much. And I'm going to miss you even more, Fern, because I can't contact you anymore. I can't send letters or call or visit. I'm so sorry, my little superhero. After I got fired, money became tight and I couldn't afford to pay the child support bills."

"What are child support bills?" I ask Raymond.

"They're money that a single parent gets from their ex-husband of wife to help raise their kid. If you don't pay it, you can get in trouble with the law."

My face must turn white, because Raymond says quickly "But it's okay, Fern. Your dad would never stop paying child support." A flash of anger bursts through me, because Raymond just doesn't get it! He's not Daddy! He hasn't done the stuff that Daddy did with me!

"He *did* stop!" I scream, causing Raymond to jerk the car forward. "He *did* stop!"

"Okay, okay!" Raymond says. He stops the car and puts his arms around me. "Do you need to talk about it?"

"No. But you're wrong. He *did* stop. You don't know Daddy like I do. He wouldn't do this to me! He wouldn't!"

"I'm not sure I understand", Raymond says. "What do you need right now?"

You need to finish the letter, Fern. It's for the best.

"I need to finish the letter", I tell Raymond.

"All right", he replies, and starts driving again, slower this time.

"The thing is, Fern, I'm in trouble. If I don't pay the child support bills, very serious things could happen to Me. I won't tell you what, because they're not going to happen. Because I'm on the run. That means I'm out of my apartment. I'm traveling somewhere so people won't recognize me. I am introducing myself under a new name. I've shaved off my beard. If you saw me, you probably wouldn't recognize me."

This is wrong. I will always recognize Daddy.

"I can't tell you where I'm going or who I am. I can't tell anyone."

I start to cry again, but this time I try to be quieter about it. Daddy can't even tell *me* where he is! Or *who* he is! And I'm his kid! His little superhero! Not anymore, though.

Raymond looks over at me, but keeps driving.

"You may have noticed that the letters I've been sending you have no return address. That's because I don't want my address out there any more than it has to be. You can't tell a soul about me, Fern. Don't tell anyone where I am or who I am. Don't try to find me. Don't mention me. I'm so sorry, my little superhero, but starting now, I can't be your Daddy anymore. Love, David."

I am on automatic. I refuse to think about what I am just read. Robotically, I open the box. Inside are cans and cans of Sandalwood Summers aftershave, the kind Daddy wears, with a note that says "Thought you might like these".

I uncap one and smell it, and that's when it all hits me. Daddy isn't my Daddy anymore. He said so himself. And if I don't have a Daddy and I don't have Holly, that means that I only have Mommy, who is mean and wants to kill me. I reread the last line of the last letter.

"Love, David".

That part hurts the most. He doesn't even want me to call him Daddy anymore. Just David, like he's a stranger. He doesn't want to be my Daddy anymore.

I cry harder, and Raymond puts a warm hand on my shoulder.

"Are you sure there's nothing you want to talk about?"

"He's not my Daddy anymore", I sob.

I'm crying too hard to explain, so Raymond pulls over and I let him read the least letter. I see his face crumple as the words zoom into his brain. When he's done, he hugs me.

"Oh my God, Fern", he whispers, "I'm so sorry about this." He hold me tight for a long time in the car that is surrounded by fog in the middle of nowhere.

"He'll always be your Daddy", Raymond finally says. "Whether he wants to be or not. And he'll always love you."

"Then why did he say those things?" I ask.

Raymond sighs. "It sounds like he's really going through a rough patch right now. But that's no excuse. The most honest answer I can give you, Fern is that I really don't know."

"I hate him!" I say. "I do! He left me!"

"You have a right to be angry", Raymond says. "You can hate him if you need to."

Raymond tells me some more stuff then, about Daddy and love and anger, but I'm only half-listening because I am suddenly very tired. I feel the car start to move again.

I am in a room, standing on a chair. The room is white. There are two of those wooden stands. I think they're called podiums. I am standing on one, and Holly is on the other. We are both looking out into the room, which is filled with men. We are trying to find Daddy. Each man steps up to us and we say "Yes, you might be Daddy" or "No, you're just a creep. Go away."

Holly makes most of the calls, while I just stand there, waiting for the familiar face to come into view. I'll recognize Daddy. I know I will. There are hundreds of men in the room. Suddenly, I think I see someone who looks like Daddy standing in the corner. I leap off my podium and run over, but by the time I get there, he's all the way on the other side of the room. I try to go after him, but he's always a few steps ahead of me, and when I call out "Daddy! Daddy!" He doesn't answer.

I shove through the mass of bodies, but Daddy is impossible to catch. Then I hear yelling. I crouch down on the floor because I am scared. It is Daddy's voice.

"LEAVE ME ALONE, FERN! I AM NOT YOUR DADDY ANYMORE! GOT THAT? STOP TRYING TO LOVE ME, BECAUSE I'M NOT GOING TO LOVE YOU! I DON'T CARE WHAT HAPPENS TO YOU! JUST GIVE UP ALREADY! I'M NOT GOING TO BE THERE FOR YOU ANYMORE! IT'S OVER!"

Then a door slams, and the room fills with the smell of Sandalwood Summers aftershave. I feel something stop inside me, and I wake up. It turns out that the thing that stopped was Raymond's car. There is sun coming in through the windows, lighting up the inside of the car. The fog is gone. I blink my eyes open. The brightness is surprising.

"You're awake", Raymond says softly. "How do you feel?"

"Sad", I say. "Daddy was yelling at me in my dream. He didn't love me anymore."

"But that's just a dream", Raymond says. "You have to remember that. Dreams aren't real. Especially bad ones."

"How long did I sleep?" I ask.

Raymond looks nervously at the 7-11 we are parked in front of. "A few hours. We're here at the police station. I didn't want to wake you up. When you're ready, we can go inside."

"I'm ready."

"You're a brave girl", Raymond says, taking my hand as he helps me out of the car.

The police station is cold and quiet. A woman in a police officer uniform sits at the front desk. Raymond says something to her, and she nods.

"I'll get right on it", she says. "But things tend to run slow here."

Raymond comes over to me. "Sit right here in this chair, Fern, and I'll get you a snack, okay? It might be a while before someone can help us."

Raymond brings me a bag of barbeque potato chips and says quietly, "I have to go to the bathroom, Fern, but I'll be right back. The woman at the front desk will make sure you're okay while I'm gone. It'll only be a minute."

I nod, not looking up from my chips. I feel safe here, like nothing can hurt me.

But I am wrong.

Look out the window, Fern. Run, run, run!

I peer through the glass panes and my heart stops in my chest. It's Mommy. She's running toward the door and fake-crying, from what I can tell. The police woman is looking down at some papers on her desk. Quietly, I put down the bag of chips. Raymond said no one would hurt me, but Mommy can fool the police, I know she can. And then I'll be taken home and...

No, you won't. Not if you run. Go! Now!

I sprint out the door. I'm a fast runner, but as I dart through the cars in the parking lot, the cold stinging my cheeks, I can feel someone behind me. I run, into the road, into the trees surrounding the police station. I hear the police woman yelling far behind me, and I slow a bit. Has she caught Mommy?

But no. I feel bony arms around my waist, and I am being lifted up, up, up into the air and carried like a sack of potatoes through the parking lot, where Mommy dumps me into the back of her car. Brian is sitting in the front seat, crunching on a bag of Cheez-Its. He laughs when he sees me.

"Help!" I scream, and even though Raymond and the police woman are pounding on the glass of the windows and struggling to open the car door, Mommy's too powerful. She's got the windows closed and the doors locked. And now she's driving away, with me screaming in the backseat.

CHAPTER
40

Raymond and the police are right behind us, but Mommy's too fast. I keep screaming, even though I know it won't do me any good.

"Shut up!" Brian snaps. "We came all this way to find you, you know."

"What?"

"When I couldn't find you after my appointment, I went home. Brian said you were with Raymond. This morning, I used my Phone Finder on my iPhone to track where Raymond's phone was. That's how I knew where you were. And it's over, Fern. This time it's over."

That's when Brian lurches out of the front seat, spilling Cheez-Its everywhere. He's got a bottle of pills in his beefy fist, and he's heading straight towards me.

"Stop!" I yell. "What are you doing?"

He holds me down by my neck, so it's hard to breathe. Mommy laughs.

"You're in so much trouble", she says. "You have no idea, you little piece of shit. No idea."

She laughs again and shakes something in her hand. It rattles. It's a bottle of pills

"You know. I'm pregnant", she says. "You know about Holly. You know what I'm doing to you. So, really, you know too much."

"What?" I choke out.

Brian grabs me tighter, so tight I must be turning purple. If I were Green Arrow, I'd shoot him right in the chest with my magic arrow and drain all his power. Then he'd *have* to let me go. But I'm not Green Arrow, so I can't do that. Instead, I moan helplessly as Brian sinks his body into me, sitting on my legs so I can't even kick him.

"I'm having a baby", Mommy says. "And do you know what that means for you, Fern? Your time is up. David is history. I don't need you as a piece of him anymore. This new baby will get me what I need. I think she'll have chronic salt poisoning."

I scream, the only sound I can make. Mommy can't do this! She wouldn't! She's my Mommy! She's supposed to love me!

"You know, I've tried to love you", Mommy says. "But I just can't. That's why I'm okay with doing what I'm about to do."

Brian unscrews the bottle cap with two fingers.

"Sleeping pills", Mommy says. "It's the easiest way to go, Fern, believe me. Much easier than Holly. That kid struggled and suffered when I smashed that pillow over her face, but you're lucky. No pain. Just sleeping...forever."

Help me, Holly. Please help me. Am I going to die?

I don't know, Fern. But you can't stop fighting like I did. Stand up to them. They're going to try to force those pills in you, but don't open your mouth, no matter what. If you can't stay strong...I'll see you soon, little sister.

Refusing to believe the last thing Holly told me, I clamp my mouth shut. I'm never opening it, never! They're not going to win! But Mommy just laughs.

"You think you're pretty damn smart", she says. "Brian, the nose."

"Huh?"

"*Plug* the *nose*, you idiot!"

Brian's greasy finger pinch my nose, and all of a sudden, I can't breathe at all. I feel like I'm drowning, slipping slowly under water. I won't open my mouth. Brian holds a white pill over me, ready to drop it in when I give up. But I won't. My cheeks puff out, trying to get the slightest bit of air. Maybe if I just take one breath, I'll be too fast for him. I could hold on another minute with one breath. I open my mouth, and the pill tumbles in. Brian hold my jaws together, pressing down a lot harder than he needs to. I have no choice but to swallow. The bitter pills sticks in my throat. I begin to cough, choke with my mouth closed.

"Don't wait for her to open her mouth to breathe", Mommy snaps. "Just open it for her."

So that's how I taste the salty, sweaty grease of Brian's fingers in my mouth, prying open my jaw. I try to bite him, but his fingers are too slippery. Another pill down.

I'm not giving up! I won't let them do this!

But Holly doesn't answer. There is no one to help me, not even in my head. It becomes a torture pattern. Brian opens my mouth, puts the pill in, and closes my mouth and holds my nose until I swallow.

Please save me, Holly.

Three pills.

What is happening to me?

Four pills.

Daddy? Won't someone come back?

Five pills.

I feel weird, Holly. All fuzzy inside.

Six pills.

Save me, someone, please save me.

Seven pills, and then I spiral into nothing, nothing, nothing. Colors spin in front of my mind, and I close my eyes. The last thing I remember thinking is *I hope I can open my eyes again, Holly. Please don't let me see you if I wake up.*

I am standing in the clouds. At first, I wonder how that is even possible, but then I decide that maybe clouds are very strong and they can hold me. But I know that isn't true. Then how...?

I look around me. I see nothing in every direction, except a purple-streaked sky full of stars. That clouds I am standing on are silver. They feel like a cross between marshmallows and feathers. The night air warm, blowing my hair around. My hair? I touch my head. My blond hair is back, like it never even left. For the first time, I realize I am alone, and I get scared.

"Hello?" I yell. "Anyone there? Where am I?"

In the distance, I start to see a shape walking toward me, very slowly. Then it starts running, and I can see that it is a person. My sister Holly. She is crying and laughing at the same time as she hugs me. Her hands are warm as they press into my back. I am still wearing Raymond's sweater.

"You're here", Holly says, tears dripping onto the sweater. "You're really here."

She steps back so I can look at her. She's small, like me, with dark brown hair in braids, just like I've seen her with in my dreams. She is barefoot in the clouds. But there's something different. Her white nightgown isn't stained with blood anymore. Instead, it's shiny and full and silky-looking.

"I missed you", she says. "I missed you my whole life."

"Am I in Heaven?" I ask. "Am I dead? Where am I?"

"Yes to the first question", she says. "Sort of. And no to the second. This isn't *exactly* Heaven, but it's close. I'm just visiting here. I've visited here lots of times. To see what it's like. But I never stay, because I have to be in *actual* heaven a lot of the time. It's beautiful there, Fern. I can't even describe it. It's like everything I love in one place." "You didn't answer all my questions", I tell Holly.

"Not 'where am I?'. So where am I really?"

"You're kind of in-between dying and living", Holly says. "If you fight long enough, you'll get to go back to earth. But if you don't, you can stay here with me."

"I want to go back", I say.

"Are you sure?" Holly looks like she might cry. "You could stay here with me, Fern. I've never had a sister I actually got to see."

"Me neither."

"But you will", she says. "Either way. If you die, I'll be your sister. If you live, the new baby will. If she's a girl, I mean."

"But won't you always be my sister?" I ask.

I see sparkles in Holly's eyes, silver sparkles. Then I realize they are tears, only not regular tears. Heaven tears.

"Of course I'll always be your sister", Holly whispers. "I love you, Fern. I've guided you through this. You think I would give up on you now?"

"But if I live, will I still see you?"

"In dreams, yes. And in your head. But not like you're seeing me now. Come here. There's something I want to show you."

I walk over to where Holly is kneeling. I feel lighter, like I'm nothing, or like I could fly. Holly dips her hands in the soft clouds and clears at patch of them away. There is something underneath. I kneel next to her and look down. It's me. In a white hospital room on a bed. I am nearly bald. Tubes are sticking out of my body. I look like a robot.

There are beeping machines and doctors surrounding me, talking very loud, but I can't hear them. I can just tell they're shouting. Some of them touch me, putting their hands on my chest or face. If they're touching *me*, how come I don't feel them? In the corner of the room, I see Raymond. He's talking to a doctor, moving his hands a lot like he always does. The doctor looks familiar, but I'm not sure why.

"What *is* all that?" I ask Holly.

"That", she says, "is what's happening right now in room 666, floor three of the Penn Brook State Hospital."

"But how come I can see myself? It's not like a mirror, because I don't have all those tubes when I'm here, and I have hair also. Why is it like that?"

Holly shrugs and smiles. Then she takes me by the hand. "Before you decide what to do, I want to be with you just a little longer." The sky is purple and blue now, with stars that seem a thousand times brighter than the ones on earth. Or are they the *same* as the ones on earth? I'm not sure. Holly leads me across the squishy clouds to the very edge of...something. The clouds stop here, and we are peering down at a dizzy, spinning planet.

"That's the earth", Holly says. "I know it doesn't make sense, but really, when has anything ever made sense?"

I sit next to her and dangle my feet over the edge of the clouds. I am not afraid of falling here. I don't know why. Holly doesn't speak. She points to a star shooting across the sky, and I know that means "make a wish".

So in my head, I think, *I wish I could live again. But not with Mommy and Brian. With Raymond.*

Holly doesn't ask me what I wished for, and I don't ask her, even though I have a pretty good idea of what it was.

I wish you could stay, Fern.

Yes. That must have been it.

"You have to decide now", Holly tells me. "Do you want to go back? It's going to be hard, if that's what you want to do. You're going to have to fight harder than you've ever fought before. And even then, it still might not work."

I look at my sister, so happy to be with me. I look at the beautiful sky and stars and the silvery clouds.

"What do I have to do?"

Holly looks down at the world below us.

"You have to jump", she says.

For some reason, my brain doesn't start screaming.

"I thought I have to fight", I tell her.

"You do", she says. "You have to fight the fear of jumping. And if you make it back, you'll have to fight even harder to stay there. But I think you can do it. In fact, I know you can. You're so strong, Fern. I wish I could have been more like you."

She throws her arms around me, hugging me tight.

"I'm ready", I whisper after a while. "I'm ready to jump."

I stand on the edge of the cloud and look at the sky around me. It's beautiful here. The world isn't nearly as pretty as almost-heaven. My bare toes poke over above the cloud, and my heels rest firmly on it.

"I can give you a push", Holly offers. "Please. I never got the courage to jump myself, so I lost my chance. So I want to help you do it."

"Okay", I say.

"Don't close your eyes", she tells me. "I've heard the ride down is absolutely magnificent."

"I love you", I whisper.

"I love you too", she replies. "Be strong."

She puts her hands on my back and I feel my sister pushing me into thin air.

"Be strong, little superhero", she calls, and then I am falling.

At first, I think I fall fast, zipping past the purple sky and the stars and the clouds. But I don't feel dizzy. I just feel light. Then I think I slow down, like the feeling when you're jumping out of an airplane with a parachute and the parachute suddenly opens. But there no parachute attached to my back. I fall slower, my feet kicking as I get closer and closer to the spinning planet. What had Holly said? *If* I make it back? I think I'm going to crash, but I don't close my eyes, because I feel like I'm falling through a rainbow.

Well, Holly, I might see you soon, after all.

Then the planet seems to zoom right toward me, and I am falling, falling, falling, right into the center.

At first there are the colors. Lots of white, and some blue also. I don't know what the colors mean, they just *are*. Then come the voices. I hear them, and the colors move around, but I can't see any people yet. They come later. The only person I can see is Holly. She visits me a lot, but I can't exactly say how much, since time is all gone. Everything is all gone. Until one day, I open my eyes. There is someone standing right over me. A doctor. A can see his nose hairs and they are very long. When he sees me open. My eyes, he presses a button on a little machine he's wearing and talks into it.

"Nurses, doctors, all on floor 3. Fern Kyros is awake. I repeat, Fern Kyros is awake."

I hear footsteps, lots of them, but I don't know who's coming. I wonder if my voice works.

"Where am I?" I ask the doctor with the nose hairs.

"You're in the hospital", he replies. "You're a fighter, kid. You almost didn't make it."

I feel tubes in my arm and something in the back of my throat. I am hooked up to all sorts of things.

"What do you mean, I almost didn't make it?"

Just then, a crowd of people in white and blue come into the room.

"It's a miracle", Dr. Nose Hair tells them. "An absolute miracle."

My head feels like it's been put in a blender and turned on high speed. "Excuse me", I say, trying to shake the tiredness out of me, "but *what's* a miracle?"

An older nurse with white hair grasps my cold hands in her warm ones. "*You're* a miracle, child. Do you know what you just went through?"

I shake my head.

"Beatrice!" says a voice toward the back of the crowd. "Please. She's not ready to know what...I...I think *I* need to be the one to tell her. Later."

"By all means, Dr. Ray", Beatrice replies. "After all, you're the one who saved her life."

"Raymond?" I ask. I can't see him. Things have started to get all fuzzy around the edges, and my eyes feel heavy.

"I'm here, Fern", Raymond says.

"I'm tired", I tell him. "Will you stay with me until I fall asleep?"

Raymond looks at the other doctors and nurses. "Stay with the poor child", says Beatrice. "I'll cover your front desk shift."

"Thanks, B." I feel the bed sink down a little as Raymond sits. I offer him my hand, and he takes it, squeezing tight. Then I drift off into someplace I don't know. I am not anywhere in my dreams. There are just swirls of color and laughter and glitter.

"Lucy In The Sky With Diamonds". That's what my dream is, with Holly's voice in it, saying **Keep fighting, Fern. Keep fighting**.

When I wake up, all the doctors and nurses are gone except for Raymond, who is still sitting on my bed.

"Where is everyone?" I ask.

He shrugs. "In different places. Most of the doctors and nurses you saw before were working on other units. They just came in because they had heard about you. They were concerned."

"What happened?" I feel a little bit more awake now. I try to sit up, but Raymond tells me to lie down, because if I raise my head, the machines all go crazy beeping.

"What happened?" I ask again, once the machines are quiet.

"Well, the police and I managed to chase down your mother and Brian", Raymond says. "You were in the car with them, but by the time all the police cars blocked off the road to catch your mother's car, they had given you the sleeping pills. They confessed to it. At least, Brian did. Your mother wouldn't say anything. You looked unconscious, so the police called an ambulance and they brought you here. You've been in a coma for about three weeks."

"What's a coma? Is that like when you're dead?"

"Sort of, yes."

"Like being in almost-heaven", I say.

"What's that?" Raymond looks confused.

"Nothing", I smile. Then I think of something scary and awful that makes me feel sick to my stomach.

"Where are Mommy and Brian?"

Raymond sighs. "This is going to be difficult to hear, Fern. They were both convicted of medical, physical, and emotional child abuse. A judge made the final statement about a week ago. Your mothers in jail for life, Brian has forty years."

My brain feels zapped. "So I'll never see her again."

It isn't a question, because I don't want an answer. But Raymond answers me anyway.

"No, Fern, you probably won't see her again. At least, not before you turn eighteen and have the right to make your own decisions on those matters."

I think about Mommy in one of those striped prisoners uniforms like the kind on TV. She would probably freak out if she had to wear horizontal stripes, because she told me once they make her look fat.

"Is she okay?" I ask.

"That's not yours to worry about", Raymond replies. "But yes, she's doing okay. They're going to give her some therapy and treatment, and hopefully things will get better for her."

"What about Brian? I don't ever want to see him again."

"You won't have to", Raymond says. "Don't worry about Brian." I am nervous to ask the next question. "What about Daddy?"

"The police have spent the last few weeks trying to track him down", Raymond says. "Since your mother is in prison and you don't have any other relatives, he would get custody. But he's hidden his tracks pretty well. The police have given up looking."

"In the letters, he said he was going somewhere so he didn't have to pay child support, because he couldn't afford it", I say. "He said he looks different and he got a different name. I didn't know you can get a different name. Can you?"

"If you're over eighteen, then it's possible", Raymond replies.

"Oh." I try to keep my tears in, but one leaks out the side of my right eye. "Raymond? Do you think they'll ever find him? Do you think he'll come back?"

Raymond takes a deep breath. "You want the truth?" he asks, "or some candy-coated version that most adults would give you?"

I remember one time when Daddy and I were on the swings at the park, pretending to be superheroes. He was Batman, and I was Green Arrow. "Defender of Justice and Truth!" I yelled as I pumped my legs so the swing would go higher and higher. "Defender of Justice and Truth!" Daddy agreed with a yell. Then, suddenly, his face got serious. "That's important, Fern. Always tell and ask for the truth. Even if you think you can't handle it. Even then. Especially then."

"Okay", I had said, and I pumped my legs even higher, the tips of my green sneakers almost touching the big, blue sky.

CHAPTER
41

I can feel my eyes fill with tears, and before I know it, I'm crying so hard I can barely breathe. The machines around me start beeping, and I doctor comes rushing in and shoves a plastic thing over my nose and mouth. The tears leak into it, and I can taste them. Salty. I fall asleep after that, and in my dreams are locked cages with bars, and Mommy and Brian trapped in them, like birds in a cage.

When wake up, there is a tray of food in front of me, and Raymond is gone. I examine the food. I'm very, very hungry, but what if the food is poisoned? What if Mommy snuck in here and put salt or sleeping pills or that thing called "ethanol glycol" in it? "Excuse me!" I yell as loud as I can. No one comes. I look around the room. Machines, bed, food tray, tubes. Then I notice a little red button on the side of my bed that says "CALL DOCTOR". I press it, and a doctor comes in. Dr. Warner, the man I saw talking to Raymond when Holly and I were in the silver clouds. Dr. Warner walks toward me, smiling.

"Hello, Fern", he says. "What can I do for you?"

"Is this food poisoned?" I ask.

"No. Why would it be poisoned?"

"You never know", I whisper. "I can assure you one hundred percent, Fern, that food is absolutely not poisoned. It may not look very appetizing, but that's the way hospital food is."

Suddenly, I want to hug him, so I do. He looks startled.

"What's this for, Fern?"

"You were the first one", I whisper.

"The first one?"

Now he just looks confused. He's old, though, and old people get confused a lot, so I'll have to explain it to him.

"You were the first doctor who was nice to me", I say. "You tried to make me better. Thank you."

"Oh, Fern", he sighs. "I'm so glad you're all right. You're a special kid, you know that? A real special kid."

The he takes something out of the pocket of his long doctor's coat. Daddy's oil shirt. He hands it to me, and I lay it out on the bed, almost afraid to look at it.

"No more throw up stains", I say finally.

"Nope." Dr. Warner smiles. "I took it home with me and spent quite a while scrubbing them off. I left the oil stains, though, because I figured those were part of the shirt."

"They are", I say. "This was my Daddy's shirt. It's the only thing I've got left of him. They can't find him anywhere, and he doesn't even know where I am or what happened. It's like he turned into a ghost."

"I'm very sorry", Dr. Warner says.

"And Mommy's in jail."

"Yes", he sighs. "I know."

"So who will I live with?" Dr. Warner shakes his head. "I don't know, Fern. I'm not a court judge. But right now you're in the hospital recovering, so you need to be resting and eating that food."

I ask him again if it's poisoned, and he says no.

"Then *you* take a bite", I tell him. "Take a bite from each thing on the tray. Take a sip of the milk, too. *Then* I'll eat."

So Dr. Warner does, even though he says it's against the hospital rules.

That night, when all the lights are out and the only sounds I hear are soft beeps, I sense someone standing by my bed.

"Hello, Fern", Holly says. She is wearing the bloodstained nightgown again. She looks tired.

"You did it", she says. "I'm proud of you."

"Thanks", I say. "I still miss you, though."

"I know. I miss you too", she says, twirling a braid around her bony finger. "It would have been fun to live in Heaven together. But you made the right choice. You're not like me, Fern. You're brave."

"But I *am* like you", I insist. "Because you were brave too."

Holly doesn't say anything, and for minute I think she's gone. But then I feel her cold hands in mine. She lies next to me on her back. She's not touching me, but I can feel the cold coming from her body.

"I'm glad she's in jail", Holly says, her voice tight. "She deserves to die in there."

"Who, Mommy?" I ask.

"Yes", she says. "I hate her. You should too."

So I try. I lie there in the darkness and really try to hate Mommy.

"After all she's done to you, you *should* hate her", Holly whispers.

I try, but I can't. I can't hate Mommy.

"I can't", I tell Holly. "But I really, really don't like her, if that's enough." Holly squeezes my hand.

"It's not", she says. "But don't worry. I have enough hate in me for both of us."

"Thanks."

"But aren't you *mad* at her? You almost died, Fern! I hate her for doing that! I HATE HER!"

Holly is screaming now, and I tell her to be quiet, because someone will hear, but she just screams louder. It sounds like a siren, right next to my ear, splitting it in two. She screams until I hear her run out of breath, and then I don't hear her at all anymore. I roll over and bed and realize that she is gone.

The next morning, Raymond brings me my breakfast on a tray. I groan a little bit when I see the Ensure, but Raymond says I'm "malnourished and emaciated", so I need to have two Ensures every day. The rest of the breakfast is okay though, except there are lumps in the oatmeal and little brown things also. And they're not raisins, either, because I tasted one and spit it out.

"Was I screaming last night?" I ask Raymond nervously, stirring my oatmeal to try to get the lumps out.

"No", he says. "I was here last night, and no one told me you were screaming. Why? Did you have a bad dream?"

"Sort of", I say.

"What about?"

"Well, it wasn't *bad*, exactly, but...Holly visited me last night. She told me...stuff. And then she started screaming."

"What did she say? I mean, if you want to tell me. You don't have to if you don't want to."

I think for a minute. "I don't think Holly would want me to."

"Okay", Raymond says. "Fern, when Holly visited last night, were you dreaming?"

I scrunch up my face. "I don't know", I say. "She was screaming really loud, and if no one heard her, does that make it a dream?"

"That's something I want you to think about", Raymond replies. "Finish your oatmeal, please."

"I think it might be poisoned. Also, there's got to be something bad in the Ensure. Nothing can taste that awful on its own."

Raymond sighs. "Dr. Warner told me about this", he says. "Am I gonna have to take a bite from each thing on that tray before you'll eat?"

"Yes."

"Okay", Raymond says. "If it will make you feel better." He takes a bite of my oatmeal and shutters. "How can they actually call this stuff food?"

"Raymond", I ask, "Why aren't you at work? Won't you get fired if you don't go?" "I *am* at work", Raymond replies. "I work at the children's unit at this hospital, remember? And I specifically asked to be assigned as your doctor. So don't worry, I'm not getting in trouble. I just thought you might like to see a familiar face instead of someone new."

"Thank you", I say. "And I've got something for you", Raymond says. "I'll be right back, okay?"

He leaves the room, and I take out Daddy's old oil-shirt, which I've been sleeping with. Daddy loved me. He loved me and he left. I wonder if I hate him. Raymond comes back into the room, carrying the box and letters from Daddy.

"I've got the diaries, too", he says, pulling them out of his pocket. "I don't know if you want this stuff, but..."

"I want it", I say. "It's all I've got left."

A few days later, Holly starts visiting my room, and we read the diaries together. She tells me more things than she could ever have written about herself. She's a lot like me. We both hate cooked tomatoes and people who lie. We both love Astronomy and Popsicles. I tell Holly that as long as I drink my Ensure, I get Popsicles whenever I want them.

"That's the life", she says. "But not even close to Heaven. You'll see when you get there."

"But not for a long time, I won't get there", I say.

"Right." She smiles and turns the page.

Rereading the diaries with Holly teaches me just as much as the first time I read them. With every sentence, Holly offers comments. I have to hold her back, though, from ripping up Mommy's diary, since she tries to grab it from me some nights and tears and bite out the pages. She's sort of like a wild animal sometimes, one who was never loved. Then I realize she never actually *was* loved by anyone except Daddy. No wonder she's so mad. After I realize that, I try to be more "understanding and empathic", as grown-ups say.

Each night, I ask Raymond for a piece of paper to draw on, and I draw a picture of Mommy. And every night, I let Holly tear the picture up. One day, Raymond comes into my room, carrying a box wrapped in green paper.

"Is it Christmas already?" I ask.

Raymond laughs. "No, but it's the middle of November, halfway between Christmas and your birthday. I got this present a while ago for you, but I kind of missed you birthday, since so much was going on."

I take the package and unwrap it carefully, because I want to save the green paper to draw on tonight, so Holly can rip it up. Wrapping paper is more fun to rip than regular paper. I set the wrapping paper on the side of my bed and open the box. Inside is a brand-new stuffed rabbit. Suddenly, my mind flashes back to Pox, his head torn off, lying on the floor. My eyes fill with tears.

"Do you...do you like it?" Raymond asks quietly. I lift the rabbit out of the box, all clean and white and new. It looks at me sadly, like it's saying "Please love me."

"I love it." I hug the rabbit tight to my chest. "It's perfect. Thank you."

Raymond grins. "You're welcome. So what are you going to name it? Please not something stupid like Mr. Rabbit."

"Not a chance", I say.

"Good. Raymond looks relieved. "You know what? You never actually told me how your old rabbit got his name. Pox, right?"

I can't believe Raymond has such a good memory. The first time I was in the hospital, I remember him asking, but I never got the chance to tell him. So now I do. I tell him the whole story. And then I ask, "What was the name of what Mommy did to me? What was that word?"

"Abuse?"

"No, not that. It started with an M."

Raymond strokes his beard. "Munchausen syndrome by proxy?"

"Yes!" I say. "That was it. "I'll call my rabbit Proxy."

Raymond laughs. "You're one in a million, Fern. One in a million."

He laughs all the way to the door, where he says, "I've got to go get more IV fluid, I'll be right back."

Then he starts laughing again. I'm not sure what is so funny, but I'm glad he is happy. I snuggle up with Proxy and stroke his soft ears. I smell him. Winter Pine aftershave.

Two days later, a woman who I do not know comes into my room. She tells me her name is Sarah. She is young and pretty and carrying a clipboard, where she writes down what I say.

"Who are you?" I ask. "I'm Sarah", she says.

"I know that. You just told me. I mean, who *are* you? How come you're here?"

"I'm a social worker", Sarah replies. "That means I'm here to talk to you about your situation. I'm here to help. Raymond has told me a few things. He says you're having trouble eating."

"Not trouble", I say. "I just want to make sure the food isn't poisoned."

"Mmm-hmm." Sarah scribbles something down on her clipboard. "What about the nightmares?"

"They're not exactly nightmares", I tell her.

"Can you explain one?" she asks, but I shake my head, because I don't really like the idea of my dreams being written on that clipboard.

Sarah sighs. "Okay. We might as well move on, then. Fern, as you know, your mother is in prison. So that means you can't go home. Do you know what foster placement is?"

"Like adoption?"

"Yes, it can eventually lead to adoption, but in this case, it means you would be staying with a family for the time being. They may have kids, they may not. It could be any family."

"I don't want any family", I say. "I don't want anyone at all except for Holly."

Then Sarah asks who Holly is, so I have to explain the whole thing. The entire time, she's writing on her clipboard, which makes me nervous. When she's done writing, she says, "I know foster placement isn't your ideal situation, Fern, but it's the very best thing for you right now, okay?"

"Who would I stay with?" "Well, we've got a few people who are interested, but we'll let you know once we've made the final decision."

"You mean I don't get to decide *at all*?"

"The family will be very nice. Trust me, nothing like what your mother was like. They won't leave you, either. I promise you'll like them. And the baby will stay with the same family! Won't that be fun?"

"The baby?" I ask.

"Your mother is pregnant, Fern", Sarah says.

"I know that", I tell her. "But why isn't Mommy keeping the baby? Will she hurt it like she hurt me?"

"She might", says Sarah. "Which is why we're taking the baby away to keep her safe."

"*Her?*"

"Yes", Sarah smiles. "It's a little girl."

I am shocked. A little girl. I'll have a little sister soon.

Holly, I hope I can be as good to her as you were to me.

And I get an answer right away.

You will be, Fern. Besides, you'll be there for her. I was never there for you.

Sarah asks me why I'm staring into space. "I'm talking to Holly", I tell her. Then Sarah says she wants me to see a doctor, even though I say I'm already at a hospital, and aren't there plenty of doctors here?

"This isn't the same type of doctor", says Sarah. "This doctor will help you with your feelings. It's called a therapist. His name is Doctor Griffith. He's very nice."

"Are my feelings sick?" I wonder.

"No, but Doctor Griffith will help you get over all that you've been through", says Sarah. "You'll start to see him once you're out of the hospital. He'll help get rid of Holly's voice, too."

No! Holly, don't go, not matter what Dr. Griffith says!

Don't worry, Fern, I'm not going anywhere.

The next day, I wake up from a nap and find an envelope sitting next to my pillow. Raymond peeks his head in the door.

"Oh good, you're awake", he says. "What this envelope?" I say. He grins. "Open it up and find out."

The envelope was written on by a kid, I can tell. It says "To my friend Fern. From Leah."

"How did Leah know I was here?" I ask.

"Well", Raymond smiles, "you can thank Blue for that. She works at multiple locations, too, and she also happens to work with Leah quite a bit. At Leah's last appointment, she gave Blue this envelope and told her to make sure you got it. So Blue gave it to me, because I had told her what had happened. And now here it is."

I rip open the envelope, and a single picture falls out. I pick it up. It's a glossy photo of Leah, standing in the woods. Behind her is the most beautiful fairy house I've ever seen. She is holding a piece of notebook paper with the words "Thank You, Fern." She is smiling, and I can see the gap between her teeth.

"That was a great thing you did", Raymond says softly. "I can't think of a single kid besides you who would do that."

"I can", I say. "Holly would do it. She'd do it in a second."

"You're right", Raymond says. "From what I know about her, she probably would."

We are quiet for a while, and then I ask, "How are my other friends? Sammy and Katie and Antonio and Abby and Celia. Are they okay? Do you know them?"

"Unfortunately, I don't", Raymond says. "But I can give their names to someone who might be able to track them down."

"Okay." I think of Celia's feeding tube and Sammy's wheelchair with the dragon stickers and Antonio, dancing with me. "Please find them."

"I'll do my best", Raymond promises. He gets me a piece of tape so I can hang up the picture from Leah.

That night, I look at it for forty-three minutes before I fall asleep. Holly is next to me on the bed. She is sitting cross-legged. The bottoms of her feet are really dirty.

"You need to show someone the diaries", she tells me.

"Who?" I ask.

"You'll know when the right person comes. Trust me. But you need to show them to someone. None of the people who sent Mom to jail know about me. Think about how much more trouble she'd get in if they knew she actually *killed* someone."

"Do you *want* her to get in more trouble?"

Holly grins. "Yes. But you have to anyway, Fern. It's the right thing to do. They should know."

"But the diaries are private. I don't want to give them away."

"Please do it. For me?" The next morning, I hear loud voices outside my room. It's Sarah and a man I don't know.

"I just came from the prison", Sarah says. "I was talking to your mother about the baby."

The man standing next to Sarah smiles at me. I still don't know who he is.

"What about the baby?" I ask Sarah. I ignore the man, because he looks kind of like Santa Claus with his beard, and Santa Claus isn't real, so maybe this man isn't real, either.

"We were discussing what will happen once the baby is born", Sarah tells me.

"What *will* happen?"

"Well, the baby will stay with you in your foster home. We talked about that already. But-".

"Wait a minute", I protest. "Why do we keep calling her *the baby*? Doesn't the baby have a name?"

"Yes", says Sarah. "You're mother's already decided on that. The baby's name is IV."

I gasp as I look at the tube connecting my arm to a bag of liquid.

"No!" I scream. "Not IV! Not a hospital word! No!"

"Fern!" Raymond grabs my hand. "Fern! Calm down. She means "Ivy", like the plant, not "IV" like the tube in your arm. Ivy. The plant. Like Fern. Ivy and Fern."

"And Holly", I say.

Show her, Fern. Show her the diaries.

I take the two diaries off the nightstand.

"Maybe you should look at these."

"Diaries?" the man asks.

I squint at him. "Who are you?"

"Oh! Oh, my gosh, I completely forgot to introduce you!" Sarah exclaims. "Fern, this is Dr. Griffith. Dr. Griffith, this is Fern, the girl you'll be working with once she feels better."

"Where's your doctors coat?" I ask Dr. Griffith. He's only wearing a suit and tie.

"I'm not that kind of doctor", he says. "But I'm looking forward to getting to know you, Fern."

"Okay", I say, because I am sort of looking forward to getting to know him, too. He seems nice, even if he looks like Santa Claus.

"Please look at the diaries", I say. Sarah and Dr. Griffith both look at Raymond, who nods.

"Go ahead. Read them."

So Sarah and Dr. Griffith bend over Holly's diary and skim through the pages. When they're done with Holly's diary, they pick up Mommy's without looking at me. Raymond and I glance at each other. We aren't sure what to do. I hug Proxy.

Please, Holly, was this the right thing to do?

Yes.

After twelve minutes, Sarah closes the diary and clears her throat. At first I wonder how she can read so quickly, but then I remember the bookmarks. I've folded down all the pages that described how Mommy was hurting me and Holly, the not-boring pages.

"We have to show this to the judge", Sarah says. "A piece of evidence like this is...well, it's a remarkable insight."

She takes the two diaries and puts them in her briefcase.

"Wait!" I gasp. "Don't just take them! They're all I've got left of Mommy and Holly! Please!"

"They're pretty important to her", Raymond agrees.

Dr. Griffith nods. "We can photocopy them, Sarah. Fern, we'll give these back tomorrow, okay?"

I nod. I decide that I like Dr. Griffith a little bit more.

A day later, I have the diaries back, just like Dr. Griffith says. It's a good day, because it's snowing outside. Raymond comes to work late, though, so in the morning a very mean nurse takes my blood pressure and all those other tests. When Raymond finally comes in, he's covered in snow, but he's smiling.

"Sorry I'm late, Fern", he says. "I just had to...work something out. You'll hear about it later today, I believe. In the meantime, I've got some news for you."

He sits in the chair that visitors are supposed to sit in. "I've managed to track down your friends!" Raymond says. "You can send them letters, if you like. Sammy, Katie, Leah, and Abby are at home. Antonio is recovering from another leukemia treatment at the Children's Hospital in Malden, and Celia's been having problems with her feeding tube. She's in a treatment center in Hamilton."

"Are they all okay?" "All the ones at home are", Raymond replies. "And I know that Antonio is fine, he's just very tired and weak. But Celia's been having some problems getting nutrition through her tube. They're taking care of it, though. I asked, and the doctors at the institute told me they expect to start regular leukemia treatments within a month. That afternoon, between bites of my lunch, I write letters. Lots and lots of letters. The first one is to Leah.

"Dear Leah, This is Fern. I am glad you got to go see the fairy houses. It looks like fun. Write and tell me all about it. I have something to tell you. You may be mad at me for this, but I don't really have cancer. My mom just pretended so she could get money and also lots of attention. Right now, I am in the hospital and my mom and Brian are in jail because they tried to kill me with sleeping pills, but I am okay. I miss you so much. I hope you get better very, very soon. Your Friend, Fern Kyros."

I explain the same thing in the letters to every one of my friends. I hope they won't be mad at me.

They won't, Fern. It's Mommy who's done something wrong, not you. If they're mad at you, then they're not real friends anyway.

After dinner, Raymond comes in to take my tray and the letters, so he can send them where they need to go. A man in a suit and Sarah follow him.

"I've got something to ask you", Raymond says. "Judge Silla is the judge supervising your foster placement. And when your mother was arrested, I asked him something. And today, it was confirmed. Judge, would you like to tell her?"

Judge Silla smiles. "No, Raymond, you go ahead."

Raymond takes a deep breath and wipes his hands on his pants like they're all sweaty.

"Are you nervous?" I ask. "Why are you nervous?"

Raymond's hands are nearly shaking. "I was wondering something, Fern", he says. "Do you know what I was wondering?" I shake my head. His smile grows wider, like a stretched rubber band. "How would you like to live with me, Fern?"

I can't remember how loud I screamed, but it was loud enough to bring three nurses and two doctors running into my room. Tears trickle down my face as I hug Raymond tight, smelling Winter Pine and hope and love and just plain happiness.

"Yes", I whisper. "Yes, please."

Raymond's cheeks are wet, and I realize that he's crying too. "As soon as you feel better", he says. "We'll fix up a room in my house for you and Ivy. With green wallpaper and superhero posters. Whatever you want. And you can go to school, too. Third grade."

I laugh, feeling my heart full with a thousand colors that aren't black and gray and scared.

"You'll go home in a week", Sarah says. "If you're still doing as well as you are now."

Raymond opens his doctor's briefcase and pulls out a notebook with a green cover.

"I got this for you", he says. "And I have a feeling you'll know exactly what to do with it."

I imagine myself on Raymond's car, not hiding, just going home to the tree in his yard, where I'll climb and find shapes in the clouds. And I'll go to school and come home again and help take care of Ivy. I won't have Daddy, but right now, I have all I need.

That night, I can't sleep. I'm still shaking with excitement, so I open my green journal and write.

"December 3rd. I am going home with Raymond, Holly. He's going to be my foster dad. I think I will really, really like it. Thank you, Holly. Thank you so much for everything. I'm sorry you had to die. But you were brave. You may not think you were, but I see it so clear it's like a smack in the face. Ivy will, too. I'll tell her all about you, Holly, because she deserves to know about both of her big sisters. I love you, Holly. Promise never to leave me, okay? It was fun in Heaven with you, but now I'm going home. But if I need you, promise you'll be in the clouds when I look up from the tree at Raymond's house."

And even though I can't see her, I still hear her reply loud and clear:

I promise. You did a good job, little superhero.

ABOUT THE AUTHOR

L auren E. Richards is a junior in high school. She has always loved writing and has won nine awards for her work at the Scholastic Art And Writing Awards. After she graduates college, she would like to be a child psychologist. Lauren lives in Massachusetts with her family and three cats.